KATE
SCHUMACHER

THE CALL OF THE SEA

THE GRAIL CYCLE

1

Paperback: 978-0-6454030-4-6

Hardcover: 978-0-6454030-6-0

Ebook: 978-0-6454030-5-3

First paperback edition: 2023

Edited by Danikka Taylor - https://www.taylormademedia.online/

Cover design by Franziska Stern – https://www.coverdungeon.com

Map created by Rachael Ward - https://www.cartographybird.com/

For more information, please visit https://www.kateschumacherauthor.com/

or Instagram: @kate.schumacher.writer

For all those seeking their path who are yet to peel back the layers and discover who they are -
Keep going

TO THE READER

This story has been written for an adult audience. Within these pages you will find content that may be triggering, including forced marriage, forced sexual situations, physical assault and violence, discrimination against those from different backgrounds and those from LGBT+ communities. People who have suffered religious trauma may also find some of the story content distressing.

A NOTE FROM THE AUTHOR

This story has been one I have wanted to write for a long time. I have been obsessed with the Arthurian legends since my childhood (mum, I blame you) and have seen every movie and TV variation of the stories. I have also read a lot – whether it be fictional retellings or non-fiction surrounding the characters and the places where the stories are set.

I have drawn on a lot of different source material to write this story in order to settle on my own interpretation of the characters and the tales that surround them. TV shows and films have been a great place to start, to see how others have interpreted the characters, but I have dived deep into literature as well: *Le Morte d'Arthur,* by Thomas Malory; *Idylls of the King,* by Alfred Tennyson; *Vita Merlini,* and *The History of the Kings of Britain,* by Geoffrey of Monmouth; *The Mists of Avalon,* by Marion Zimmer Bradley; *Arthurian Romances,* by Chretien de Troyes; *The Sword in the Stone* and *The Once and Future King* by TH White; and *Gawain and the Green Knight,* amongst others.

The Grail Cycle is my reimagining of the Arthurian legends. You will find familiar characters, settings and symbols common within the plethora of Arthurian stories, but I wanted to do something different with them, and present those things you know in a different way. Within this series, you will find Arthur, Lancelot and Guinevere. You will find Merlin and the Lady of the Lake and Mordred. You will find Morgaine Le Fey. You will find the quest for the Grail, the Knights of the Round Table, and Camelot.

But you may not recognise them at first glance.

Because you will also find pirates and syhrens and mythical creatures of the sea. You will find folklore elements from ancient mythologies. You will find Gods and Goddesses and a world on the brink of change. You will find magic and mystery, prophecies and a complex land with differing perspectives on how to view the world. And you will find an interwoven, complicated story with characters who need to find themselves before they can be what they are destined to be.

This is a story of discovery, of belonging and the search for identity, of finding your power and learning how to use it.

I hope you enjoy it.

Pronunciation Guide

People

Jenyfer - Jennifer
Ordes - Or/dez
Lamorna - Lar/morn/a
Jalen - Jar/len
Iouen - I/oh/an
Carbrey - Car/bray
Ulrian - Ol/re/ann
Bryn - Brin
Niniane - Nin/ee/aine
Aelle - Ay/la
Tahnet - Tar/net
Katarin - Kat/ar/en
Tregarthen - Tree/gar/then
Ankou - An/coo

Sheleitari - Shay/leet/ar/ee
Syhren - siren

Places

Teyath - Tae/ath
Cruithea - Crew/i/the/a
Mahwenia - Mar/when/e/a
Kernou - Ker/know
Calledun - Cal/ee/dun
Sacellum - Sack/ell/um
Lyonesse - Lie/on/ess

CHAPTER 1

Jenyfer kept her eyes on the slice of blue sky above her. The dream lingered – as it had been lingering all through the morning and into the creeping dark of the afternoon, sitting in the corner of her mind, like it had been for almost a week.

Each time it was a little different, but three things remained the same: the sacrificial stake, music and a ship. The same ship that was now sitting where the ocean met the sky. It had been there when she woke that morning, as if pulled from her dreams. Premonition tugged at Jenyfer's insides but she swallowed it away, sitting up and brushing the sand from her back.

The music in her dreams was the same music that had haunted her for as long as she could remember. The song had started as a whisper, a scratching of words in the corner of her mind, each syllable bending and shifting with its own simple melody, until it settled beside her heartbeat and nestled there, living inside her.

But music was forbidden and songs that lived inside people's heads were a sign of the Beast. So, Jenyfer kept it caged, although she could not keep it silent. There was power in her song, in the way the melody melted against her throat, the way the rhythm flowed through her, begging to be released.

'Are you listening to me?' Lamorna's voice was sharp.

'Yes, of course I'm listening.'

Her sister was watching her, Lamorna's shrewd eyes crawling over her face. Jenyfer rearranged her features and hid her shaking hands in her lap, focusing on the sea birds that hovered over the boundary between the ocean and the land, wings spread, feathers brushed with sunlight; they floated high on the updrafts, suspended between here and now. Below them, blue-green waves caressed the sand, the water infused with flecks of white as the ocean breathed, folding like windswept curtains upon a pale, golden shore. Jenyfer counted the seconds between sets, getting lost in the endless rhythm.

Beside her, her sister sighed, and Jenyfer wasn't sure if Lamorna was simply enjoying the sight of the ocean spread out like a blanket, or whether she was basking in the glory of the One God's world, unable to just *look* at something beautiful without creating a space for religious reverence.

'Do you remember the stories Aunt Tamora used to tell us about the Grail? About its magic?' Jenyfer asked. Her magic tingled and, like always, she pushed it away, down into the depths of her, where she hid her dreams. Dreams of water and music, of the cool touch of the ocean on her bare toes, of water tugging insistently at her skirt, the soft, grey fabric turned storm-dark in the growing dawn. An ocean licked with golden flame, each wave capped with a crown of fire, sparkling like jewels. A vessel that sang when she touched it. And a stone that whispered music, a man with silver eyes and a crown of bones, the sea rising to swallow the land—

'She should never have told us those stories,' Lamorna said crossly. Jenyfer didn't know if her sister was cranky about the stories or Jenyfer's lack of footwear. They were only in the garden, after all. She dug her bare toes into the sand-smattered grass defiantly while she wrestled her swirling thoughts into a false calm.

Lamorna's pale blonde hair was tucked neatly beneath her white linen cap, a contrast to Jenyfer's wild midnight mane, left loose and free to fall where it wanted and blow in her eyes. Lamorna was sitting with her knees tucked up to her chin, feet crossed at the ankles. Her back was rigid. Relaxing on the grass in the afternoon sunshine was obviously not part of the Word.

'Why not?' Jenyfer pressed. Lamorna wouldn't look at her, so she went on, digging a little deeper for a reaction, feeling wicked and sinful, like everyone said she was. 'Tamora's stories are much more exciting than the ones from the Decalogue.'

'Jenyfer,' her sister hissed, looking around in fright, as if worried one of the Konsel – or the Chif himself – might be lurking behind the wind-shorn bushes of their cliff-top garden, ready to pounce on them for their blasphemy.

Well, on Jenyfer anyway. Lamorna had never done a blasphemous thing in her life.

'It's true, and you can't deny it. The Decalogue is boring. Mind-numbingly boring,' Jenyfer emphasised. She shouldn't niggle her sister, but it was too easy and she enjoyed it. Hiding her smile, she turned away from Lamorna's scowling face and watched the ocean instead. The water sparkled in the afternoon sun, snatches of light bouncing from the top of one foam-flecked wave to another.

'You wouldn't think it was boring if you bothered to come to the prayer circle, which is what I've been trying to tell you,' Lamorna said firmly. 'You need to come, Jenyfer. People are talking.'

Jenyfer heaved a sigh. She was supposed to go to the prayer circle, as all the women in the village were, young and old, but it was nothing like the children's group, where at least there were games and people actually laughing and smiling. The women's circle was full of cranky old things, their faces like pieces of dried fruit, the skin around their mouths tight with bitterness. Or, if not them, it was young women like Lamorna, eyes blazing with a zeal that Jenyfer did not understand.

Sweat had gathered on the back of Jenyfer's neck and she rubbed at it with an irritated hand, knowing Lamorna was right. People were talking, and talk was dangerous, not only for her, but for her sister and their aunt. The last thing Jenyfer wanted was for any trouble to fall on her family, like it had on many others. The Chif and the Konsel seemed to have a nose for the forbidden.

Glancing again at the ship anchored out to sea, Jenyfer nudged her sister, pushing aside thoughts of Witchfinders and the Decalogue, and wanting to niggle a little bit more. If anything, annoying Lamorna distracted her. 'I wonder whose ship that is.'

'Who cares?' Lamorna mumbled. 'They're obviously pirates. It's best if they stay out there on their ship. We don't want their sort in Kernou.'

'It might be Katarin Le Fey!' Jenyfer said excitedly.

Lamorna grabbed her arm, as if she was expecting Jenyfer to fling herself from the safety of the garden and race down the rocky path to the beach. 'I hope it isn't. She's nothing but trouble,' Lamorna said firmly.

'Rumours,' Jenyfer replied airily. 'I happen to think she's amazing.' Jenyfer had heard Katarin Le Fey was once a wealthy lady, who turned pirate when scorned by a lover. Some said she was a faery, and others that she was not real at all, nothing but a legend designed to scare. But Jenyfer knew she was real; it was just that no one in Kernou had ever seen her. Her crew were all female, Magic Wielders rescued from stakes and bonfires around the continent. It was also said that Katarin was bound to the Witch of the Mists and the mysterious Isle of Avalon.

No one told Katarin Le Fey what to do, not unless they wanted to be sent to the bottom of the sea, impaled on her cutlass or choked with magic.

Lamorna gave Jenyfer's arm a sharp pinch. 'You would think that. And you shouldn't. She's a faery and an abomination in the eyes of the One God.'

'If the One God created the world and everything in it, He must have created the fey creatures as well.' Jenyfer rubbed at her arm. Lamorna's pinches were always hard, leaving tiny bruises. 'The mermaids and the Little Folk.'

'The fey are servants of the Beast, and those who consort with them are destined to Burn. You need to remember that,' Lamorna said piously.

Jenyfer clenched her fists. 'I hope they build the biggest bonfire Kernou has ever seen for me then.'

Lamorna shook her head in disapproval. This was an old argument and, for once, she didn't engage in it. Instead, she shot Jenyfer a worried look. 'There is a rumour.'

'What now?'

For someone so devout, Lamorna was an expert at collecting gossip, hearing things that should not be spoken about.

'Kernou is getting a visitor from the Sacellum.'

Jenyfer's heart skipped a beat and her stomach turned over.

'When?' She could barely breathe.

Don't be a Witchfinder, she begged silently. Witchfinders were notoriously skilled at sniffing out those with magic, like an animal on the hunt. If it was a Witchfinder coming to Kernou, she would have to be careful. Maybe she could feign illness when he arrived? Maybe she could—

'Soon, is all I know.' Lamorna shrugged. 'You'd know all this as well, if you bothered to go into town more,' she added. 'You spend too much time with Bryn'—she paused for what Jenyfer knew was intended as dramatic effect—'alone.'

Jenyfer's laugh was shaky. 'First you tell me to make friends, and then you tell me not to spend time with the one friend I have.'

'He's a man.'

'Really? I hadn't noticed. Thanks for pointing that out.'

'People are talking, Jenyfer,' Lamorna said, her voice dropping to barely a whisper.

'Let them talk,' Jenyfer muttered. Then, before her sister could begin her lecture, 'I know the rules.'

'Maryaine and Heath were married last month, and you know they were *just friends* as well,' Lamorna said. 'I'd heard that they were discovered in a *compromising* situation by her father and now—'

Jenyfer gasped in mock outrage and covered her mouth with her hand.

Lamorna scoffed, but her cheeks coloured. 'The point is, Bryn likes you, and you obviously like him. You can't sit still when you know he's out in the boat, watching the water from up here when you should be doing your chores and rushing off to see him the moment he gets in.'

Because I want to be out there as well, Jenyfer thought furiously. *Because I want to know what he saw, what colour the water was, what sort of fish were out there, if he saw any mermaids or—*

Her sister was still talking. 'You should be married by now. You're of age.'

'So are you,' Jenyfer snapped. Her stomach flopped again.

Lamorna tossed her head, ignoring her sister's emotion. 'I won't ever get married. Men hold no interest for me. I am going to travel to Malist and join the Sisters.'

Jenyfer gaped. 'But … you'll have to leave.'

'Yes, but I'll come back, and when I do, it will be as a Sister of the Order,' Lamorna said proudly, before she remembered pride was a sin and rearranged her face to hide her smile. They all knew about the Sisters of the One God. A group of them had even visited the village the previous year. Being a Sister meant a life of faith and devotion, a life spent at prayer and charitable work. It took years to become a Sister, but, Jenyfer thought, if anyone could commit to such obedience, it was Lamorna.

Lamorna breathed the Word, from the moment she opened her eyes in the morning to when she finished her evening prayer. But, if Lamorna did leave Kernou to become a sister, Jenyfer would never see her again. Sisters lived in the Coventry in the city. They did not have guests, not even family, and rarely travelled.

Neither of the girls had ever been anywhere – they had never left their town. Kernou was nestled in the Bay of Calledun, the coastline around them a rugged and jagged assortment of rocks like broken teeth, sheltered coves where the water was aquamarine and warm, and small bays and hidden caves, full of deep, dark mystery. Creeks ran from the hills to trickle into the sea, and the beach was scattered with boulders and pebbles, with long stretches of rock that reminded Jenyfer of a table-top, the surface littered with holes that captured the water that swallowed the beach at high tide.

Below them, the waves continued to pound against the sand and a warm, briny scent crept through the air. Jenyfer could always sense the sea. No matter how far from the shoreline she was, the sound of the waves was inside her, echoing through her blood and shifting the rhythm of her heart until it matched the soothing swell of the ocean.

Jenyfer had no idea how big Teyath was, and probably never would. There were old folk in town who had never travelled further than the shoreline unless they were fishermen, born to cast nets and rip the bounty of the ocean from the waves. She plucked strands of grass from the ground and gazed out at the sparkling ocean, at the ship that lingered on the horizon. It was a large ship, the largest she had seen recently. *There would be room on there*, she thought, then swallowed the dream away.

Lamorna stood abruptly, shaking her skirts free of sand.

'I want to go places, too,' Jenyfer said with a sigh, tossing her fistful of grass aside.

'Where?' Lamorna demanded, hands on the swell of her hips. Lamorna was all curves and soft flesh, where Jenyfer was built like a boy, tall and lanky, her limbs long. In all her time wandering the town and gathering gossip, Jenyfer wondered if her sister ever noticed men staring at her. Probably not. She had bound herself to a nameless, faceless God.

'I don't know. Just somewhere,' Jenyfer answered, and the song that lived inside her soared in agreement. It was a calming song, deep, and as smooth and steady as the ocean. She couldn't ever make out any words, but she liked it, the way it sat in her mind, like a lullaby, even if it was forbidden. She'd tried to sing it once, to remember the notes that clung to her, but her voice wouldn't cooperate and Tamora had commanded her never to sing again, so Jenyfer hadn't, not even the tunes Lamorna tried to teach her about the Word and the One God.

It was nearing time to prepare dinner, so Jenyfer stood as well. They would be needed in the kitchen. She cast one final look at the ocean, a flash of blue in the growing amber light, and, as she was turning towards the cottage, something moved in the corner of her eye.

A tiny face was peering at them from within the branches of the faery shrub, bursting into flower like it did every month. Jenyfer gripped her sister's arm tightly. 'Lamorna! Do you see him?' She indicated the shrub and the wizened face that was watching them with interest. 'It's a pisky!'

Lamorna did not even look at the shrub. She pulled her arm free. 'I can see nothing, and neither can you, Jen,' she added sternly. Jenyfer watched her sister stalk back to the cottage, then lowered herself to her knees in front of the faery shrub. Lamorna hated that shrub, believing it nothing more than a pagan symbol, a sign of their heathen past, calling it eldritch and unnatural. She hated that it flowered all year round, when other things died and slept over the cold months. She had wanted Tamora to pull it out, but their aunt refused, demanding if Lamorna was so confident in the One God that she was willing to risk the wrath of the Other Ones, she could do it herself. Lamorna wisely decided she wasn't that pious yet, although Jenyfer often caught her scowling at the shrub.

She dropped to her knees and smiled at the pisky. It grinned at her, then vanished as a bang echoed around the garden. Lamorna had slammed the back door to the cottage. With a sigh, Jenyfer stood, dusted off her skirt, and followed her sister inside.

In the simple kitchen, Lamorna was talking about the women's prayer circle, trying once again to convince their aunt to go. Her sister's voice went on and on as Jenyfer tied an apron around her middle and joined her aunt at the table. Tamora rolled her eyes and passed Jenyfer a bowl of peas to shell. Jenyfer had collected them that morning from the garden, before the sun was high and the peas suffered in the heat.

'I have my own circle, Lamorna, you know that,' Tamora said softly.

She meant the women who came to sit with her and drink tea, to discuss the Word. When they came, the girls were ordered out of the house; even Lamorna, who knew the Decalogue inside out, her copy of the Book never far from her hands.

Jenyfer snuck a look at her sister, but Lamorna was busy at the stove, setting the kettle to boil.

Jenyfer knew there was more to her aunt's *prayer* circle. She had followed Tamora once, when the moon was dark, slipping from the cottage into the night. Her aunt had gone to the stone circle on the hills above the town. Jenyfer watched as Tamora strode into the middle of that circle and waited and, soon, others joined her, the women stepping from the night air like ghosts. They were wearing hooded cloaks but, as they began to speak, Jenyfer recognised their voices.

Tamora had raised them since Lamorna was a newly born babe, screaming her welcome to the world, their mother lying with unblinking eyes and the sheets soaked in her blood. Jenyfer shouldn't remember that day, but she did. A fleeting glance was all she had of her mother's body before she was pulled away by strong hands.

First their father lost to the sea, and then their mother to the birthing bed.

'—I've been telling her that she needs to come,' Lamorna was saying.

Tamora nudged Jenyfer. 'Yes, Lamorna. Jenyfer will go with you, won't you, Jen?'

'I guess,' Jenyfer muttered. She glanced sidelong at her aunt. Tamora's face was impassive, but Jenyfer could almost feel the truth of her aunt's thoughts pushing against her brain. Tamora hated the Decalogue and the Konsel as much as Jenyfer did.

Lamorna nodded, pleased with her success, and swept from the room. Jenyfer waited until she heard the back door close before dumping her unshelled peas on the table.

'Please don't make me go.'

Tamora sighed, dropping her own peas back into the bowl and rubbing at her face. 'You have to play the game, Jen. Just as I do,' she added, her voice low.

'Why don't we just leave?' Jenyfer asked, keeping an eye and ear out for her sister.

'And go where?' her aunt asked.

'Cruithea,' Jenyfer whispered. 'The High Priestess—'

Tamora gripped Jenyfer's wrist. 'What do you know about her?'

'Nothing,' Jenyfer muttered.

'Keep it that way,' Tamora said softly, releasing Jenyfer's wrist. 'Your song?'

'Unchanged,' Jenyfer replied.

'Good.' Her aunt nodded, picking up the peas and continuing her task as Lamorna swept back into the room, carrying an armful of tomatoes and wearing a cross expression.

'You were meant to pick these, Jen,' she admonished. Then she noticed Jenyfer and their aunt's faces. 'What's going on?'

'Nothing, Lamorna,' Tamora said, standing and moving to the stove. 'Let's get dinner prepared.'

Jenyfer remained seated, her fingers automatically moving over the peas, while her mind floated out to sea and her song crooned away sadly.

Chapter 2

Jenyfer woke with her heart hammering and her mouth dripping. Wiping her face on her sleeve, she sat up, blinking at the sharp slice of moonlight that shot through the gap in the curtains. Her pillow was damp, her hair hanging lank around her face, the long strands sluiced with sweat. Or water. She ran her hands over her face, fingers trembling. Her cheeks were wet and when she licked her lips, she could taste salt.

The same dream. She was tied to the stake at the end of the beach. Jenyfer rubbed at her wrists, feeling the sting of the rope. She knew what the dream meant, even if she didn't want to admit it. She was going to die. She needed, now more than ever, to get out of Kernou, but a woman on her own... Jenyfer swallowed. Bryn would help. She had no one else, and when it was morning, she'd track him down and bully him into taking her up the coast. He'd never said no to her before.

Or if not up the coast, she'd make him take her to that ship, the one she knew – without having to look – was still out there.

Around her, the cottage was silent, her aunt and sister sleeping the soundless sleep of those who didn't get woken at night by dreams of water and death. She glanced at Lamorna. Even in sleep, her sister was beautiful, with her plump lips and porcelain skin. Lamorna never snored or drooled through the night.

Jenyfer pulled the simple linen curtains wide and rested her fingers on the window sill; a breeze smelling of the sea came racing inside and she closed her eyes and breathed deep, sucking the salt and brine into her lungs. Her heart was still pounding, so fiercely it was almost painful, mingling with the dizziness that washed over her like waves. When she withdrew her hands to tuck them into her lap, wet fingerprints were left on the weather-smooth timber of the window sill. Quickly, she pulled the curtains back into place, hiding the evidence of... what? Sweaty skin? The result of the strangely warm night air?

Keeping her movements small and one eye on her sister, Jenyfer slipped out of bed. She didn't bother with her boots, but grabbed her coat from the floor, sliding her arms into the sleeves as she moved towards the door. In the hall, she paused, holding her breath, eyes shifting to her aunt's door. Swallowing the guilt that tickled her throat, satisfied Tamora was sleeping, Jenyfer crept through the small house, careful not to bump the table or knock a chair or spill the milk left for the Other Ones.

Sitting by the fire, tiny hands held to the glowing warmth, were three piskies. The little faeries resembled old men, with their lined faces and hairless skulls. Jenyfer ignored them, as she should. Tamora had schooled both girls in the ways of the Small Folk when they were younger – it was best to let them go about their chores, and never thank them, for the Small Folk were strange in their ways and viewed thanks as an insult.

Jenyfer eased the front door open just far enough to slide her body into the night air; any further and the door would creak, and she would be discovered.

Outside, the moon was full and high in the sky, lighting the world with silver and white. Pulling her coat tight, Jenyfer hurried across between

12

the garden beds, making for the place in the fence where the palings were loose. The white blooms on the faery shrub glowed like tiny lights in the darkness. Careful not to disturb the shrub, Jenyfer slipped through the fence and followed the well-worn path from her cottage to the water. The shrubs and bushes that grew alongside the path were small and weather-worn, the rocks coated in moss and lichen, the granite always damp, no matter the season.

The sand was cool beneath her bare feet as Jenyfer ran along the shoreline, dodging the reaching arms of the water, a game she used to play with the sea when she was a child and was allowed down here. She would have to remember to wipe her feet clear of sand before returning to her bed. Her salt-tangled hair was easily explained; a bed full of sand... not so easy to lie her way out of.

Sneaking out of the cottage to visit the beach always gave Jenyfer a little thrill. No one walked the shoreline in the dark anymore, and especially not under a bloated moon, but Jenyfer was not just being rebellious. She *had* to come. If she didn't, she was twitchy and annoyed, and the middle of the night was the only time she could enjoy the ocean like this. The magic under her skin demanded this one thing of her.

Jenyfer did not know much about magic or the Old Ways. She was a child when the One God swept into their world, and such things were of no concern for a girl more focused on collecting shells and flowers. But she knew that under the Old Ways, people had been free to choose what they believed and magic was an accepted part of everyday life. If the Old Ways still held firm in Kernou, Jenyfer would not have to fear her magic. She would not have to fear the Pit, or the Beast, or eternal damnation.

She did not ask questions of her aunt, fearful that speaking those sorts of things out loud would be a ticket straight to the stake, or the pyre, if the Konsel were feeling generous. Jenyfer hadn't decided which way would be the best to die – with her lungs filled with water, or her flesh slowly burning and peeling from her body. She had seen a burning once and, out of everything about that morning, it was the smell that had stayed with her, burrowed beneath her skin like a permanent reminder.

Yet her aunt Tamora was the only one she could talk to, even if, when they did talk about magic, it was in whispers, or in sentences half-spoken for fear of discovery. Jenyfer swallowed. Her sister scared her; that was a thought she would only admit down here, in the darkness with the sea stroking the shore. She didn't believe Lamorna would ever march into the town and spill her sister and aunt's secrets all over the place but, sometimes, the way Lamorna spoke, the way she acted, the way she knelt for hours on the hard stone floor... Jenyfer could not be certain, so she was careful.

Out past the breakers, the water was still, a mirror that reflected the silvery face of the moon. The sky was clear, but Jenyfer knew that, by morning, silvery-black clouds would cloak the world and the ocean would boil and writhe beneath the storm. People used to believe it was the storm demon who brought the rain and winds that lashed their world. Now, the villagers considered the Old Ones and the Small Folk servants of the Beast, who dwelt in a fiery pit and consumed the souls of sinners – as Lamorna was fond of reminding her family.

Jenyfer paused, her breathing sharp, and squinted at the ship on the horizon, but the vessel was too far out for her to know which ship it was. She'd been joking, trying to get a rise from her sister, but part of her wished it was *The Night Queen* – but it was possibly Tymis Merlyni's *Excalibur*.

The tide was beginning to shift. Jenyfer watched the mysterious ship for a moment longer, and then turned away. The moonlight glinted on the wet sand, painting it silver and white. As Jenyfer ran back along the beach, her shadow raced beside her, a crisp black outline. Water crept over her toes; it was cold but, as the ocean kissed her skin, the song inside her burst to life. Smiling, she let it sweep over her, until the magic she kept hidden in her veins thrummed in warning. Jenyfer glanced over her shoulder, then darted away from the water, flinging herself into the nearest bushes.

A fishing boat was approaching the beach, skimming in on the tide. There were four men seated in the boat, but she couldn't make out their faces. No one glanced down her end of the beach and Jenyfer relaxed. Instinctively, her magic slunk away, leaving droplets of water on her palms. She had no idea how to use it, did not understand a thing about it, and had never worked up the courage to ask her aunt. It was better to pretend it didn't exist.

Two of the men jumped out, helping drag the boat onto the sand, grunting with the effort. Water swirled around their bodies. The men in the boat were struggling to lift something wrapped in what looked like canvas. Jenyfer narrowed her eyes, wishing she was closer as the bundle was eventually hefted over the side and into the arms of the waiting men.

'… heavy…'

'Did you expect it to be light?'

'Wait until they see!'

The last voice dripped with excitement that Jenyfer recognised and as he lifted his face to look up at the moon she saw his features clearly. Bryn. She hadn't known he was out on the water tonight. He usually told her when he was going out.

The other men jumped from the boat, rushing to help with the weight of whatever they carried. Jenyfer frowned. No wonder they were excited. She'd never known anyone to bring in a catch that large before, but why was it wrapped in canvas and not a net?

The men shuffled up the beach towards the village, their prize held awkwardly between them. One of them stumbled; his end of the catch fell to crash into the sand.

The canvas fell away and Jenyfer had to slap her hand over her mouth to stop from crying out.

The fin that was bathed in moonlight was bigger than the fin of any fish she had ever seen. The scales were iridescent blue, shimmering as silver as the sand. Cursing, the man who had stumbled hurried to secure the canvas, but not before Jenyfer saw that fin twitch and an unearthly screech split the night.

A mermaid.

CHAPTER 3

Kernou clustered around the beach almost desperately. From the deck of *The Excalibur*, Ordes watched the first rays of the dawn strike the grassy hills behind the town, then shoot between the simple buildings and across thatched roofs towards the ocean. The light broke onto the sand and painted the beach and the sea surrounding the ship with flames that faded quickly. Sunrise was always over too fast.

His father stood further along the deck. Tymis Merlyni was watching the town as well, his shrewd gaze sliding over the cottages and the lone fishing boat, resting at an angle against the beach, like it had been parked there in haste. Ordes had seen no one near the boat, the fishermen long gone by the time he appeared on deck.

The town was a strange place, ruled over by Ulrian Tregarthen. Ordes' eyes lingered on the cliff face at the far end of the beach. He couldn't see it, but he knew that at the end of the beach, wedged between the rocks, was a wooden stake, the same sort found in each village along the coast.

His stomach turned. The stake was for Magic Wielders, people like him, considered unnatural, servants of the Beast.

Belief in the One God had slowly spread like a poison from the Sacellum in Malist, Teyath's capital. Ordes had never been there, and wasn't in a hurry to visit. The city was full of Witchfinders – the Shaleitari, men, and sometimes women, trained to sniff out magic. The irony was not lost on Ordes. To be able to smell magic on another meant possessing magic, but it seemed the One God and his followers did not object to a Magic Wielder who served them.

What had those people been offered, to turn on their own?

Ordes had barely slept the whole time they'd been marooned in the Bay of Calledun. According to his father, he'd never been restful when the water was still. Even as a babe, Ordes preferred it when the sea was wild and rocky, when the waves tossed the ship from one foaming crest to another and the men hung their heads over buckets. Tymis would stand on the deck with his infant son in his arms and let the storm wash over them until Ordes was snoring on his shoulder.

Tymis had always been a god-like figure in himself, but Ordes knew he wasn't a god, just a man, as flawed as any other, as driven as the rest of them with the same desires and wants.

'Why here?' Ordes asked, his gaze remaining on Kernou as his father came to stand beside him.

'I don't know. *The Excalibur* brought us here, like she brings us anywhere, and there is always a reason,' Tymis answered, running his hand through his shoulder-length dark hair. The water was calm and still around them, the sails limp; while not becalmed, the ship had drawn them to this spot and now, they had to wait.

'Have you ever thought to ask her to be a little clearer?' Ordes mumbled.

Tymis chuckled, reaching out to ruffle his son's hair, like he used to when Ordes was small. He said nothing, not needing to.

After spending his life on board the magical ship, Ordes knew her as well as his father did. The ship guided them, leading them where she wished. *The Excalibur* was a fey ship, ruled by laws not of this realm, and her crew were therefore ruled by her and all aboard were blood-sworn to Tymis, Ordes included. He had taken the oath willingly, like all the crew had. It was always made clear whenever they took on a new man that the blood oath was voluntary, but Ordes was yet to meet a sailor not willing to drop to one knee and open the skin of his palm when Tymis Merlyni asked him to. Such was his father's power over men; in him, they saw a leader.

A gentle breeze skimmed the water, reaching over the railing to tickle the skin on the back of Ordes' neck. He wanted to turn around but forced himself to be still, to not look over his shoulder, to ignore the lilting voice that tugged at his insides like a song he couldn't ever remember hearing.

Somewhere behind them, shrouded by mystery and folklore, was Avalon, the Isle of Mists and the realm of Ordes' birth. Avalon was a place of magic and wonder. The island could only be seen in that liminal space just before dawn, or at twilight, when the veil between the worlds thinned and the mists parted. As a young man, Tymis found his way through the mists, washing up onto Avalon's shores after his boat sank. The Witch of the Mists, Niniane, had tended his wounds and allowed him to stay. He stayed for years, caught in the space between the realms, but eventually grew restless and wanted to leave. The way Tymis told the story, he escaped the island by stealing one of Niniane's ships, taking his infant son with him.

As punishment, Niniane had bound Tymis' magic.

Ordes did not know his mother; she was from Avalon, a servant of the Goddess. When he looked in the mirror, he saw a face cast from the same mould as his father. He had his father's eyes, his colouring, his messy, slightly wavy hair. But the structure of his face – the high cheekbones and straight nose, sharp jaw and the unnatural smoothness to his skin

– it was a fey face, features gifted by his mother, along with the pointed tips of his ears.

He'd also inherited her magic and most of the time, he muddled through. His father had taught him the basics, but magic was mostly intuitive. Ordes could use his magic to move objects or light a lantern, float his dirty plates across the room or pick his clothes up off the floor. He could control the way the wind moved and hold water in the air with his mind. Fire eluded him, and while water was fickle and hard to hold, Ordes could manipulate it in all its forms with ease. Water moved with its own purpose – it always found a way. It might take centuries, but the wave would wear down the rock eventually. He liked that about water; it was determined, stubborn. And patient.

The Excalibur's crew knew what Ordes was and, if anyone had a problem sailing with a fey Magic Wielder, the nearest port became their new home. There had been no concealing Ordes' magic when, as a seven-year-old, he had managed to conjure a dog made of water after one of the sailors had described the animal Ordes had never seen. He wanted one, and a magical child who wanted something usually found a way to get it. He'd kept his water-dog for a week, until he fell ill from overuse of his magic and his pet vanished back into the ocean from which it had come.

Part-fey, part-human.

At times, Ordes didn't feel like either.

He rubbed at his eyes. Sometimes, he wished he could pluck them from his head. The crew trusted his faery eyes to warn them about mermaids and syhrens and whatever else lurked around Teyath's coastline. He could see the things humans could not. He saw the Bag Noz, the boat of the Otherworld, which often passed by on the way to the island of Lyonesse and the portal to the realm of the dead. Ordes saw the faeries of the sea – the selkies and water horses – and the faeries of the land. He'd seen piskies flitting around villages at night, doing the chores no one had managed to complete during the day. He'd seen the storm demon, and he'd seen the Night Riders astride the moorland ponies of Newlyn. He'd saved a man from being pisky-led into the forest outside Arcdon, where the poor soul would have danced until his death. And he'd heard the Iannic-ann-ôd and their ghostly calls along the shoreline at night, as they tried to tempt fishermen to their doom.

Teyath was a land crawling with fey creatures, yet somehow, somewhere along the way, people had closed their eyes to the Little Folk. The land would never be free of faeries, no matter how much the Magister of the Sacellum wished it. The Little Folk were tied to the land, to the sea, to the fabric of the world. They had existed before humans, and would continue to exist long after they had gone.

Tymis smothered a yawn and stretched luxuriously. The morning sun had crept into the sky and the mists had lifted, revealing an ocean as smooth as glass and as still and silent as a graveyard. No ripples marred the surface and the water was clear, shot through with sunlight. Ordes could see the sea floor below them. Small fish darted, bursts of colour and speed, and the water-smooth pebbles that littered the sand were as shiny as jewels.

His father left him with a gentle slap on his back. Below deck, Ordes could hear the rest of the crew begin to wake. Soon, they would all be topside with him, mumbling about the lack of wind while the night watch went to catch some rest.

Ordes couldn't resist any longer. He turned to face the open ocean, finding nothing but clear skies and smooth water. Avalon had hidden itself for the day, but it was waiting, somewhere out there. Fishermen told tales of seeing spires and castles beneath the waves, or glimpses of them through the mists, but he'd never seen any sign of the island – the one fey thing he truly wished to see.

On the horizon, where the ocean met the sky, a fin broke the surface of the water, sunlight glimmering off the iridescent green scales. Mermaid, or syhren, Ordes couldn't be certain. Both were deadly, for all their allure and beauty, but he'd choose to tangle with a mermaid over a syhren any day.

Ordes sighed, wishing the damn ship would make her reasons clear soon. For all his impatience, he was his happiest on the water, with the sun on his face and the salt air kissing his skin.

Tymis had told him that, the night he was born, the sea around Avalon had risen, the tide higher than it had ever been. Ordes thought it was bullshit, just a stupid story a father told a son, to make his younger-self think he was important in the grand scheme of the world and its mechanisms. According to his father, when Ordes was a week old, he had taken his baby in his arms and stood waist deep in the cool shallow waters off the coast of Avalon, his mother watching from the soft sands of the beach behind them, and there, all manner of sea creature and faery had come to see the child.

Kayrus – the ship's helmsman and navigator – came above deck, blinking in the bright morning sun, Iouen on his heels. Kayrus nodded in Ordes' direction and headed to the quarterdeck, where Ordes knew he would stand with one hand on the wheel even though they weren't going anywhere. The ship might set her own course, but she still needed steering and Kayrus had been with them long enough that he was used to *The Excalibur* and her ways.

The Excalibur was the jewel of the seas; Ordes had never seen a more spectacular ship. Not even *The Night Queen* could compare – Kat's ship was impressive, but she was smaller, with two major sails instead of three. *The Excalibur* was faster, built for speed and manoeuvrability. She had two gun-decks and twenty cannons, three fully-rigged masts, and a crew of almost seventy men – some of whom Ordes couldn't name. They'd just taken on board a further ten sailors at Newlyn last month.

The Night Queen was Niniane's invention as well, and she carried a dozen cannons and a crew of over forty women. *The Night Queen's* one advantage was Katarin and her magic, magic she knew how to wield. Ordes wondered how much better *The Excalibur* could be if he could harness his magic properly, but he'd probably never know. Whenever he used it for anything more than turning on the lights, he had the sense there was *more*, like he was just skimming the surface of something, but he'd never been able to push past that barrier and dig deeper.

Without turning from where he was examining the horizon, Iouen grunted. 'I suppose, while we're here, you'll find some reason to go ashore.'

'Won't we all?' Ordes asked in response. It had been some time since the men had been off the ship.

'Not me. Not in this place, anyway,' Iouen added scornfully. 'All the rum in the world isn't worth the trouble.'

Ordes turned his gaze back to Kernou, filled with a sudden desire to know just what was happening in that town.

CHAPTER 4

There was a strange sort of pleasure that came from maintaining a lie, to first cultivate it and tend it as carefully as the most delicate of flowers. Arthur Tregarthen wasn't naive enough to be unaware of the dangers, but every time he managed to look his father, his Chif, in the face and lie, a spark danced along the length of his spine to tickle the back of his neck – the knowledge he had made it through one more day, the lie intact and the truth still veiled and hidden within the deepest parts of himself. It always gave him a well-earned burst of courage.

But that never lasted long.

Arthur was on his knees, his father beside him, hands clasped and heads bowed before the altar. Almost as long as the table in their kitchen, the altar was dressed in deep red cloth, as soft as the first breath of the summer sun. It dripped with candles – seventy of them. Arthur knew. He counted them each time he had to light them, wishing that, somehow, one or ten would vanish throughout the day. Seventy tiny flames flickered, the light a blazing welcome to the One God in the otherwise dark room and darker house. Arthur had spent many hours before the altar, crouched on the stone until his knees were bruised and the muscles in his shoulders were ready to crack like dried mud.

The words of the One God fell from his lips; he spoke them with relish, with devotion, in the way that was expected, but they were empty words, holding no meaning for Arthur at all. His voice chimed in alongside his father's, a softer counterpoint to Ulrian's harsher tone. Even when worshipping his god, Ulrian managed to be stern.

Arthur's legs hurt. His hands hurt where they were clasped at his chest. He couldn't remember how long they'd been kneeling. He could feel the approaching dawn, that intense heat, that energy, hovering behind the hills in the east, preparing itself to strike into the sky and bathe the world in light after a night of darkness.

Arthur was on borrowed time. He was dancing with death; the ultimate truth of his lies.

He went to the men's prayers with his father and recited the Decalogue. He placed his forehead on the cold stone floor before the altar, while his stomach turned and his heart beat so hard and fast it was painful. He was reverent and respectful in all things, but the fear of discovery was a living thing, squirming and burning his insides, burrowing through the core of him until sometimes he wasn't sure if any of it was real. If this life was a dream, Arthur was begging to wake up.

Ulrian wanted Arthur to be Chif, only Arthur did not want that to be his future. He had never wanted it, but had spent his life being reminded of his duty. If only he wasn't his father's son. Sometimes, Arthur wished for nothing more than to be a simple fisherman, but the one time he had suggested he could go out on the water and learn, his father had laughed, and then sternly reminded him of his sworn role.

Arthur had sworn nothing, not in earnest. He lied to his father, he lied to the One God. The way Ulrian would look at him sometimes had Arthur wondering if the One God did indeed speak to his father.

Knocking echoed through the house. Arthur paused in his prayer, but Ulrian did not stop.

The knocking continued.

'Father...'

Ulrian did not falter, not even to admonish his son. Arthur swallowed, clasping his hands tighter as he stumbled over the words while the knocking sounded again, harder this time, more insistent, each echoing thump burrowing into Arthur's brain. He could feel the words of the Decalogue twisting on his tongue.

Three more knocks, before silence and prayer spread through the house.

Eventually, Ulrian finished and rose to his feet, his movement fluid and smooth. If Arthur hadn't been there with him, he'd have never believed his father had been crouched on the stone floor before the One God's altar for hours.

He knew, though, that his father believed physical pain was a tool to bring them closer to the One God, closer to the beauty of the next world, a world offered in promise to those who were faithful. Arthur had seen the marks on his father's back. He had seen the whip, held in Ulrian's own hand, and had watched as his father opened the flesh between his own shoulders until the stones were slick with blood.

That morning, ten-year-old Arthur knew for certain the One God was not the God of beauty and strength, for what beauty was there in bloodshed and pain, and what true strength was there in a hand that flexed with violent darkness?

His father explained it as transcendence.

The knocking began again.

Arthur fidgeted.

Ulrian gave him a stern look, a reminder that his punishment would come later, before he turned from the altar and swept from the room. His footsteps resounded through the cold and still house. Arthur stood with a groan, casting a hateful glance at the altar. Quickly, he extinguished those seventy candles before he smoothed his hands over his shirt and hurried after his father, his knees aching and his shoulders stiff.

In the hall, the door was thrown wide, the light of the morning sneaking inside, illuminating the four men gathered on the doorstep. None of them had crossed the threshold. Ulrian stood with his hands held stiffly by his side; the only sign he would give the men that they had interrupted his moment with the One God.

One of the fishermen removed his woollen hat, holding it between large, scarred hands that could probably crush Ulrian's skull if he wanted. But the man lowered his eyes and when he spoke, his voice was reverent.

'Apologies, Chif, but we have something you should see.'

His words opened the gates for the others, and they all spoke at once, fear and excitement colouring their voices. Arthur drifted closer, staying behind his father.

'... mermaid...'

'What?' he gasped. Ulrian glanced over his shoulder, saw his son lurking in the shadows, and frowned. Arthur didn't care; he moved closer, his father's eyes on him. Arthur arranged his face into a mask of disgust. 'I want to see it.'

'Why?' His father demanded.

'To see that which the One God declares unnatural and not meant for this world,' Arthur replied, as he should. Ulrian held his eyes before he nodded, turning back to the fishermen. Behind the man who had spoken first, Arthur could see a large shape wrapped in canvas.

Ulrian stepped out into the brisk morning air, Arthur following him. The fishermen moved aside to let the Chif pass; Ulrian crouched beside the canvas, his head tipped to one side, before he stood and gestured for Arthur.

Arthur approached, his stomach in his throat and his tongue thick as nerves grabbed hold of him. His father nodded, waving at the canvas shroud and Arthur understood – it was for him to unwrap, a present from the One God. Swallowing, he dropped to his still-aching knees on the cobblestones outside their home and reached for the corner of the canvas, peeling the cloth back like the skin of a ripe fruit.

He froze, the wrongness of what lay before him echoing through the thundering of his heart. Ulrian rested his hand on Arthur's shoulder and squeezed, mistaking his son's stillness for devout disgust. Instead, Arthur was burning inside as he stared at the mermaid, at her pallid skin and blank eyes, the long torso, the naked breasts, gills positioned beneath the rib cage and the long tail, scales a dull grey.

She was beautiful, but she was dead.

He sat back on his heels, unable to look away from her face, his father's voice a distant thing, Ulrian's tone both delighted and disgusted as he praised the fishermen for catching her, for putting an end to what the One God deemed should not be.

'Mermaids – indeed, all the Other Ones who remain – are vestiges of the Old Ways,' Ulrian was saying. 'The One God will see the end of all those things he is not pleased with, for His way is the New Way, and He is preparing the world for those who will come after us. It is our job, men, to be faithful and to do all we can to help in His plans.'

As the men murmured their agreement, Arthur glanced quickly at each of their faces. He stopped on the face of Bryn Hawkens. He knew Bryn. They had played together as children, when things were simpler and they were all innocent of the true ways of gods and monsters and men. Bryn met Arthur's gaze, and looked away.

'Who caught her?' Arthur heard himself ask.

One of the older men clapped Bryn on the back, and then he was being dragged forward to receive a blessing from the Chif on behalf of the One God.

CHAPTER 5

Jenyfer dreamt of the sea but, sometimes, she wondered if the sea was dreaming of her. The connection she felt to the water, the rhythmic push and suck of the waves, the shifting of the sand on the ocean bed, was so strong at times that she wasn't sure if it was her or the sea that was sleeping.

With her head as foggy as the coastline before dawn, Jenyfer sat at the kitchen table nursing a cup of tea. Tamora flitted around in the background, her deep red hair bundled awkwardly beneath her plain linen cap. The pot on the stove pumped the scent of herbs into the air as Tamora mixed Jenyfer's nausea tonic. Her stomach was rolling particularly violently this morning. The nausea was a familiar part of Jenyfer's life and Tamora's tonics worked; but no one knew about them, except Lamorna. Jenyfer knew that, once, her aunt had been a healer and midwife to the town. But then things had changed and the only medicines people were allowed were the bitter powders and tonics dished out by the Konsel apothecary.

Jenyfer was finding it hard to concentrate on anything. Her inner song swirled inside her, loud and insistent, giving her a headache to accompany the twisting of her stomach.

The front door swung open with a dramatic flourish and Lamorna, wild-eyed and hard-faced, stomped inside. Her sister's bed had been empty when Jenyfer woke and, seeing the basket Lamorna carried, Jenyfer realised she'd been at the market, just as she remembered it was supposed to be her task this morning.

Lamorna dumped the basket on the table so hard the teapot rattled and Jenyfer clutched her cup tighter. The dreams of water and waves were still flowing around her head and her tongue was thick, her eyes dusted with sand and salt.

'They've got it on display, like some trophy,' Lamorna was saying. She unpacked her basket, slamming each apple and potato on the table in her disapproval – Jenyfer wouldn't call it anger. Lamorna didn't get angry; she disapproved, and most of the things she disapproved of began with Jenyfer's name. Jenyfer was the older sister, yet somehow, whenever Lamorna was around, she felt like a child.

Tamora reclaimed the apples and set them in the bowl beside the teapot. 'You'll bruise the fruit,' she scolded gently. 'And what are you talking about?'

'The fishermen brought it in the other night and it's strung up in the market square, right in the middle so there is no way anyone could miss it – not that they would with such a crowd gathered around it. It's completely unnatural and against everything the One God—'

'Lamorna,' Tamora cut in, her voice soft but firm as she drained Jenyfer's tonic into small brown glass bottles.

Jenyfer rubbed at her face as her sister smoothed back non-existent stray strands of sunlight coloured hair from her severe knot.

'A mermaid.'

Jenyfer dropped her cup. Hot tea spilt across the table. She sat, frowning, as her aunt tutted and wiped up the mess. 'What mermaid?'

Lamorna turned blazing blue eyes on Jenyfer. 'I thought you'd know. I thought Bryn would have told you, considering he was the one to catch it yesterday morning.'

'I haven't seen Bryn since...' Since you snuck out and watched his boat come in, a little voice whispered. 'I thought that was a dream,' Jenyfer whispered.

Tamora was frowning as Lamorna sighed in disapproval. 'You went out? Again?' Tamora said more than asked. She already knew the answer.

'She is going to bring nothing but ruin on us all,' Lamorna announced piously. '"A woman should not wander—"'

'Not now, Lamorna!' Tamora interjected, squeezing the dish cloth tightly. 'Did anyone see you, Jenyfer?'

'No.' The mermaid was real! She was real. Forgetting her nausea, Jenyfer pushed her chair back and hurried for the door, barrelling past her sister, who had attempted to block her path. Lamorna cried out in objection but Jenyfer didn't stop.

'Where are you going?' Tamora called, her voice worried.

'I need to see for myself,' Jenyfer muttered.

'Her hair—'

'Not *now*, Lamorna, for the Sea's sake.'

'The One God...'

Their voices fell away as Jenyfer broke into a run, scattering stones and sand as she raced towards the town, her heart in her stomach and her stomach in her throat.

A thousand people, give or take, called Kernou home. Most were fishermen, or craftsmen – the town was equipped with a blacksmith and baker, a fishmonger, and a cloth merchant. Children learnt their lessons at home, crowded around kitchen tables while their mothers attended to the household chores. When she was a child, between lessons, Jenyfer remembered being able to run freely through the streets, or along the beach, or over the hills and across the moorland that overlooked the neat cottages.

This was before the Chif and the Konsel decided that running wild was not something the One God approved of, not even for children. Jenyfer wasn't sure how old she was when she had started sneaking from the cottage at night, but it had been the tension that built and burnt inside her, threatening to spill over, that drove her. When her shoulders had become so tight she could barely move, not even to tend the vegetable garden or the beehive they kept at the end of the yard. Lamorna would not go near the bees, so it was up to Jenyfer. But tending bees when she was a ball of tension was not always easy – the tiny creatures seemed to sense when she was agitated, and that was when they would sting her.

Most of the homes in Kernou were simple cottages, the sort found in any seaside town in Teyath. The One God did not approve of wealth, although Jenyfer thought that was a lie. She had never been inside the Chif's house, but she had stood outside it more than once, soaking up every detail – from the manicured garden beds bursting with blossoms, to the thick thatch on the roof and the walls, washed so white they were almost blinding in the midday sun. The Chif's fence was in perfect condition, the house far enough from the ocean wind and sea-spray that the damp could not chew on the timber. The windows were framed in dark wood, the front door solid oak, shining in the sunlight.

But what struck Jenyfer the most was how large the house was, at least three times the size of her cottage. She'd wondered how many bedrooms there were and had been still wondering about things like how big their dining table was, how many fireplaces there were, long after she'd been shooed away by an old woman she'd assumed was the housekeeper.

Now, Jenyfer only ever looked at the Chif's home when she was sneaking past it on her way up the hill, where the ancient stone circle lay in the middle of the moor. In summer, the moor was covered in purple heather and white cottongrass. The hills were the best place to find burdock, which was good for digestion, as well as juniper, rosemary, orange cloudberries, and blackberries. There were hares and grouse on the moors, red deer, and plovers, whose nests were architectural wonders.

And the stone circle was the place to find korrigans. Jenyfer didn't go there often – while she never felt threatened by the shape-shifting faeries, she was highly conscious of the danger they posed. There was a wildness about them, and they spoke in riddles most of the time, when they bothered to speak at all, but Jenyfer was drawn to them, to what they represented – power, and freedom. No one would dare tell a korrigan what they could wear or where they could go.

Jenyfer had never gone further than the circle. Beyond the moors, the land fell away into a steep valley before rising slowly, the grassland giving way to granite tors and boulders that folded over one another, the rock dark with age and moss.

The mountains rose into the sky on the other side of the valley. Sometimes, their tops vanished completely beneath the thick fog that crept down their sides and over the valley to kiss the moor and tumble into the town. When the wet mist rolled in from the sea, Kernou was lost under a thick grey blanket.

As she approached the first of the houses and slipped between them towards the market square, Jenyfer could feel the heartbeat of the ocean thrumming beneath the ground, which was shifting and rolling beneath her feet in perfect timing with her stomach. She swallowed as she approached the crowd gathered around an ornate stone cross, the symbol of the One God. It had been brought all the way from the Sacellum in Malist and unveiled with much ceremony and flourish. The cross was accentuated with a circle that intersected the arms and stem of the structure. The four arms of the cross represented the people in the four corners of the world, and the circle, a shape without beginning and end, symbolised the One God's endless love for all his servants.

Jenyfer hated it. The structure loomed above the people clustered at its base, staring and pointing, their whispers and murmurs about abominations cutting into Jenyfer's ears. She pushed her way through the crowd, not caring who she elbowed and not listening to their mutterings.

She had to see.

The mermaid was indeed on display, her long arms tied with thick rope, stretched out from her body on the large cross. The torso of a woman, with bare breasts and a slender waist led to a flowing tail where her legs should be. The night Jenyfer had seen her, her scales had shimmered with the moonlight. Now, they were a dull grey, all the light and shine drained with the horrible fate she had suffered. Her skin was tinged with blue, and her hair was the colour of the ocean under sunlight. There were gills below her prominent rib cage, and a terrible gaping wound, the flesh torn like paper, the dried blood around it a dark blue.

Jenyfer's breath hitched but she forced herself to look at the mermaid's face, at the slit-like nose and large, fish-like eyes. Eyes that were blank and staring at nothing in death. There was webbing between the mermaid's fingers.

A mermaid. A child of the sea.

A faery.

Jenyfer swallowed the lump that lodged in her throat. Even the song branded into the very core of her was silent.

A hand descended on her shoulder, making her jump.

'I was going to come and see you later.' Bryn's deep brown eyes were on the mermaid, sandy-coloured hair wild with the wind. He smelt of the sea and she guessed he'd not long returned from the water – he was dressed in a heavy woollen jumper and pants. His strong fingers dug into her skin and she wanted to cringe away from him, but she made herself stay still.

'To brag?' Jenyfer snapped, unable to help her anger. She still needed to ask him to get her away from Kernou, but now she knew he was not the one to help her, not after this. 'Did you really do this?'

Bryn nodded, his face alight with excitement and pride. 'Isn't she hideous?'

'No,' Jenyfer said quietly. 'She's beautiful.'

Bryn looked around nervously, but it appeared no one else had heard Jenyfer's words. 'Jen, she's not natural. You know that.'

'I know what the Chif and his God want you to think,' Jenyfer hissed under her breath.

Bryn ignored her tone, puffing out his chest and standing up straighter, his face full of boyish pride. 'I'm the first to catch one. Ever. Imagine that? The Chif said I was special.'

'Why couldn't you just leave her alone?' Jenyfer asked. She could feel the tears brimming in her eyes and blinked them away, not understanding why she was upset. She wiped her wet palms on her skirt and curled her hands into fists, trying desperately to reign in her anger, her disgust at what Bryn had done. They'd grown up together and had been friends for as long as she could remember, but, at this moment, she may have been standing next to a stranger. Seeing him so proud of what he had done, what he had murdered, made her want to tear his eyes out.

'A spectacular catch, Bryn,' boomed a voice behind them. 'The One God is pleased.'

Slowly, Jenyfer turned around to face Ulrian Tregarthen. The Chif was tall, his dark hair recently cut severely short. His strong brow was folded into a little frown, and his deep blue eyes bore into hers. He was dressed in his usual rich red coat, starched white shirt and dark vest with gold buttons running neck to navel. Jenyfer lowered her eyes, taking in his polished boots and neat trousers.

She wondered if the Chif had ever worked a day in his life. Behind him, lingering and looking as uncomfortable as he always did in his father's presence, was Ulrian's son, Arthur. Jenyfer caught his eye. He raised his eyebrows and gave her a polite smile, quickly smoothing it from his face as Bryn folded his arms. She did like Arthur, probably more than Arthur liked himself. He was quiet and gentle. For all his wealth and the grand house, she didn't envy him at all.

The Chif was still looking at her. 'You remember what the One God says, Jenyfer Astolat, don't you?'

'That God made man in his image and anything else is an abomination and a creature of sin,' she parroted, trying to pull up a shred of the piousness her sister possessed. She forced herself to swallow and meet his gaze, to ignore the feeling of ropes around her wrists, to ignore the feeling of the sea washing over her toes. 'It was right for Bryn to catch it and bring it here, for everyone to see that which He doesn't approve of.'

The Chif narrowed his eyes briefly and Jenyfer's heart pounded so loudly she was certain he could hear it. Eventually, he nodded. 'Be certain to attend the women's prayers tomorrow evening, Jenyfer. It's been reported to me that you have not been attending the circle in your neighbourhood. I hope you have been praying at home.'

'I have,' she said, schooling her face into the sort of expression Lamorna might wear. 'Every day.'

'Good girl,' the Chif said approvingly. 'The One God sees all and He will be pleased. Have you learnt the hymns?'

'No,' Jenyfer answered bluntly.

'She doesn't sing,' Bryn explained; his hand came to rest on her shoulder again, a strangely possessive action. 'She can't.'

'Bryn!' she hissed.

'It's alright, Jenyfer. The One God encourages honesty in all things. You do not need to be angry with Bryn. The Decalogue says to forgive others their mistakes, to not be proud and place yourself above others,' the Chif said smoothly.

Jenyfer opened her mouth but Bryn's hand tightened on her shoulder, so she simply nodded, lowering her eyes until the Chif had turned away, his hand on Arthur's shoulder as he steered his son from the square. Jenyfer let out a breath of relief.

'You lied to him,' Bryn said in a strange tone, one that had her suddenly worried, but she shook her head and folded her arms across her chest, shrugging away from his touch.

'I don't care.'

'The One God will know.'

She glared at her friend. 'I don't give a shit what the One God knows or doesn't know,' she snapped. 'What has gotten into you? Since when were you a believer, Bryn?'

He indicated the mermaid. 'Since I pulled *that* from the sea.'

She grabbed him by the arm, practically dragging him through the square, people scattering out of their way, their eyes burning through Jenyfer's dress. When she glanced over her shoulder, Bryn's face was amused, which only made her scowl and tighten her grip on him, pushing through his jumper to dig her nails into his skin, her scowl transforming into a smug grin when he failed to hide his hiss of pain.

When they were far enough away from everyone, she let him go, whirling to face him, jabbing her finger into his chest. He frowned at her.

'You're shittier than usual. What's going on?' he demanded.

'Is there a Witchfinder coming?' Jenyfer asked bluntly.

Bryn held her eyes. 'I don't know.'

'You do,' she insisted, taking a step closer to him. 'Lamorna heard you've been sharing a table with some Konsel men in the tavern most nights. What's that all about? The last I knew, you thought they were all idiots.' Two women carrying baskets hurried past, their eyes darting to Jenyfer and Bryn, no doubt noticing how close they stood, and how Jenyfer's hair was unbound and everywhere. She glared at them and they averted their eyes. When they had gone, she shoved Bryn hard enough that he stumbled back. 'Tell me what's going on. Why are you spending time with the Konsel?'

'For the Sea's sake, Jenyfer,' he said, and she didn't miss the slip of the tongue, the Old Ways' saying on his lips. 'Your sister needs to stop her gossiping. Who I share a table with is no one's business but mine.'

Jenyfer held his eyes, heart thundering. Bryn was the only person to know what she was. He was the only one she had ever told and she'd considered him an ally. But if he was drinking with Konsel men...

'Have you told them about me? Your new friends?'

His face blanched. 'Why would I do that?' He shook his head. 'I can't believe you...'

'I saw you, the night you brought the mermaid in.'

Bryn grabbed her by the upper-arms and gave her a little shake. She scowled but his face was deeply worried. 'You're going to get yourself killed,' he whispered. 'And I won't be able to stop it, no matter who my friends are, Jen.'

'You don't have to protect me,' she shot back, but a chill walked up her spine at his words. Jenyfer pulled herself free and turned her back on him, hurrying along the sand towards the path that led to the cottage.

At the other end of the beach, the stake waited. Jenyfer rubbed at her wrists and ran all the way home.

CHAPTER 6

That night, Jenyfer's dreams were terrible things filled with blood and salt water and a vessel of stone. She woke with sand in her mouth, the bedclothes drenched, music swirling through her head. The front door snapped closed and she dressed quickly, hurrying downstairs.

This time, it was her aunt who returned with news on her lips. Tamora's face was pale and she ushered both girls into the kitchen; Lamorna made tea while Jenyfer sat and rubbed at her weary eyes, trying not to fall asleep sitting up. She'd drunk her tonic and now fiddled with the bottle, enjoying the smoothness of the glass against her skin.

When they were all seated around the table, nursing cups of herbal tea, Tamora looked from one girl to the other, her face pinched and tight, her glorious red hair hidden beneath her simple linen cap. Her hands trembled where they held the cup and, suddenly, Jenyfer was wide awake, her belly squirming and her breathing shallow.

'What is it?'

'A body was found on the beach this morning,' Tamora said quietly.

'Was there an accident?' Lamorna asked, pouring herself a second cup of tea. Jenyfer didn't really care for the tea her sister brewed, it was too bitter. She always snuck a second spoon of honey when Lamorna was not looking, wanting to avoid any argument about the One God and his rules for living frugally – even though the honey came from their garden and they had enough in the pantry to last months.

Jenyfer set her cup to the side, watching her aunt closely. 'What happened?'

'There is no easy way to say it – but by the time either of you go into the town the news will have spread,' Tamora said with a little sigh, the frown between her eyes lingering. 'Arthur Tregarthen found the body this morning while out walking. It was Will Sanderson. He's a fisherman, you girls won't know him.' She sighed again and poured herself a second tea while Jenyfer and Lamorna waited patiently for her to sweeten it, Jenyfer noting Lamorna said nothing about the extra spoon of honey Tamora added. 'At first, Arthur assumed he had drowned. Will had gone out alone last night, and you know that is never a good idea.'

They knew. It was how their father had arrived at his watery grave.

'When Arthur turned Will's body over... he was missing his eyes, and it seemed his tongue had been torn out.'

Lamorna gasped and covered her mouth with her hands.

Jenyfer frowned. 'What does it mean?'

'What do you think it means?' her sister demanded. 'Obviously, some horrible sea-demon has—'

'No one knows for certain, Lamorna,' Tamora said wearily.

Lamorna picked up her cup and took a little sip. 'I bet that horrible ship and that *horrible* Katarin Le Fey are involved. Everyone knows what she does to the men she catches.'

Though Lamorna said it with horror, Jenyfer could only think that if Katarin Le Fey *had* got her hands on the fisherman, he must have done something to deserve his fate.

Tamora would not allow either of them to go to town that day, so Jenyfer spent most of it in the garden, tending the flowers and the faery shrub. Jenyfer's thoughts lingered on the mermaid and her stomach turned again as she saw those dead eyes and the wound decorating her flesh.

After a simple dinner of bread and cheese, Tamora extinguished the lanterns and sent them to bed. Jenyfer watched her sister kneeling by the bed, hands clasped to her chest as she prayed to the One God. She turned away as Lamorna finished up, rolling to face the wall and burrowing into her blankets, and waited until Lamorna had climbed into bed and blown out the candle before opening her senses to the night.

On the beach, below the hill their cottage rested on, the ocean swelled and played against the sand. Its wild rhythm bent and twisted its way into Jenyfer's heart, where it slowly shifted until it settled alongside the regular tune of the song that beat in her blood. When she was certain her sister was sleeping, she slipped from bed and padded from the room, coat in hand.

Jenyfer knew she shouldn't go out, not after what had happened to Will, but the mermaid... she wanted to say sorry for what had happened to her, to tell the sea to forgive them – forgive Bryn, for what he had done. Although terribly angry at him, Jenyfer told herself it wasn't his fault. Somehow, he had changed and she had failed to notice. She would notice it now, she vowed, and bring him to his senses... somehow.

It was dark out, only a slither of moon to light the world around her, but Jenyfer knew her way to the ocean with her eyes closed. She drifted down the sandy path, avoiding rocks, the grass reaching out to twine around her ankles. Once she reached the sand, she paused, her eyes swinging the length of the beach before her. She was alone, with nothing but the sea for company.

Jenyfer set off along the shoreline. She hadn't known Will; he was just another man tied to the ebb and flow of the water, to the shifting of the tides. Just another man who went about his life, and now, something had taken that life. Jenyfer plonked herself down on the sand, not caring that her dress was getting wet as the water lapped at her toes, skimming further to caress her backside. She sent a silent prayer to the sea for Bryn, and for her sister, not knowing why she included Lamorna – only that it felt right.

At the far end of the beach the rocks crowded against the base of a cliff. Jenyfer couldn't see it, but she could feel the stake beckoning to her, suggesting she tie herself to it now and save them all the hassle.

The sea was restless, the waves coming in set after rolling set, no pause given between them to catch a breath. Beyond the breakers, the nameless ship still waited, a dark outline against a star-littered sky. Jenyfer chewed her lip. She could steal a boat, row out there... except she couldn't row. She couldn't even swim.

Something broke the surface of the water. A head. Jenyfer held her breath as the creature came closer to shore; the force of the waves increased for a moment, then stilled, and she scrambled to her feet in shock. From the shallows in front of her, a woman's head emerged, followed by a torso, long silver hair plastered across her breasts and flowing down her body.

A syhren.

Jenyfer's heart stopped, then surged as the syhren stood, the silvery scales of her tail fading away until two long, slender, very human-looking legs appeared. The syhren watched her, the colour of her eyes hidden by the darkness around them. Jenyfer couldn't move, couldn't look away, utterly transfixed by the strange magic of the syhren. She had nothing to block her ears and she sent a silent plea into the night that the syhren wouldn't open her mouth and sing. Even though it was mainly men the syhrens sang to their doom, they had all been taught to never listen to their music.

The faery of the sea came closer, those powerful legs moving through the swirling water with ease.

Jenyfer tried to stand, to run, but her legs wouldn't move.

Caught in the syhren's stare, she could only watch helplessly as the faery stopped where the waves left patterns of white lace on the dark sand. She was so close. If Jenyfer leant forward, she'd touch her. She wriggled her toes, digging them into the sand instead.

The syhren dropped to her knees, still with her eyes on Jenyfer's face.

The faery did nothing, just looked, her strange eyes moving over Jenyfer's face; faint music floated through the air, delicate and sweet, like an invitation. Then, as quickly as she arrived, the syhren was gone, slipping beneath the waves. Moments later, a tail flipped free of the water.

Heart hammering, Jenyfer stared at the water. Lightning suddenly lit up the sky and she jumped, but in that flash of bright light, Jenyfer could see a silvery head, far out to sea, still watching her. Thunder rumbled and a storm rolled towards the shore with unnatural speed. As the first raindrops pounded the sand, Jenyfer turned and ran.

Her sister was awake, perched on her bed with her hands folded neatly in her lap, when Jenyfer tumbled through the door, panting and terrified. She skidded to a halt as Lamorna lit the candle that sat on the small table between their beds. Outside, lightning streaked across the sky, the thunder so close it made the cottage shake.

'What have you done?' Lamorna asked, her voice low.

Jenyfer wiped her hands on her dress. She was soaked to the waist and dripping water.

'You're going to get us all killed,' her sister said, still in that low voice.

'What are you talking about?' Jenyfer managed breathlessly.

Lamorna tossed her head. 'The One God knows what you are. I know what you are. Soon, if you're not careful, the whole town will know, and they will come for you. And us, as well – we'll be punished for being your family.'

Jenyfer's heart was pounding, the wild rhythm of a storm-lashed sea. She realised absently that her inner-lullaby had stopped. 'And what am I?'

Her sister spoke between her teeth. 'Witch.'

CHAPTER 7

Ordes was certain *The Excalibur* was playing with them. Why she'd brought them here, to this slice of coast on the western side of Teyath, was still unclear. It was dark and stuffy inside the tavern, the lanterns burning low, windows a tightly shuttered barrier, closing the building off to the world outside. Ordes didn't know why he was here, only that he'd woken that morning with a desire to go ashore. From the moment he'd set foot on the sand, pulling the boat up behind him, he had felt eyes watching him – some human, some not – but, beneath that, something tugged at his insides.

The group of fishermen who occupied the table nearest to him hadn't called for more drinks, nursing the same cups for the last half an hour. Ordes finished his rum and motioned to the young man behind the bar for another, his ears open to the murmured chatter around him, *about* him. They didn't realise he could hear every word, his faery ears more attuned than theirs – faery ears he kept carefully hidden beneath the length of his hair. He was certain the chatter would be less murmured and more shouty if the good people of Kernou realised they had a faery wandering around.

For a moment, Ordes thought about standing on the bar and announcing who and what he was for all to hear. He could handle them. A quick bit of magic and they'd be on their arses and he'd be gone; but he'd also heard the whispered talk about a delegation from the Sacellum due to arrive soon. It was probably best to avoid trouble.

The other interesting thing he'd overheard was that a body had washed up a few mornings ago, missing its eyes and tongue. That intrigued him. Waterhorses usually ate everything. Kelpies and mermaids had the potential to be dangerous but mostly stayed clear of humans, and there hadn't been a sea serpent in these waters for years. That left syhrens, but removing body parts was not usually their way, either.

Sighing, he set his mug aside and stood. The men at the table next to him paused in their talking, their eyes raking over him, before they turned away. He thought briefly of Kat and where she was right now. They hadn't caught sight of the *Queen* in over a month. Did she know about the Sacellum's visit, he wondered. Would there be someone tied to the stake for Katarin to rescue? Or did they burn them, here?

Ordes left the toasted air of the tavern behind and stepped out beneath a night sky littered with stars. The moon was just cresting the cliffs behind the town, a tiny slice of light against the blackness of the night. It was a short walk from the tavern to the beach.

The town was organised around a cobble-stone market square, with the tavern on one side and some guild houses on the other – a blacksmith, a bakery, a fishmonger, and shipwright. Beyond the main square, cottages with thatched roofs and stone walls dotted the landscape, some clustered close together, others set further back. The cottages climbed the gentle hillside, until the gradient of the landscape became too steep.

Rubbing at his face, Ordes groaned, realising the tide was yet to come in. He'd sit in the small boat and wait it out, he supposed. Better to be out here in the sea air, with the stars blanketing the sky, than in that mournful tavern listening to bullshit about the One God, dead mermaids, and rumours about his father.

He strolled across the square, pausing at that horrid cross. The body of the mermaid was gone, but Ordes could feel her, like an afterimage. He could smell the brine and fish scent of her, and the scent of her rotting flesh hung over the village like a cloud. He made himself face that cross, to remind himself of the horrors people were capable of. He could imagine her strung up there, her long body dangling like a fish on a hook. He wondered how they caught her. Mermaids were sly and sneaky things; he couldn't imagine one of them being tricked by a baited line or being careless enough to become tangled in a fishing net.

Hopefully, she managed to sink her sharp little teeth into at least one of them as they hauled her overboard. They would have been surprised by her weight. Mermaids looked like they were made of air, the way they moved through the water, but they were heavy, made of sharp bone and thick, sinewy muscle.

It would have been a horrible way to die, drowning in air as men drowned in water. For a moment, he considered going back into that tavern and thrashing the living shit out of everyone in there. He'd happily bruise his knuckles and unleash his magic to teach those men a lesson. Whether they'd been the ones to pull the mermaid from the sea or not, by letting them hang her up like a trophy, they were complicit in her death.

But, justice or not, it would make things harder for his father, for all the men on the ship, and for those with magic. He'd heard stories of Magic Wielders in other parts of the continent swept away in the dead of night, never to be seen or heard from again. The Shaleitari were good at their job, and their numbers were growing. From what Katarin had told him the last time they met, Cruithea was the promised land, the safe haven for Magic Wielder's. Kat had helped dozens escape their fate, ferrying them across the waves to the forests of the north.

Even the Shaleitari stayed away from Cruithea – the Inborn were lethal, both with their magic and their weapons.

Movement in the corner of his eye made Ordes drop a hand to the dagger at his hip, before he relaxed and grinned. A pisky. The little faery grinned back, showing off his toothless gums, before he beckoned and vanished between the bakery and the blacksmith, moving like a shadow. Ordes followed. The pisky led him to the edge of town, the cottages all dark for the night.

He was about to ask the pisky what it was playing at when it pointed.

Hurrying up the grassy slope, behind the last row of houses, was a woman. Her cloak was the colour of the night sky but, with his faery eyesight, Ordes saw her easily. He bit his lip, intrigued about the sort of woman who'd be running around Kernou in the dark, when all good girls were tucked up in their beds. He looked around for the pisky, but it was gone.

'Alright then,' Ordes mumbled softly, setting off after the woman.

As the breeze blew her scent towards him, the magic in his veins surged to life, recognising her for what she was. Kindred. A Magic Wielder. And a faery. That last realisation stabbed at him, urging him on, his heart stuttering. He quickened his pace, keeping his feet light and undetected, magic curled in his palms and danced like lightning over his knuckles.

The woman moved quickly, making no sound and leaving no prints in the sandy ground. She was practically running as she crested the hill and rushed out onto the moor. Ordes stopped, dropping to one knee and tucking himself close to the wind-shorn shrubs. In the weak light, he could make out a stone circle, the menhirs catching shards of moonlight and holding them so that the rock glimmered silver and white. It was the sort of place the Magic Wielders of old would have worshipped, and he was surprised the Chif had not torn the stones down. But old superstitions die slowly, and maybe there were still other gods to anger.

The woman paused just outside the perimeter of the stone circle. Her dark hair was unbound and flowing over her shoulders like a blanket. She glanced over her shoulder and he caught a glimpse of a pale face, full lips, and eyes that appeared silver. He made himself still, calling on his magic, letting it deepen the shadows that surrounded him – like stealing snatches of the night to wear as a cloak. Satisfied she was alone, the woman squared her shoulders and stepped inside the circle.

Immediately, the earth beneath Ordes' feet began to hum, and the breeze blowing in from the ocean intensified. He watched her place her hand on the menhir in the middle of the circle. The air around her shimmered and, then, a sound like tearing sailcloth split the night.

She was no longer alone.

Standing with her were three others – females, as tall as she was, with flowing hair that shimmered with silver and captured starlight. Their skin was like moonlight on the water and, as he watched, their unnaturally beautiful faces shifted in and out of focus.

Korrigans. Faeries of the land and the water. Ordes didn't know much about them, except that they were dangerous, predatory shapeshifters with the power of compulsion over humans.

He watched, fascinated, as the woman and the korrigans seemed to be talking. On the breeze, he could hear music and he closed his eyes, unable to help it, and that mysterious melody slipped beneath his skin, mingling with his magic, which thrummed and twisted in time with the notes.

Without warning, the pisky who had led him from the village appeared beside him, making him open his eyes with a jolt. The little faery bounced up and down on his heels, looking between Ordes and the woman.

'What do you want me to do?' he asked the pisky.

A mischievous grin split that ancient face before the pisky clicked his fingers and vanished. Ordes sighed and rubbed at his eyes. Piskies annoyed the life out of him.

His vision swirled as the world around him suddenly shifted; something hooked him behind his navel and left him crouched in the stone circle, a korrigan on either side and one behind him. The dark-haired woman stood in front of him, her arms folded. The wind pulled at her hair, whipping it around her face. Not a crease marked her pale skin and her pert nose was dusted with a faded constellation of freckles that he thought were cute, but it was her eyes that struck him. In the moonlight, they glimmered like a storm-kissed ocean, silver and blue and fierce.

She stared at him; a little face peeked at Ordes from behind a menhir. He scowled at the pisky, then turned back to the woman.

'Well,' he said. 'This is unfortunate.'

'How did you... were you following me?' Her voice was pitched low, lower than he was expecting. There was fear oozing from every part of her. Ordes swallowed and stood, keeping his movement slow and steady. The faeries would probably rip his throat out if the woman asked it.

'I was curious.'

'Curious?'

One of the korrigans poked him in the back with something sharp and his knees gave out. He was propelled towards the earth so quickly he was surprised he didn't fall through it; he tried to stand but the korrigans magic held him firm, vines snaking from the ground to grip his arms and ankles. Ordes glanced up at the woman, who was looking down on him, her bottom lip between her teeth.

'I'm not going to hurt you. You can call off your bodyguards.'

'You can see them?' Her voice was sharp.

'Why, can't you?'

The woman shook her head, her expression panicked. 'How can you see them?'

'Am I not supposed to see them?'

She shook her head again. 'I don't know anyone else who can see them, except...' She let her voice trail off.

'He has magic,' whispered one of the korrigans. 'Different magic. Old magic.'

The woman's expression had shifted from fear to outright terror. 'You need to go.'

'You don't need to be afraid of me,' he affirmed softly, at the same time wondering what the korrigan had meant about his magic.

The woman's sharp eyes crawled over his face. 'Who are you?'

'I'm from *The Excalibur*,' Ordes answered.

'A half-truth,' one of the korrigans hissed. 'A half-lie. Let us kill him, strip the flesh from his bones and feast on his insides.'

Ordes heard the faery lick her lips again; he swallowed, falling back on the only weapon he had in the moment – his shitty sense of humour. 'Although I don't mind a brawl, and I'm sure I'd taste fantastic, there's no need for violence, ladies.'

'Cheek.' The sound came from the air around him, hissing and scraping along his spine like claws. The korrigan put her mouth close to Ordes' throat and *sniffed* him. 'He smells like something long forgotten, a place out of time and a time out of place.' Her voice dropped, so only he could hear it. 'Faery of the Isle, you're a long way from home. Does your mother know, I wonder, where you carry your bones?'

Ordes turned to face the korrigan. Her pale eyes stared back at him, swept their way over his features. She smiled and licked her lips.

'What do you know about my mother?' he asked her.

She stroked the side of his face. A jolt went through him at the touch of her fingers on his flesh. 'One foot on the land, one in the sea. Born of two realms, yet outside of each you be,' she purred, then gripped him by the chin and forced his face from hers. 'No more questions.'

The woman had her arms wrapped around herself; the wind set her hair dancing about her face again, a halo of black burnished with moon-silver. 'Let him go,' she told the faeries. Suddenly, he was free, the korrigan's magic sliding from his skin like water.

Ordes stood, wiping his hands on his thighs as the woman watched him. 'No one knows that you're a Magic Wielder,' he murmured, looking at her closely. 'Do they?'

She pushed past him, striding from the stone circle. He felt rather than saw the faeries disappear, a ripping of the air. The woman darted through the darkness and he had run to catch her.

'I meant it,' he said, sliding in front of her and blocking her path. 'You don't need to fear me.'

'I need to go home,' she muttered.

'Wait,' he implored as she stepped around him.

She paused, glancing at him over her shoulder.

'Why are you so frightened?'

Her eyes were wide, skin silver-white in the moonlight. 'You know nothing about this place, do you?'

The shadows around them seemed to grow darker, deeper. 'Let me walk you home.'

'I'm fine on my own. Go back to your ship.' She turned away from him again. Before he could stop himself, he rushed after her, feet sliding in the sandy dirt, and caught her arm. Even through her clothes, he could feel her magic. There was something off about it, like it was being held back by something. He let his magic slide beneath her skin, delicate, gentle, keeping his face clear once he understood what it was – she'd been bound. Her magic was tied up in spells and, he realised, she had no idea; but those binding spells were coming apart at the seams. They didn't have long – *she* didn't have long – before that magic made itself known.

She shook herself free with a little growl. 'What do you want?'

'Just to make sure you get home,' he answered.

She sighed, continuing down the path without another word. He followed, and she ignored him. She walked with her arms folded around herself; but he could see her hands, curled into fists and tucked against her sides. They didn't speak. She led the way around the outskirts of town, ducking between buildings and shadows, making him wonder just how often she snuck around at night.

As they approached the last row of buildings, she suddenly stiffened. 'What is it?'

'The Konsel's guards,' she whispered. 'Up ahead.'

'Guards?' Ordes whispered back.

Her eyes cut to his. 'I told you you knew nothing about this place. We have to hide – well, I do, and you probably should too, pirate.'

'Whatever you say, witch.'

She scowled and slipped into the shadows, tucking herself against the wall of a cottage, motioning for him to follow. He did, sliding next to her. Her arm pressed against his – he could feel the heat of her skin, and her magic, through the fabric of her sleeve.

As the guards came closer, she held her breath.

It wasn't dark enough. Ordes flexed his fingers and the shadows around them deepened until they were thick and opaque, like the morning mist that cloaked the ocean before dawn. The woman didn't take another breath until the guards' footsteps had long been swallowed by the night.

Ordes let his magic fade.

They looked at one another. Without a word, she pushed herself off the wall and hurried away. He followed her along a narrow path that wound lazily upwards, until a cottage came into view. No lanterns burned in any windows. The wind blew in from the ocean, sharp and salty.

'This is where you live?'

'Yes,' she said, stopping at the wooden gate. She hesitated, resting her hand on the gate, and turned to him. 'Can you teach me? What you did back there.'

'I'm not sure...'

'Please.' She turned imploring eyes on him and he groaned.

'I can't resist a pretty face,' he said. 'Fine. When do you want to do this? Should I just knock on your door and ask to see you?'

She put her hands on her hips and tried to look stern, but a smile played at the corners of her mouth. 'I wish you could. The look on my sister's face would be worth it. But no. I can meet you somewhere. Tomorrow night?'

He looked at her curiously. 'How do you know I won't kill you?'

Delicate brows lifted. 'You would have done it already, wouldn't you?'

He smirked. 'Alright, I'll play. It's your town. You tell me where and when, and I'll be there,' Ordes replied. Maybe this was why *The Excalibur* had parked herself in the Bay of Calledun – this woman, and her hidden magic.

The woman pushed open the gate, carefully, so no sound eased from the hinges. He raised his eyebrows. 'Just how often have you done this?'

'Often enough, although I usually use the back gate. At the end of the beach, near that horrible stake, is a cave. It's private. No one will see us. Now go away.' She didn't wait to see if he did what he was told, hurrying along the stone path and disappearing inside the dark cottage.

CHAPTER 8

The Konsel were meeting in the main room. It was a large room in the centre of the house; no windows lined the walls, and it was stuffy and dark. The cross of the One God was nailed to the wall behind Ulrian's head, peering down at them all. Arthur eyed it with distaste, then turned his face away before his father saw.

Arthur had recently been invited to attend Konsel meetings. Preparation, his father told him, for when he was Chif. Only, Arthur did not want to be Chif. He did not like the six men of the Konsel – all old and bloated with self-importance. He had never seen any of them without their red Konsel coats, and wasn't sure he'd recognise them if he passed them in the street.

Ulrian sat with his hand on his copy of the Decalogue. The book was perfectly bound in the best leather, golden thread wound through the spine and emblazoned the front with the symbol of the circle and cross.

Arthur closed his eyes and clasped his hands at his chest as his father recited the prayer, Ulrian's voice ringing as loud and clear as a bell through the darkness of the room. Arthur and the Konsel's collective voices chimed in below it.

'Friends,' Ulrian began, his eyes sweeping over the men assembled before him. Ulrian sat at the head of the long table, its surface polished to a brilliant shine. Arthur could see his reflection in it, if he looked long enough – but studying one's reflection was a sign of vanity, so he lifted his gaze to his father, who continued, 'I have recently received word from the Sacellum, from the Magister.'

The Magister was the Head of the Sacellum, the House of the One God. Arthur watched his father closely. It was Ulrian's deepest wish to meet the Magister, to have the man visit Kernou and see the great work they were doing in the One God's name.

'The Magister has bestowed a great honour on us.'

Arthur snuck a look at the Konsel. Their faces remained composed, not a slither of noticeable excitement in their eyes at Ulrian's words. 'We shall soon be receiving a Witchfinder in Kernou,' Ulrian continued. 'He shall be most welcome in my home, and we shall show him how devout and committed Kernou is to the One God.'

Arthur's heart stuttered, convulsing sharply in his chest, shifting so quickly he could not hide his gasp.

'Son?' Ulrian's eyes drilled into Arthur's face.

'It's nothing,' Arthur mumbled. 'I'm just wondering why the Magister feels the need to send a Witchfinder. There are no Magic Wielders in Kernou, are there?'

'There are Magic Wielder's everywhere.' The speaker was Morley, an elderly man with a shock of white hair and eyes that seemed to wobble in his head when he spoke. 'The Magister does us a great honour.'

'That he does,' Ulrian agreed simply.

'Of course,' Arthur managed. His throat was painfully tight, and all he could think of was Jalen. Jalen, whom Arthur knew had magic. Jalen, with his soft blue eyes and windswept sandy hair. Whose very presence turned Arthur's insides to a burning mush. He kept his face composed. 'Does the Konsel suspect someone?'

'We have someone we have been watching,' Ulrian answered, his tone indicating he would not speak the name of the person the Konsel had already decided was guilty. They did not need a Witchfinder for that.

After the Konsel had gone, Arthur and his father remained seated in the hall. Ulrian was oddly silent, drumming his fingers lightly against the table-top. A frown rested between his heavy brows. Arthur studied him as much as he dared, wondering anew, like he did almost daily, at this man who was his father. He knew only small details of his father's life before he became Chif. The position was an elected one, not a familial one, and Ulrian had managed to win the people of Kernou over to obtain the position. Now, he was schooling Arthur for the job.

The only prayer Arthur had was they elected someone else.

Ulrian had grown up in Kernou, the Tregarthen family being well-regarded and respected tradespeople. He had been expected to continue in the family tradition, taking over the apothecary from his father, but the young Ulrian had bigger dreams. Leaving Kernou, he travelled over the mountains to Malist. It was there, from what Arthur understood, that he first heard the Word of the One God, bringing the new religion home when he returned.

Arthur knew nothing more than that, and he had never asked. Every question was met with a similar answer – 'It was the will of the One God.'

His father's eyes found his. 'You don't approve of the Sacellum sending us a Witchfinder?'

'It is the will of the One God,' Arthur intoned. 'So it is also my will.'

Ulrian inclined his head in approval. 'You will make a good student at the Sacellum,' he said simply.

'What?' Arthur blurted.

'I am sending you to Malist, Arthur,' his father replied. 'You will study the Word with the best tutors. You will immerse yourself in the pages of the Decalogue and, when you return, you will be ready to guide the people of Kernou.'

Arthur licked his lips, keeping his eyes on his hands, clamped tightly in his lap.

'Yes, father.'

Heart thundering dangerously, Arthur made his way out the back door of his house. On the hill behind was a flat rock, spread like a table-top over the earth. In the early morning, Arthur liked to sit there, facing the ocean, the sun rising behind him. From there, he could see the whole village, the whole of his world. He could watch the light strike the yellowed thatch of each roof, each white-washed stone wall, and he wondered what was going on between those walls and beneath those roofs. How many others were like him, how many others had impure thoughts invading their heads and urging them to do things they should not? From the rock behind his house, Arthur could see that light stretch like a golden finger, through the cobblestoned streets, until it reached the village square where, like a breath exhaled, it expanded to fill every corner of the space, alighting on the wooden cross of the One God.

But he was not headed for the rock today. He sucked in a breath of cool evening air and turned towards the town, spread out before him like an offering. Walking quickly, he was relieved to meet no one. The shops were long closed for the day and darkness was settling sleepily over Kernou.

Once, there was no cross looming over the village square. Authur could not remember a time when the cross and the One God were not a presence in his life; but he imagined that, in years past, before his father fell to his knees in front of an altar covered in glowing candles with the Word falling from his lips like rain, Kernou had been a different place.

He knew that, once, the Old Ones were worshipped, along with the demi-gods and the Small Folk of Teyath.

But no one spoke of those things anymore, especially not Arthur. He did not ask questions.

Arthur sighed and rubbed at his face, at the mouth that had only that morning spoken the words that burnt all the way to the very core of him. The words that marked him as sinner, as tarnished, a stain on this world that his father was determined to remove.

A man shall not lie with another man...

Jalen had advised him to run, but Arthur couldn't bring himself to do it. It wouldn't be as easy as Jalen seemed to think. To gather a bag and slip away in the night was one thing for an ordinary person, and it did happen – much more than Ulrian cared to admit. But for Arthur... he would be hunted down like a wild animal, brought back to suffer whatever justice his father and the One God decided on.

And Arthur knew what that was.

His eyes had read that passage in the Decalogue more times than he liked, always drawn there, to the fate that he may one day be subjected to. Would it hurt to burn, he wondered? Would his own father murder him for his God? He knew Ulrian was buried so deep in the One God's pockets, it wouldn't matter what Arthur did to atone for the sins his father so deeply condemned.

Once, when Arthur was small, a man had been brought to his house. He was not very old, perhaps younger than Arthur was now. Arthur did not know his name or even remember his face, but he remembered why he was there. Arthur had watched the man be led into the main hall. No one bothered to shut the door, so ten-year-old Arthur saw everything unfold.

Ulrian and the Konsel had held the man down and poured buckets of seawater over his head, one after the other, not stopping even when the man had almost drowned. They had burnt the soles of his feet with their candles, his screams drowning out their low recitation of the Decalogue.

Then, they had left him in the dark for days without food or water, someone always on the other side of the door, whispering the Word through the solid timber.

The man had left, limping, and Arthur had never laid eyes on him again.

When he had asked his father what the man's sin had been, Ulrian had simply picked up the Decalogue and read aloud from it. 'A man shall not lie with another man as with woman, for such acts are for heathens and sinners and shall be punished, for the Word is the Law and the One God is power and might.'

Arthur shivered and pushed those memories from his mind. He passed the closed shop-fronts and hurried through the empty square, not stopping to glance at the stone cross where they had tied the dead mermaid. He passed the tavern, the shutters pulled tight, the murmur of voices easing through them. Turning right where the sand began to reclaim the streets, he kept going, moving quickly through the darkness. He needed no lantern to light his path. He walked this way in his dreams most nights.

At the edge of town, soft light burning in the windows, was a small house. Arthur paused briefly, glancing over his shoulder, his eyes darting into the shadows, looking, as always, for eyes watching him back. With a quick intake of breath, he pushed the door to the house open and slipped inside, his father's last words that day lingering in his head, burrowing themselves in his blood, echoing so fiercely they rattled his bones.

Jalen was sitting at his simple wooden table, a bowl of soup before him. Steam rose from the bowl to curl around Jalen's ruggedly-handsome face.

'You're eating; I'll come back,' Arthur mumbled.

'Arthur.' Jalen chuckled. 'Sit down. Have you eaten?'

Arthur shook his head, sinking into a chair, legs trembling, shoulders tight. But when Jalen climbed to his feet and bustled around the small kitchen, Arthur couldn't help the smile that crept across his face at the sight of the other man, his scruffy blonde hair and sharply cut jaw, preparing food for him.

The Old Ways did not care if one man loved another.

Jalen set the bowl down before Arthur and returned to his seat on the opposite side of the table. Arthur's stomach flopped as Jalen's bright blue eyes met his, Jalen's smile smothering the fear in Arthur's belly, even if only for a moment. Jalen reached up to rub at the back of his neck, a gesture Arthur knew meant nerves, because he did it too.

'Eat,' Jalen told him gently, so he did. They didn't speak through their meal; Arthur barely tasted a thing, too busy sneaking glances at the other man over his bowl. His lips tingled. One kiss, stolen, and he'd thought about nothing else for two weeks.

Arthur cleared his throat. 'I attended a Konsel meeting this morning.'

Jalen's eyebrows rose and a smirk tugged at his mouth. 'That must have been riveting.'

'You have to be careful,' Arthur said tightly. 'The Sacellum is sending a Witchfinder.'

Before meeting Jalen, Arthur had known nothing about the world of magic, and they had known each other for months before Jalen let Arthur see who he truly was. Arthur was under no delusions about how much of a risk Jalen had taken and realising that, knowing Jalen had trusted him enough to share his secret, had opened a door in Arthur's mind, one he hadn't known was closed.

Not only had Jalen opened up the world of magic to Arthur, he had opened up the truth of who Arthur was to himself.

And Arthur had struggled to live with that truth ever since.

The more he learnt about magic, the more the layers of the Word wrapped around his thoughts peeled back as a new way of thinking, a new way of looking at the world, emerged. Arthur could see the connection between everything – how water fed the earth, how fire created as well as destroyed, how air fuelled fire, and how sunlight breathed life into the trees and plants of the forest. He could understand the power of the

Old Ways, could see why the Old Ones and their magic had been so revered, and could see all the spaces that worship of the One God did not penetrate.

Where, in the Word, was the space for the natural world? Without it, the village and its people would starve. Yet the Word all but denied its very existence by omitting to account for the intricacies of nature. It became clearer than ever that his father and the Konsel had it wrong.

Jalen got up, clearing their bowls from the table. When he returned, he didn't sit back down, but stood behind Arthur, resting his hands on Arthur's shoulders tenderly. Arthur closed his eyes, leaning back against the firm muscle of Jalen's stomach.

'I wasn't sure if you would come tonight,' Jalen said, his fingers stroking the back of Arthur's neck. Arthur closed his eyes, leaning into the touch, the callouses on Jalen's fingers sending tingles shooting through his body. 'You're worried – about more than the Witchfinder,' Jalen observed.

'My father is sending me to Malist, to the Sacellum.' The words were a whisper, torn from Arthur's throat. 'I won't go,' he added. 'I'll run away before the carriage comes for me.'

'When?' Jalen asked. His fingers had stilled.

'I don't know. Soon, no doubt.'

Jalen sighed and moved away, back into the kitchen area, returning with two mugs of mead. He pressed one into Arthur's hand.

'At least, if you smell like mead, you can say you visited the tavern,' Jalen joked, but his tone was wrong, tight. 'Do you want me to come with you, when you make your grand escape?'

Arthur's heart soared, and then crashed back down to earth so quickly it hurt. He turned the mug around and around between his fingers. 'I just... it won't be easy. My father watches me. And if it isn't him, it's one of the Konsel he has set to guard me. It's ridiculous. This is the only time I am free from it. When I'm with you.'

Jalen smiled, reaching out to run the tip of his finger along Arthur's forearm; Arthur shivered. Little touches, that's all they were, but they made him burn with all the ferociousness of a forest fire. 'I heard you were the one who found Will.'

'It was awful,' Arthur said. He had never seen a dead body before, let alone one that had been mutilated. He hadn't known Will Sanderson well, but knew he was a father, with two young boys destined to take over his boat when it was their time. He wondered whether they still planned to do that, considering how their father met his end.

'I'm sorry you had to see that.'

Jalen was a fisherman, and like every man who took to the water, he had a slightly different approach to life and death. Each wave has the potential to bring about our deaths, Jalen had said once.

Arthur knew most fishermen could not swim. No one swam. The waters were filled with faery creatures who would rip out your throat. Or so they had been led to believe.

Jalen sat back. 'The ocean has been unsettled since Will. Lightning and storms. The sea is angry, churning. The clouds are painted yellow on their bellies. The men think it will be a rough season.'

'You will be careful out there?' Arthur asked, feeling his cheeks heat.

Jalen's smile was soft. 'Of course.'

'I have to go,' Arthur said regretfully. 'I've been here too long already. Please be careful,' he added, reaching over to grasp Jalen's rope-roughened hands between his own soft ones. 'The Witchfinder...'

Jalen nodded. 'Won't find me. I promise, Arthur.'

CHAPTER 9

Jenyfer wandered the town square, following in her sister's wake. Lamorna moved through the crowd of morning shoppers with a confidence Jenyfer didn't possess. She envied her sister for being able to just fit in. Lamorna carried a large wicker basket over one arm; they had already visited the baker and the fishmonger. It was vegetables Lamorna was looking for now.

Some of the stalls were packing up and Lamorna quickened her pace.

'Come on, Jen. You know Mr Chigwin won't wait for us. I can already see him reaching for his boxes. Oh, he's seen us. He'll wait, but hurry up!'

Lamorna dashed across the cobblestones, the wind catching her dress and making it billow like sails around her legs. Jenyfer watched as she scrambled to hold her cap in place with her spare hand, turning to toss Jenyfer a glare as she did so. Jenyfer was not wearing her cap, and the wind had pulled pieces of her hair free, throwing the long black strands around her face. Smothering a sigh, she made her way to Mr Chigwin's vegetable stall, hanging back while Lamorna bartered for carrots, handing over a small jar of honey as payment while Mr Chigwin pretended not to notice Jenyfer standing there.

Her thoughts wandered. She'd fallen asleep with the pirate's face in her head, and it had still been there when she woke. Her skin had been twitching and tingling all day, her magic nudging at her, as if it couldn't wait until nightfall.

She could barely wait either.

The sensible part of her told her she was being careless. He was a pirate. She knew nothing about him, not even his name, except that he had magic. Like her. For the first time in her life, she had an opportunity to learn more about what lived inside her. She could ask him questions and not worry if he told anyone.

He could also possibly report her to the Chif or slit her throat, but she pushed those thoughts away. The risk was worth it. A smile spread across her face and she looked up at the midday sun, wishing the day would move quicker.

Basket brimming, Lamorna took Jenyfer's arm and steered her back across the square.

'What are you smiling about?' she asked Jenyfer.

'Am I not allowed to smile?'

Lamorna narrowed her eyes suspiciously. 'Whenever you smile like that, it makes me nervous. It generally means you're about to do something stupid.'

Jenyfer laughed. 'It's a nice day, Lamorna, that's all.'

Storm clouds threatened the blue expanse above them. Lamorna snorted, but said nothing. As they passed the bakery, the door swung open and the pirate stepped out. Jenyfer froze, her smile widening. She hadn't really been able to see what he looked like before, but now, she could fully appreciate the tone of his skin – like rich, raw honey – and his eyes, which were an unusual silvery-blue. His dark, shoulder-length hair was loose, strands dancing around the sharp line of his jaw, teased by the wind. Scuffed leather boots, dark long coat, and a crisp white shirt – missing several top buttons so a glimpse of his chest could be seen – marked him clearly as *not from here*.

He in turn swept his eyes over her; the corners of his lips twitched. Lamorna, who missed nothing, tugged Jenyfer out of the way.

'Don't look at him!' she hissed, practically dragging Jenyfer across the square. 'He's a pirate.'

'Yes, Lamorna, I must have missed that, but even you can't dispute the fact he's incredibly handsome,' Jenyfer said with a sigh. She risked a glance over her shoulder. The pirate was watching them – he winked, making Jenyfer stifle a giggle.

Her sister tossed her head. 'He's trouble.'

'Know him personally, do you?'

'Do you?' Lamorna shot back. She looked back the way they had come, then made a noise of satisfaction. 'He's gone.' She turned her gaze on Jenyfer again. 'I know you're up to something, and don't pretend otherwise.'

Jenyfer rolled her eyes dramatically as they began the walk up the hill to their cottage. 'You've seen through me. I guess I have to tell you my plans then.' She leant her head close to her sister's. 'That pirate is my lover and we're going to run away together.'

'I don't know why you say things like that,' Lamorna scolded. 'Whatever you're doing is undoubtedly wrong. You never think, do you, about how your actions reflect on us?' She began crossly, but had to stop when a voice called out behind them.

Bryn was hurrying up the path after them.

'Oh good,' Lamorna said, untangling her arm from Jenyfer and planting her hand on her hip. 'You can tell her not to be so stupid. She'll listen to you.'

Bryn frowned, his eyes moving between them. 'What's going on?'

Jenyfer folded her arms. 'Nothing, Bryn. Lamorna is just being dramatic, as usual.'

Lamorna huffed, turning towards the cottage. 'Don't be long,' she ordered, stomping her way up the path.

Left alone with Bryn, Jenyfer's shoulders tightened further, but he was watching her and she knew she had to say something. 'How was the water this morning?' she asked him, listening with one ear as he told her about the catch. She hadn't forgiven him for what he'd done, and the words were out of her mouth before she could stop herself. 'Should I expect to see another faery strung up in the square tomorrow?'

Bryn's face darkened and he narrowed his eyes. 'Why do you always have to do that?'

'Do what?' Jenyfer demanded hotly.

'Turn everything into something... that you don't like!' he snapped.

His anger made her frown. It wasn't like him to be angry with her – exasperated maybe, but not angry. Her own anger squirmed away inside her. 'Because there is something seriously wrong with this place, Bryn,' she said in a low voice. 'It's alright for you, because you're a man, but for someone like me, someone with magic,' Jenyfer paused, lowering her voice. Bryn visibly flinched. It wasn't something they spoke about often.

Jenyfer looked away from him, out over the ocean where, on the horizon, *The Excalibur* lingered. Eventually, Bryn sighed and shuffled his feet; she dragged her gaze back in time to watch him pull his hand through his hair. A gesture she knew well – a gesture that meant he was nervous.

Bryn cleared his throat. 'Jen, we should talk. I—'

Lamorna's voice echoed down the path. 'Hurry up, Jenyfer. I'm not doing your chores today. Aunt Tamora says you need to see to the bees.'

'Better go,' Jenyfer told Bryn quietly. 'The bees need me.'

She didn't wait for a reply, leaving him standing on the path, but she felt his eyes on her back until she'd opened the gate and slipped out of sight.

Ordes had been waiting at the cave for what seemed like hours. He sat on the rocks and watched the water, dark with the night and full of secrets. He hadn't told anyone what he was really doing, letting them think he was visiting the tavern. His father would call him a fool, and no one else would understand.

He wasn't sure what he was doing, either, but there had been something in her eyes, a desperation combined with defiance, that made him agree to this. He probably wasn't the best person for the job, but he was here. And he was intrigued by her magic – he could still feel it, a tingle in his fingertips, different to his own. The more he thought about it, the more certain he was that she had faery blood. Apart from Kat, he'd never met another faery. Something inside him squirmed, delighted, but he pushed it away.

Another hour ticked by. The moon slipped a little closer to the horizon. Just as he was about to give up and return to the ship, the woman appeared, climbing nimbly over the rocks, her dress lifted free of her bare feet, bunched in one hand while she used the other to steady herself.

Ordes stood as she approached. 'I was beginning to think you weren't coming.'

'Sorry. My sister took forever to fall asleep,' she said, letting her dress fall and dusting her hands on her hips. She met his eyes briefly. 'Thank you for waiting.' She glanced over her shoulder and he knew it wasn't the waves she was watching. 'Let's go inside.'

He followed her into the cave. Faint moonlight slanted through a small gap in the roof, throwing stripes of silver light across the sandy floor. 'Should I light a fire or something?'

'No. Someone might see.'

'You're not supposed to be here, are you?' Ordes asked, watching the way her eyes kept darting to the cave's entrance, as if she expected someone to come charging through.

She drifted past him, towards the back of the cave and the deep shadows. 'I'm not supposed to be anywhere, except doing what I'm told and waiting around for some man to make the mistake of wanting to marry me,' she said bitterly.

'You don't want that?' Ordes asked. He couldn't see her face, but he could feel her eyes.

'No. I don't want that at all.' She walked around the perimeter of the cave, running her fingers along the water-worn walls. 'I hate it here,' she divulged softly. 'The town. I want to leave. Take me with you?'

'On the ship?' Ordes exclaimed. Her eyes burnt in the darkness. He rubbed at the back of his neck. 'I can't. I'm sorry.'

She sighed. 'I didn't expect you to.'

They stared at one another, until she shifted her weight. 'I don't know your name.'

'Ordes,' he told her.

She nodded, coming closer to hold out her hand for him to shake. 'Jenyfer.'

Jenyfer's skin was warm, her grip strong, her magic a vibration beneath her skin. Her hair was as wild as it had been that night he'd seen her in the stone circle, her eyes glinting aquamarine under the moonlight filtering into the cave. Her lips were red, like berries, the lower one plump and ripe looking. Kissable, he decided as her eyes moved over his face, as if taking in every detail.

'I've never seen anyone with silver eyes before.'

'Family trait,' Ordes said. 'Yours are like sea-glass and storms. They're beautiful.'

She let go of his hand abruptly and wandered around the cave again. 'Will you show me your magic?'

'You want to see some tricks?'

'Not really.'

'Then what are we doing here?' Ordes asked.

Jenyfer turned to face him, her expression fierce, thirsty. 'I want to *know* about magic. I want to understand it. Where does it come from? Why doesn't everyone have it?'

Ordes chuckled. 'If I'd have known you wanted a history lesson, I'd have brought you a book.'

'A book?'

'Sure. I can bring one next time.'

'About magic?'

He nodded.

Her face lit up, snuffed out by a dark wave just as quickly. 'We're only allowed to read the Decalogue. If I was caught reading a book about magic...' she trailed off.

'No books then,' Ordes said, understanding but wishing he didn't. 'Alright, I'll answer your questions as best I can.'

She didn't come any closer to him, pressing herself against the cave wall. 'Where does it come from? What can you do? How did you know you had magic? What does it feel like? What about faeries? How many types are there? Have you seen them all?'

Ordes burst out laughing. 'That's a lot of questions. But okay, one at a time.' He sat down; Jenyfer copied him, but stayed on her side of the cave. She was wary of him. He guessed she wouldn't be very smart if she wasn't.

She was waiting expectantly, her eyes on his face, her gaze so intent it made his cheeks heat. No one had looked at him the way she was in a long time. It was like she was trying to see inside his head, like whatever came out of his mouth was about to be the most important thing in the world.

He cleared his throat. 'Magic comes from the world around us, from the Old Ones who are of the earth and the air and the water.'

Her question came at him like cannon fire, sharp and quick. 'Where did they come from, and how many are there?'

He shrugged. 'I don't know where they came from, but I can tell you who they are. The Green Knight – the God of the Earth. Inanna, worshipped mainly in Cruithea - she is the Goddess of War and Fertility. Morrigna, the Goddess of Fate. Melodias, the Master of Songs and Death, the God of the Seas, and Niniane, the—'

'Witch of the Mists,' Jenyfer said, excitement colouring her tone. 'What does she do? What's her job?'

'She is the guardian of the fey, of all magic.'

'She must be the most powerful then.'

'Why do you say that?'

'Well,' Jenyfer answered, sitting up a little straighter. 'She lives on Avalon, doesn't she? Which is a magic island, isn't it? And you've just told me she is the one who protects magic and the faery creatures, so I just assumed... every other Old One you've mentioned is connected to one realm – like the earth, or the sea – but Niniane must be connected to all of them, in some way.'

Ordes sat back. 'I actually hadn't thought about it like that before.'

Jenyfer blinked at him. 'You hadn't?'

He shook his head. 'No.'

She launched into her next set of questions. He couldn't remember the last time he'd spoken so candidly, and had such a captive audience. Jenyfer barely looked away from his face the whole time he spoke, and several times he'd found himself stumbling over his words as he told her about mermaids and syhrens, sea serpents, the selkies that lived on the southern coast, the waterhorses that lived in streams and rivers, and the boggles that lived in the peat swamps on the other side of the continent. She knew about piskies and, of course, korrigans.

Then she'd asked him about the sea, a wistful note in her tone. She wanted to know about dolphins and porpoises, about seals and the way they moved. She wanted to know if he'd seen otters.

The questions eventually stopped. Silence dropped between them as they studied each other from their opposing sides of the cave, the sea tumbling over the rocks outside.

'You're brave,' Ordes said finally. Her eyebrows lifted. 'To come here, to meet a man you don't know, to ask the sort of questions you've asked. How do you know I won't tell your Chif?'

She held his eyes. 'I don't. How do you know I'm not going to kill you?'

Ordes shrugged. 'You don't seem like the killing type.'

Jenyfer smiled. 'Maybe I like to play with my food before I eat it.'

He laughed, and her smile widened. She sat back again, resting against the cave wall. 'Why did you really come here?'

'I know what it's like to have questions you want answered,' he replied simply.

She considered this, tapping her fingers on her knees. 'And did you get your answers?'

'Not really,' he said. 'I have a question for you. This One God—'

Jenyfer made a face.

'You're not a believer I take it?'

'No, but my sister is. A passionate believer.' Jenyfer fiddled with the length of her hair. 'I'm reminded of how many rules I'm breaking almost daily, and there are so many rules, and all of them ridiculous. What does it matter if my hair'—she paused, tugging at a chunk of hair—'is loose?'

'I like your hair,' Ordes supplied. He expected a blush, but she just shrugged. 'And the other rules?'

Her expression darkened. 'Men can run about and do whatever they like.'

Ordes frowned. 'There's different rules for men and women? Why?'

Jenyfer hesitated before continuing. 'I overheard my aunt talking once – she thinks it's about control, but, also, it's about destroying belief in the Old Ways, which gave women power over men, over everything. The Chif and the Konsel – all men – just want power. They enjoy it.'

'Your sister? The other women in the village? They're happy with this?' Ordes' thoughts had strayed to Katarin. She'd have a field day in this place. Maybe he should mention it.

Jenyfer sighed. 'My sister needs someone to tell her what to do and now she has a nameless god to listen to. She never used to be like that. We were all made to attend prayers as children. I guess, after a while, she started to believe. When it's thrown at you from all directions, woven into every aspect of your life... I don't hold it against her. She was young, impressionable. She's not as cynical as I am. I just wish she'd open her eyes and see things for what they really are.' Jenyfer leant forward, her eyes pinned to his face. 'We're prisoners here. I want to be free to make my own choices – I want to choose who and what I believe in, what I wear, where I go, how I spend my time... can you see why I want to leave this place?'

Ordes nodded. 'I can, yes.' He tapped his chin. 'Tell me about your friends up there on the hill.'

'The korrigans?'

'Yes.'

Jenyfer settled back against the cave wall. 'I like going there, to the stone circle. There is this energy that I can feel there, different to the sea though. I like the water more, but I like being with the korrigans. We don't usually talk. I just like to watch them.'

'They're dangerous,' Ordes said softly.

'Only to people they don't trust,' she said, a small smile tugging at her mouth.

'And they trust you?'

She nodded. 'I don't know why. I've never been scared of them. I know what they are, what they are capable of doing, but they've never tried to hurt me. Maybe because I just let them be.'

Jenyfer stood abruptly. 'I have to go. I've been here too long.' She was almost at the mouth of the cave when she paused, glancing at him over her shoulder. 'Thank you, for answering my questions. And for listening.'

'No problem.'

She hesitated, then, 'Tomorrow night?'

'Sure.'

He saw a flash of a smile in the darkness, then she was gone. When he made his way outside, there was no sign of Jenyfer, not even a footprint left in the sand – the shifting tide had already washed away any evidence of her passing.

Chapter 10

Jenyfer's scrambled brain had decided that Ordes was the most handsome man she'd ever seen, not that she'd seen many men outside of her town. His skin was smooth, no lines etched into the space around his eyes. His cheekbones were high and strong, his jaw sharp. He was unrealistically beautiful, like something out of an old fairy tale. Sometimes she found it difficult to look at him.

She had no idea how old he was; while it made her curious, she didn't ask. It wasn't important. She was here to learn and he'd been more than happy to answer all her questions each night they met up. Her head was so full of his words she'd been unable to concentrate on anything else for the last three days, burning the porridge and then snipping herself while cutting flowers from the garden.

Tonight, she had something to tell him.

'The Sacellum is sending a Witchfinder,' she said softly. Lamorna had told them that morning, her face creased with concern. Their aunt had been agitated all day as well, and no one had spoken of it since Lamorna shared the news. They all knew what it meant.

'Are you scared?'

'No.'

'You should be, Jenyfer,' Ordes told her. 'They're dangerous. When does he arrive?'

'In a few days, according to my sister,' Jenyfer answered. 'I'll be careful,' she added. They were sitting on opposite sides of the cave again. Part of her wanted to go and sit beside him, so she could see his face better. He had an expressive face, she'd decided. He smiled often, frowned when he was concentrating, and bit his lip before he answered her questions, as if trying to decide if his words would be enough. The other part of her brain told her to stay where she was, but it was hard to listen to that part when her inner song had barely stopped singing since the moment she met him in the stone circle. The only time it was quiet was when he was talking.

She shook her hair back. 'I don't want to think about it. Tell me how magic works.'

'I don't know exactly. It's part of us – part of who we are.' Ordes waved his hand through the air and an arc of water appeared from nowhere, hanging suspended above his palm, before it vanished.

Jenyfer's mouth dropped. 'That... how did you do that?'

'I wish I had an answer for you, some way to describe it, but I don't. I think about it, and I can make it happen. It's always been that way,' he said softly. He glanced at her curiously. 'What can you do?'

Jenyfer's laugh was humourless. 'I can hide it so it doesn't get me killed. That's why I have to get out of here. I don't know how much longer I can hide it, and now that a Witchfinder is coming...' She sat back and closed her eyes, a small sigh escaping her. 'I feel... twitchy. Restless, like the sea before a storm. It feels like there is something inside me, and it's trying to get out.'

Outside the cave, the waves threw themselves against the rocks.

'Can you teach me?' Jenyfer asked quietly.

'How to use your magic?'

She shook her head. 'No. How to hide it. How to control it. How to push it away so no one will ever know it exists, especially now.'

'I don't think I can do that, Jenyfer,' Ordes said slowly. 'It's not that I don't want to help you – it's just... I've never had to hide it, so I don't know how to teach you to do that. And,' he paused and rubbed at his face, 'you probably shouldn't. Magic is meant to be used. You can't just push it away and pretend it isn't there. It's part of you.'

'You're not listening—'

'I am,' he said gently. 'But I can't do what you're asking. I'm sorry. Stay away from the Shaleitari.'

'The Shaleitari?'

'It's what they call Witchfinders in Cruithea,' Ordes said. 'It means "they who devour".'

She frowned. 'Devour?'

'Think about it – the Shaleitari must have magic themselves, to be able to sense it like they do. And what do they do with the Magic Wielders they capture? Do you think they simply kill all of them?' Ordes replied. 'People, no matter where they come from or who they are, like power. There are rumours about the Shaleitari stealing magic before disposing of its owner.'

By the time Jenyfer crawled back into her bed, she felt weighed down, drowning, disappearing under the threat her magic posed. To learn there was no way she could get rid of it... she swallowed, tucking herself beneath the blankets, rolling onto her side to stare at the curtains shifting in the night air, her brain flying, trying to come up with all the possible ways she could avoid the Shaleitari. There would be a town meeting, a welcome to Kernou. She would be expected to attend, like everyone; not going would only cast suspicion.

When Jenyfer closed her eyes, all she could see was the stake at the end of the beach. Her song was silent, as if it, too, knew it was running out of time.

They didn't talk about magic or faeries or the Old Ones. They sat side by side this time, tucked just inside the mouth of the cave. Jenyfer hadn't said much, but her mouth was turned down at the corners and she poked furiously at the sand with a stick.

Her desperation ate at him. Out of everything she'd asked of him, there were two things Ordes couldn't deliver – help her get out of Kernou, or help her hide her magic forever. All he could do was mumble a sorry, and accept her curt nod in return. And there was something else, some question she wanted to ask him but hadn't. He could sense it, swirling around her.

As the moon started to move towards the horizon in the east, Jenyfer sighed and stood, wandering deeper into the cave. She glanced at him over her shoulder.

A tiny nervous smile played on the corners of her mouth.

'What?' he said, climbing to his feet.

She cleared her throat, turning to face him. 'I bet you've kissed heaps of girls.'

Out of all the things she might ask him, he hadn't expected that. 'A few, yes.'

'How many?'

Ordes laughed. 'I don't know. I didn't keep count. Why? How many boys have you kissed?'

'Just one, and it wasn't because I wanted to,' she said, shrugging. 'He thought he was going to die and didn't want to die without being kissed so...'

'So you obliged,' Ordes finished.

Jenyfer shrugged again. 'I didn't like it much, but now, I don't know... I think it would be different. I was just a kid then.' She glanced at him, and then away again. 'Would it be different?'

'I don't know,' he said. 'Maybe.'

She sighed. 'Before I end up married off to some man I don't even like, I'd really like to kiss someone, just to see.'

'Got anyone in mind for this kissing?' Ordes teased.

'Yes,' she said simply. 'You.'

The wind left his lungs. 'Me?'

She nodded, but said nothing, just looked at him.

'Jenyfer...'

'It's okay, you don't have to,' she said quickly, dropping her gaze. 'I just thought...'

Ordes bit his lip, then crossed the sand to stand in front of her. She glanced up, then blushed at his nearness, but held his eyes. He watched her throat move as she swallowed. 'Why me?'

'You make me feel comfortable,' she said quietly. 'I don't even know you, but I feel comfortable when I'm with you.'

'I feel the same,' he murmured.

She moved a little closer to him. 'You do?'

He could only manage a nod. Silence fell between them, but neither of them moved away from the other. The sea whispered outside the cave, this space where Ordes had been more open and honest than he had with anyone for a long time. The waves stroked the shore, fingers of water sliding between the rocks and then back out to sea.

Jenyfer sighed. 'It's okay,' she said softly, and went to step away, but his hands moved on their own, palms coming to rest, one on her cheek, the other the back of her neck. His skin tingled where he touched her. Jenyfer's eyes were huge in the darkness, and he could hear the racing of her heart, hear the way her breathing had changed. He didn't say anything, just moved closer, until their bodies were almost touching. Slowly, hesitantly, she let her hands rest on his waist.

'What sort of kiss were you looking for?' he asked.

'There are different sorts?'

'There are,' he whispered. Her fingers tightened.

She swallowed. 'Whatever you want to give.'

Ordes managed half a laugh. 'That's dangerous, giving me that sort of freedom.'

'Why?'

He couldn't find the words, so he tucked a piece of hair behind her ear, and just kissed her.

The moment their lips met, he felt it. A spark. Energy, shooting between them and curling beneath his skin, and he wondered if she felt it as well. Her arms closed around him, one hand in the small of his back, the other moving along his spine. He kissed her gently, softly, because he imagined that was the sort of kiss she wanted; but what he wanted was to crush her to his chest, wind his hands through her hair and, now that he'd started, never stop kissing her.

But he did. Slowly, Ordes pulled away. Jenyfer's eyes were closed, her lips slightly parted, glistening in the faint light that made its way into the cave. She swallowed, and opened her eyes.

He had no idea what to say. The way she was looking at him... he wanted to walk her backwards, press her against the wall of the cave and kiss her again. He wanted to feel the heat of her skin on his, to feel her lips on his throat, to...

Ordes took a deep breath, let his hands drop, and took a step backwards.

A tiny frown crossed her face. 'Did I do something wrong?'

'Gods no,' he breathed. 'But I'm worried if I don't put some distance between us right now I...'

'Oh,' she whispered. Even in the darkness he could see the blush on her cheeks.

He cleared his throat and took another step away.

'Well,' she said softly, 'I should go.'

He expected her to leave immediately, but this time, she waited for him, and walked with him to the edge of the water, where the ocean crept over their toes. They walked close together; her hand brushed his briefly, sending a wave of heat flowing through him.

'Where's your boat?'

'Out there.'

'So how did you get here?'

He winked, but it lacked his usual humour. His insides were a mess, his thoughts scrambled, his body thrumming. 'Magic.'

Jenyfer was watching the water; a tiny smile tugged at her mouth. 'Of course.'

'Tomorrow?' Ordes asked, his stomach twisting when she shook her head.

'Not tomorrow. My sister is more suspicious than usual. The night after, though. Let's try that. But, once the Witchfinder gets here, you probably should stay away, just in case.' Her cheeks were still flushed, but she flashed him a smile, then turned and hurried along the shoreline. He watched her until she'd vanished into the bushes at the other end of the beach, to reappear on the rocky path leading to her cottage, and he was left with the gentle lapping of the sea against his boots.

He hadn't lied to her. There was something about her that drew him in. Her magic, perhaps; or perhaps it was her longing, her yearning to understand what she was. He took a deep breath, thinking about what had just happened between them. *That* had not been his intention at all but, now that it had happened, it was all he could think about.

Ordes waited out the next day and night on the ship, unable to stop his eyes moving towards the land, then sweeping along the beach and up to the headland, where a simple cottage hunched against the oceanic wind.

He'd gone over it a million times, all the possible ways he could smuggle her onto the ship and keep her hidden from his father and the crew, but it wasn't going to happen. Apart from hiding her under his bed, there was nowhere on the ship that wasn't used, nowhere that Jenyfer could possibly remain undetected until they docked somewhere else and he could sneak her off.

And then what? He thought. She'd be eaten alive by the first person who came along.

'She not interested anymore?' His father's voice cut into the swirling of his thoughts.

'What are you talking about?'

'Come on, Ordes. You've been gone most nights, you're doe-eyed—'

'I am not,' Ordes protested, his stomach tightening, but his father ignored him.

'—and suspiciously cheerful. Although, at the moment, maybe cheerful is not the right mood. Gloomy, perhaps.' Tymis leant his hip against the railing and folded his arms. 'What are you doing?'

'There's a girl—'

'You get caught messing about with girls in that place and they're likely to tie you and her to that stake and leave you for the tide,' Tymis warned.

'It's not like that, not really.' In a quiet voice, Ordes told his father about Jenyfer.

'So, there's a Magic Wielder running around under the Chif's nose?' Tymis said, then chuckled. 'She's out of your league, son. Way too smart for you if she's managed to survive in that place.'

'Are you done insulting me?' Ordes grumbled. 'She wants to leave.'

Tymis' humour faded. 'We can't take—'

'I know,' Ordes said. 'And so does she. She asked me to teach her to suppress her magic instead.'

'I hope you told her why that was a bad idea,' Tymis said.

'I told her I couldn't do it. She's already been bound – though she doesn't seem to know that. Someone has her wrapped up in spells, but they're coming apart at the seams. She's powerful,' Ordes added, 'and she's scared.'

'You care about her,' Tymis stated.

Ordes said nothing. He did, and he wouldn't lie about it, not to his father, who knew him better than anyone else. Ordes stared moodily at the water; he flexed his fingers, causing droplets to rise from the surface like a swarm of insects. He let them dance around, then fall back into the ocean.

'A Shaleitari is arriving in Kernou soon.'

'Shit.' Tymis sighed, his gaze moving to the shoreline. He groaned and let his head fall into his hands. 'How much space does one girl take up?'

'What?'

'Just her. She isn't bringing her friends or her dog, understand?' he said, then walked away.

His father left him to count down the seconds until night fell the following evening and Ordes made his way across the bay towards the cave, barely able to contain his excitement, imagining the look on her face when he told her.

Jenyfer was waiting for him this time, perched on the sand in the middle of the cave.

'I didn't think you were coming,' she said. Her bottom lip was plumper than usual and he wondered if she'd been chewing on it. He couldn't stop looking at her mouth. 'How long are you staying for?'

'You mean tonight?'

She shook her head. 'When will *The Excalibur* leave?'

'I don't know,' Ordes told her, easing himself down to the cool sand next to her. She shifted a little closer to him, until their shoulders were touching. 'The ship is magic. She does what she wants, goes where she wants, and we just go along for the ride.'

'A magic ship?' Jenyfer whispered. 'I'd love to see her.'

He said nothing, and they sat and watched the ocean, visible through the mouth of the cave. The water seemed restless tonight, waves tumbling over themselves, one after another, smashing with a roar into the rocks and tossing a wall of spray into the night air. Ordes wanted to slip his arm around her, but before he could do anything, she sighed and rested her head against his arm, sending his heart racing. He swallowed, and made himself speak.

'Any questions for me tonight?'

Jenyfer shrugged. 'No. I just want to sit. I don't think you understand how amazing it is to just sit with someone without worrying they're going to notice something isn't right with you. Without having to be fearful. Thank you.'

'You talk as if we're not going to see each other again,' Ordes said quietly.

'After you leave here, we probably won't, will we?'

He was unable to stop from smiling. 'Well, make sure you pack light.'

She blinked at him, and then her eyes widened in understanding.

Ordes stretched his legs out in front of him, crossing his feet at the ankles casually. 'You won't need much – just a few clothes. Everything else you'll need is already on the ship.'

The sound of the waves tonguing the rocks answered him. He snuck a look at her face – confusion, wonder, fear, and, beneath it all, hope. 'But if you've changed your mind...'

'I haven't,' Jenyfer finally breathed, her eyes sparkling in the weak light. 'When?'

'I'm not sure. I think it would be best if you and *The Excalibur* vanished at the same time,' Ordes said with a frown. 'Although, that's difficult to predict. I said the ship was magic? She chooses where we go and how long we stay. Who knows? Maybe you're the reason we're here.'

'Me?' Jenyfer whispered.

He shrugged. 'Why not?'

She gnawed on her fingernails. 'So, how will I know when we're leaving? Oh,' she exclaimed. 'I could always leave some things here, hidden so no one will find them. It's mostly boys from town who play around the rocks and the sea caves, and they're mainly interested in poking things in the rock pools.'

Ordes grinned and Jenyfer grinned back, a devious, cheeky grin that he liked, before she stood and dusted her backside free of sand. She didn't argue when he walked the length of the beach with her, but her eyes darted towards Kernou lurking in the darkness. Moonlight was splashed over the world, coating the water silver. The sea was calm; it washed over Jenyfer's bare toes and Ordes' boots, soft and gentle. At the end of the beach, where the path began its journey to her cottage, she stopped, turning to face him.

They were standing close; he could see the freckles on her nose in the moonlight.

'Are you sure you can take me with you?' Jenyfer asked, gazing first at his face, then shifting her eyes out to sea where the ship waited. Gently, he took her hands in his, running his thumbs over her skin.

'My father allowed it.'

'You sail with your father?' she asked, and he caught a wistful note in her tone.

'He's the Captain,' Ordes confirmed.

Jenyfer's face changed – it became wary, guarded; she slowly slipped her hands free. 'Your father is Tymis Merlyni?'

'Does *this* mean you've changed your mind?' Ordes asked.

'No.' She sighed, glancing out to sea again. 'I don't want to leave my family, but this place... they'd find out what I was, eventually, and then... I'll take my chances with a magical ship and her Captain.'

'Two nights from now,' Ordes said. 'Meet me at the cave?'

Jenyfer nodded. The wind blew her hair around her face like a cloud. She laughed, pushing it away. A piece clung stubbornly to her cheek. Ordes reached out and brushed it away and her eyes snapped to his, her gaze burning him alive. He swallowed, tucking the errant hairs behind her ear, his fingers lingering on her skin as her breath hitched, then deepened, and she turned her cheek into his palm, not taking her eyes off his face.

Before he could do anything else, panic washed over her features, and she shoved him, sending him tumbling into the bushes behind him.

'What the—' he began.

'Shut up and stay out of it, please,' she whispered, and the urgency in her tone made his blood turn to ice and had him reaching for the dagger at his hip, his magic gathering in his palms. Coming across the sand were three figures – men, by the way they moved and the spread of their shoulders.

'Miss Astolat.' The voice was deep, dripping with authority.

'Chif Tregarthen.' Jenyfer's voice was pleasant, as if she was greeting the Chif in the village square on market day, and not on the beach in the depths of the night.

Ordes could see the Chif from where he sat crouched in the darkness. He was tall, and, despite the hour, dressed like he was ready for the day's business in an impressive cloak and leather boots. Behind him were two more stern-faced men, bearing the cross of the One God on chains around their necks.

'Miss Astolat, would you care to explain what you are doing?' the Chif went on.

Fuck, Ordes breathed. His grip on the dagger tightened.

Jenyfer tossed back her hair. 'I couldn't sleep, so I thought I'd get some air.'

'There is plenty of air around your cottage, is there not?'

'Yes, there is,' she said. Ordes caught the hint of a tremble in her voice. 'But...'

She was stalling. She shifted her weight from one foot to another and Ordes thought for a wild moment, she was going to turn tail and run, but she squared her shoulders and lifted her chin. 'I was meeting someone.'

He stared at her in disbelief.

'Who?' The Chif's voice was low, grandfatherly, but Ordes could pick out the danger in it. Ulrian Tregarthen took a step closer to her; she held her ground, did not step away, even when he was close enough to touch her. Ordes held his breath – everything she had told him about the town and what things were like smashed through his brain.

'Who were you meeting?'

Jenyfer said nothing, folding her arms around herself and holding the Chif's eyes, her proud expression never faltering.

The Chif's lips barely moved when he spoke. 'His name?'

She hesitated and the Chif sighed. 'Jenyfer, you know the rules as well as anyone else. The One God does not look favourably on those who engage in acts of lust.'

'No,' she said, a hint of defiance in her voice.

'His name, if you please.'

For a moment, Ordes thought she wasn't going to speak and he shifted onto the balls of his feet. With magic and dagger, it would take him less than a minute to dispose of the Chif and his men, but he hesitated. He'd never killed a man before. He'd never had to. Before he could do anything, Jenyfer sighed.

'Bryn Hawkens,' she said softly. The Chif turned to the men behind him and nodded. They immediately made their way back towards the town. Ulrian held out his arm, not taking his eyes from Jenyfer's face. After a moment's pause, she linked her arm through his.

'Come. I will escort you home and we will speak to your aunt.'

As she was led away, Jenyfer didn't look back. Ordes stayed where he was until she had vanished from sight. He should follow her. He should do something.

But he didn't.

CHAPTER 11

Jenyfer was ordered inside, ordered to rouse her aunt and sister from their beds, to ask them to dress and make themselves decent, and then invite the Chif into their home. She did as she was told, heart thundering, stomach heaving. She was going to vomit, she knew it, could feel it creeping up to coat the back of her throat as she lit a candle with trembling hands and walked slowly down the dark hall to her aunt's room. The silence swelled with her breath, the world shifting and shaking beneath her feet.

When Tamora opened the door and saw the look on Jenyfer's face, she sighed. 'Please tell me you didn't.'

'I'm sorry,' Jenyfer whispered, and then bent double and emptied her stomach in her aunt's doorway. Tamora sighed again, her hand falling to rub Jenyfer's back. With her face hidden by her hair, Jenyfer told her where she had been, not mentioning Ordes or the fact she'd been meeting him almost every night for a week. Even her aunt, who forgave her so much, would not understand the risk Jenyfer had taken.

'But I lied,' Jenyfer said quickly, standing so fast her head spun. 'I wasn't meeting Bryn. We're not... we never have been... seas damn it!'

Tamora sent her to wash her face, change her clothes, and wake Lamorna. When they were all dressed and downstairs, she took a deep breath and opened the front door to their simple home, inviting Ulrian Tregarthen and some of the Konsel inside. Jenyfer sat at the table, trying not to vomit again, Lamorna beside her wearing her most disapproving expression. Jenyfer turned away from her sister to glance quickly at the Chif and the Konsel members. Bryn was standing between two of the men, his face confused, his hair a mess.

With them, his red cloak like a beacon, was the Witchfinder – the Shaleitari.

Jenyfer swallowed tightly; she caught her aunt's eye. Tamora's skin was bloodless, her spine stiff, while Lamorna fussed about, asking did the men want tea? Warmed milk? Water?

The Chif shook his head and sat, not waiting for an invitation; the Witchfinder stood behind the Chif. The other men remained standing and they seemed so much taller, so stern and powerful in that moment, that Jenyfer's heart sank.

Ulrian directed Bryn into the last seat at the table. Still puzzled, he did, shooting Jenyfer a quick look, and she sat there, unable to deny it, unable to say anything, completely powerless as the Chif recounted her lies to her family and to Bryn, whose face turned the colour of old milk. The Chif took Bryn's expression as confirmation he was as guilty of this false sin as Jenyfer was.

The Chif did not introduce the Witchfinder. He didn't have to.

'The One God is very clear on matters like these,' the Chif said firmly. 'As you know, women are transgressors and the bearers of sin.' As he said it, Jenyfer noticed her aunt clench her fists, her face tight, but Tamora said nothing. 'It is not Bryn's fault that he was led astray by this woman, but it is his fault for allowing himself to be driven by his lust. In doing so, he put aside his faith in the One God and the Decalogue.'

Bryn hung his head. He still hadn't said anything. Jenyfer's heart felt like it would explode as the Chif turned his attention to Bryn.

'This is your chance to deny the claims,' he said simply. 'Has Miss Astolat spoken true?'

Please, Jenyfer begged. *Please. Put it together and work it out, Bryn. Don't choose this moment to be dumb.*

Eventually, Bryn lifted his head. He nodded, just once.

'You know what this means?' Ulrian asked quietly.

It was Lamorna who answered. 'It means they have to marry.'

Silence echoed through the cottage. Jenyfer couldn't breathe. Her mouth was full of sand and then, it flooded with water that threatened to spill over her chin while, inside, her song was screaming, protesting while she couldn't.

Tamora cleared her throat and addressed the Chif, avoiding looking at the Witchfinder. 'Surely not,' she argued softly. 'They made a mistake, Chif Ulrian. A silly, childish mistake, one that I can guarantee my niece will not make again.'

Jenyfer held her breath, her eyes shifting from her aunt to the Chif. The Witchfinder stared at her so intently, his dark eyes branding her skin, she felt her stomach turn over. She dropped her eyes, focusing on her hands, clenched tightly in her lap.

They who devour.

If she ran, how far would she get?

The Chif was speaking again. 'I'm sure you mean that, Ms Rosevear, but the very fact that your niece was out at night when she should have been in her bed makes me wonder just how much control you have over her. Without a man in this house... I worry that Jenyfer needs a firmer hand,' he said, his voice calm. 'She obviously needs guidance that you have failed to give. A husband will give her that.'

Tamora did not argue; she glanced at Jenyfer, who did not raise her head. She could feel the Witchfinder's eyes on her still, digging into her scalp as if trying to see inside her, and she forced calm over herself, thought about her magic as a tiny ball, tucked deep inside where no one could find it.

'The Decalogue is very clear,' the Chif continued calmly. 'And if we let this incident pass without consequence, who is to say that others will not make the same "mistakes"?'

No one said anything. Jenyfer could feel the blood moving through her veins. Her inner song had gone silent, and its absence drowned her.

'They will be married,' the Chif confirmed.

Slowly, Jenyfer lifted her head. Bryn looked across at her, his expression unreadable. He nodded calmly.

The Chif's smile did not reach his eyes. 'That's settled then. In two days' time, you shall become man and wife under the eye of the One God. Come, Bryn. There is much we need to discuss with you.' Ulrian turned his dark gaze on Tamora as he stood. 'I trust, Ms Rosevear, that I can leave instruction on the Decalogue to you? You understand how important this task is?'

Tamora inclined her head stiffly. 'I do.'

'I will make certain my sister listens and absorbs the Word,' Lamorna stated, her blue eyes shining. She looked absolutely thrilled with the whole situation.

Ulrian smiled. 'Of course you will. I have no doubt about it, Lamorna. You have been the most willing pupil.'

'Wait,' Jenyfer blurted. Lamorna tutted, but she ignored her sister. 'I want—'

'Miss Astolat, if I were to give you one piece of advice before you are wed, it is this: you must learn to hold your tongue, and remember a woman's place,' the Chif said, his voice cold.

Jenyfer stood. The Witchfinder's eyes were glued to her. 'I need to speak with Bryn.'

Displeasure crossed Ulrian's face, but he quickly arranged his expression into the one he usually wore – proud, reverent and calm. 'That is not allowed.'

'You're forcing us to get married. The least you can do is give me a moment to talk to him,' Jenyfer begged as Lamorna sucked in a breath and the members of the Konsel shook their heads.

Ulrian smoothed his hands over his clothes again. He was barely containing his anger, and it gave Jenyfer a little spark of delight to see it. She wondered what Ordes would say in a moment like this, but quickly pushed the feeling aside and made sure her expression was contrite. She did not have to pretend to be frightened. Her tongue was coated with fear.

The Chif opened his mouth, but Tamora cut across him, her voice smooth and calm. 'I think, under the circumstances, the One God would allow them this,' she said, holding Ulrian's gaze. 'I will chaperone, if it is needed. I will make sure my niece behaves herself'—she turned her eyes on Jenyfer, a warning in their brown depths—'as the One God requires.'

The Chif swallowed. He didn't want an argument – Jenyfer could read that in his face – not in front of the Konsel and the Witchfinder, who he would want to think the people of Kernou were under his thumb. He nodded, just once, and demanded Jenyfer and Bryn step into the garden only, and that Tamora and one of the Konsel supervise this conversation.

Jenyfer hurried from the room. In her mind, she gave the One God and his Chif the finger, a gesture Bryn had taught her and she'd used once on her sister, suffering a week of lectures for it.

Outside, the moon had begun her descent, slipping closer to the horizon. Jenyfer hovered near the back door, grabbing Bryn's arm when he finally emerged. She dragged him towards the faery shrub, making sure her aunt and the sour-faced Konsel representative could see them.

'Thank you,' she whispered.

'You're stark-raving mad,' Bryn whispered back. 'How did this happen?'

Jenyfer sighed and recounted her story, again leaving out the most important details, but Bryn scowled, leaning his face close to hers.

'You have to stay away from the water, Jen. And now I'm caught in your lies. And there's a bloody Witchfinder in your house!'

'You didn't have to—'

'You'd rather I said nothing? By the Word, Jen – I care about you, even if you don't care about yourself. I've always cared about you,' he said in a low voice. Jenyfer's skin prickled. In all the years she had known Bryn, he had never sworn on the Decalogue. His brows were drawn together and there was fear on his face – for her, for both of them maybe – but beneath it there was something else Jenyfer couldn't identify, something that made her want to take a step back.

She didn't. The Konsel man was watching them and she didn't want to show any sort of fear in front of him. She needed to be strong. A few more days and she would be free of this place, marriage or not. She would not let this stop her from leaving.

Bryn ran his hand through his hair. Neither of them said another word – they just looked at one another, until he cleared his throat and stepped away from her at the same time that Ulrian appeared in the garden. He gestured for Bryn to join him and the men left, Bryn swept away with them, and the world was suddenly quiet and empty again.

Jenyfer trudged back inside and down the hall to her room, the room she had shared with her sister their entire lives, the room that would be hers for only two more nights. She could feel the Witchfinder's presence in their home like a dark cloud as she pushed the door open and sunk onto her narrow bed, running her fingers over the familiar coverlet.

'This is stupid,' she announced.

Her aunt and sister joined her moments later, the former looking at her with pity, the other with such dripping piety it made Jenyfer want to slap her. No one spoke, and the air hummed with unsaid things. Eventually, Jenyfer folded her arms and huffed.

'They can't really make us get married,' she declared. 'Can they?' She turned to her aunt, but Tamora was fidgeting and her expression was one of worry.

'You made your bed, Jenyfer,' Lamorna declared. 'Now you have to lie in it.'

Jenyfer glared. 'Do you hear yourself?'

Her sister smoothed non-existent wrinkles from her clothes. 'At least, this way, you won't be able to make trouble. You will be the property of your husband and you will answer to him and the One God.'

'This isn't fair,' Jenyfer whispered. 'Tamora—'

Tamora's eyes flashed. 'What did you think would happen? I told you not to wander. I told you. Your sister is right. You will need to do this and you will stay out of trouble, Jenyfer.'

'But—'

'Lamorna, make some tea, please,' Tamora instructed quietly. Lamorna nodded obediently and left the room. When her short, sharp footsteps had faded, Tamora rubbed at her face, looking older than she ever had. Jenyfer felt a twinge of guilt.

'I'm sorry,' she said.

'I know, and I know you don't like this. I don't like it either,' Tamora said, her voice low. She crossed the room to pull back the curtain and peer out. 'And, now, there is a Shaleitari in our town.'

'They who devour,' Jenyfer mumbled.

Tamora dropped the curtain and spun around. 'Where did you hear that?'

'It doesn't matter,' Jenyfer said softly. 'I don't think he suspected me.'

'You wouldn't know, Jenyfer,' her aunt said fiercely. 'That isn't how they work.'

'I don't think he suspected you either,' Jenyfer said, holding her aunt's eyes. 'I wish I'd asked you about it, but I was too scared – for me, for you, and for Lamorna. Even though she'd never believe that. And now... it's too late, isn't it?'

'Jenyfer,' Tamora whispered.

'What if I can't hide it anymore? What if I can't control it?' Jenyfer asked softly.

Tamora lowered herself to the bed beside Jenyfer, taking her hands, thumbs smoothing their way over her skin, like they used to when Jenyfer was small and worried about stupid things that truly held no meaning anymore. 'You were right. I should have gotten you girls out of this place a long time ago, but there are people here I couldn't leave, people like us. But my fear has put you both in danger – brought us to this moment.'

A little gasp rushed into the room – Lamorna was standing in the doorway, a tray set with tea things held dutifully between her hands. She recovered herself, pursing her lips and marching into the room, setting the tray down on the bed next to Jenyfer. Apart from the teapot and cups, there was a plate with the sweet biscuits Jenyfer liked arranged on it. She shot her sister a look, but Lamorna would not meet her eyes. She would not look at their aunt, either.

She shook her head in disapproval and left the room.

Tamora was silent for a long time; then, so softly Jenyfer had to strain to hear her, 'You will marry Bryn and you will make do, Jenyfer.'

'But—'

'Please, Jen. Please. This is your *life* at stake. Don't you understand? He is dangerous. The Chif's power is dangerous, and I'm afraid for all of us left with magic in our blood. You've been so brave, and so very clever, my girl, keeping it secret. But you need to continue to do so. You will marry Bryn. For me. For yourself. Or you will be the next one tied to the stake for the sea to devour – or worse.'

As Jenyfer looked at her aunt's face, at the fear and the worry that coated it, she nodded.

'What about Lamorna?'

'Lamorna?' Tamora glanced towards the doorway. 'She has chosen her path, but she's still your sister. She's in there, somewhere. Beneath the dogma and the preaching, she's still there.' Tamora gave Jenyfer's hands a final squeeze and stood, smoothing down the front of her simple woollen dress. Without another word, she left the room. Jenyfer sat and stared stupidly at the wall until her sister returned. She barely blinked as Lamorna changed back into her nightdress and climbed into bed.

'I can't believe you spoke to the Chif like that,' she muttered. Jenyfer said nothing. Lamorna sighed, and then, 'It will be alright, Jen.'

'How can you be so sure?'

'Because the One God has a plan for us all.'

Jenyfer stared at her sister in the darkness, whose face she had looked at every day for over twenty years. Lamorna, who had come screaming into the world on a tide of blood, who had grown beautiful and charming, who had always been there. Their aunt was right. Regardless of what she had become, how her belief had changed her, Lamorna was still Jenyfer's sister, her blood, and regardless of what Lamorna thought or how she acted, Jenyfer knew she'd do whatever she could to protect her. From herself, if not from anything else.

She swallowed. 'Lamorna...'

Lamorna lay back and arranged the blankets over her chest. 'Blow out the candle, Jen.'

Jenyfer didn't. She could only stare, and she was still staring when the candle was gone. As the sun crested the horizon and painted the world with golden light, Jenyfer sent a prayer to the Old Ones that *The Excalibur* would wait for her, and that she would get herself *and* her sister out of this town before it destroyed them both.

CHAPTER 12

A rthur sat on the rocks, the surf pounding at his feet. He watched the waves tumble over themselves, one after another, no pause between them, their tips white foam. On the horizon, the pirate ship still lingered. Arthur wasn't sure how long it had been there. He clenched his fists. It needed to leave. He had nothing against pirates – they were just men, after all. But he hated that they were free, and he wasn't. That he was stuck in this town, bound to its fate. Everytime a ship – whether pirate or merchant – parked itself in the Bay of Calledun, Arthur came up with a million different ways he could get out there. A million different reasons he would give when he was discovered as a stowaway.

But he never tried to leave. That would take courage Arthur knew he didn't have.

Now, his father was sending him away. To a place he knew nothing about, to devote his life to something he cared nothing for, and there was nothing he could do about it. Arthur scooped some stones into his palm and tossed them one by one into the thrashing waves, imagining what it would be like to throw himself in. Was drowning quick, or was it painful? He chuckled humourlessly to himself – he didn't even have the guts to decide how he would end it all.

Arthur threw another rock into the water. Did he want to die? Sometimes he thought it would be the easiest way to escape. With a sigh, he climbed to his feet. It would be dark soon, and he needed to be home before his father sent men looking for him. Yet he still took his time walking towards the headland. The tide had shifted while he'd been sitting and brooding, water lapping at the rocks near his feet. He made his way carefully around the headland, picking a path through water-slicked rocks as sharp as teeth. A wave washed over his feet and Arthur could feel the power in the water.

He paused, straightening and turning to look out to sea. The water had grown dark as the sun slipped towards the horizon. Arthur blinked. He could hear music – a faint melody that echoed in his ears. With a shake of his head, he turned from the water and almost fell over himself in shock.

Jalen was perched on a boulder, his eyes on the ocean. 'Another hour and you'd have been stuck around there,' he said simply.

'Good,' Arthur mumbled. The sound of the waves crashing against the rocks beat in time with Arthur's heart.

Jalen stood and stretched. 'Come on. I'll walk with you.'

'Someone will see.'

'And what will they see? Two men walking along the shoreline? I'm pretty certain there is no rule against friendship, Arthur. You worry too much,' Jalen added. 'Come on.'

'I don't want to go back,' Arthur declared sullenly.

Jalen paused. 'Then don't.'

'He'll come looking for me, Jalen.'

'He'll come looking for you whether you leave now, or in a month, Arthur. You said so yourself,' Jalen reminded him. He stood too close and too far away at the same time. Arthur's fingers itched to touch him. He wanted to feel the firm softness of Jalen's skin beneath his fingertips again. He wanted to dig his nails into that brown flesh, dig his teeth into it, put his lips on his throat and...

He stayed where he was, staring back out to sea, knowing everything Jalen said was right.

'Why can't it be easy?' he whispered, his voice snatched by the ocean wind.

'It can be,' Jalen said. Arthur looked at him and sighed wretchedly, feeling torn in two. Jalen's smile was soft, understanding. 'Come on. I want to show you something.'

Arthur followed Jalen around the headland, all talk between them suspended for the moment while they found the best places to put their feet. The waves were wilder here, smashing against the rocks and coating them with spray, drenching their clothes and forcing them to press closer to the curve of the cliff. As they passed the stake, Jalen scowled but said nothing, slipping into a crack between the rocks. Arthur followed, throat tight.

The cave was small, tucked into the belly of the cliff, and Arthur wasn't sure anyone else knew of it. It was dark, the shadows cool, flowing over them like water.

They didn't speak until the sound of the ocean had faded to a dull roar.

Arthur knew Jalen felt it too, that spark that ignited whenever they were near one another. That spark that had Arthur burning in his bed as he imagined his hands were Jalen's hands. His skin warmed and his belly tightened. There were times when Arthur wasn't sure he was reading the signs correctly, or if there were even signs to read; but the way Jalen looked at him, the way his lips tugged up at one corner, the way his eyes lingered on Arthur's face – or other parts of his body – made Arthur think that yes, there was something. Perhaps it was more than attraction, more than the longing that gripped his belly, but he didn't know.

Jalen sighed, running a large tanned hand over his face. 'I don't...' he paused, his expression irritated. 'I don't like not knowing if you're safe. I don't like the idea of you being sent to Malist.' His voice was soft and low. Arthur watched his throat move as he swallowed.

'Why don't you like it?'

'Because I can't protect you,' Jalen said. There was a trace of anger in his tone, and a desperation that Arthur had never heard before. He took a deep breath, and moved closer, so close that if Arthur lifted his hand, it would rest on Jalen's very impressive chest.

'And how would you protect me?' Arthur's heart was hammering, so fierce and strong he thought he'd be sick. Jalen opened his mouth to reply, but stopped, his face folding into a frown. 'What—'

Jalen pressed his hand to Arthur's mouth and shook his head. They could hear voices, not far from their cave. They looked at each other, eyes wide and panicked. It would be okay, Arthur thought. They weren't doing anything wrong, they weren't... he swallowed. Jalen reached out and pulled Arthur into his body, wrapping strong arms around him as the shadows around them thickened and became so dark Arthur couldn't see anything. He could feel Jalen's breath on his neck, could feel the strong line of his body, and his hand, pressed firmly in Arthur's lower back.

Sweet seas.

The voices had stopped and, moments later, they were gone. Arthur didn't move, Jalen's magic wrapped tight around them. Only when they could hear nothing but the lapping of the waves and the screech of seabirds did Arthur push a breath from his lungs.

'Neat trick,' he whispered.

Jalen chuckled. 'I've got plenty more, little Chif.'

'I hate it when you call me that.'

'Really? Why's that?'

Arthur could feel Jalen smiling, even though he couldn't see a darn thing. Feeling bold, he pushed himself closer, until not a breath of air existed between their bodies. Jalen's fingers dug into Arthur's back; his other hand gripped his hip, then slid lower as Arthur saw stars, his breath stolen, his senses drowning, his body on fire.

'My mistake,' Jalen whispered. 'Not so little after all.'

It was too much. The closeness. The heat of Jalen's body, the way his breath tickled Arthur's neck, the smell of him, his hand...

The shadows were still thick and heavy around them, Jalen's magic threaded through the air, hiding them from sight.

'Show me,' Arthur whispered boldly, 'what's in your bag of tricks.'

'Arthur...'

The way his name sounded on Jalen's lips made Arthur's knees tremble.

'Say it again,' he demanded, another spark of confidence shooting through him.

'Say what?'

'My name,' Arthur groaned. His head dropped into the curve of Jalen's neck. Jalen let out an unsteady breath and Arthur almost melted as Jalen's hand found its way beneath his shirt. A shiver passed through Jalen's body as Arthur's lips touched the skin below his ear. Before he could speak, before he could say anything sensible and undo the moment, Arthur fumbled in the darkness, finding Jalen's cheeks – those beautiful, sculpted cheeks.

'Arthur.' It was a whisper this time, a mere breath.

Arthur sighed, then kissed him.

The house was dark when Arthur eased open the front door and crept into the hallway. His whole body was buzzing with what had just happened with Jalen. What they had done would see them both burnt. His belly twisted uncomfortably at the thought, but he couldn't bring himself to regret it. He had almost made it to his room when his father's voice echoed from the blackness.

'Where have you been?'

'Just walking,' Arthur stammered.

Ulrian's sigh carried from the main hall to where Arthur stood, paralysed, in the darkness. 'Come in here, Arthur.'

Swallowing his fear, Arthur stepped into the large room. His father stood by the fire, a warm, red glow encasing his tall form. He gestured to the table, a command to sit, so Arthur did.

'Where have you been?' Ulrian asked again.

'Walking,' Arthur said, his voice firmer this time. 'On the beach.'

'It is not wise to wander the shoreline at night, Arthur. You know this,' Ulrian said. 'There are rules and I expect you, as my son, to follow those rules. You need to be setting an example for the rest of the people in Kernou. It does not reflect favourably on me, the Chif, if my son cannot do what he is told, does it?'

Ulrian's voice was calm, but Arthur knew that calm was nothing but a pause, a brief moment before the storm of words that were about to leave his father's lips and attempt to drown him. He made the bold decision to speak before that could happen, doing what he always did when he knew his father could see right through him. Arthur fidgeted with the hem of his shirt; there was a small tear there, from when he'd ripped it off in the cave with Jalen.

'I want to go to Cruithea.'

'No.' The answer came as swiftly as it usually did.

'Why not? You're sending me away, anyway. I want to meet my family,' Arthur pressed. 'I want to meet *her* family.'

'Your mother's family knows where you are and they have never come for you, have they?' Ulrian challenged.

Arthur dropped his eyes. 'No.'

'And why is that?'

'Because they're heathens who have not heard the Word,' Arthur mumbled.

'Louder, son,' his father demanded.

Arthur glanced up; a small triumphant smile was pulling at the corners of Ulrian's mouth. 'Because they don't care about me.'

'No, they don't. Only the One God and myself care about you, Arthur. That is why you will go to Malist and study.' Ulrian stepped away from the fire blazing in the hearth and took a seat opposite Arthur at the table. 'Do you think I want to send you away?'

'Sometimes,' Arthur said.

'I do this for you, Arthur,' Ulrian replied, his voice low, a gentleness to it that Arthur rarely heard. He had always hoped that, beneath it all, beneath the Word and the One God, there was a man who was nothing more than Arthur's father. Not a Chif, but a parent who loved their child and wanted them to be happy. Sometimes he saw that man, but it never lasted long. He could not remember the last time his father had told him he was proud of him, or had praised him for anything.

Perhaps Ulrian was just not the fatherly type – but Arthur knew that was a lie as well, one that he had told himself over and over to try and dissipate some of the hurt that had built up over the years. He had seen his father interact with others in town. He had seen him praise others, like Bryn when he caught the mermaid. He had seen Ulrian look at others with the sort of pride a father reserves for his child.

But Arthur knew it was all false. Ulrian Tregarthen was simply pretending, able to school his expression so skilfully that no one suspected it was all a lie. Arthur wondered what would happen if the people of Kernou ever came to understand their Chif was using them, that they were nothing more than tools for Ulrian to bend and shape to show the Magister and the Sacellum how pious and devoted he was, how he should be rewarded and blessed by the One God.

And now, Ulrian had gotten his wish.

Arthur cleared his throat. 'The Witchfinder?'

'Doing his job,' his father declared. The firelight caught in Ulrian's dark eyes and they blazed with reflected flames, with the zeal that Ulrian was buried so deeply in. 'Any Magic Wielders in Kernou will be seen for what they truly are.'

'Will the Sacellum think ill of you, for not being able to find them yourself?' Arthur asked. His heart beat painfully at his bravado and he held his breath, waiting to see how his father would react to such a question, one that was almost an accusation.

Ulrian's brow creased slightly. 'The Sacellum knows how treacherous magic can be. They know that those who practice it are skilled in the art of lies and falsehoods. The Witchfinders were created for this very purpose, Arthur – to find the hidden evil among us and vanquish it, as the One God demands.'

'And if he doesn't find any Magic Wielders in Kernou?'

Ulrian held Arthur's eyes. 'Oh, I think he will.'

CHAPTER 13

Something had the townspeople in a twisted knot. A crowd was gathered on the beach, clustered tightly around something lying on the sand. Ordes knew he shouldn't go over there and look. He'd come ashore for supplies, and to see if he could find out what happened to Jenyfer. He'd thought of nothing but her since the night the Chif found her, thought about nothing except the fact she had probably thought she was saving him. He could have easily hidden them both, but he'd seen how quickly the fear had rushed into her eyes and he knew she did the only thing she thought she could – let herself get caught to keep him out of trouble.

She hadn't shown up at the cave. He'd waited all night, trying not to panic, trying to not storm his way into the town and find her. He'd made himself remain calm, returning to the ship just before dawn. *The Excalibur* was still idle in the water; every gust of wind that swept across the ocean wasn't caught in her sails, so he figured he had time before the ship decided they were leaving, but he wasn't sure how much time he had before the Shaleitari discovered Jenyfer. If he could sense her magic, a Witchfinder easily could.

Ordes arranged his long coat so that his weapon was hidden and walked steadily along the beach towards the group of men. No one noticed him approaching, not until he was close enough to lean over the shoulder of the nearest man and peer down at what had them all tight-shouldered and dressed in fear and worry.

A body. A fisherman, by the dark woollen jumper and pants.

Then there was the net wrapped around his throat, the flesh bulging and red around the fibres.

And the eyes. Removed from his head and lying next to him, pinned to the sand by thin spikes of white coral.

'That's nasty,' Ordes commented.

The man closest to him jumped and scuttled away. They all did – until there was a dead body and section of sand between Ordes and the men. He whistled, holding up his empty hands, and took a step back.

'Easy there.'

One of the men, a grizzled old thing with wiry grey hair and a face decorated with deep lines, narrowed his eyes. 'What are you doing here, boy?'

'Boy?' Ordes frowned. 'I'll have you know, I'm much older than I look. Don't let these dimples and smooth skin fool you.'

One of the men snorted, biting down a laugh, but the rest did not relax their grim expressions or the tightness in their stances. Ordes gestured at the body but, before he could say anything, the old fisherman pointed a crooked finger at him.

'What do you know about this here, then?'

'Me?' Ordes blinked.

'Yes, you. Don't think we don't know who you are or where you come from,' another man called; a ripple of murmured agreement answered him.

'Listen, I just came to get a few bottles of rum.' *And check in on someone.* Ordes gestured towards the town. 'Once I visit the tavern, I'll be returning to my ship.'

Some of the men glanced out to sea, where *The Excalibur* sat poised on the horizon, sails and anchor down. The sea was calm today, barely a wave, but the sky was cloaked in clouds, the water and the sand taking on the same grey hue. A storm was coming; Ordes could feel it in his blood, mingling with his magic and making him edgy.

The old fisherman seemed to be the group's spokesperson. His gaze shifted from the ship to Ordes' face. 'I'll ask again, boy. What do you know about this?'

'And I'll answer again – nothing.'

'Maybe it was Katarin Le Fay,' another man mumbled.

Ordes laughed. 'Kat? Nah, not her style.'

'And you know her style, do you?'

Ordes couldn't help but grin – though he quickly let that grin fall when confronted with an array of glowering faces. 'She didn't do this,' he said, then sighed. 'But believe what you will. I'm going to fetch my rum, and then I'll be out of your hair. What's left of it, anyway.'

His cheek was not appreciated. 'And just how long is your ship going to be lurking around our bay?' the old fisherman demanded pointedly. 'You've been there for over a week already.'

Ordes said nothing. They knew the rumours; they knew his father's reputation. Let them make of it what they would. He turned his back on the men and headed up the beach, the wet sand giving way to a thick layer of pebbles, the heat of their glares trailing him. He was desperate to know about Jenyfer, but couldn't just ask.

The town square was deserted, but the market stalls were still set up – bread, apples, fresh milk and vegetables, and, of course, baskets and baskets of fish. The tavern was empty except for two young men, the room dark and gloomy, the air thick and stale. The tavern keeper didn't say one word to him, handing over the bottles of rum and nodding his ruddy face at the bar, where Ordes assumed he was to leave his coin. He did so, wanting nothing more than to be out of the wretched place.

Usually, he'd be waiting for the morning when they woke to full sails and a smile from Kayrus as the ship finally got her shit together and they could move on. Now, though, he wished for nothing more than to stay where they were until he could find Jenyfer and find some way to do as he'd promised – get her out of this suffocating place.

He didn't know what to do next. Apart from marching up the hill to pound on her door, he had no idea where to start looking. The smell of fresh bread, mixed with the lingering scent of fish, sand, and the sea, made his stomach tighten. He wandered across the square towards the beach, deciding to come back when it was dark.

'Ordes,' a voice hissed, making him jump. Jenyfer was lurking in the shadow of a building, her cloak blending into the grey-day darkness. She looked around, then beckoned, darting between two buildings. He tried to appear casual as he strolled towards the narrow gap.

'Thank the seas,' he said quietly when he reached her. 'Are you alright?'

'If there was ever a time for you to take me with you, it's right now. I don't have to pack a thing. Let's go,' she said urgently. His stomach dropped at her tone; he wanted to fold his arms around her.

'Did the Witchfinder...'

'No.' She scowled, eyes darkening. 'I hate this place so much.'

'Jenyfer!' A female voice, high-pitched and urgent, rang across the square. Jenyfer groaned.

'My sister. She knows all my hiding places.' Then, she added, 'I want to take her with us.'

'What?'

'Please, Ordes,' Jenyfer whispered. 'I can't leave her here.'

He sighed and tugged at his hair. His father would kill him. 'Alright, alright. Be at the cave. Midnight,' he whispered, glancing over his shoulder. The young woman he had seen shopping with Jenyfer hurried across the stones, headed straight for them. She wore a linen cap over her hair and was carrying a basket stiffly on one arm. Her expression was one of deep-seated aggravation.

'Alright,' Jenyfer whispered.

Ordes opened his mouth but the sister lifted her chin dismissively, marching over and taking hold of Jenyfer's arm. 'What in the Word are you doing?' she hissed.

'I was just—'

'What would people think if they saw you standing here with'—she paused, her sharp blue eyes raking over Ordes, from his scuffed boots to his forehead, taking in every detail in between—'that.' She shook her head at him. 'You need to leave. We don't want your kind here,' she added pointedly.

He raised his eyebrows. Jenyfer wanted them to take this prissy cow with them? He should let it go. Jenyfer's expression told him he should let it go, but he couldn't. The fishermen on the beach had pissed him off. The tavern keeper had pissed him off, this whole village pissed him off and now Jenyfer's sister was pissing him off, too.

'Listen here, love. Someone needs to bend you over their knee and—'

'I answer to the One God, and only Him,' the woman shot back. Ordes narrowed his eyes at her, taking in the finer details of her face. She was younger than he first thought, not much more than twenty, her face not yet grown out of girlish softness. Her eyes were blue, not like Jenyfer's ocean blue, but the colour of a crisp morning sky, pale and piercing. A straight nose, slightly turned up at the bottom and full lips. Her cheekbones sat high on her heart-shaped face, and the hair he could see beneath the cap was sunshine yellow. A little young – and pretty – to be so pious, he thought.

'Lamorna,' Jenyfer said softly. 'Leave it. Let's just go home, alright.'

Lamorna showed Ordes her back. She still had hold of Jenyfer's arm and tugged, almost sending Jenyfer tumbling to the stones beneath their feet. A sense of desperate helplessness crawled over Ordes.

As she was dragged away, Jenyfer twisted her head to look at him over her shoulder. There were deep shadows beneath her eyes, ones he had failed to notice in the shade. He could do nothing more than leave. On the beach, the fishermen and the body were gone. With a sigh, Ordes headed for his boat, water splashing around his ankles. He tossed the bottles of rum into the boat, then climbed in and made his way across the water to the ship.

'Another body,' he told his father as he passed up the rum, swinging himself up the rope ladder and onto the deck. 'Eyes cut out and arranged next to his head on little skewers like a delicacy on a plate.'

Tymis frowned. 'Who are they pointing the finger at?'

'Kat.'

'Is it her?'

'No.' Ordes saw his father's sceptical look. 'She might be a bitch, and a little vicious at times, but I don't think she's really capable of something like that. What purpose would it serve her? Or Niniane?'

'What else happened? You're as white as a sheet.'

'Jenyfer.'

'The girlfriend who isn't your girlfriend?'

'I need to get her out of that place,' Ordes said fiercely, ignoring his father's shitty sense of humour. 'I'm getting her tonight,' he added, not mentioning Lamorna, then gestured at the water. 'Here's Kat. Looks like we'll have the chance to ask her about the bodies.'

The sea around them bubbled and churned, water boiling and spluttering as *The Night Queen* rose from the depths – it never mattered how deep or shallow the water was, Kat's ship went wherever she wished it. Water spilled over the *Queen's* sides and dripped from the masts, but her sails were dry, as was her crew, standing on deck.

'Morning, Kat,' Tymis called, his voice dripping with false cheer. 'What brings you by?'

Katarin Le Fey smiled. The Captain of *The Night Queen* rested her hands on the railing, dark red hair loose around her shoulders.

Tymis folded his arms, waiting. Katarin ran the tip of her finger along the railing – droplets of water beaded in its wake. They hardened into jewels the colour of the ocean under a setting sun. She scooped them up, tossed them lazily from hand to hand, before letting them drop to the deck of her ship, where they became water once more.

'What do you want, Katarin?' Tymis called. 'Or have you come to show off?'

'Just checking in,' she responded, eyes flicking to Ordes' face again briefly.

'I hope you don't have bad news,' Tymis said. 'They shoot messengers for bad news.'

'Are you going to shoot me?' she asked.

'Are you going to remove my eyes? Or possibly my tongue?'

Ordes didn't think she'd done it, but he wasn't entirely certain. She was capable of it, if she was angry enough, but he hadn't lied to those fishermen. It wasn't her style – but she might know whose it was.

Kat frowned, folding her arms. 'What are you talking about?'

'Dead fishermen,' Tymis answered. 'Two now. Mutilated and left on the beach. Was it you?'

'I don't leave evidence.' She glanced up at the clouds. 'A storm is coming, boys. You better hold on tight,' she told them, turning and returning to stand amidship.

'Is that a metaphor?' Tymis asked. She just smiled.

'Kat,' Ordes called. 'There's a Shaleitari in the town.'

'How long?' Her expression became fierce; the women of her crew were whispering amongst themselves furiously.

'Not long,' Ordes said.

She nodded. 'I'll check in again later, if you're still here.'

The Night Queen sank beneath the waves again. Ordes glanced up. Despite the stormy sky, no wind teased *The Excalibur's* sails.

Tymis turned to his son. 'If your mouth isn't too busy, maybe you can use it to ask your girlfriend number one some questions. The Shaleitari wouldn't just show up without reason. Has Kat gotten sloppy?'

Ordes shook his head. 'She isn't my girlfriend.' Katarin was many things, but she was never sloppy. Her rescues were by the book. She never got caught, and was rarely spotted, thanks to her magic and the magic of her crew.

Tymis turned to go, then stopped, shooting Ordes a hard look over his shoulder. 'Do not get caught with girlfriend number two, understand?'

Ordes nodded.

Just before midnight, he slipped into the water. No boat this time. Too slow and too noisy. He could carry two people through the sea with his magic, and he had nothing to fear from the Shaleitari – once he had Jenyfer and her sister on board, the Witchfinder couldn't touch them. Dripping with water, Ordes climbed from the sea and headed to the cave.

He waited until it was almost dawn, but neither Jenyfer nor her sister showed up.

CHAPTER 14

Jenyfer and Lamorna sat in their respective beds watching each other as the candle burned down. For over twenty years they'd shared a bedroom, with its two narrow beds with identical cream coverlets, one window, a slim wardrobe, and a small table crammed between the beds. There were no ornaments or decorations; only Lamorna's battered copy of the Decalogue sat on the table, along with a lone candle, their only source of light once night had fallen. The wardrobe – old, timber, with a creaking hinge – held the scant amount of clothes the sisters' owned.

Jenyfer let her eyes crawl around the room, watching the way the candlelight flickered against the dull white walls. The window was open, as it usually was. Jenyfer slept with it open all year round and, as the window was above her bed, she was in charge of it. She barely felt the cold, and Lamorna had long given up telling Jenyfer to close the window. Instead, she burrowed beneath more blankets when the weather turned. The eaves were wide enough that even the fiercest oceanic squall, with its teeming rain and howling wind, did not send water spiralling into the room. From the window, Jenyfer could watch the ocean, see the colours shift and bleed into one another as day turned to night and back to day. She could see the hills beyond the town where, in autumn, russet reds and browns dominated the landscape – a final pause before the trees shook their leaves free and the world succumbed to winter, when everything was grey and muted blue and woodsmoke pumped from chimneys day and night.

Lamorna was dressed for bed, the white of her nightgown glowing in the near-darkness, her golden hair falling free over her shoulders. She had not looked away from Jenyfer's face, and she had not spoken a word. The candle was half burnt down, the scent of tallow and wax enveloping the room, and their aunt had sought her bed hours ago.

Jenyfer could stand the silence no longer. 'I'm getting out of here.'

'Getting out of where? This house? No, you're not,' Lamorna answered.

Jenyfer scooted to the edge of the bed, looking into her sister's face. Candlelight coated her sister's skin golden and warm, but Lamorna's expression was as chilled as a winter wind. 'You can come as well. It's all arranged.'

'What have you done now?' Lamorna cried, wringing her hands. 'By the Word, Jenyfer, you're going to get us all killed!'

'What do you mean?' Jenyfer sat back and folded her arms mutinously.

'I know what you are, remember?' Lamorna said, her voice dropping to almost a whisper. Her expression shifted. 'They'll burn you if they find out. You know this, Jen. I don't want to see that happen.'

'Then help me,' Jenyfer pleaded. 'Help me get out of this place because I don't know how much longer I can hide it, especially not with a Witchfinder in town.'

Lamorna said nothing; she pulled her bottom lip between her teeth, brows furrowed.

'There is room for you, as well,' Jenyfer said softly. 'On the ship.'

Lamorna's eyes hardened. 'What ship? That one out there in the Bay? Full of pirates and murderers and thieves?'

'Yes, that one. Lamorna, please.'

Lamorna narrowed her eyes, then gasped. 'That pirate! I knew it. I knew you were up to no good. Has he seduced you?'

'What the... no, no,' Jenyfer said, shaking her head, ignoring the burning in her belly as her mind drifted to that kiss and away again. 'He's going to help me. Help *us* get out of here.'

Lamorna folded her arms. 'I don't want to leave. What about Aunt Tamora?'

A little pang shot through Jenyfer at the thought of their aunt. 'I'll miss her.'

'And I'll miss you,' Lamorna said firmly.

Jenyfer swallowed. 'So you won't come?'

'No, and you won't go either, Jenyfer. What about Bryn?'

'What about him? He doesn't want to marry me anymore than I want to marry him. I lied, Lamorna. I lied, and now Bryn and I are both caught up in this. I want to make it right, and the best thing I can do for him is to not be here. It's the best thing I can do for all of you,' she added quietly.

'I'm sorry, Jen,' Lamorna said. 'I can't let you.'

Jenyfer sighed, then, 'You're not scared of me? Of my magic?'

'No. The One God protects me,' Lamorna answered.

'Oh for...' Jenyfer muttered. She looked her sister in the eye. 'I will get out of this place. I'll leave, Lamorna, one way or another.'

Lamorna just nodded, and sat back, settling in to keep watch. The candle went out suddenly, a breeze rushing through the open window. Lamorna sighed, an irritated noise, then promptly lit a second candle, and just before dawn, it too had burnt away to nothing, taking with it the last hope Jenyfer had of escaping the fate that the Chif and his God had written for her.

Had Ordes gone to meet her? She wished she knew how long he'd waited. He'd be gone by now, she knew that, and another tiny slither of hope slipped away from her. With a final glare at her sister, Jenyfer made her way into the kitchen, wearing yesterday's clothes. She hadn't bothered to change. What was the point?

Tamora was sitting at the table nursing a cup of tea when Jenyfer went in. Their aunt barely registered Jenyfer's entry, her eyes distant, face tight. No steam rose from the cup clutched between her strong hands and Jenyfer wondered how long she'd been sitting there.

Jenyfer took a seat opposite her, studying her aunt as covertly as she could. Tamora had been both mother and father to Jenyfer and Lamorna, but she had never married herself and had no children. Besides her sister, Tamora was all the family Jenyfer had in the world, and now, she was being forced to leave her, to leave her home and everything she knew because she'd made a stupid mistake.

No, she thought fiercely. It wasn't a mistake. The Chif and the Konsel were the ones who were wrong.

The lines around Tamora's eyes were deep, and in the light filtering through the kitchen window, Jenyfer could see the lush red of her aunt's hair was beginning to fade. She had always thought Tamora was beautiful, that she could easily have married.

'Why didn't you get married?' she blurted.

Tamora started, then laughed. 'And what would I do with a husband? Someone beneath my feet, getting in the way. No,' she shook her head.

'But there must have been someone,' Jenyfer insisted. 'Did you have a lover?'

Her aunt laughed sadly. 'I've had no time for love affairs with two small girls to look after,' she said. Her expression shifted suddenly and she reached across the table for Jenyfer's hand. 'I wish this wasn't your fate, Jen, but it's better than death.'

Is it? Jenyfer thought.

'I was going to run away last night,' she found herself confessing. 'But Lamorna stayed awake and watched me.'

After they'd stopped talking, she'd sat there staring at her sister, thinking until her head hurt, scheming into the night, but could see no way out of it anymore, besides throwing herself into the sea.

Tamora was watching her. 'Where were you going to go?'

'I don't know. Just anywhere but here.' Standing, Jenyfer made a half-hearted attempt to tidy her hair. 'I need to see Bryn.'

'Jenyfer, I don't think that's wise,' her aunt warned. 'The Witchfinder—'

'I'll stay away from him. I need to talk to Bryn, before everything changes.'

Jenyfer left her aunt sitting at the table with her cold tea, hurrying from the cottage and down into the town. The morning sun was warm on her face and the ocean breeze whipped her hair around her head, tangling it more than it already was. She passed a few people on the path, heading back to their homes with laden baskets, but they didn't look at her. She was certain the whole of Kernou would know about her upcoming wedding and her 'indiscretion' by now, and she shuddered, but squared her shoulders as she arrived at the market square. People avoiding her was nothing new.

Jenyfer pushed her hair from her eyes and strode across the stones to the fishmongers, keeping her chin high. She'd acquired a new label, and had decided she'd wear it with pride, even if it was based on a lie. It was the only thing she had left – her defiance, her hate of the One God and his rules.

Denny, the fishmonger's teenage son, was in the shop, looking bored. He jumped up when Jenyfer burst through the door.

'Has Bryn been in?' she demanded. Bryn would have been out on the water that morning and was probably home by now, but she was not going to waste time running all over town looking for him.

Denny's cheeks coloured and he bit his lip. 'I...'

Jenyfer folded her arms and glared at him. 'He either has, or he hasn't, Denny. Which one is it?'

'What's going on out there?'

Jenyfer repressed a groan as a voice oozed into the shop front from the back room. Denny's mother, Margaret, waltzed in, wiping her hands on a cloth. She froze when she saw Jenyfer standing there. A mixture of emotions crossed her pudgy face and Jenyfer almost laughed as the poor woman tried to work out which one she would run with.

Margaret settled on passive aggression, tucking a strand of greying hair beneath her cap with flour-smudged fingers. 'If it's Bryn you're looking for, he isn't here.'

'I can see that,' Jenyfer answered impatiently.

Margaret clicked her tongue in disapproval.

'He was in this morning.' Denny finally found his voice. 'Dropped off the catch and then left. You'll find him at the bait shed, I'd say.'

Jenyfer flashed the boy her best smile, ignoring the look his mother shot her. Women about to be married did not smile at other men. 'Thank you, Denny.' She turned and left, not bothering to close the door. Her eyes shifted towards the ocean, but she couldn't see if *The Excalibur* was still there with the buildings blocking her view. Though she'd missed her chance to escape, she had one last thing to try.

The bait shed was on the edge of town, nestled where the grass and stones gave way to soft, golden sand. Jenyfer had been there before, but not for a long time. Approaching the shed, she saw Bryn lingering outside, two older fishermen whose name's she didn't know with him. Jenyfer bit her lip. If she marched up there and demanded to talk to him, it would put him in an awkward position. So, after a moment's pause, she ducked between the two nearest buildings to wait.

Eventually, the older men left, one of them slapping Bryn on the back as he went. Bryn winced, but his cheeks reddened and a strange sort of pride was scrawled across his face. He rubbed at his hair, then turned to leave, hands in his pockets. Jenyfer rolled her eyes to hear him whistling to himself.

'Bryn!' she hissed. He looked around in fright, saw her lingering in the shadows and shook his head a fraction. She waited, and he strolled casually into the dark passage where she had tucked herself.

'What are you doing?' he demanded. All the happiness had fled from his face. She grabbed at his arm, pulling him towards her so she could lower her voice.

'When will the Witchfinder leave?' It wasn't what she needed to ask, but she didn't want to leave without knowing.

Bryn sighed. 'I don't know. Don't get yourself in trouble, please.'

She jumped when his hand reached up to caress her cheek gently. He had never touched her like this, in all the years they had been friends. She swallowed, an unfamiliar sensation crawling its way up her spine, and stepped away.

Disappointment flashed across his face, and then it was gone, and he was frowning at her.

'Don't do anything stupid,' he said sternly.

Jenyfer rubbed her cheek, feeling the heat from his skin merging with hers. 'Maybe he'd like to take a walk on the moors, see the stone circle, meet some faeries... should I suggest it?'

Bryn let his head fall into his hands. 'Are you serious?'

She didn't know why, but something about his changed manner drove her to say more. 'I'd love to see it. I'd love to watch the korrigans peel the flesh from the Konsel's collective bones and eat them,' Jenyfer said viciously. 'They should eat the Chif first, because then this place would be free of his God and all his rules.'

Someone walked past their hiding place, a woman, but she was too preoccupied with the children that dashed around her legs to notice them. Bryn said nothing for a long moment - the only sounds were their combined breathing, the distant shrieks of children and the pounding of the waves on the shore. The sea was rough today.

'This isn't how I wanted it to happen,' Bryn mumbled. 'But what am I supposed to do, Jen?' he asked, pulling at his hair in frustration. 'I can't say no. I've got to make up for it.'

'Make up for what?' she demanded, while his other words swam around her head.

This isn't how I wanted it to happen.

Wanted what? Jenyfer opened her mouth to question him, but Bryn put his face close to hers again, so close she could see the freckles beneath his tan. 'For your lies. For disgracing myself, even though I did nothing at all.' He sighed and stepped away. 'You think you're the only one who's been affected by this? You have no idea. I had to atone for my sins – and yours.'

Jenyfer swallowed. 'Bryn—'

'They've instructed me,' he said. 'The Konsel and the Chif. I've been told exactly how I am to treat you.'

'And how is that?' A coldness crept over her at his words, and her mouth went dry even as water beaded on the skin of her palms. Hurriedly, she wiped her hands on her dress, but Bryn didn't notice. His face was deeply conflicted, more pained than she'd ever seen it, even when he'd broken his leg and the healer set the bone. She'd been with him that day, they'd been playing on the rocks near the stake. The sea had been wild, the waves throwing themselves against the shore, mist and spray coating them. A rough set had rolled in, and, seeing what would happen, Bryn had pushed her out of the way and let the sea throw him about like a piece of driftwood.

Thirteen-year-old Bryn thought he was going to die, and she believed him, kissing him on the mouth when he'd begged her not to let him go to the Otherworld without ever being kissed. That had been the first, and last, time she'd kissed anyone. Until Ordes...

'If you don't consent,' Bryn began, his voice soft, 'I can...'

Jenyfer said nothing, not sure she wanted to hear it. Her body had gone numb.

Bryn let out a breath, not looking at her when he spoke. 'I can take you by force, if I must.'

The rational part of Jenyfer's brain was not surprised in the least, but the other part, the wild and wicked part – the defiant, disobedient part – had her pressed against the opposite wall to Bryn, as far away from him as she could get. 'You will not touch me like that,' she hissed. 'If you do... I'll throw myself into the sea, Bryn.'

'You think I want to do that?' he said quietly.

'No,' she said eventually. 'Then we lie about it. We say we did, and no one will know.'

Bryn shot her a quick look, holding her eyes this time. 'They want proof.'

The sheets, she realised quickly. They wanted to see her blood on them, the proof that Bryn had fulfilled his duty, whether she desired it or not. She shook her head, a dark and bitter laugh creeping up her throat and into the air around them. 'Why doesn't the Konsel just invite themselves to bed with us? Seas damn it!'

Beneath her skin, her magic stirred, but she pushed it down, pushed her inner song away, willed it to be silent, for *once*, so she could think. 'Then we find an animal, use its blood. We could—'

Bryn stepped forward and caught her face between his hands. 'I promise not to hurt you.'

She shoved him, sending him flying back into the wall. A gasp of pain left his lips. Jenyfer narrowed her eyes. 'What's wrong with you?'

'Nothing.'

'Liar. What happened?'

Bryn scowled. 'I told you – I had to atone.'

Something squirmed deep in Jenyfer's belly. 'Turn around and lift your shirt.'

He shook his head, so she spun him around and pulled his shirt up, exposing his back, and sucked in a shocked breath at the angry red welts that criss-crossed his skin. She'd heard stories, whisper and rumour, but had never seen the evidence of it herself. She wanted to vomit. 'Did they do this to you?'

Bryn pulled his shirt back down and turned to face her again, his cheeks red. 'I did it to myself.'

Jenyfer knew what he left unsaid. He'd had no choice. It was all her fault. She'd done this to him – her lies had done this. She may as well have whipped him herself. Shaking, she grasped his hands. She had planned to ask him to row her out to *The Excalibur*, but now, she didn't want to leave him in this place either.

'Then we leave,' she said. 'We get Lamorna, get in your boat, and we go. We can go wherever you want. Anywhere but here. There's a ship out there. We can row out to it and—'

'We can't,' Bryn interrupted softly. 'It's too late to run. They'd find us – and then they'd punish you, Jenyfer, not me. You know this.'

She swallowed, her throat tight, her heart feeling like it would explode from her chest and splatter on the stones at their feet.

'Is marrying me really such an abominable fate?' he whispered.

'I need to go.'

He let her, and she ran for the ocean, tearing along the beach, her vision blurring. On the hill above her, her aunt's cottage was a white-washed smear against an achingly blue sky.

Jenyfer paused. She glanced towards the end of the beach, where the cave lay, filled with her secrets and everything Ordes had told her. She scanned the horizon, looking for anything, a rowboat, some sign that he hadn't given up on her. But there was nothing.

She walked into the water and the sea closed over her ankles, gripping her with cold fingers.

Then, she remembered she couldn't swim.

CHAPTER 15

When Arthur woke, his head full of dreams that would see him Burn, there was a pisky perched on the end of his bed, his tiny fingers tugging at Arthur's blankets. Arthur scrambled upright, heart pounding in terror, not taking his eyes off the faery. The pisky had skin the colour of fallen leaves, a hooked nose, and long limbs. Each finger, Arthur noted, had an extra joint. The little creature blinked at him, then dropped the blanket and bounced off the bed, scurrying towards the door.

'Wait,' Arthur said, his brain fit to explode. He was seeing *faeries*! In his house, of all places. The pisky waited, cocking his head to the side, watching Arthur intently through liquid-black eyes. He beckoned, and Arthur threw back the bedclothes and dressed as quickly as he could, the pisky watching him the whole time.

Arthur's heart was thunder in his chest, sinking into his stomach and hammering there so forcefully he thought he'd vomit. He eased the door of his room open and peered down the hall, first in one direction, then the other, but the pisky didn't wait, darting out into the darkness.

'Come back,' Arthur hissed. He heard a giggle in response and, swallowing his nerves, hurried down the hall after the faery, who was waiting for him near the door to the Chif's official room. Arthur came to an abrupt stop.

He wasn't allowed in there. No one was.

The pisky, however, cared nothing for Ulrian's rules. The faery winked at Arthur, then shoved the door open with more strength than he should have, considering he was only as tall as Arthur's knees.

Truly panicked, Arthur dashed into the room to find the pisky standing on his father's desk. Made of oak, the desk was polished to a high sheen, and the pisky seemed to be studying his reflection, tipping his head to one side and then the other. He hopped around the desk, scattering papers and writing tools.

Arthur made a dive for the ink pot before it was split across the desk. 'Get down,' he whispered.

The pisky giggled, but did as he was told, bounding from the desk to sit on Ulrian's grand chair, running his twig-like fingers over the arms with interest. Arthur breathed a sigh of relief, setting the ink pot right and organising the papers back into their neat piles as he glanced around the room. Bookshelves lined one wall, virtually empty except for copies of the Decalogue. A small cupboard made of oak sat on the opposite side, a candle in a sconce resting on top of it. Arthur averted his eyes. He knew what was in there.

The pisky was now standing on the chair, tugging on the knob of the desk drawer, the lines on his little face deeper with his frown. 'What do you want with that?' Arthur came around to the other side of the desk, his heart beating so loudly he was certain his father could hear it from wherever he was in the house.

This was so dangerous.

He needed to leave, but the pisky, the faery, had picked up a letter opener and was trying to prise the drawer open. Arthur frowned at him.

'Can't you just magic it free?' he asked, remembering the things Jalen had told him about the Small Folk.

A giggle, then a snap of his fingers, and the desk drawer sprung open. Before Arthur could stop him, the pisky dove inside, rustling around like a rat. Arthur kept one eye on the door, the other on the pile of papers shifting in the desk drawer as the pisky dug about.

'What are you looking for?' Arthur asked.

A piece of paper floated free, fluttering to the lush carpet beneath Ulrian's desk. The pisky's head popped out of the papers. He blinked, then looked at the paper. Swallowing, mouth like sand, Arthur bent and collected it.

'You want me to read this?'

The pisky just blinked at him. Arthur sighed. The sooner he did what the faery wanted, the sooner it would leave and he could get out of here. He turned the paper over, and froze.

It was a list of names, mostly female, with their ages and dates written next to them in his father's neat hand.

The earliest date was... Arthur frowned. The day before his birth date.

The next was just over a year later, the name not one he recognised. He let his eyes trail down the page.

Myfanwy Enys. He had known her.

Had listened as she'd been accused of witchcraft, had watched as she was tied to the stake and given to the sea while her mother wept. The whole town watched... and did nothing.

And the girl before her. Ellowen Sholl. Also a witch.

Feeling sick, Arthur looked again at the very first name – Morgaine Tintagel. He traced the words with the tip of his finger, wondering who she was. There was no age listed with her name. Frowning, Arthur bit his lip. There were no Tintagels living in Kernou. As far as he knew, Tintagel was an old Cruithean name, so how had—

'What are you doing here?'

Ulrian's voice was like a slap across the face. Arthur jumped and dropped the paper. The pisky, he noticed, had vanished, leaving him to face his father's wrath.

The Chif strode into the room, eyes everywhere, looking for evidence of Arthur's transgression. 'Well?'

'The window,' Arthur stammered. *Stupid.* 'It was open and I thought I should close it and—'

'You lie,' Ulrian said. His voice was low, filled with certainty.

Arthur swallowed, sweat gathering in his armpits and on the back of his neck. 'I…'

Ulrian sighed, turning and closing the door. The sound of the lock clicking into place echoed ominously through the room. 'I don't know what I did to anger the One God,' he said with deadly softness. He strode purposefully behind the desk while Arthur skittled out of the way. Ulrian bent and collected the papers from the ground. 'I don't know why He decided to grant me a liar and a sinner for a son.'

'Father—'

'He tests us in many ways,' Ulrian continued, still in that calm voice. He set the papers back in the drawer and closed it gently. Arthur could do nothing but watch as his father then approached the small cupboard. His stomach clenched. Droplets of sweat made their way down his cheek.

'Don't.'

'Lying is a sin, Arthur,' Ulrian said simply, reaching into the cupboard. 'And sins must be punished.' He turned around. Held between his large hands was the whip. The same one Arthur had witnessed his father using to open the skin on his back. 'Take off your shirt.'

'No.'

Ulrian's eyes flashed. 'Do as you are told, Arthur.'

'I'm your son,' Arthur said, trying to make his voice strong, trying to have courage, but he could hear the waver in his tone just as his father could. He had spent so many years living with fear as a companion, he didn't know how to be strong. 'I'm your child.'

'We are all children of the One God,' Ulrian said, running his fingers over the whip. 'We all must chastise our bodies, to remind us of our sins and our vile human natures. This is what the One God asks of us, Arthur.'

The whip, three leather thongs tipped with nails, was held gently, reverently, in Ulrian's hands. 'Remove your shirt. The One God demands your sacrifice, Arthur. He demands your blood as a sign that you truly love Him.'

Outside, a storm suddenly ripped and clawed at the world. Wind grabbed at the Tregarthen house and the windows of Ulrian's official room rattled as thunder split the sky and rain pelted onto the roof.

With his father's eyes boring into his, Arthur took a deep breath and removed his shirt.

Ulrian held out the whip. 'You will do it yourself.'

Chapter 16

Jenyfer didn't have much to pack. They lived simply, as everyone did, as the One God decreed they must. She owned some clothes and shoes, and – apart from her collection of shells and smooth rocks and delicate feathers she'd found on the beach – there was nothing else Jenyfer could call hers. Her sister had declared shells and rocks and feathers were childish fancies, and not things a married woman needed.

What Jenyfer needed was a plan, but her brain was nothing but fog, her inner song screaming so loudly her head was pounding and she thought she'd vomit.

She sat on her bed and stared out the window. The sea was spread below her, the vista one of the most familiar things in the world, and that would be taken from her as well. She stared and stared, committing everything to memory, adding it to the layers that already existed. How the water brushed against the shore, white foam slicked across the sand before it vanished, and how the light caught on the surface of the water. The ocean was rough today, waves rising and smashing into one another.

A lone fishing boat sat past the breakers, the men aboard no doubt waiting until the sea was calm until they tried to come to shore. White birds screeched their displeasure at the day and the sky was a muted grey, clouds strung across it, their undersides dark with fury.

Good, Jenyfer thought, sending her own prayer to the sea. Drown this place.

Lamorna was helping her pack. A small trunk lay open on Jenyfer's bed. It would carry her belongings out of this cottage, the only home she had ever known, and into her new life. Lamorna hummed to herself as she put Jenyfer's hairbrush into the bottom of the trunk, followed by her nightdresses and a soft, woollen blanket that had belonged to their mother. She frowned and rearranged the items so the blanket was at the bottom.

'You don't have to do this,' Jenyfer said, the first words she had spoken to her sister in days. Lamorna had betrayed her, more than once, Jenyfer thought.

'It's my duty,' Lamorna responded simply. 'You're my sister.'

Jenyfer said nothing.

'You didn't eat this morning, or at lunch,' Lamorna said gently as she laid a copy of the Decalogue in the trunk. Jenyfer didn't comment on it. She didn't want the argument, not today, not when her life was being ripped away from her and everything had fallen well and truly outside of her control.

Not that she had any control. Not that any of them did.

In less than an hour, she was getting married. Her sister had always told her her mouth would get her in trouble and, now, it had gotten her into the deepest trouble possible. She didn't know why she'd lied to the Chif that night. She hadn't been thinking – she'd been worried about Ordes being discovered, even though, too late, she realised she didn't need to be.

He was a Magic Wielder. A pirate. Perfectly capable of defending himself.

Jenyfer glanced out the window to where the sea lay as if in waiting.

'Jen?'

Jenyfer ripped her gaze from the ocean. 'What?'

'You need to eat,' her sister chided gently.

'I can't,' Jenyfer snapped. Her stomach was rolling, hands trembling. She thrust them into her lap, horrified when her skin became wet. Ordes had told her she should be able to control that but, at the moment, her thoughts were too scattered to control anything. Her sister didn't notice, too busy with her task.

'I know you're worried, but you needn't be. It really is quite simple,' Lamorna said. 'You do as he says. You keep the house, cook the meals, clean the linen. And if he wants to lie with you and you don't... well, it doesn't matter because your job now is to please your husband.'

The rolling in Jenyfer's stomach intensified. 'You have got to be joking.'

Lamorna shook her head. 'It's what the One God demands, Jenyfer.'

'The One God can kiss my arse,' Jenyfer muttered mutionously, but her sister heard. Lamorna planted her hands on her hips and pursed her lips but, for once, she didn't argue. She shook her head, moving around the room, pulling Jenyfer's clothing from the drawers and laying them gently, almost reverently, in the chest.

'Women are the bearers of sin. They are transgressors and they will hold their tongue and submit to the rule of their husband, who she was created to serve,' Lamorna quoted solemnly. 'You will do as your husband demands of you.'

Jenyfer stood, slamming the lid of the chest closed, almost snapping her sister's fingers in it. 'Don't quote those stupid bloody rules to me!'

Lamorna stepped back, eyes flashing. 'You have brought this on yourself.'

'I didn't do anything wrong!' Jenyfer cried, throwing her hands in the air.

Lamorna's voice was soft but stern. 'Bryn will soon be your husband and you will be his property. You will wear respectable clothing at all times, be modest and control yourself, Jenyfer,' she added more firmly.

Jenyfer stared at her sister. 'How can you think this is alright? How do you even know the One God is real and that he really wanted this for us?'

'He only wants us to love Him and—'

Jenyfer took her sister by the shoulders, staring into her bright blue eyes imploringly. The afternoon sun slanted through their window, painting the side of Lamorna's face and her hair burnished gold. 'It is no god of mine that takes away my voice and my freedom,' Jenyfer whispered. 'Can't you see what's happening? Don't you feel it? Are you happy to be a slave?'

'The Decalogue says we shall have no other gods but Him.'

'For fuck's sake, Lamorna,' Jenyfer spat, releasing her sister and dropping onto the bed. It was exhausting. She'd watched Lamorna and many others slowly falling under whatever spell the Chif was casting on the town with his words and his prayer circles and his seas-damned speeches. She'd watched her aunt's face tighten whenever Lamorna read aloud to them from the Decalogue, and she watched how, gradually, the women and girls were seldom seen anywhere that was not the market square or the women's prayer circle. 'It's not right.'

Lamorna sighed and sat beside her. Gently, she took Jenyfer's hand in hers. 'You will be fine. Bryn will take care of you, Jen. You're lucky. He's a good man.'

'Is he?' Jenyfer said. 'Because lately, he seems like the rest of them.'

'Are you talking about that mermaid again?' Lamorna's voice was sharp and she clicked her tongue in disapproval. 'He lied for you.' She held up her hand when Jenyfer opened her mouth. 'He did. I don't know what you were doing out that night. I don't want to know if you were meeting someone or if you were... he saved you, and you need to remember that.'

'They made him whip himself, Lamorna. The Chif and the Konsel. I've seen the marks. They're horrible – red and angry and... and it's my fault it happened.' She gripped her sister's hands, staring into her eyes. 'Don't help them do this to me. To Bryn. Help me get out of here, please. Come with me, Lamorna.'

Lamorna pulled her hands free and stood, smoothing away invisible creases in her simple linen dress. 'You need to get ready. I'll get Aunt Tamora. Get dressed, Jen.'

When her sister had gone, Jenyfer stared at the dress laid out for her on Lamorna's bed. It had been their mother's, her best, the dress she had worn when she married their father. Jenyfer didn't remember either of them, but she wondered if they had been happy, and whether they married because they loved one another.

Of course they loved one another. The One God and his rules had not snuck inside the town like a poison when her parents were alive. The Old Ways had no rules, no scriptures that must be obeyed, save one – if it harms no one, do as you will. How much simpler things were, Jenyfer thought, her eyes on her mother's dress.

And now, she had lost her freedom, the power to choose. She couldn't see what was so wrong with walking the beach in the darkness, or crossing the moor to step inside a stone circle with the korrigans, creatures that came from the earth. She didn't see what was so wrong with being able to say no to a man, or let her hair run free down her back.

Jenyfer was still frowning when Lamorna and their aunt came in. Lamorna tutted to see her sitting there, not yet dressed, not yet ready to be dragged from one world, kicking and screaming, and thrust into another that she had no desire to enter.

But Jenyfer wasn't sure she had the energy to kick and scream, not when she was surrounded on all sides, caged and trapped like an animal. If she bared her teeth and showed them her claws... she didn't know what would happen.

The sacrificial stake came to mind and she shuddered.

Tamora looked at her sadly, and nodded. 'Get dressed, Jenyfer.'

Sighing, Jenyfer rose from the bed. She let her sister pull her plain linen dress over her head, let her take up their mother's glowing white gown, obediently lifting her arms. Then she let Lamorna comb her hair and tie it into a tight knot at the base of her skull. When her sister was done and a white cap was placed over her hair, Jenyfer wanted to cry.

It was her wedding day, and she didn't even know what she looked like.

Mirrors were a symbol of pride.

There were no mirrors in their home anymore.

The wedding was conducted at the Chif's home. The Tregarthen home was richly decorated with lush rugs and tapestries depicting the natural world – a reminder of what the One God had created for His children.

Lamorna was instructed to take Jenyfer to a small room that was connected to the main hall by a short corridor. It was a dark room with no windows, and the silence that clung to that small space was deep and miserable. Jenyfer frowned and plucked at the hem of her sleeve in agitation as she stepped into the room, while Lamorna hovered in the doorway.

'It will be alright, Jen,' Lamorna said. 'You will be married, and I will become a Sister.'

Jenyfer said nothing.

Lamorna fussed over the sleeves of Jenyfer's gown, slapping Jenyfer's fiddling fingers away. 'I heard that, in Malist, the Sisters of the One God are beloved by the people of the city for the work they carry out in His name,' she said. The single statement was tinged with pride and Jenyfer, in her sorrow, jumped on it.

'It sounds like you want to be a Sister so people will like you, Lamorna. Isn't that a sin? Desiring the favour of others?'

Lamorna tossed her head. 'There is nothing wrong with wanting people to respect you for the things you do, especially if it helps them.'

'Yet you worship a god who considers you nothing but chattel,' Jenyfer spat. 'Does the Chif respect you? Does he care what you do for him and his god?'

'I—'

'You know he doesn't. He only cares if your acts, your sacrifices, benefit him,' Jenyfer went on, lowering her voice. 'Him, the Konsel, anyone in this place – they don't care about *you*, Lamorna, not like Aunt Tamora and I do.'

Lamorna's cheeks had grown pink. 'You don't care about me,' she said fiercely. 'If you did, you'd stop running around doing foolish things that get us into situations like this.'

'It is the One God and his stupid rules that are to blame for this,' Jenyfer shot back, her voice rising. Good. She didn't care if they heard her down the hall.

'The Witchfinder...' Lamorna stammered.

'I don't care,' Jenyfer hissed through her teeth.

Lamorna opened her mouth, then closed it and shook her head. 'I know what this is,' she said, her voice soft, gentle. 'You're nervous.'

'No. I'm furious.' Jenyfer clenched her fists, feeling water coat her palms. 'If I could drown them all, I would. And maybe I can. I don't know. Maybe I should try. Should I, Lamorna? Should I drown them all? Let my magic do what I can't?'

Lamorna narrowed her eyes, then shut the door in Jenyfer's face, locking her in the darkness. Jenyfer bit back a sob, all her anger fading, replaced with nothing but blank despair. How far would she get if she ran? And where would she run to, anyway? Cruithea? It was at least two weeks' walk through the forest, and she didn't know where she was going. Tears pricked her eyelids and she rubbed them away with the heel of her hand.

They might be forcing her to do this, but they would not see her broken. She would go into this with her head held high. How she would get out of it was a mystery, but she would, somehow.

Time ticked on. Jenyfer had no idea how long she was left in the dark room. She focused on her breathing, on keeping the magic that lived beneath her skin still and compliant. She could no longer hear the waves or the beating heart of the ocean, and her inner song was unusually quiet. She'd give anything to hear it right now, hear that familiar melody pick its way through her brain.

She tried to hum a few bars, but her voice failed her, the sound that came from her lips as defeated and weak as the rest of her.

Her thoughts shifted to Ordes. Where was he now? Had he come for her? Or had he stayed out there on his ship, as free as the birds that glided from the headland each morning to plunge head-first into the water? The natural world was simple, existing in a cycle that continued year after year, season after season. There didn't seem to be anything powerful enough to interfere with that cycle.

Jenyfer closed her eyes, letting her mind drift, feeling it leave this house and the darkness within, and float across the soft sand of the beach, over the waves and the sparkling water. If only she'd been able to see what lay beyond the horizon she stared at everyday – but, now, she knew she never would. Her life would be forever woven into the threads of this town.

Maybe Lamorna was right, and it was Jenyfer's fault she was in this situation. If only she could take back the words she said to the Chif that night, but it was too late now. At least she was alive. But was that really better?

The door to the little room was flung open with a level of drama that belonged to no one but Lamorna. She was smiling, her face radiant, eyes almost glowing with excitement, their argument and Jenyfer's nasty words clearly forgotten.

'If you're so pleased about this, you can take my place,' Jenyfer muttered.

Lamorna ignored her, reaching for her hand and drawing her down the corridor and into the main hall. Jenyfer swallowed. Gathered at the end of the hall was Tamora, her face sorrowful, Arthur Tregarthen, who looked like he was going to be sick, and Bryn, his back to her. Jenyfer's steps slowed as she recalled those lurid red marks on his skin.

Standing before an altar, adorned with candles and red cloth, was the Chif. Light poured into the room from the ornate stained-glass window behind him, crowning him in a display of gold and red that Jenyfer did not think was coincidence.

The Witchfinder was not present; Jenyfer breathed an internal sigh of relief.

Ulrian did not smile as Lamorna escorted her sister towards the small party. He simply watched Jenyfer, his dark gaze crawling over her face. A shiver walked her spine and her steps faltered again. Lamorna tugged harder on her arm, practically dragging her the last few metres. Bryn didn't look at her; his eyes were on his feet, but Jenyfer heard him swallow. She glanced at him from the corner of her eye. A bead of sweat was making its way slowly from his temple to the line of his jaw.

'Let us begin,' the Chif said with soft reverence. Jenyfer wondered if she should faint, or pretend to, but she knew it would do no good. They had sealed her fate.

In his large hands, the Chif held a copy of the Decalogue, which he opened to his marked page, clearing his throat before he spoke again. 'The Decalogue contains the Law, the Word of the One God in all His glory. May we be thankful for His blessing.'

Lamorna echoed the Chif, Arthur's soft voice chiming in. Jenyfer said nothing.

'With the authority of the One God, today I bind Bryn Hawkens and this woman to the sanctity of marriage.'

I don't even have a name anymore, Jenyfer thought. She could feel herself slipping away, could feel her mind shifting. Something inside her was clamouring to get out, to escape, to run screaming. She wanted to plunge headlong into the ocean, or pitch her body towards the rocks from the top of the cliffs. She wanted this to end before it began. She wished she'd had the foresight to conceal a knife beneath her sleeve. She wondered what they would have done if she'd pressed a blade to her own throat.

But that was another thing she couldn't change.

Her breath hitched as the Chif went on, but she barely heard him, the words washing over her, attempting to bend and shape her, remould her into the sort of woman the One God would be proud to call one of His children.

'A woman shall be submissive...'

'A woman's desire shall be for her husband and he shall rule over her...'

Jenyfer kept her eyes on her feet, and closed her heart.

Soon, too soon, Bryn lifted her hand into his and, together, they walked like two people condemned from the Chif's house and into the growing night.

Bryn's cottage was small, but it was neat and tidy and warm. A fire blazed in the hearth and candles were lit on the mantle. Set beside the hearth was a large metal cooking pot, a hook dangling over the flames. The cottage had only two rooms – an open space that served as kitchen, dining room and bedroom, the bed hidden behind a section of rough curtain, and a smaller room for bathing. Bryn crossed the room to pull aside the curtain, revealing his bed, *their* bed now, Jenyfer supposed. Although it wasn't, she realised. It was his, as was everything in this cottage, including her things, and her. Anger bubbled up inside her at the knowledge that not even her clothing belonged to her anymore. Her chest had been delivered. It sat at the foot of the bed, the lid firmly closed, as if it, too, did not want to be there.

Jenyfer could not take her eyes from that bed, such a simple piece of furniture that dripped with assumption and expectation. She pulled her arms around herself, rubbing them, feeling her skin beneath the sleeves of her mother's gown pucker and pull into gooseflesh. She was aware of Bryn taking off his coat and hanging it on the peg on the back of the simple wooden door while she continued to stare at the bed. Outside, wind tugged at the corners of the cottage, moaning through the cracks and crevices in the walls.

'It isn't much,' Bryn said simply, gesturing vaguely around them. 'But it's enough. Isn't it, Jen?' His voice had a piteous note of hope in it.

Jenyfer made herself nod. That he would even ask that meant there was still something of the person she knew inside him. It was proof that he did actually care about her, and that he did want her to be happy. She realised dully that she'd never been in his cottage before. It wasn't allowed for a woman to enter the home of a man who was not her father, brother... or husband. 'It's fine, Bryn. Really.'

He came towards her, hesitantly, as if worried she would run screaming into the night, but didn't make any move to touch her.

Jenyfer took a deep breath. Maybe, just maybe, he wouldn't make her do this. But she thought about the marks on his back and bit down a sob. Would they make him hurt himself again, for failing to do what was expected of him? Would he be punished, for her, again?

She found herself unable to look at him, which she'd never done before. She had always met his gaze, met his smiles and his words, with confidence. But, now... she focused on her feet, hidden beneath the hem of her mother's dress. There was dirt on the fabric, she noticed. That would have to be cleaned – and soon – before it stained.

Bryn slid his finger beneath her chin. She jumped. He smiled at her, a soft smile. 'You're here now, and you're my wife. We will just have to make the most of it.' He gestured towards the bed, his cheeks slowly colouring.

She stepped away from him and his face fell a little. 'I don't want—'

'We have to, Jenyfer.'

She shook her head, then remembered what he'd told her – his *instructions*. Swallowing, she folded her arms around her middle. 'Will you force me then?'

Bryn ran a hand through his hair. 'I don't want to. I don't want this either.'

'I think you do,' Jenyfer snapped, the words rushing free without thinking. His hand on her shoulder, the other men slapping him on the back, that strange pride on his face.

She'd known Bryn her whole life and she watched his face as he didn't deny her words, as he came closer to her.

'Jenyfer... I don't want to hurt you. Please.' It was a whisper. Silence dropped between them. Jenyfer could hear the sea pounding against the shore.

It could be worse, she knew that. If it was any other man, the deed would probably have been done by now, regardless of what she wanted, regardless of any fear she had.

'Let's go to bed,' he mumbled, glancing at her quickly and then away. Before she could say anything, he crossed the room to blow out the candles. Jenyfer waited as the fire-kissed darkness of the cottage slowly encased her. It was probably better this way, but part of her had wanted to see his face. She kept her eyes on his back as he pulled the curtains closed. He glanced at her over his shoulder; she looked away quickly and sat on the edge of the bed.

The bed dipped as Bryn claimed his place next to her.

Neither of them moved for a long moment, and the only sound was the crackling of the flames mingling with Jenyfer's tight breathing. She jumped when Bryn reached up to remove the linen cap and untie the knot of her hair from the nape of her neck, letting it tumble down her back. He ran his hands through it, petting her like he would an animal. 'This was always going to happen, wasn't it? I was going to ask you anyway.'

'What do you mean?' Jenyfer whispered.

'Us. This marriage. You must have known how I felt, Jen,' he said, voice low; he held her face between his hands, which were larger than she'd ever realised. Somehow, Bryn had changed, in more ways than one. Jenyfer didn't know why she never noticed it, never noticed the boy become a man. Never noticed him look at her as *more*.

Bryn likes you, Lamorna's voice reminded her.

'Bryn,' Jenyfer began softly, gently, trying to search for the right words. 'I—'

Then his lips were on hers and she didn't know what to do, didn't know whether she should open her mouth or put her arms around him. If she should touch him at all. So, she sat there, let him kiss her, just wanting it to be over. But his kisses became hurried, barely giving her time to breathe between them, before his hands were under her dress and he guided her onto her back. Her muscles tensed and her breath hitched as he touched her in places she hadn't even touched herself.

Was she supposed to like it? No, she wasn't.

Panic closed over her mind as Bryn shifted his weight on top of her and she felt him fumble with the buttons on his pants. He was heavy, heavier than he looked. Jenyfer wriggled around.

'You're squishing me,' she managed.

'Sorry.' Bryn repositioned himself, shifting his weight off her torso, balancing on his elbows and knees. His breathing was tight. 'I'm sorry, Jen.' He reached between their bodies and, then, there was a sharp stabbing pain between her thighs.

Jenyfer closed her eyes as he began to move.

She had made her bed, now she must lie in it.

The following morning, when Ulrian Tregarthen and two members of the Konsel swept into the tiny cottage to inspect the marital bed, she turned her face to the wall to stop herself from clawing their eyes out.

CHAPTER 17

Without wind cupping the sails, there wasn't much for a ship's quartermaster to do; which left plenty of time to think in between daily chores. Ordes had already spent more time than was necessary in the ship's hold sorting through cargo that didn't need sorting. Now, he was sitting on the deck, bored out of his skull.

Iouen sat with him. A former cabin boy from the merchant fleet that sailed regularly from Malist, Iouen had been onboard *The Georgiana*, one of the Portsmouth Trading Company ships, when it was attacked by pirates not long after leaving port on its way to The Vale. Rather than surrender, the crew had chosen to fight, a decision that left most of them floating face-down or bleeding out on deck. The pirate ship had scuttled *The Georgiana*, and Iouen was sent back to shore to spread the word about the bloodthirsty Captain Marsh and the crew of *The Black Rose* in every tavern he could.

The pirates had given Iouen a nasty gash down his cheek to remember them by and, once his wound had healed, the young man decided crap pay from Portsmouth Trading wasn't worth his time; so, like many others, he turned to other ventures. Tymis had picked him up in Skulls Rest and Iouen had sailed with *The Excalibur* for over ten years. Iouen and Ordes were around the same age, and Ordes always suspected it was his son's need for a friend that made Tymis take the thirteen-year-old Iouen on.

The rest of the crew came from various places – they were thieves and criminals, destined for the gallows in Malist, men simply bored of their lives pulling fish from the ocean, or men unhappy with their previous pay. Unlike Katarin's crew, none of the men were Magic Wielders, except Ordes. He didn't flaunt his magic, except when they engaged an enemy ship. Then he got to really let go, stretch his magical muscles. It was thrilling, to feel such power flowing through him, and in the aftermath of those moments he always thought of his father and his bound magic. What would it be like to lose something that was so instinctual, so inherently *his*?

That made him think of Jenyfer.

He'd tried to convince himself she'd simply changed her mind, but his gut told him that wasn't correct. He glanced towards the town, the whitewashed buildings gleaming in the sun.

'You aren't thinking of doing something stupid, are you?' Iouen asked.

Ordes ran his hand through his hair and sighed. 'Something is wrong.'

'With that town? You bet there is,' Iouen muttered. 'But that's not what you meant, is it?'

Ordes said nothing, keeping his gaze on Kernou.

'If she means that much, go and get her,' his friend declared softly.

'It's not that simple,' Ordes answered, sitting back and resting his weight on his elbows. He closed his eyes, letting the heat of the sun sink inside his skin. 'I could be worried about nothing. She could have simply changed her mind and decided not to leave,' he murmured, more to himself than Iouen, but his friend nudged him, making him open his eyes and sit up.

'What does your gut tell you?'

'That I should go and get her,' Ordes said. 'There's a Witchfinder in town.'

'You're not scared of a Witchfinder, are you?'

'Of course I'm not, but I am scared that if I go bursting into that town looking for her it would put her in danger. I should never have agreed to meet with her in the first place, but I couldn't resist.'

'She's pretty, then?'

'That's not the point,' Ordes argued. 'She was so scared the night I met her, yet she still had the courage to ask me to help her. I admire her for that, and even more for showing up to meet me. I know what it's like, Iouen, to have questions and to need answers. But it was more than that,' he said, shaking his head. 'I can't explain it. It feels like I know her, like I've met her before, which is impossible, because I've spent my life on this bloody ship and she's spent hers trapped in that bloody town.'

Iouen was looking at Kernou. 'If it were me, I'd go get her.'

'Yes, because you have no sense of self-preservation,' Ordes said with a smile. 'Remember that last encounter with *The Black Rose*? You took on Marsh, Iouen, and he would have gutted you if—'

'If you and your magic hadn't saved me.' Iouen gave Ordes a curious look. 'Why didn't you kill him? I know about your oath, but you could have, easily, yet you didn't.'

'I won't use my magic to kill,' Ordes answered quietly. 'You know that.'

Iouen blinked at him. 'You're the worst pirate in history, you know that, right?'

'Fuck off.'

Iouen chuckled. 'We've been stuck here for too long. The men are restless. Even Kayrus is getting grumpy,' he said, glancing over his shoulder to where the navigator stood at the helm, one hand on his hip, the other on the wheel. 'What are the Captain's plans?'

'You know as well as I do that we're at the mercy of the ship,' Ordes said. 'If the men are restless, give them something to do. You're the boatswain, Iouen,' he added.

'And as boatswain, I'm letting you know, quartermaster, that the men are agitated.'

Ordes raised his eyebrows. 'If this was any other ship, I'd be asking you about their intentions towards their Captain – but as it isn't, and they've all sworn the blood oath to my father, I'm not going to ask.'

Iouen ran his hand over his shorn head. 'Okay, no need to get testy.'

'Supplies?' Ordes asked.

Iouen shrugged. 'Enough to last, although it's been a long time since we got a prize.'

'And the last was enough to keep the men's pockets full,' Ordes pointed out. 'Tell them...' He sighed. 'Tell them we'll move on soon, head south, to Skulls Rest. That should give them something to look forward to.'

'Lie to them?'

'Yes,' Ordes snapped, then rubbed at his face. 'Sorry.'

Iouen sighed. 'Look, go get your girl before we wake up one morning off the coast of Carinya or somewhere further away. If you don't, you'll regret it forever, Ordes, and then you'll be pissed-off and we'll all have to wear it, won't we? At the very least, go and find out what happened to her. Maybe she did simply decide your mug wasn't worth looking at anymore, or pointed ears weren't her thing, or maybe...'

Both men turned their eyes back to Kernou. Ordes swallowed. The sensation that something was very wrong had dug itself inside him the night Jenyfer didn't show up and had not let go. Now, it burnt, twisting like a dying thing in his belly.

CHAPTER 18

Bryn's face was haunted, a frown resting between his brows. He shut the door behind him with a firm snap, quickly closing off the slice of the outside world that rushed inside. Jenyfer rose from tending the fire, wiping her hands on her apron. A week. It had been a week. She reminded herself of how much time had passed each morning when she woke. The days bled into one another with a speed that frightened her. She was terrified of waking one morning and finding it had been a year, then two, her life well and truly passing her by like water through her fingers.

Was *The Excalibur* still out there? She hadn't seen the sea, so she had no idea.

The Witchfinder was still in Kernou. Jenyfer could feel him, his dark presence lurking at the back of her mind. Lamorna told her he was going door to door throughout the town, but had so far found no trace of magic. She didn't say it, but one look at her sister's face and Jenyfer knew they were thinking the same thing – how long until the

Witchfinder came here, to an unassuming cottage on the far side of town? That look was the closest Lamorna would ever come to admitting she was worried.

Bryn sighed and pulled his jumper off, tossing it onto the bench.

'What is it?' Jenyfer asked. She remained standing by the fire, letting the heat of the flame coat the woollen skirt she wore. She'd just broken another rule, she knew. Don't ask questions of your husband. She'd broken a lot of rules over the last seven days. Rules she didn't even know existed, but Lamorna had come almost every day after Bryn went out in his boat and lectured Jenyfer on the Word. She also brought Jenyfer's tonics, the small, brown glass bottles bringing with them a sense of something familiar that anchored her.

Lamorna's teachings were enough to make Jenyfer's head spin, but she preferred it when her sister was there, even if she was dribbling nonsense from the corner of her mouth and sometimes avoided looking Jenyfer in the eye. It was in those moments when Jenyfer knew Lamorna had not forgotten their argument and the words Jenyfer had spat at her before the wedding. Even so, she looked forward to Lamorna's visits. Neither of them had given any words of apology, but they wouldn't. Both were stubborn, but Jenyfer knew their aunt was right – the Lamorna who had once been a happy, smiling child, full of life and questions, was still there.

Lamorna had not asked and Jenyfer had not mentioned what it was like to be married. The cottage was dark and quiet without Bryn, but when he was there... she swallowed, pushing it out of her mind.

The second night they'd lain together she said no. Or at least she tried to, but the word stuck in her throat and she nearly choked on it; instead, she had closed her eyes and imagined she was somewhere else while, beneath her, the bed rolled like it was floating at sea.

Now, she watched Bryn intently, the way he moved, the way he pulled his hand through his hair and rubbed at his face. Those were gestures she knew but, since becoming his wife, she'd seen things in him that she hadn't known existed. Her muscles would tense when he was near her. He'd not apologised for hurting her on their wedding night. He'd not spoken of it at all – and she hadn't brought it up.

The Bryn she had grown up with would have listened to her. He would have said sorry. He would have asked her permission.

But this new Bryn, this man who was now her husband, gave her no indication he cared about her feelings at all. She had thought that he did, that first night, but she realised quickly she'd been wrong.

She didn't know this man, not anymore.

'There's no fish,' Bryn said finally.

'What do you mean no fish?' The old Jenyfer would have made a joke out of it, and he would have laughed with her. The old her would have smacked him in the arm and told him there was nothing to worry about, but the new her stayed on the other side of the small kitchen while he stared at her, his expression hard.

'We didn't catch a thing,' he said in a quiet voice. 'Nothing. And yesterday, and the day before. Nothing.'

'Maybe you've picked the wrong spot?' Jenyfer said.

Bryn shook his head. 'You don't understand. No one has caught anything substantial since Will...' He rubbed at his face again. His eyes had lost the hard glint and now he just seemed tired. 'There were a few bad days, but no one thought anything of it, but now... I don't know. And the sea has been rough, the storms fierce. It's almost like...' His voice trailed away.

Jenyfer chewed on her lip. Her inner song was humming away, louder, stronger than it usually was. It had been like that for a few days, but she'd barely registered it, her head too caught up in this new world and new role she found herself inhabiting. She cooked three meals a day for her husband. She cleaned the cottage, went to the market most mornings, avoided the Shaleitari, and sat with her sister. Her blood itched. She had not set foot on the sand or laid eyes on the ocean since the afternoon of her wedding. She washed the clothes and the linen, scrubbed the floors, and lay beneath her husband, shutting her eyes and closing her ears to the sounds he made.

'There's something else, isn't there?' she said. Bryn looked away, but not before Jenyfer caught a glint of something in his eye. 'Bryn? Tell me.'

His eyes flashed to hers, and then away. 'Don't command me, Jenyfer. It's not your place,' he added, but then sighed heavily. 'The men are worried. They think... they think the sea has been cursed. They think the storm demon is angry. It's superstitious nonsense.'

Jenyfer thrust her hands behind her back. Water beaded on her fingers. She wiped them on the back of her dress. 'You never thought it was superstitious nonsense before.'

'That was before,' he shot back, then, 'There's a meeting tomorrow.'

'What for?'

'The Konsel wants everyone in the tavern. There is to be an announcement. But you're not going to go.'

Jenyfer frowned. Her heart was hammering, sweat had gathered under her arms and between her breasts and, in her mind, she could feel the wind on her skin and the rope around her wrists.

She folded her arms. 'I'm going.'

Bryn shook his head. 'You're my wife now.'

'You don't own me, Bryn,' she reminded him forcefully. It was a reminder to herself as well – the One God was *not* her god, and he didn't own her, either. She held Bryn's eyes, watched the emotion rush across his face as he tried to figure out what to do, what his role was, how Bryn the husband should act.

'I forbid it,' he said finally.

Jenyfer couldn't help it – she laughed. 'You *forbid* it? Do you hear yourself? What has happened to you? The man I knew, my *friend*, would never—'

Bryn stepped closer to her, anger splashed across his face. 'I've been trying to help you for years, but you've been so insistent on doing whatever you wanted, no matter the consequences. How you haven't gotten your aunt and sister into trouble, I don't know,' he said. 'You've forgotten your place, Jenyfer. At least now, as my wife, I can make sure you do the right thing. I can make sure you're safe. Have you forgotten about the *Witchfinder*?'

Jenyfer just stared at him as every muscle in her body twisted itself into knots. Her spine was rigid with anger – at him, at herself, because he was right: she'd been rash and foolish, had risked her family's safety. Her magic tingled and she flexed her fingers. Something wanted to break free. She could feel it writhing beneath her skin – and her song was deafening.

'I'll admit I made a mistake,' she said coolly.

Bryn's face relaxed a fraction. 'Good. That's a start—'

'I made a mistake in believing you were still my friend,' Jenyfer continued bluntly. 'I've been so blind. Everyone keeps telling me how lucky I am, that you're a good man, but you're not, are you? You're just like the rest of them. I just couldn't see it before now.'

Bryn's face darkened with outrage, his fists curled.

'Are you going to hit me?' Jenyfer said quietly, defiantly. Her song had stilled but it was there, waiting, as was her magic. She could feel it, hovering like a snake about to strike.

Ordes had said all he had to do was think about what he wanted, and his magic did the rest. Perhaps it was the same for her. If Bryn raised his hand to her, she would find out.

Bryn glared at her until, eventually, he turned and stormed from the cottage.

The townspeople crowded in the tavern. It was the only building large enough to contain such an audience. The room was silent – no one gossiped, and no speculations were voiced. Jenyfer let her eyes sweep over the members of the Konsel, sitting at the head of the room behind a long wooden table, a fire blazing in the hearth behind them. The firelight deepened the shadows on the men's faces; their eyes were hidden and Jenyfer shivered as she took her seat between her aunt and her sister, noticing Arthur Tregarthen sitting to the side of the room, back pressed against the wall, pale and sickly looking, like he'd rather be anywhere else.

But Jenyfer wouldn't worry about the Chif's son, not now. She leant close to her sister. Her insides were a twisted mess. Bryn hadn't spoken to her since their argument, and she hadn't paid him a shred of attention, although she was still wound as tight as a knot, and her magic still slithered around and pushed at the confines of her skin. 'Why are you here?'

'I was asked for,' Lamorna whispered. 'The Chif requested my presence.' She tried, but could not keep the pride, the reverence, from her voice. A shiver skittered down Jenyfer's spine. She tried to catch her aunt's eye over Lamorna's white-capped head, but Tamora was looking at the Konsel, and at the Witchfinder hidden in the shadows, only the length of his red cloak visible.

Chif Ulrian cleared his throat and stood. 'People of Kernou. I know that word would have spread by now, and that fear has taken root among you. I know some of you are wondering if the One God is punishing us, that He is unhappy with us. Why else would the sea not be providing for us? I ask you all to double your prayers, and keep the needs of the town above your own, for the One God knows and sees all, and He is ever-watchful.' He paused, adjusted the stiff collar of his shirt. 'We need to show the One God that we are devout and that we hold Him in the highest regard. We have had a Witchfinder with us for some time now. He has been here on the orders of the Magister, and you would have seen him dutifully going about his good work, searching for the heathen among us.'

Jenyfer could barely breathe, but a frown pulled at her face. Bryn had told her not to come. He'd told her to stay away. As the Chif continued his speech, she could hear the beat of the waves on the shoreline, their constant, shifting rhythm steady, as if waiting to see what was to come.

Unease clawed at Jenyfer's belly. She swallowed, and looked sideways at her sister. Lamorna's hair was neatly combed and hidden beneath her cap, her skin glowing in the dim tavern light, her eyes as blue as a calm ocean. Next to her, Jenyfer was a wild tangle.

The Witchfinder stepped from the shadows. A few people gasped. The man did not take a seat at the long table, nor did he acknowledge the Konsel or the Chif in any way. He walked around the table, turning to face the townspeople with a flourish of his cloak.

When he spoke, his voice was soft, yet it rang with power, racing to fill every corner of the room. 'Good people of Kernou, you have been most welcoming and most gracious. I do not wish to reward your hospitality with terrible news, but I am afraid to inform you that there is a witch amongst you.'

A collective gasp echoed around the room.

Tamora reached around Lamorna's back for Jenyfer's hand, squeezing it tightly.

'Such a creature has gone undetected for some time. She has been clever, hiding her foul magic and presenting a face of obedience and devotion, designed to fool you all,' the Witchfinder said.

Jenyfer frowned.

The crowd waited, collective breaths held, until the Witchfinder's voice rang out around the room.

'But, a witch comes in many forms, and it is part of her sorcery to convince you she is something she is not. This woman has fooled you all for years. She has recited the Word alongside you, her foul tongue tainting the lessons the One God wishes us all to learn, and tainting the wisdom He has imparted to all His children. Such is the way of a woman, and such is the way of a witch.' He paused, his pale eyes sweeping into every corner of the room, touching on every face. Eventually, the Witchfinder's gaze came to rest on Jenyfer. She froze, but the man's eyes moved from hers. 'Lamorna Astolat.'

Tamora sucked in a breath. Jenyfer blinked. Her heart stuttered. Words rushed to the tip of her tongue and then fled.

'Lamorna, please stand and approach the table,' the Chif commanded, his voice soft, regretful. Lamorna pushed back her chair and stood, her face filled with terror, and Jenyfer found her voice. It rose from her throat with a mind of its own.

'No!' she shouted. People hissed in shock. 'No,' she repeated, ignoring Tamora's hand on her arm, ignoring the whispers and the looks of those around them. She leapt to her feet and grabbed her sister's hand. Lamorna's eyes brimmed with tears and Jenyfer shoved her sibling behind her.

They would not do this.

The Witchfinder's eyes bored into hers.

Jenyfer shook her head. 'You have no proof.'

The Chif raised his eyebrows. 'Are you questioning the word of the Witchfinder, he who has been sent by the One God to uncover evil among us?'

Lamorna was sobbing. Jenyfer clutched her tighter, barely registering that their aunt had risen from her seat as well. 'I'm not a witch,' Lamorna choked. 'I'm not.'

'You can't do this,' Tamora implored.

'I won't *let* you do this,' Jenyfer hissed as her magic readied itself beneath her skin. She raised her voice, making sure it was loud enough that every person in the room would hear her. 'You sent me into a man's bed without my consent. You forced him to mutilate his flesh in the name of your God. You can't deny it – I've seen it. What sort of god demands blood and pain? What sort of god condemns the innocent?'

Lamorna's nails dug into Jenyfer's wrist but, for once, her sister did not reprimand her.

'Jenyfer,' Tamora mumbled, fear lacing her tone, her skin blanched of colour. 'Stop.'

Ulrian Tregarthen stood. Jenyfer kept her eyes on him, her chin lifted defiantly, but he did not spare her a glance. He cleared his throat, the sound too loud in the stunned silence of the room.

'Lamorna, please approach the table.'

Anger like Jenyfer had never felt raced through her like a wave. She felt it in her blood, in her bones, and the deepest parts of her churned like a violent ocean. Something crackled in her head; the floor heaved beneath her. Spots danced in her vision, patterns of foaming lace and water under sunlight.

She fixed Ulrian in her gaze, and when she spoke, her words were low and filled with all the malice she could muster, all the anger and rage that was coursing through her. 'I curse you, Ulrian Tregarthen, and I curse this town. May the syhrens pull you from your boats into your watery grave. May the Night Shepherd deny you entry to the Otherworld, and may Ankou stalk your every step until the day you breathe your last.'

Silence fell, a deep, thick silence that rang with the power of her words.

Jenyfer kept her eyes on the Chif.

The Witchfinder smiled.

Ulrian shook his head sadly. 'It will be as the Witchfinder has stated. Lamorna Astolat will be gifted to the sea.' He glanced at Bryn, his unspoken words branded clearly on his face.

Punish your wife – or we will.

CHAPTER 19

Night announced herself with a breath and a sigh, a curtain of blackness draped over the world. The sea was still, the darkness a silent comfort. Ordes let the oars rest and leant over the edge of the rowboat, dangling his fingers in the water. The light of his magic sparked silver in the darkness, like moonlight on water. He watched his fingers, the way they glistened beneath the water, like pearls.

'I see you're still looking to lose your fingers,' a gruff voice said.

Ordes didn't turn from the water. 'You worry too much.'

The sailor grunted. 'One day, boy, a syhren will pull you in and drown you.'

'I was born with a caul on my head. I can't drown,' Ordes replied.

'Tested that theory have you?'

Ordes straightened, shifting to face the grumpy old sailor. Carbrey had been with *The Excalibur's* crew for as long as Ordes could remember. 'You were the first to join my father, weren't you?'

Carbrey narrowed his eyes. 'What are you fishing for?'

'Nothing,' Ordes said, turning his gaze back to the water.

'It's not natural,' Carbrey mumbled. 'Your fascination with the water.'

Ordes managed a smile. 'You're a sailor, Carbrey, surely you have a fascination with the water.'

'Not me,' the old man affirmed. 'I can't swim.'

'You can rest easy, old mate. I'll not let a syhren get her hands on me, or a mermaid. I'll steer clear of the Bag Noz and the Iannic-ann-ôd.'

Carbrey's glare was as sharp as moonlight. 'You can joke all you like, Ordes, but them things be true.'

'I know,' Ordes said simply. 'Believe me, I know.' He lifted his hand and allowed a little of his magic to sneak free – drops of water dangled from his fingers like silvery-blue jewels. Carbrey muttered to himself, his strong arms never faltering as he rowed them closer to shore.

The time Ordes had spent with Jenyfer had been liberating. He hadn't had to hide anything about his magic – she wanted to know everything, and had listened as he explained what he knew. She'd watched as he'd demonstrated things when he didn't have the right words, and he'd showed off quite a bit, enjoying himself. He had felt so free, even though there was nothing really holding him down, no metaphorical chains around his neck, not like there was around hers. A pang went through him as he thought about her, followed by the sharp burn of failure.

He should have taken her from that town the moment she had asked him.

If he was half as brave as he thought he was, he'd just march in there and get her, Witchfinder or not.

Newlyn came into view; the lights from the village stretched across the surface of the water like a glimmering trail of fire. *The Excalibur* was still anchored off the coast of Kernou. The journey from the ship around the headland to Newlyn took hours. Ordes could have used his magic to help them along, but he knew Carbrey didn't like it, so Ordes rowed alongside him like any ordinary man.

He cleared his thoughts, giving the old sailor a fond smile as they steered the rowboat alongside the wooden jetty that reached like a solitary finger into the sea; there were other boats moored there and several ships were anchored further out to sea – two sloops and a brigantine, though not as large or grand as *The Excalibur*. The waters around the beach were too shallow for a large vessel to dock. There was no sign of *The Night Queen* yet.

Carbrey's face was stern. 'Dawn. No later, boy.'

'I won't be that long.'

Carbrey's bushy eyebrows lifted. 'Oh? So I shouldn't worry about getting comfortable then?'

'No. I'll be back soon.' Ordes climbed from the boat and onto the jetty, standing a moment to let his body adjust to the firm timbers beneath his feet. While he never had an issue finding his legs, he preferred the rolling deck of the ship to the solid mass of the earth. He preferred to keep light on his toes, dancing with the sea and all she threw at them.

Newlyn was a town favoured by pirates and smugglers as well as merchant ships; a town on the borders, it was caught between the Old Ways of Cruithea and the shifting allegiance of the rest of the continent.

Ordes walked the short distance from the jetty to the tavern slowly. He'd never lived in a town, never spent his life anywhere but the sea. As he walked, his eyes roving over the neat timber and stone cottages on the far side of the main square, he wondered what it would be like. What would he do? Find a woman willing to put up with him, get married, and have a bunch of ratty half-breed kids like he was?

Jenyfer's face flashed into his mind again. He shook his head and quickened his pace.

The tavern was filled to bursting when Ordes entered. A fire crackled merrily in the hearth on the far side of the room, and every table was occupied with sailors and townspeople, some with a girl on their lap, some a boy. His eyes lingered on a woman's naked back, on the bearded man whose face was buried between her breasts; his belly tightened, and then he remembered he wasn't here for that this time.

By the time he had made it to the bar and sat down, Elaria, the tavern keeper, had a drink in front of him. She rested both elbows on the bar, leaning over to offer him a view of her ample cleavage.

'She's not here.'

Ordes rapped his fingers on the bar. 'Not yet.'

Elaria straightened with a smile, toying with a piece of blonde hair. 'If she doesn't show...'

'Sure, love. Why not?' Ordes noted the extra swing in her hips as she walked away from him to dunk mugs into a bucket of water, cleaning them with a stern expression, her eyes sweeping over the men and women clustered within the walls of her establishment. Elaria had run this tavern for the two years Ordes had been coming in here, at the same time every month, with the same purpose.

Katarin Le Fey.

It was *The Night Queen* that would surface from beneath the waves without warning, pulling alongside merchant vessels and fishermen, ready to enact revenge on the men aboard those ships. Katarin's grudge against humans was well-fortified, though he'd never asked her why she hated them so much. Kat wasn't one for small talk.

Ordes had asked himself a million times what the point of all this was, this game he was playing with Katarin, beyond exchanging insults and information, as limited as it was. He knew, of course, but it was difficult to admit he was searching for acceptance, for belonging. He was a faery amongst a bunch of humans; men who, he knew, had their own reasons for taking to the seas. But it wasn't enough to stop Ordes being so deeply aware that he was different. Katarin was like him, a fey creature caught up in a world of humans. Though he knew he'd never sit down and have a deep and meaningful conversation with her about the purpose of life and their place in the world, he kept coming back to see her all the same. Like drawn to like.

The Captain of *The Night Queen* was closed off, guarded, and she had never let him in. Ordes had thought once that maybe he loved her, but he knew he didn't. He loved what she was – confident, strong, in control of herself. Katarin was a person who knew what she wanted, who reached out and snatched it from the world, whether the world wanted to give it or not. And, every now and again, she decided she wanted Ordes.

The drunk sailors were on to their third shanty and Ordes was three spiced rums down before the tavern door flew open. He glanced over his shoulder to watch Katarin stride into the room, the tails of her black long coat swishing behind her with the usual dramatic flair. Ordes chuckled. The Captain and his father were more alike than either of them cared to admit. He turned his smile on his drink and waited.

Long, casual steps crossed the floor. He heard her greeting a few of the sailors; heard their mutterings and her satisfied laugh. Katarin was feared, and she played on that fear whenever she could.

Ordes didn't turn around, drumming his fingers against the rim of his mug. A body pressed into his back, and a breast, if he wasn't mistaken, was crammed against his head. He forced himself to smile as her hands came to rest on his shoulders. She gave them a squeeze, fingers digging into his muscles, a reminder – and a promise. She dropped gracefully onto the stool beside him.

'Kat,' he drawled. 'Twice in ten days. Did you miss me, love?'

'Call me 'love' again and I'll shove that mug so far up your arse you'll be eating it for breakfast, Ordes.'

'We're doing breakfast are we?' He angled his body towards hers, playing the game, like he always did. 'Let me buy you a drink and you can shove whatever you like, wherever you like, afterwards.'

Her lips twitched, dark eyes twinkling in the light from the lamps that hung suspended above them as she signalled for a drink. Elaria had gone, replaced by a young girl Ordes had never seen before. The look on her face told him the girl knew exactly who was sitting in front of her. She wasn't scared – it was excitement mixed with a strong dash of admiration that flashed across her pretty features as she looked at Katarin.

Kat nodded her thanks; the girl refused her coin. She didn't refuse Ordes', though, holding out a hand for his money, the other planted on her hip. Kat chuckled and shook her head, the beads that decorated the lengths of her dark red hair clinking gently, almost musically, with the movement. She shot him a look, one slash of a brow raised, her lips curled at the corners, the barest hint of a smirk.

'You here for business, or pleasure, Ordes?'

It was like walking the edge of a very tall, crumbling cliff, and the best thing about Katarin was he never knew if she'd pull him to safety or push him off. Despite being desperate to form some sort of true connection with her, Katarin scared the life out of him. She was powerful, ruthless, and dangerous, capable of killing him, slitting his throat in his sleep and gutting him like a fish.

She was watching him from the corner of her eye, waiting for his response.

This had been their game for two years. Flirt, fuck, and then usually fight. But he wasn't in the mood for it. Katarin was watching him, picking up on his mood.

'What's wrong with you?' She turned to face him, crossing long legs in front of her. Her foot rested against his calf muscle, hovering there, before she dragged the toe of her boot higher until she reached the back of his knee, then, slowly, so slowly, dragged it back down again, setting a fire under his flesh that he made himself ignore.

'I'm not doing this tonight,' he said in a low voice.

Kat frowned. 'Ordes—'

'You're going to have to find some other poor sucker to torment, because it's not going to be me,' he said.

Katarin rested her elbow on the bar, letting her cheek fall into her palm as she watched him. 'Something's happened.'

'No, I just don't want to do this.'

'You've met someone.'

'Kat,' he warned.

'Alright,' she said, holding up her hands. 'No need to get testy.'

Two years of this game, and he didn't know any more about her than when this first started, and she constantly surprised him. He'd been expecting her to rip his head off for rejecting her. Ordes had met her by accident and was, like most people, immediately caught up in the whirlwind that was Katarin Le Fey. Katarin had him buy her the best drinks in the house, then let him kiss her and put his hand under her shirt before she held a dagger to his throat and told him how it was going to be between them. It always ended with him naked and on his back as the Captain of the legendary *Night Queen* rode him as thoroughly as her ship rode the waves.

Except this time.

Katarin drained her mug. Elaria had returned, and Ordes was aware she was watching them curiously. The tavern keeper had been a sideline participant in this game for as long as he and Kat had been playing it. Elaria filled Kat's mug, holding out the jug for Ordes, but he shook his head, waiting until she had moved away before he spoke.

'So,' he began.

Katarin raised her eyebrows and drummed her nails on the side of her mug. 'Are we going to have an actual conversation, Ordes?'

'Something like that.'

'Alright. I'll play.' She took a sip of her drink, giving him an interested look, one that he knew meant she was looking for information. 'Tell me,' she said, tucking a chuck of hair behind her ear. Like his, Katarin's ears were slightly pointed. But, unlike him, she didn't hide it. 'What does your father know about the Grail?'

Ordes smiled. 'The Grail? Come on, Katarin. You can do better than that.'

Katarin shrugged. 'I thought you believed in the Treasures?'

The Treasures of the Gods consisted of four things – the Sword of the White Dragon, the Bow of Truth, the Singing Stone, and, lastly, the Grail. Ordes had grown up on a diet of stories about the Gods, the Treasures, and the different realms of the world. Tymis had relished telling them, and Ordes had memories of his father's theatrics being put to good use to entertain a small boy with magic in his veins. Those stories always made Ordes feel comforted; it was much easier to believe in magic, believe in what he was, with those stories swimming around his head.

Tymis had told him that, long ago, the Treasures of the Gods had gone missing, and no one, not even those who once held them in their hands, had been able to find them. Apparently, the Treasures would not reveal their locations until the Once and Future King appeared. This man, whoever he was, was destined to reshape the land, to save magic.

'What do you want with the Treasures?'

'Niniane is looking for them.'

'Why?'

Another shrug. 'I'm just her blood-hound, remember?'

'You know I didn't mean that,' Ordes mumbled.

'You meant it well enough at the time.'

'You'd just thrown me out of bed – the sun wasn't even up.'

Katarin smiled. He wasn't sure if she was remembering that morning the same way he did – she'd not only thrown him out of bed, she'd thrown him out of her room half-naked and freezing. She pushed her mug aside and stood. 'Come with me.'

'I already said—'

'I need to tell you something.' She lowered her voice, her eyes darting around the tavern, blazing in the dim light, a shimmer of her magic mingled with the warm brown. Ordes watched Kat's face, the warring emotions that flashed across her features, before she leant forward, as swift as a striking snake. Her lips were almost touching his. Her breath tickled his mouth; she flicked her tongue over his bottom lip. 'But not here, alright?'

She didn't wait to see if he agreed, sauntering away from the bar. He followed her into a dark corner, finding her already seated with her boots on the table, her body positioned so she could see every person in the room.

'I've been north,' she said quietly as he sat. 'To Cruithea. Did you know Magic Wielders are disappearing?'

'What do you mean disappearing?'

'I mean just that – they're being taken from their homes across the continent and are never seen or heard from again,' Katarin answered.

'Who's behind it?'

'Rumour is, they're being taken to Malist,' Kat said.

'To the capital? Why?'

'Morgause's spies have seen them entering the Sacellum, and not coming out again.' Katarin waited while a man stumbled past them. 'There are Witchfinders everywhere, Ordes. More than ever before. The Shaleitari have been recruiting up and down the east coast.'

He swallowed. 'What does the Sacellum want with Magic Wielder's?'

'That's the most worrying part,' Katarin said.

They fell silent, each caught in their thoughts. No one knew exactly what went on behind the stone walls of the Sacellum, the headquarters of the One God. Belief in the Old Ones and the Old Ways had died out in the city years ago – it was a place where buildings had grown as thick as a forest, a place of stone and noise. There were no faeries there, no Small Folk. The Sacellum had started as a religious order, but had quickly grown to become something more – some of the men who had joined the crew last month spoke of the spread of the Sacellum's power. The eastern half of the continent had fallen to the One God many years before; now, after what Jenyfer had told him, Ordes knew things were more dire than anyone had thought.

Jenyfer's face pressed into his mind. 'Kat, I've a friend in Kernou and with the Shaleitari around...'

'You think she's in danger?'

'Who said it's a she?'

Katarin just raised her eyebrows. 'Want me to rescue her?'

'I don't know,' Ordes said quietly. 'I'm going to go ashore later to find out what's happening. She was supposed to meet me and she didn't show up.'

'Ordes—'

'He won't catch me.' He stood, pressing a kiss to Katarin's forehead. 'See you next month?'

Katarin nodded. 'Be careful.'

'You too.'

Carbrey grunted when Ordes showed up, accepting the bottle of rum he handed him without a word. He could feel Carbrey's eyes combing his face as he jumped lightly into the boat and settled himself on the hard bench. As they pulled away from the jetty, Ordes glanced over his shoulder. Lights winked in the darkness.

'You look like shit,' the old sailor commented when they were heading towards the breakers. Ordes sighed, sitting back, crossing his ankles and rubbing at his face.

They didn't speak as the boat pushed over the first line of breakers, Carbrey's arms as sure as the water, as rhythmic as the waves. Ordes took the second set of oars, watching Carbrey's face as they approached the next wave. Carbrey's forehead was folded, wiry grey hair sticking out at all angles from beneath his skullcap. He wore the simple clothes of a sailor – linen shirt and dark blue vest, baggy grey trousers, no shoes. He shot Ordes a quick look as they drew closer to the break.

He'd never ask for it, so, without a word, Ordes pulled his oars, held out both hands and closed his eyes. He felt the boat pause, then surge forward, borne on its own wave, pulled from the bed of the ocean by Ordes' magic. When he next opened his eyes, they were in open water, the beach a strip of white sand glowing in the darkness.

They glided past the headland and into the Bay of Calledun.

'What's going on over there then?' Carbrey muttered, narrowing his eyes and peering into the darkness. Flaming torches dotted the beach.

Ordes twisted to glance at the headland, and opened his faery eyes, letting his vision sharpen as the dark coat of night slipped away and the world became lighter.

A crowd was gathered on the beach and his heart pinched. A woman, gold hair billowing around her, was tied to the stake wedged between the rocks below the cliff face. Water kissed her feet as the tide shifted but she was calm, reverent almost. He frowned, then gasped. Jenyfer's sister. His eyes swept the beach frantically as another voice rose, strangled with terror and anger.

'Stop,' Ordes ordered.

'We can't do anything,' Carbrey reminded him, but he stilled the oars.

A woman was struggling in the arms of a man who was having difficulty holding her. Ordes narrowed his eyes, then sucked in a breath, his heart pinching. Jenyfer. Her feet were bare and she twisted and writhed with a ferociousness, a desperation, that made his blood burn. The man holding her cursed and called for help as she dragged him along the beach with the strength of her despair. Other men joined him, until Jenyfer was forced to stop, unable to break free of them all, but she fought, arms swinging, feet lashing, until they pulled her to the ground.

Four men. One woman. Ordes ground his teeth. His magic stirred, curling in his palms.

Still, Jenyfer fought, managing to elbow one of them in the nose and rise to her knees, her arms pulled tight behind her back. As Ordes watched, she tipped her face to the sky and screamed, the sound raising the hair on his arms. Beneath the boat, something glimmering silver and blue shot past as the water became as smooth as glass, as still as the night, under the rippling wave of Jenyfer's voice.

Ordes felt it in his blood, the change that came over the ocean, and he dragged his eyes from the sea to the beach where Jenyfer still screamed, the sound a guttural cry of anguish and power that tore across the water.

Near the rocks, where Lamorna was bound, a silvery tail broke the surface and Ordes watched in mute disbelief as a syhren emerged from the water, pulling herself onto the rocks and shedding her tail for legs. The faery of the sea, shining silver hair tumbling down her back, ripped Lamorna from the stake, kissed her on the mouth, then dove into the water, the town's gift to the ocean wrapped securely in her arms.

It was only after the syhren and Lamorna had vanished beneath the waves that Ordes realised Jenyfer had given up fighting.

The men had let her go, all but one, who still held her arms while the others looked at her in fear. Jenyfer sat calmly with the water curling around her. Behind her, red cloak kissing his ankles, was the Witchfinder.

CHAPTER 20

Mist shrouded the ocean. The water was still completely flat; nothing stirred the surface or broke through from the depths. As Ordes watched, a gentle breeze skittered across the water, teasing tiny peaks to life and parting the mists. The lights of Kernou faded as dawn crept over the world and footsteps approached him from behind.

Ordes had stood there all night, chewing his lip, not daring to look away from the town.

'Did you sleep?'

His father's voice was soft.

'No.'

'You are not to go ashore again, Ordes. Promise me.'

'Jenyfer—'

'You can't help her. I know you want to, but you can't.'

The men would wake soon, and they'd spend the day working on menial tasks, watching the sun creep across the sky while they waited for *The Excalibur* to make it clear why she had brought them to this place. The anchor was down and they wouldn't be going anywhere until the sails filled with a breath of wind that the ship would pull from nowhere.

Ordes had no idea how Jenyfer had called a *syhren* to the beach.

Syhrens were powerful beings. Born of the sea, they were capable of seducing men with their voices; sailors would stuff their ears with cloth or wax when a syhren was near. Those unfortunate enough to get close to a syhren would be dragged to a watery grave. They could control the winds, luring ships close to rocky shores – many of the wrecks that littered the ocean bed were there through a syhren's power. According to legends, the sea faeries lived on the rocky island of Lyonesse, believed to be hidden in the mists like Avalon was. They were shapeshifters, as he'd just seen firsthand, and answered to Melodias, the King of Lyonesse, guardian of the portal to the Otherworld. Ordes couldn't help the girl pulled beneath the waves – especially not if she'd been taken to Lyonesse – but Jenyfer... he chewed his lip. None of the men would help him, especially if it meant going against the Captain, so he'd have to use his magic instead.

Ordes rubbed at his face. 'They'll kill her, because their stupid god will demand it.'

'Ordes,' Tymis began, his voice low.

Ordes turned to his father, his hands held out. 'She's like me. Would you let them kill me?' he asked. Water curled in his palms, droplets spinning in a vortex before they bound themselves together and formed two perfect spheres. Tymis stepped forward and closed his hands over Ordes', the watery spheres collapsing between their palms and dribbling down their arms. They stood that way in silence, the waves lapping gently at the ship, until Tymis let go and pulled away, turning to face the water again, his arms folded.

'I'm not going to let them take her,' Ordes promised in a low, fierce voice. 'The other girl? The one the syhren took?'

'I don't know. To Melodias, I'd guess, though what the Master of Songs and Death wants with a human girl is beyond my understanding,' Tymis muttered.

'A lot of things are beyond your understanding,' Ordes mumbled.

Tymis ignored him. 'What did Katarin have to say?'

'The Shaleitari have increased their ranks, and Magic Wielders are disappearing. They're being taken to Malist, to the Sacellum, and no one ever sees them again. Kat also asked about the Grail,' Ordes added.

Tymis' eyebrows shot up. 'Did she now?'

Ordes had always thought it was nothing but a fairytale, but now... he flexed his fingers; silver light danced across his knuckles, before he let it sink into his skin. 'Is it true?' he asked his father. 'Magic is in danger?'

'Why do you ask?'

'You used to tell me stories,' Ordes said with a shrug.

'I did,' Tymis said. 'But they were not stories, Ordes. They were truths. I don't always talk because I like the sound of my own voice,' he added, his lips curling in a wry smile and Ordes found himself smiling back. His father didn't smile a lot. Tymis was cranky and moody most of the time – a mystery. Ordes knew nothing of his father's life before he was born and Tymis escaped Avalon, taking them both to the seas. He knew nothing of his father as a young man – and he wanted to know everything, but wasn't sure how to ask.

He had to start somewhere, he supposed, needing to distract himself until night fell again. Now, when everyone else was sleeping and he stood watch with his father while dawn cracked the sky, was as good a time to ask as any. But, before Ordes could give voice to his questions, a breeze that smelt of damp earth brushed his cheek. He frowned as mist rose around the ship, mist that was tinged with green and brown and shot through with flecks of gold. He tensed as Tymis' hand dropped to the weapon at his belt. Ordes readied his magic, pulled it through his veins to let it coil in his palms, fingers flexing, the air around his hands shimmering.

The sky grew darker, storm-dark, and everything stilled, as if all the air in the world had been sucked away. Thunder rumbled and lightning ripped across the sky. The air was suddenly filled with the scent of leaves and wet earth, of rich soil and sunshine. Clouds raced in and swooped low to the ship, swallowing everything in their path as the seabed thrummed below them. The air was a kaleidoscope of green and gold and brown, swirling before their eyes, until it froze and began to crack.

A hand reached through that crack, peeling back the mist like skin, until a shape emerged from the earth-tinged air around them. A man's head, crowned in leaves, skin like bark, was followed by a body, limbs long and clothed in underbrush. His feet were those of a deer, and brown fur crept up his legs.

Ordes sucked in a breath.

An Old One.

'The Green Knight,' Tymis murmured. 'To what do I owe this honour?'

'Don't think to flatter me, Tymis Merlyni.' The voice that spoke was as warm as sunshine, dripping with amusement.

Tymis inclined his head. 'Apologies. I forgot my manners. It isn't often that one of the Old Ones pays me a visit.'

The God laughed, the sound like wind through the leaves. Ordes started as the Green Knight's attention swung to him. He was unable to look away as the God of the Earth studied him, fern-green eyes scanning his face. 'He looks like you,' the Old One mused. 'Have you told him?'

Tymis scowled. 'No.'

'Told me what?' Ordes demanded.

'Is that why you're here?' Tymis said, his gaze on the God. He folded his arms. 'To remind me of things I know more about than you? What do you really want?'

The Green Knight threw back his head and laughed again. 'You've always intrigued me, Tymis. I don't know many men who are as bold as you. Very well,' the God said. 'I want you to rescue the girl.'

'It's too late. Melodias has her,' Tymis replied.

'Not her. The other one,' the Green Knight said sharply, like Tymis should have known this. Ordes sucked in a breath; the eyes of the God flickered to him briefly, then back to Tymis. 'The Magic Wielder. You need her.'

'Why?' Ordes asked. Hope was swelling inside him. His father would help now – Witchfinder or not, even Tymis would not go against the wishes of an Old One.

'There is a prophecy. Surely your father has mentioned it in one of his stories?' The Green Knight chuckled. Tymis looked like he'd reach across the deck and wrap his hands around the Old One's throat. But the God was unperturbed. 'Rescue the Magic Wielder. I give her to you to protect.'

Ordes opened his mouth, but nothing came out.

'She needs your help,' the Green Knight added. 'Rescue the girl, find the King who Shall Be, and find the Grail.' He glanced at Tymis. 'One who stands between the worlds—'

'Shall bear the weight of them both,' Tymis finished with a resigned sigh.

The Green Knight's eyes brushed Ordes' face, before the Old One vanished.

Ordes was sitting with his father in the Captain's cabin, head still reeling. The Green Knight – the God of the Earth – had just stood on the deck of their ship and had a casual chat with his father, like they were old friends, and had just given Ordes a job. He should be in a rowboat. He should be on his way to shore, but there were so many questions burning their way through Ordes' head, so many thoughts he needed to unravel, but he didn't know where to start.

Outside, the water was painted pink and gold with the dawn. Tymis smiled. 'Well, you get your wish. You get to rescue the damsel in distress.'

'Why me? Why would the God of the Earth ask me to do this? And what did he mean, had you told me? Told me what? Who made the prophecies? And why did an Old One tell *you* to find the Once and Future King *and* the Grail?' The questions poured out one after the other, tumbling over each other and becoming a jumbled mess in the air between Ordes and his father.

'What—'

Tymis held up his hand. 'That's a lot of questions, son.'

'That's all you're going to say?'

'I told you there was a reason we were here and now, at least, we know what it is.' Tymis sighed and rubbed at his face, his eyes weary, worried. 'So it begins. Three sets of hands upon the stone, one set of hands to pass alone,' he murmured.

'That's the prophecy,' Ordes said, 'the one you used to tell me when I was a kid?'

Tymis nodded. 'You thought I was making it up, didn't you?'

'A story about a King who was promised and the most powerful Magic Wielder in the world, who had his magic stolen by a witch...' Ordes shook his head. 'How do you know an Old One?'

Tymis tapped his fingers on the top of the desk, his expression thoughtful. 'What do you think about, when you think about your future?'

Ordes resisted the urge to scream. It was one of his father's tactics when he was evading the truth – answer a question with a question. He knew that if he wanted answers, he'd have to first give them.

He'd spent his life following his father around, like the rest of the crew. He crawled out of bed each day with a smile, but he knew it was a mask. He'd worn it so long that it was sometimes difficult to distinguish which of the two faces he wore was his true self. He was a Magic Wielder who barely knew what he was doing. There always felt like there was more beneath the surface of him that he couldn't, didn't know *how*, to reach. Ordes knew he should be happy – he was free, after all, but how much of that freedom was actually real?

Tymis was watching him, patient, especially for him.

'I feel like I'm waiting for something to happen,' Ordes confessed, frowning at his words. 'But I don't know what. It's like my life is on hold, out here on the water, like I'm hiding from something and... I don't know, not doing what I'm supposed to be doing.'

Tymis was silent. Ordes could hear the water lapping at the hull, could feel the gentle movement of the ship beneath them.

'I've watched you grow from an annoying kid to a man I'm proud to call my son,' Tymis began. 'I wasn't sure what sort of father I'd be, Ordes. It was never something I'd planned, but once you entered the world, it was like everything suddenly made sense to me. But maybe I did make a mistake – maybe I should have left you with your mother. I've robbed you of part of your heritage. I was being selfish, if I'm honest. And, in my arrogance, I thought I'd be able to give you everything you needed.' Tymis paused. 'But I'm a Magic Wielder without my magic – I didn't think of how that would impact you, and I should have.'

Ordes swallowed, throat tight. His father rarely spoke with any degree of candour, and he was often left wondering how much of what Tymis said was truth, and how much wasn't.

'What are you thinking?' Tymis asked him softly.

Ordes shook his head, but there it was again, that feeling that there was something else he needed to be doing. 'What did the Green Knight mean?' he asked again. 'About me?'

Tymis sighed. 'I'm not going to insult your intelligence by saying I don't know. He was talking about the prophecy, and your role in it. Perhaps it is nothing more than rescuing a Magic Wielder from her death,' Tymis said softly. 'Things are changing, and not for the better. So, for now, do what the Old One has asked of you and save the girl. Help her.'

Ordes had never doubted the existence of those forces outside of the realm of men. If a God gave him a job, who was he to ignore it?

'I'll go ashore tonight.'

Tymis was frowning. 'Don't let them catch you, understand? You might not think it, but you are more important to me than a ship, or the Grail, or recovering my magic, Ordes. Why do you think I took you when I left her?' His voice dropped, so quiet Ordes had to strain to hear it. 'She barely knew you were there, until you weren't.'

Ordes swallowed; something dug into his stomach, something dark and with claws. He'd always thought it, but never asked, too afraid of the answer. 'She didn't love me at all, did she?'

His father's face was cast in shadow, the rising sun behind him. 'She did, in her own way. You have to understand – she's a faery. Time is different for her. And faery children don't need mothering the same way human children do. Sometimes, I think she forgot that you were human as well. I named you, did you know that?'

'You did?'

Tymis chuckled. 'Yes. She wanted to call you Lancelot.'

Ordes blinked. 'What sort of name is that?'

'It means "god-like". I thought that was too heavy a thing to place on a baby's shoulders. Names are serious things – they can end up defining who we are,' Tymis explained, then sighed wistfully. 'Part of me misses the Isle, and your mother. There's a lake on Avalon. One of the most beautiful places I've ever seen. Mist dances off its face, and it's bordered on one side by willows that kiss the water, which is as clear as crystal and full of all manner of wondrous fey things. You were born on the edge of that lake, Ordes.'

'I was born in the water?' Ordes whispered. His magic stirred.

'You were born between the realms. Between the land and the sea.'

Something shifted inside him. 'Why didn't you tell me?'

His father shrugged. 'I don't know.' Then, 'Be careful, son.'

CHAPTER 21

It was madness. Utter madness – and Arthur was powerless to stop any of it from happening. He'd watched his father, eyes shining, as Lamorna Astolat had been sentenced to death. He'd watched helplessly as Lamorna, the most devout of all his father's followers, was bound by the wrists to that dreadful stake, the townspeople gathered on the beach to witness her death, the Witchfinder in his rich red cloak standing passively as Lamorna was left for the sea.

Lying in bed as the dawn crept closer to the horizon, Arthur closed his eyes, unable to prevent the images from flying through his head, as they had been throughout the night. He had watched as the sea crept closer to Lamorna. The wind had made streamers of her hair, tossing it around her face like a halo of burnished gold. She had pleaded and begged, reciting the Word, strangely beautiful in her faithful fight, but she may as well have been throwing words into the wind.

Arthur had wanted to climb onto the rocks and shake her until her pleas became desperate screams. Maybe then they'd listen to her. Maybe then they'd realise a mistake had been made.

It was Jenyfer who had screamed for her. Jenyfer who had fought tooth and nail to reach her sister, to be held back by her husband and the other men. Jenyfer, dark hair wild around her shoulders, her expression one of feral rage, had screamed, and screamed, and screamed.

And revealed to everyone that she was a Magic Wielder.

Arthur thought of Lamorna – pretty, pious, devoted – and wondered, not for the first time, why it had been her the Witchfinder selected.

It hit him like a punch. Lamorna was bait. The hushed conversation he'd overheard between his father and the Witchfinder two days ago... the Witchfinder had suspected someone, but could not prove it, so Ulrian had orchestrated the whole thing.

Arthur squeezed his eyes closed tighter – he could still hear it, Jenyfer's scream, could still *feel* the power it held. A collective gasp had rushed through the waiting crowd as a syhren had emerged from the water like something out of myth, and Ulrian... Arthur recalled the look of utter triumph on his father's face. The Chif had torn his dark eyes from the faery to Jenyfer, collapsed on the sand, her head thrown back as she laughed while her sister was pulled beneath the waves.

Jenyfer, who was now sitting with her hands and feet bound, a cage made of the strongest iron surrounding her. Arthur hadn't bothered asking what would happen to her. He already knew.

She had two days before she was taken to Malist, to the Sacellum.

He'd never taken the time to get to know her – to get to know anyone in the town outside of his role as their future leader – but he had felt it, a sharp tug below his navel as her scream ripped across the world.

With the Witchfinder still in town, sleeping in the room down the hall from Arthur, everyone was being watched; Arthur knew without having to get out of bed that there was a guard outside their home, and that the man was armed, just like the man who was standing watch over Jenyfer.

Dread coiled in his stomach. He couldn't let this happen. There had to be a way to stop this from happening. Swallowing, Arthur opened his eyes and sat up, the wounds on his back protesting as he stretched. There was nothing he could do for Jenyfer, but maybe there was someone else who could help. He hurried out of bed and dressed quickly. Surely, Bryn wouldn't be headed out onto the water today, not with his wife locked up and sentenced to die.

The Konsel had wanted to burn her. Arthur had overheard his father, his words dripping with relish, as he and the Konsel planned the bonfire that would obliterate the witch under the eye of the One God. One more Magic Wielder, one more nail in the coffin of the Old Ways, but the Witchfinder had other plans.

Arthur took a deep breath, leaving his room and marching down the hall, trying to be confident, to seem like he was in charge of something as he flung open the front door and stepped into the glow of the morning, his chin held high.

The guard, a burly man who had worked for his father for years, jumped as Arthur appeared on the step. 'The Chif said—'

'I have business to attend to, with the blessing of the One God,' Arthur lied.

The man frowned. 'You are not to leave the house.'

'Are you questioning His will?' Arthur didn't give the man time to argue. Heart pounding, he swept past the guard and did not look back, even though the skin on the back of his neck burnt and the sharp tang of fear filled his mouth.

The main centre of town was deserted, a wind smelling like stale seaweed dancing between the buildings and licking the stones. In the square, Arthur sucked in a breath as Jenyfer lifted her head from where it had been resting on her knees. He held her gaze, his heart pinching at the despair on her face, but in her eyes he could see blatant defiance and, beneath that, triumph. He admired her, the courage she had shown as they dragged her away. She hadn't fought them then; she'd simply smiled the whole time, her eyes bright, cheeks pink and hair swept with the wind.

Jenyfer dropped her gaze and Arthur hurried from the square.

Bryn wasn't on the beach – for the first time since Arthur could recall, there were no fishing boats on the water, nothing but the gulls whirling on the wind, and the empty stake, where Lamorna Astolat's body should be.

Arthur found Bryn in his cottage, sitting at the small wooden table with his head in his hands. Arthur didn't bother knocking, going straight in. There were unwashed dishes scattered along the simple bench, and the fire was out, the place cold and dark. He sat opposite the man he hadn't had much more than a casual conversation with since they had grown out of their childhood dreams and simple friendship, before Arthur had been ordered to put aside such things and learn to be his father's son.

Bryn looked up at him, pain etched across his face.

'Did you know?' Arthur asked him.

'She told me,' the other man said softly. 'But I didn't really believe her.'

'What are you going to do?' Arthur asked.

Bryn frowned. 'What do you mean?'

'Are you just going to let the Witchfinder take her? It isn't her fault for being what she is, Bryn. You know this,' Arthur added, resting his hands on the table. 'You could help her.'

'Let her go, you mean?'

'Yes.'

Bryn stared at him, eyes wide and wild; Arthur held his breath, waiting, but, eventually, Bryn's expression shifted and he shook his head. 'A witch is an abomination in the eyes of the One God.'

It was Arthur's turn to stare. 'She's your wife. Your friend. You can't seriously think she deserves to die?'

'If it is what the One God deems to be right, then it is right,' Bryn said softly.

Arthur let silence fall between them. Eventually, he sighed, standing and walking out of the cottage, leaving Bryn to his misery and the conscience that would one day catch up with him. There was nothing Arthur could do and he was again reminded of how powerless he was. He shivered. Since the beach, since Jenyfer's scream ripped across the world, something had been pushing at him from the inside out. He didn't know what it was, only that it felt alive and filled with urgency.

He returned home, where he spent the day wandering the dark house. His father was with the Konsel and the Witchfinder in the main hall, no doubt going over whatever lofty speech he would deliver before they bundled Jenyfer into a carriage and took her away.

As night shrouded Kernou, Arthur heard the front door open and close. He crept into the hallway, then the kitchen, the main hall, where voices eased beneath the closed door. A quick glance out the kitchen window told him the guard was still there, so he returned to his room, pushing the curtains aside and opening the shutters.

The moon was hidden behind a layer of clouds, the world cloaked in blackness. Something moved in the darkness, something small, cat-like, darting through the shadows on all fours. Arthur lost sight of it and then, a face was peering at him from the other side of the window.

The pisky showed his pointed little teeth, and knocked.

Arthur opened the window. 'You again,' he hissed at the faery. 'What do you want? Do you know how much trouble you got me in?'

The pisky said nothing, jumping down from the sill. He bounced experimentally on the bed, then tugged on Arthur's shirt sleeve. The faery pointed at the window, scrambling back through before Arthur could say anything. The pisky beckoned urgently and, without thinking any further, Arthur climbed through the window and into the night.

He skirted cottages with fires blazing, warm golden light creeping beneath doors and between shutters, led by the pisky, who danced and skittered along on its tiny legs. The faery was quick, a miniature whirlwind that slipped through the darkness towards the beach, and the cave where Arthur and Jalen had spent a glorious few hours together. The pisky bounded up the rocks and raced into the cave. With a quick glance over his shoulder, Arthur followed.

Jalen was sitting on the sandy floor. He stood when Arthur entered, conjuring a ball of pale light in his palm. The pisky stood near his feet like a pet. 'Thank you,' Jalen told it, and the faery sketched a bow, then vanished. Jalen chuckled. 'Funny little things they are.'

'I thought you weren't meant to thank them?' Arthur managed.

Jalen shrugged. 'Not every superstition is true, Arthur.'

Arthur swallowed, not knowing what to say, and then Jalen opened his arms and Arthur crossed the space between them in two strides and fell against his chest. Nothing mattered anymore except for the heat of Jalen's body and the feeling of his hands in Arthur's hair, stroking the back of his neck, moving over the flat plain of his stomach, his touch burning and cooling at the same time.

Arthur pulled back and stripped his shirt off.

'Arthur....'

'I don't care,' Arthur whispered. 'My father, the Konsel, the One God. I don't care anymore. I'm sick of looking over my shoulder. I'm sick of hiding what I am.' He cupped Jalen's face between his hands and took a deep breath before closing the gap between them and pressing his lips to Jalen's.

'I dreamt of you,' Jalen said, his voice soft in the darkness.

'Did you?' Arthur murmured. They were curled together in a nest of their clothing, the night air cooling the sweat on their skin, Jalen's magical light hovering above them, stroking their bodies with silvery light. Arthur rolled over and buried his face in Jalen's neck, fingers walking down his chest to graze the soft skin of his lower belly.

Jalen chuckled. 'You've got a dirty mind, little Chif.'

Arthur bit him, then kissed the hurt away. 'What did you dream about, then?'

Jalen hesitated, then sighed lightly. 'Have you ever heard of the Grail?'

'Of course – but it's a fairytale, a myth, a heathen symbol.' Arthur shook his head.

'It's real,' Jalen confirmed.

Something inside Arthur began beating, a steady, pulsating rhythm; and that thing beneath his skin squirmed. His arm tightened around Jalen's middle. 'How do you know?'

'I just do.'

Arthur pulled his bottom lip between his teeth and chewed on it. 'What does it have to do with us?'

'With you, you mean.' Jalen shifted so he was lying on his side. He propped his head onto his elbow, tracing the line of Arthur's cheek with a strong finger. 'In my dream, I saw you with it. You were the Chif, but not the Chif.'

Arthur swallowed. 'Okay, so what does that mean?'

'It means you need to find it.'

'No one knows where it is, Jalen,' Arthur said softly. 'But even if they did, what am I supposed to do with a cup?'

There was a flash of teeth in the light-tinged darkness as Jalen grinned. 'It's not really a cup,' he replied. 'More like a bowl. And I don't know. I only know what I saw – you, but not as you are now. You were older, and you had the Grail, and, in it, you held the land.'

A deep twisting of his stomach made Arthur suck in a breath. 'Kernou?'

Jalen shook his head. 'No. Teyath.'

'That doesn't make any sense.'

Pale light coated the side of Jalen's face, silver shadows painted on the sharp lines of his cheek and jaw. 'Not yet it doesn't, but it will, eventually.' He dropped a kiss to Arthur's forehead. 'You should go, before they realise you're missing. Before they hurt you again,' he added, reaching around Arthur's shoulder to touch, so lightly, the wounds on his back. 'If they touch you again—'

'I did this to myself,' Arthur said softly. 'It was my punishment. For my sins. My father put the whip in my hands and did not let me stop until he was satisfied.'

Jalen said nothing, just continued to stroke the skin on Arthur's back, then the curve of his shoulder, down his arm, back up again.

'I'm ready to leave this place. As soon as possible. Two nights from now the Witchfinder will take a Magic Wielder to Malist. While my father and everyone is distracted, I'll leave. Meet me here,' Arthur added.

Jalen nodded. 'And then?'

'*We* leave this place.'

CHAPTER 22

The salt and brine of the ocean infused the evening air and a cool breeze skittered through the square. Jenyfer's cell was located conveniently beneath the cross – it loomed over her, menacing and powerful. Looking at it made her shiver, so she turned her face away, studying the bars of her cell instead. It was more like a cage, she thought, running her eyes over it, then decided it didn't matter what she called it – she was on display as much as the mermaid had been. The cage was mounted on a wooden platform on wheels, the iron thick. Iron, for guarding against faeries. Rope was wrapped tight around her ankles and wrists. The man guarding her kept his back to her, as if looking at her would cause some horror to befall him.

Jenyfer couldn't help wondering where the cage had come from. Had the Chif and the Konsel had it stashed away somewhere, waiting for someone like her? Or had the Witchfinder brought it with him, hoping he'd find someone to lock inside? She'd spent the day sitting in the cage, the sun beating down on her, and her skin was as dry as old paper. With a groan, she rubbed awkwardly at her face, then shifted around, trying to make herself more comfortable. The ropes hurt, and her backside was sore. She'd been let out twice to relieve herself, then shoved back in. Her aunt had tried to see her but had been sent away. People had been allowed to linger and gawk at her as long as they liked, whispering behind their hands and shaking their heads. Bryn, however, had not been to see her and she grit her teeth as she was submerged beneath a flood of hot anger.

After the meeting in the tavern that had decided Lamorna's fate – after the accusation from the Witchfinder – Bryn had practically dragged Jenyfer through the streets, not caring that she wanted to see her sister, not caring that she was crying and begging him until her begging turned into a seething silence. Bryn had thrown her inside the cottage, his face mottled with outrage, but, before he could dish out any of the punishment the Chif had instructed, Jenyfer threw the heavy iron kettle at him and then hurried across the living space to lock herself into the small bathing room. She shoved the washstand in front of the door ignoring Bryn's voice, his demands that she come out; and she hadn't slept one bit, sitting against the wall with one eye on the door while her magic screamed and pushed and *pushed* at her.

She'd come out only when she could feel night approaching, and Bryn did not try to speak to her. He did not try to stop her from going to the beach, but then... Jenyfer scowled. She wanted to break his fingers, every one of them, break every part of him that had touched her.

Flexing her fingers as much as she could, Jenyfer felt that surge of strange power run through her again. She hadn't known what she was doing on the beach – she had acted on instinct alone, and let her magic take control. As the water had crept closer to Lamorna, there had been a roaring in Jenyfer's ears, a burning in her blood, and that inner song had become more powerful, pulling at the very core of her, urging her to reach deep inside and release... something.

She hadn't expected anything to happen. Her scream had been one of frustration, of powerlessness, filled with the anguish and the anger that had been swirling around inside her since the night the Chif had sealed her fate, that anger only continuing to build in the week she spent as Bryn's wife, and then, after Lamorna had been sentenced to die, Jenyfer's head had been filled with the smashing of waves. On the beach, when she handed over control to her magic, her skin had tingled, thousands of tiny knives stabbing at it, and a strange sort of calm had come over her.

She was as shocked as anyone at what emerged from the water.

A syhren. And it had taken Lamorna. Jenyfer let her head fall into her hands. Was her sister dead, drowned anyway? She had no way of knowing but, as she'd sat on the beach, the sea swirling around her, her blood sang and danced and that song, that song that lived in her was joyous, a symphony that sounded like triumph.

Then, they dragged her away and threw her in here, wet and dripping and still laughing. The Chif's eyes had been hard, and as they'd locked her in, he put his face close to the bars.

'The One God knows what you are,' he'd said, his voice low, for her ears only.

'And what is that?' Jenyfer had managed.

His lips had curled in what she thought was satisfaction. 'An abomination.'

The Witchfinder came to see her as night struck, the man's eyes crawling over her face. He was tall and slim, as slender as a woman, with milk-pale skin and hair cropped short. He wore the same blood-red cloak she'd seen him wearing as he paraded around the town square; and the same haughty, self-important expression.

'Interesting,' he murmured.

Jenyfer said nothing.

The man stepped closer to her, showing no fear. 'There is something different about you,' he continued. 'Something I'm not familiar with. It's no worry, though. We shall soon discover what sort of magic lurks beneath your pretty skin, Miss Astolat.' His eyes moved over her again, a smile pulling at his thin mouth. 'Yes, I look forward to it very much.'

Jenyfer shuddered and pressed herself into the back of the cage. The Witchfinder chuckled and left; she watched him until he and his red cloak had bled into the darkness.

The night grew colder. The moon was waxing to full again; silvery light splashed over the town, the buildings licked with moonlight, the shadows around them deep. In the distance, the sea pounded against the shore. The water was restless, and Jenyfer was restless as well. Her blood still swirled and sang and, when she licked her lips, she could taste salt. Her belly twisted, making her feel ill with anticipation and the air was charged, like it was before a storm, but there were no clouds.

Her stomach rolled. She didn't want to know how the Witchfinder would discover her magic. She didn't want to think about what awaited her. No one had said what was going to happen, but she figured there were two options – the stake and the sea, or the pyre and the flame. She'd already run her hands over every inch of the bars of her cage – her fingers had tingled when she touched the cold iron. Magic, she'd realised with shock, then shook her head at her naivety. Of course the Witchfinders had magic – how else would they be able to do their jobs so well? She remembered what Ordes had told her and shuddered again.

Jenyfer licked dry lips. 'Hey,' she called to the guard, nothing more than a fisherman who had been granted an overly important job. 'Am I allowed a drink of water?'

'No water,' he grunted back, then suddenly stiffened; he drew the knife he carried at his hip and moved into the darkness.

'Oh, come on. I'm pretty sure the One God wouldn't deny a lady her last drinks.'

Jenyfer blinked, then scrambled awkwardly to the edge of the cage, eyes straining. She heard a muffled thump, followed by another, and then silence, as deep and dark as the ocean.

Ordes stepped into the flickering lantern light surrounding the cage. White teeth flashed against the honey-brown of his skin as he grinned. 'Hello, witch.'

'Hello, pirate,' Jenyfer whispered.

He ran his hands over the bars of the cage; the air around his knuckles shifted. 'While I do like a woman tied up, it's usually to a headboard. This is ridiculous.' He sighed, rubbing at his cheek with long fingers. 'Give me a moment.'

A shiver walked Jenyfer's spine. 'Be quick about it.'

He laughed, then motioned her away from the bars. Jenyfer shuffled away, moving to the back of the cage, expecting him to pull a knife or something from within the folds of his long coat, but he put his hands on the lock.

His brow furrowed. 'Magic.'

'Hurry,' Jenyfer whispered.

She held her breath as he muttered to himself. The air around his hands shimmered; an audible click filled the air and the lock dropped to the ground. Ordes caught her eye as he swung the door open, withdrawing a dagger from the scabbard at his hip. He bent to slide the blade through the ropes that bound her ankles. Jenyfer held out her wrists and she sighed with relief as the ropes fell away. He straightened, offering her his hand.

'Come on. You've got a ship to catch.' He tugged on her hand, supporting her as she crawled from the cell. Her knees were stiff, her legs tight with tension. Standing had never felt so good, but when Ordes closed his arms around her she froze, terror flooding her, her senses reeling, brain screaming. She wanted to shove him away, but she also wanted to collapse against his chest and sob.

Slowly, he pulled away. 'Jen, what—'

'Let's just go,' she whispered, and, although he frowned, he did not try to touch her again, leading her quickly away from the cage. They passed the body of the guard, lying face-down on the cobblestones.

'Is he dead?' Jenyfer asked quietly.

Ordes nudged the fisherman with the toe of his boot; the man groaned.

Jenyfer swallowed. Her feet were bare and she was wearing nothing but a linen dress. It was cold and, without a word, Ordes shrugged off his coat and handed it to her.

'Thank you,' she said, slipping it on. It was warm from his body and smelt like the sea. The sleeves hung past her hands and the coat reached below her knees, but she didn't care, burrowing gratefully into the fabric. He didn't have to remind her to be quiet, or quick, and they moved swiftly, passing between the buildings like shadows, staying clear of patches of moonlight. As the beach and the ocean came into view, both glimmering silver in the moonlight. Jenyfer felt her magic tingle again.

Someone stepped from the shadows and Jenyfer found herself hauled backwards so quickly she gasped. Ordes kept his arm in front of her while his hand dropped to the weapon at his hip.

'Stop,' Jenyfer said quickly. He didn't move, so she gave him a little shove. 'It's my aunt,' she added. Ordes slowly stepped aside as Tamora hurried over, her distinctive red hair concealed beneath the hood of her dark cloak. Her eyes shifted from Jenyfer's face to Ordes.

'Who—'

'He rescued me,' Jenyfer said quietly. 'He's from *The Excalibur*.'

'Jenyfer...'

'I know him,' Jenyfer said softly. 'He's... a friend.'

Tamora regarded Ordes, and then Jenyfer, with concern. 'You can't ever return to Kernou, not now. He will hunt you,' she said, meaning the Witchfinder. 'I wish... You are different, Jenyfer. Your magic is different to mine, to any Magic Wielder I've ever known. It's tied to the sea and the sea alone, that's all I know. That's all your mother knew.'

'My mother?'

'Yes. Trust in the sea, and trust in what is inside you.'

Jenyfer opened her mouth to reply, but her aunt crushed her to her chest instead. A lump lodged in Jenyfer's throat. She breathed in the familiar scent of lavender and mint as she realised she had lost them both – Tamora and Lamorna. Her family.

'Lamorna...'

'You did what you thought was best,' Tamora mumbled.

Jenyfer pulled back. 'But I had no idea what I was doing!'

'I know, Jen,' her aunt said softly. 'I know.'

'Will you be alright on your own?' Jenyfer managed, her voice not coming out as strong as she wanted it to. She swallowed again. 'How did I do it? That syhren. I don't understand.'

Tamora ran a pale hand, fingers long and marked with callouses, down Jenyfer's cheek. 'I wish we had time. You need to find Avalon. Niniane can help you,' Tamora said firmly. 'But Jenyfer, do not, *do not* go to Lyonesse. No matter what. Stay away from the Master of Songs and Death.'

Jenyfer nodded, a shiver darting the length of her spine. She had no wish to visit the portal to the Otherworld. Tamora's eyes moved over her face again and she took hold of Jenyfer's hands, grasping them tightly. Her fingernails dug into Jenyfer's palms.

'Promise me,' Tamora breathed.

'I promise,' Jenyfer's head was spinning, and she didn't feel connected to her body anymore. She was floating above it somewhere, looking down on herself, so small and fragile-looking, and her aunt, so strong and fierce.

'We have to go,' Ordes interjected quietly, and Jenyfer was flung back into her body, back into the reality of the situation.

'Wait,' Tamora ordered, then her lips were moving soundlessly. Jenyfer gasped as her body tingled from head to toe, a prickling sensation running over her like waves. She blinked, feeling strangely light and clear-headed. Her aunt looked at her sadly. 'I had to,' she explained in a low voice. 'I did it to save you. I don't know what will happen now. It could rush out of you, or it could trickle out. I wish I could tell you what to expect.'

Jenyfer frowned. 'What do you mean?'

'She bound your magic,' Ordes said quietly. 'And now, she's released it.'

Tamora stared at him, her eyes shifting over his face with more interest than before, reading something there that Jenyfer could not see. 'You're from Avalon?'

'Not anymore. We have to go,' Ordes repeated firmly. Jenyfer's mouth dropped open; tears blinded her vision but she couldn't speak. She had no words – even if she did, she didn't know where to start.

'Look after her,' Tamora said, squeezing Jenyfer's hands again. Sparks shot through Jenyfer's skin, burrowing down to the bone. Her aunt's magic, Jenyfer realised. She'd never felt it before. Tamora was still speaking, her voice low. 'If you don't, if anything happens to her...'

'It won't,' Ordes replied gently, while Jenyfer's head spun. Her insides hurt. It was too much – too much to take in. She blinked the tears away, wanting to see her aunt's face. Tamora touched her cheek once more, then turned and hurried away, swallowed by the darkness in seconds.

Jenyfer didn't realise she was crying until a chilly breeze caressed her cheek, lingering where her aunt's fingers had just been. Sniffing, she wiped at her face, brushing the tears away as Ordes strode down the beach towards the sea, checking over his shoulder that she was following. Jenyfer stumbled along numbly, frowning when she realised there was no boat waiting for them.

'I can't swim,' she mumbled. In the distance, outlined by silver light, she could see *The Excalibur*.

'We're not swimming.' Ordes walked into the water, the waves lapping at his boots before they closed over his knees. He lifted his arms, palms facing the water, which stilled and then pulled back; it rushed out into the ocean, a wave in reverse, and returned bearing a rowboat on its foaming crest. The boat came to rest at Ordes' side.

'Come on,' he called, leaping in gracefully.

Jenyfer picked up the hem of her dress and followed him into the water, gasping at how cold it was. She was soaked to the waist by the time she reached the boat. Ordes reached over the edge for her arms, hauling her in like she weighed nothing at all. This time, when he touched her, an involuntary shock shot through her body. His eyes were wide. He'd felt it as well, but he looked away from her, busying himself with the oars. She could feel his confusion, his hurt, and she wanted to explain – but she did not want him to know what had happened with Bryn, what she'd been made to do. Shame coiled in her belly but she pushed it away. Shivering, Jenyfer wrapped her arms around herself and settled in the boat, her head spinning.

The sound of the ocean was louder than usual and her skin still tingled. She blinked, then frowned. Everything was clear and sharp. She could see every detail of the night-soaked world around them.

She shoved her trembling fingers between her knees.

Her aunt had bound her magic. Kept it contained and never told her, but why?

'You're from Avalon? You didn't tell me that,' she said quietly.

Ordes shrugged. 'I haven't been back there for a long time.'

'So you're not just a Magic Wielder? You're a faery?'

'Part-faery – my father is human.' He sighed, then, 'Seas be damned.'

A shout echoed across the beach. Coming towards them was a small crowd of men, armed with flaming torches and whatever they could carry as a weapon. Jenyfer could see Bryn at the head of the group and betrayal speared through her again, as sharp as knives. With him was Ulrian Tregarthen and other members of the Konsel. Standing beside them was the Witchfinder, his pale face glowing in the darkness. Jenyfer's stomach turned over.

'The One God does not permit a witch to live,' the Chif called.

Jenyfer bristled. It was because of the One God she was in this situation. 'The One God can kiss my magical arse,' she shouted rebelliously. Behind her, Ordes laughed and, slowly, the boat began to shift into the first set of breaking waves. She didn't know if he was rowing or using magic and she didn't turn to look, keeping her eyes on the men on the beach.

Anger replaced any grief she had been feeling at leaving her aunt and her home, any grief at what had happened to her sister. Jenyfer gripped the sides of the boat with both hands. Trust in the sea, her aunt had said, so she would. She took a deep breath, pulling the scent of the waves into her blood.

'I curse this place. May the sea rise to swallow it,' she hissed.

Ordes sucked in a breath; the boat broke through the second set of waves, and was headed for the third when the sea bed beneath them trembled. The men on the beach were nothing but pale faces in the darkness, their torches bright against the night.

A wave rose in front of the boat, pausing briefly, before it surged towards the beach. The men cried out in alarm, turning and running towards the village, but the water was faster. The wave, as tall as three men, smashed into the sand, scattering bodies and extinguishing torches, before it pulled back into the sea and vanished.

Jenyfer gaped.

Ordes was laughing again. 'You just got a whole lot more interesting, if not frightening.'

She turned to him; her hands were shaking violently, her stomach tight and the magic in her veins was singing in delight. She pushed it away. 'I just want to find my sister.'

'She's—'

'She's not dead,' Jenyfer snapped.

'I was going to say she'd be with Melodias,' Ordes said simply. 'And your aunt just told you to stay away from him. But, if I can get you to Avalon, I will.'

'Thank you,' Jenyfer said quietly. 'And thank you for saving me.'

'I should have listened to you and got you out sooner,' he said.

Jenyfer said nothing, the lump in her throat so thick she was struggling to breathe.

'Can you row?' Ordes asked.

Jenyfer had never rowed in her life, but she took hold of the second set of oars, Ordes throwing instructions at her while she struggled and muttered under her breath. Soon, they were skimming across the water,

Jenyfer's muscles burning, her eyes filling with tears again as she realised what he was doing – distracting her. With each stroke of the oars, with each burn of her muscles, Jenyfer had something else to focus on. It didn't matter that it was temporary.

No one in that town deserved her tears, she decided, taking a deep breath and pulling on the oars once more, pushing the wave of emotion aside as all she had ever known became nothing more than a blur on the horizon.

CHAPTER 23

Arthur knew he should have been grateful. Jenyfer Astolat had been magicked away in the middle of the night. There would be no pyre, no stake, and the Witchfinder would leave empty handed.

He rubbed at his face in frustration.

Making his own great escape was going to be much more difficult now. He was aware of time ticking forward, seconds becoming minutes, then hours, until the day had almost been sucked into darkness. Jalen would be waiting for him. Arthur had packed a small bag with some clothes and some food that no one would notice was missing and it was squirrelled away beneath his bed.

Ulrian had been raging all day – he and the red-cloaked Witchfinder had spent hours at prayer. Arthur had not been invited to join them, but he'd pressed his ear to the closed door, listening as his father's voice rose and fell in angry desperation as he asked the One God what to do, how to manage this issue, how to console the Konsel and the people of Kernou.

For the first time in his life, Arthur had heard fear in his father's voice.

The Konsel had arrived at noon, sweeping importantly into the house, and reported that *The Excalibur* had vanished. There would be no retrieving the witch. They had crowded around their Chif and wondered whether the One God would punish them. What should they tell the people? They had questioned Tamora Rosevear, who claimed to know nothing. Keep watch on her, Ulrian had ordered them.

It was there, his ear pressed to the door, that Arthur's stomach sunk into his shoes.

There would still be a prize for the Witchfinder to take back to Malist. The One God demanded it, and so it would happen. Who it would be was not yet decided.

'We need to show people that they cannot escape the One God's justice,' Ulrian had declared; it was all too easy for his son to imagine his eyes gleaming, his cheeks flushed, while the Witchfinder nodded in satisfaction.

Arthur returned to his room, his father's words bouncing around his head almost painfully. They settled behind his eyes and stuck in the back of his throat, sinking into his stomach to join the anxiety and fear that already lived there, twisting and writhing like a pit of snakes. Arthur wished he had more courage. He wished he'd been able to be like Jenyfer.

The sun was moving steadily towards the ocean; soon, it would be swallowed by the sea, the dying rays painting the water with golden fire. Arthur needed to go. With the Konsel still here and guards still at the doors, he would have to leave the bag. They would make do. There would be food they could gather along the way to wherever they were going. North, he decided quickly. They would go north, to Cruithea. Jalen would be safe there.

It would be colder in the north, so Arthur dressed as warmly as he could, layering as many shirts as possible over his slim frame. He could not leave the house wearing his coat. It would raise suspicion. He stuffed his pockets with a chunk of dark rye bread. A snack, nothing more, but he could walk with a snack, couldn't he?

Heart hammering, Arthur forced himself to take a steady breath, urging the bile to settle back in his stomach. He should have eaten earlier, but he'd been caught in the grip of nerves for days – weeks, even – and his appetite had vanished. He ate one meal with his father, as usual, maintaining his normal routine.

Taking a deep breath, Arthur eased open his bedroom door and poked his head into the hall. The house dripped with silence. Frowning, he hurried towards the main room, finding his father and the Konsel gone. A quick glance out the window from the kitchen showed the guard had left as well. He opened the front door, his eyes sweeping the garden before he stepped outside, muscles bunched with nerves, but no one called out. Arthur allowed a small smile to cross his lips. He could do this. He could actually do this. He rushed back inside, collecting both his bag and coat, and hurried from the house, but instead of heading into the village, he turned for the trees that crowded the gently sloping land behind his house. They would provide cover almost all the way to the headland, the cave, and Jalen.

He moved quickly and as silently as he could, ducking between the spindly trunks and slipping around the bushes. The sun inched closer to the horizon. Jalen would wait for him.

As he neared the beach, Arthur paused. Through the trees, he could see his father standing near the waterline, arms folded. Arthur hesitated. Ulrian never went to the beach. Arthur shook his head and turned back towards the headland. He would have to climb the hill and approach the sea cave from the other side.

Before he'd taken another step, a man suddenly stepped onto the path before him, then another. The filtered light sneaking between the trees glinted off the gold crosses at their throats. The Konsel. Arthur clenched his fists, the fear surging beneath his skin.

'Your father requests your presence, Arthur Tregarthen.'

'What—'

Something hit him from behind, knocking him to his knees. Arthur was grabbed by both arms and dragged, his head spinning, from the trees onto the beach. His feet scrambled over the ground, trying to find purchase, to anchor himself to something so he could fight; but the men were strong, fishermen, with burly arms and broad shoulders.

They hauled him across the sand and dumped him at his father's feet. Ulrian looked down at him, his eyes sweeping over the coat and the small pack slung over Arthur's shoulder. The Witchfinder, red cloak like a blazing fire, stood beside him. He said nothing, his strange eyes walking over Arthur's face.

'Going somewhere, son?' Ulrian asked.

Arthur swallowed the bitter taste of defeat. Slowly, he stood, dusting the sand from his knees and palms. His ears were ringing and the wounds on his back stung with sweat. 'Just a walk.'

Ulrian's eyes passed over the obvious bulk of extra clothes. He said nothing, placing a strong hand on Arthur's shoulder. 'The One God can be merciful, Arthur,' Ulrian said softly. His grip on Arthur's shoulder tightened. The wind pulled at their hair and clothes, ripping through the fabric to bite at their skin. Ulrian, one hand on Arthur's shoulder, one hand on his lower back, slowly turned his son to face the headland.

A group of men approached. Arthur recognised several members of the Konsel, and several of the fishermen from the town, including Bryn. His heart sank. Between the men was a dusting of hair the colour of the sand under sunlight.

Jalen.

Arthur sucked in a breath.

'Bryn Hawkens has claimed you advised him to free the witch,' Ulrian said in a measured voice. 'Is it true?'

'No,' Arthur lied. 'Why would I suggest that?'

Ulrian's dark eyes did not leave Arthur's face. 'You think you can continue to lie to your father? To the One God?' He said, a cruel smile curling his lips. 'The Decalogue is very clear, Arthur.' Ulrian's voice remained calm, dripping with absolute devotion, and beneath that devotion was disgust.

'Please,' Arthur found himself whispering. 'Don't do this.'

'The One God does not suffer a witch to live,' Ulrian said, his eyes shining. He bent his head close to Arthur's, so that his breath touched Arthur's cheek. 'And man shall not lie with man as he would with woman.'

A shudder wracked Arthur's body and his father's fingers dug into the muscle of his shoulder. 'I'll do anything you want,' he whispered.

'There is nothing you can do that will atone for this sin,' Ulrian replied. 'You were seen,' he hissed, that calm facade finally cracking, gesturing to where Jalen stood, hands bound, between two men. Arthur kept his eyes on his feet; his father gripped his chin, forced his head up and around, forced him to look. He could see the blood on Jalen's face, the bruise that coloured the shape of his jaw, and his stomach turned over.

'Please,' he said again.

Ulrian smiled as the Witchfinder made his way towards Jalen and the men. 'You get to watch, son. You get to watch as the One God's justice is carried out. The Sacellum will still have a prize – Kernou will not disappoint.'

Jalen wasn't fighting. Why wasn't he fighting? He was standing still and silent between the men. Feeling Arthur's gaze, he looked across the sand that separated them.

Their eyes met, and in that moment, Arthur heard Jalen's voice in his head, as warm as sunshine and as fresh as rain in summer.

Find the Grail, Arthur. Be who you are supposed to be.

Ulrian's hand squeezed, the pressure of his fingers sending shooting pain through Arthur's shoulder, down his arm and into the very tips of his fingers. The Witchfinder had reached Jalen. The man stood with his arms folded; they were too far away for Arthur to hear what words were spoken.

He wanted to cry out but his voice had fled, lost somewhere in the storm of horror that rushed through his head. He could do nothing but watch as Jalen was taken to the boat, as he climbed in, graceful even with his hands bound. He sat between Bryn and another man, still not fighting, and he remained still and calm as a third man climbed in beside the Witchfinder and took up the oars while two others waded into the surf, pushing the boat towards the breaking waves.

Why isn't he fighting? Arthur thought desperately.

'Use your magic!' he shouted suddenly. Ulrian started, releasing his grip enough for Arthur to pull free. He ran along the beach, ignoring his father, ignoring the cries of the Konsel. He didn't know what he would do against the Witchfinder and the fishermen, but he had to try.

Ulrian crashed along the beach after him. Arthur braced himself, but his father did not strike him, just closed his hand over Arthur's shoulder again.

'You see,' he whispered, his voice somehow rising above the sound of the breaking waves. 'Justice will be done.'

Arthur took a step forward, and then stopped.

Something rippled across the world.

He felt it, a tingle that brushed his skin, that crawled inside him.

The thing he called fear squirmed inside him.

The air became charged; storm clouds raced across the sky from all directions, a mosaic of grey and green and yellow, until they collided – directly above Jalen's head. Arthur heard the men cry out. Lightning danced through the clouds and thunder rumbled, so loud and fierce it shook the land.

The sand beneath Arthur's feet shifted.

The Witchfinder reached for Jalen.

A ferocious wind ripped across the water, lifting the waves into peaks, churning the sea into soup and throwing the waves against the shore. Above them, lightning smashed its way through the clouds, chased by thunder that shook the earth in its rage.

One of the fishermen raced away, his hands held up to the sky.

'It's the demon!' he cried. 'The storm demon has come for us!'

'Nonsense,' Ulrian shouted. 'It's a storm, nothing more.'

Arthur kept his eyes on Jalen. As he watched, Jalen's sandy-coloured hair lengthened and became the colour of seaweed. His skin darkened, until it was as brown as the eels the fishermen brought in. He lifted his hands, flinging his arms out and fingers of lightning reached from the clouds to land in Jalen's outstretched palms.

The Witchfinder screamed and fell back, his hands over his face.

The fishermen gathered on the beach were cowering beneath their weathered brown hands. 'The storm demon! We are being punished!' one cried. He turned and stumbled away; the Konsel men grabbed him, but could not hold him.

'Let him go,' Ulrian yelled as the sand beneath them shifted and rolled.

Arthur took another step.

Jalen smiled. He raised a hand; forks of lightning leapt from his palm to decorate the darkening sky. The wind increased, racing across the beach and Arthur closed his eyes against the force of it. Thunder growled, bouncing through the air, rebounding from the cliffs and, by the time Arthur opened his eyes, Jalen had vanished.

CHAPTER 24

Dawn on the ocean was different to the land. The water stretched from one corner of the world to the other. Clouds hung low on the horizon, the misty green hills dotted with blotches of white. Peach and tangerine hues licked the water and painted the underside of the clouds with pink. The world was silent, the ocean calm, its surface a mirror. Jenyfer could see her tired and irritated face from where she hung her head over the railing. Her skin was milk-pale, her hair a wild tangle, midnight streamers dangling towards the water.

Sighing, she straightened, resting her hands on the railing and watching as the sun shot over the horizon. The sails snapped in the wind as *The Excalibur* cut a graceful path through the sea. She'd been onboard less than a day, but already, Kernou wasn't even a speck on the horizon.

Her head hurt. Every part of her ached. She rubbed at her temples, going over the previous night in her mind, when Ordes had pulled her still wet and shivering, head spinning and hands tingling, onto the deck of *The Excalibur*. Jenyfer had just sat there, her senses completely overwhelmed. Whatever her aunt had done to her...

She could smell *everything*. Salt and sand, the warmth of a sun long-faded, the sweat of the men who were peering at her suspiciously. Fruit and bread, candle wax, sulphur from flames extinguished. She could smell leather and wet wool, the wind and her own fear.

Jenyfer looked up to find a man peering down at her, moonlight gilding him silver. Instinctively, she knew who he was – power rolled off him in waves. His authority, his confidence, but beneath it was the trace of old magic – some instinct told her the Captain of *The Excalibur* had not used any magic for many years. His expression not altering at all, Tymis Merlyni reached out a long-fingered hand. Trembling, Jenyfer took it, letting him lift her gently to her feet. He looked her up and down, studying her with an intensity she didn't understand but made her stomach twist.

'Interesting,' he said.

'What's interesting?' she whispered. His voice was rich and melodic, warmer than she was expecting. His skin was dark, the moonlight revealing a network of fine lines around silver eyes and a full mouth. Brown hair brushed his shoulders, decorated with the occasional bead of bone. His fingers held hers firmly; there was a tattoo on each one, resting between knuckle bone and joint. She studied them – symbols she had never seen before – to avoid looking at his face.

'You are. Get back to work,' he called to his crew, shooting the order over a strong shoulder. He released Jenyfer's hand. 'It's not forever, understand?'

Despair shot along her spine. 'You're just going to dump me somewhere?'

He chuckled softly. 'What did you expect? Charity? I'm a pirate, love. We don't do charity.'

'Yet you did,' Jenyfer countered softly. 'You rescued me.'

'A favour, nothing more,' he answered swiftly.

She wanted to ask about magic, about Avalon, but stored the questions away for another time, knowing anything he said would be lost in the turmoil that swirled around her mind. Wind danced across the deck, making her shiver. She burrowed deeper into Ordes' coat and wrapped her arms around herself. 'What do you want me to do while I'm here, then?'

The Captain's heavy eyebrows lifted. 'Do?'

'I want to be useful.'

'Ever been on a ship?'

'No,' she admitted. 'But I can learn. Anything. I don't want to be a burden.'

'You don't look strong enough to lift yourself let alone anything else.' He fingered his chin, eyes sweeping over her in a way that made her stomach squirm and made her regret asking. Eventually, he sighed. 'You want to do something? Half the men on this ship haven't fucked a woman, or anything, for months.'

Jenyfer recoiled, taking a step back.

Tymis laughed softly. 'No? Then stay out of the way and keep to yourself. The men would rather me throw you to the ocean. Women don't belong on ships, especially women with magic.'

'What about *The Night Queen*?' Jenyfer asked boldly. Something tightened in the Captain's face. He turned and walked away, long coat swishing behind him like raven's wings.

'Don't mention that ship to him. It's a bit of a sore point.'

Jenyfer turned around. Ordes was leaning casually against the railing of the deck, those silver eyes, so like his father's, glinting in the moonlight.

'Why?' She was not nearly as brave as she thought she was; her voice trembled. This was what she had wanted but, now that she was here, surrounded by men she didn't know, men who were tough and world-weary... fear clawed its way into her belly.

'Because Katarin can use her magic and he can't.' Ordes gestured at the ship. 'Don't worry about what he said either. He has a deplorable sense of humour. You don't need to be afraid of anyone.'

'Who says I'm afraid?' She'd have to try harder to hide it, to push it down, like she was used to doing. She could sense eyes she couldn't see, combing her from bare feet to her unruly hair. There were others on the deck in the darkness. Jenyfer shivered again, wondering just how many men were on the ship, remembering the last man she thought she could trust.

Ordes smiled, and his voice was soft when he spoke. 'Everything about you screams how afraid you are. But forget everything you've heard about pirates – we're actually a charming, decent bunch on this ship.'

Jenyfer schooled her expression. She could feel the water beginning to leak from her closed fists, hidden deep in the sleeves of his coat. She lifted her chin. 'I'm not afraid.'

Ordes' smile was hesitant. 'Come on. I'll show you where you can sleep.'

She had no choice but to follow him below deck. As they descended down the narrow ladder and darkness closed above her head, Jenyfer took a deep breath, trying not to panic. She had never spent much time in confined spaces, and it was so dark and still in the belly of the ship, the waves lapping against the hull. Ordes took down a lantern hanging from a hook, and lit it with a wave of his hand. He caught her eye briefly, then looked away, continuing into the darkness, the lantern light painting everything golden and warm.

He stopped at the last door along a narrow passageway. 'You can sleep in here.'

Beyond the simple door was a large cabin, with a comfortable looking bed, a table and a wooden chair, an armchair covered in clothing and a small wardrobe and dresser tucked against one wall.

'Whose cabin is this?' Jenyfer asked.

'Mine.'

Her stomach clenched. 'Yours? But—'

'It's fine,' Ordes said simply, stepping up behind her, forcing her to move into the cabin. 'I can sleep with the crew for the moment, until we sort something out for you. We're without a medic at the moment, so you can probably use that cabin, but it's a bit of a mess. I'll get one of the boys to tidy it.'

Jenyfer shook her head. 'I'll manage in the medic's cabin.'

Her muscles were bunched tight, spine rigid. Something flashed painfully through her mind. She pushed it aside, chewing on her lip. 'I don't want to put you out of your cabin.'

'Jenyfer,' Ordes said softly. 'It's the least I can do.'

She swallowed and came further into the cabin, slowly, one foot in front of the other. 'I... fine. But I don't want to kick you out of your bed, so,' she paused and took a deep breath, lifting her eyes to his, trying to pull up a shred of the false bravery she was feeling fifteen minutes ago. 'We can share.'

His eyebrows rose. 'I've been told I snore and hog the bed.'

'I don't care. I'm not taking your bed from you. You've done enough, getting me out of that cage and getting me here,' she added. He was watching her, his expression closed, eyes shining silver in the dim light.

He pulled his hand through his hair again. 'Alright. If that's what you want. Are you hungry?' he asked.

'A little,' Jenyfer whispered. Ordes told her he'd bring food and the moment he was gone, she rushed across the room and bolted the door. She sighed, her stomach twisting, her heart bruised and broken, before she swallowed and plonked down onto the bed. The coverlet was simple – white with pale grey stripes cut across it – and clean. It was comfortable, well slept in. Absently, she ran her fingers over the sheets, wondering how she was going to do this – share his bed, lie there as if nothing had happened between them, and as if nothing had changed in her. But she was changed, she knew it. Changed in ways she didn't want to speak about and, even if she did, she didn't think she'd be able to find the right words to convey what was swirling through her mind, or to explain the way she felt like vomiting, the sharp bite of anxiety whenever a man looked at her – even Ordes, who had given her no reason not to trust him.

Jenyfer was still wet; a quick hunt through the clothing dangling from the armchair and she found a shirt, but nothing else that looked like it would fit her. The shirt would have to do. She stripped off Ordes' coat, followed by her wet clothing and pulled the shirt over her head. It hung to her knees, the material softer than it looked. There was nothing she could use for a belt, so she pulled the blanket from the foot of the bed and wrapped it around herself, then curled on her side until someone knocked lightly on the door, then louder when she didn't respond.

Sleep was hanging just over her shoulder. Yawning, Jenyfer pushed herself upright and stumbled across the floor as the ship pitched suddenly. Gripping the wall for support, she opened the door.

Her eyes fell on the beaten silver tray grasped between two large hands, the fingers misshapen, a ring glinting against golden brown skin. There were tattoos on his fingers, like the ones the Captain had. She hadn't noticed them before in all the time they'd spent together, and wasn't even sure they'd been there. She reached out a finger and touched one of the symbols – a series of lines crossed and woven together. Ordes stood still, letting her touch. Her fingertip tingled.

'Why didn't I see these before?'

'I hid them,' he replied.

'Why?'

'Later,' he said gently. 'I'll answer all your questions later. You need to eat and sleep.'

On the tray was a bowl of stew, steam billowing from the surface, and a plate of crusty bread. Jenyfer sighed in gratitude and her stomach let out a loud grumble. Ordes stepped past her into the cabin, shoving things aside and setting her meal down on the top of the table. He ducked back into the passageway, returning with an unlit lantern. He placed it beside the tray, and clicked his fingers; the flame inside roared to life and slowly, the cabin filled with warm light.

He flashed her a grin, his eyes finding her bare legs. His expression shifted again.

'You need clothes.'

'My dress will dry.'

He shook his head. 'We'll find you something in the morning, but for now—' Those silver eyes travelled the length of her body. 'You managed to find a clean one?'

'What? Oh yes,' she mumbled, tugging at the shirt, embarrassed. 'Sorry.'

He grinned. 'My bed. My shirt. Anything else you want?'

Jenyfer shook her head quickly, cheeks heating, pulling her arms around herself.

Ordes cleared his throat and gestured to the food. 'Eat. And then sleep. I'll try not to disturb you when...'

She nodded. When he was gone, Jenyfer demolished her food. Then, she crawled into Ordes' bed and prayed that the gentle movement of the sea would lull her to sleep.

Jenyfer was not alone on the deck. There were several sailors sharing the crisp morning air with her, all working and doing their best to ignore her. She kept her eyes on the water; it was easier for her, and probably easier for them. The deck was silent and she wondered was it always like that, or was it her presence that had disrupted their lives. She had no idea what people did on a ship, having never been on one, except for her father's small fishing boat when she was a child.

The Excalibur was huge. It had three masts that towered into the air, square sails that hung symmetrically across them. Jenyfer knew from talk around the town that the system of wires, ropes and chains that attached the sails to the masts was called the rigging.

Around her, the men worked; a group of them were washing down and scrubbing the deck, while another group were hauling on the rigging, one man suspended up the mast like a bird. Others were greasing and oiling, varnishing and scraping away at things she couldn't name.

Ordes strolled towards her, his gait casual. The ship rocked suddenly; Jenyfer gripped the railing for support, but the pirate just grinned and kept his feet.

'You have to learn to dance with the sea, Jen,' he said. He was dressed much the same as the sailors in dark brown trousers and a linen shirt. The wind pulled at his shoulder-length hair, lifting it from his head in a halo of midnight burnished gold by the rising sun. He looked different in the bright sunlight, with the ocean surrounding them. More real, she decided. In the cave, it had just been the two of them, caught together in the darkness, sharing stories, but now, in this new world, he was like a stranger to her again. She wondered if he was feeling the same about her.

'Did you sleep alright?'

Jenyfer looked out over the water again. 'Yes. You didn't come back?'

'I did, but only for a few hours.'

She glanced at the sails straining against the masts, at the men working. She didn't know any of their names. 'Did you sleep?'

Ordes stood next to her, his eyes trailing over her before he turned his gaze to the sea. 'I slept fine in the chair, don't worry. I didn't want to disturb you.'

'Oh. Thank you. Where are we going?' Jenyfer asked. She wanted to ask why he didn't claim his bed, but part of her was glad he didn't. It had been stubbornness that had made her demand they share the bed, but the reality was she hadn't wanted him there, that close to her.

'The ship sets her own course. We'd been sitting in your bay unable to go anywhere, until you ended up on board. The minute you were on this ship, those sails filled with wind and we were off,' Ordes answered.

'But that's—'

'Very interesting,' he said.

Jenyfer swallowed, recalling the Captain's words. 'Will they really throw me overboard?'

'The crew? Not unless the Captain orders it.'

Silence dropped between them. Jenyfer turned back to watch the ocean sparkling in the morning sun; a white bird hovered over the water. She kept her eyes on it as it hung there, suspended in the air, before it wheeled away with a harsh cry.

'Why haven't you been back to Avalon?'

'More questions?'

'Sorry.' Asking questions meant Jenyfer didn't have to answer the ones she was asking herself. It was a distraction, but she was deeply curious about him, his father, the ship, magic... she flexed her fingers. A droplet of water emerged, then sank back inside her skin. She swallowed, taking a deep breath, instantly regretting it. The smells! And her eyes hurt. The world was too big, too bright. The sound of the waves slapping at the hull of the ship was unbearably loud. She couldn't hear her inner song over the noise of the world around her.

She wasn't sure Ordes was going to answer, but he sighed and rubbed at the back of his neck. 'I'm blood-sworn to the Captain – my choice,' he added softly.

'If he's the Captain, what are you?'

'The ship's quartermaster. Basically, I run this ship while my father gets all the credit, and a much better cabin.' Ordes ran his eyes over her quickly. 'Clothes. Come on.'

Jenyfer blushed. She was still wearing his shirt, the blanket draped around her shoulders like a cloak. Her hair was a wild tangle, dried salt speckled through it. Wordlessly, she followed him below deck once more. They passed some of the crew heading topside. They nodded to Ordes, and most avoided looking at her.

Her stomach twisted. Ill-omen or not, she was free, she was alive, and she was safe enough for the moment; but once Tymis had decided she'd outstayed her welcome, then what? She'd never been alone before – her aunt and her sister had always been there. Jenyfer's throat tightened. She had to find Lamorna but had no idea how to bring it up. She knew she couldn't ask, not yet. She needed to earn the right to ask for their help, so she would make herself useful. Tamora had been a healer – maybe it ran in the family? Maybe there was some instinct there that Jenyfer hadn't tapped into yet. She dug furiously through her memories, trying to recall which herbs her aunt used to treat which affliction, but her brain was still a muddled mess and her senses were overwhelmed.

Ordes stopped in front of a pile of crates. Muttering to himself, he lifted the lid off one, pulling out a bundle of clothing, handing them to her one item after another, and by the time Jenyfer returned to the cabin, she had two pairs of men's trousers that were slightly too big for her, a belt, several bone-coloured linen shirts, a dark short coat, and a pair of scuffed boots, also too big.

She dressed, then sat on the bed, not knowing what else to do. This ship was now her life-line, her chance at something else, something more. It was stuffy in the cabin, so Jenyfer pushed open the porthole and gazed out.

Outside, the sun sparkled on the face of the water. She let a smile crawl over her face. In that reflected light, she could see hope, and in the rich smell of the sea, there was promise.

Now, all she had to do was work out how she would get to the Isle of Mists and work out where her sister was, and how to find her. Jenyfer flexed her fingers again, watching the water bead on her skin like perfect jewels as, inside her, her song was singing.

CHAPTER 25

Arthur crouched behind a stack of crates on the wharf, the smell of fish and seawater burrowing into his nostrils. He'd made it to Carinya, four days north of Kernou. He'd stopped in Newlyn, the next village along the coast, after managing to find his way through Vidarra Forest without getting lost. He spent the night tucked against the back wall of the tavern, shivering in the crisp air, and was moving again before the sun was up, sleeping the next night tucked into a narrow gap between two boulders on the edge of Celivale Grove. His belly was empty and he was fighting sleep, but he needed to keep going.

He was being followed, but he needed to rest, to eat and sleep, to recharge, and then... he had no idea.

After Jalen had disappeared, seemingly swept up in that magical storm, Arthur had been dragged along the beach by his father, Ulrian's hand fisted in Arthur's shirt, then through the town, not caring if anyone saw them, the Witchfinder trailing them, hands held to his face, moaning in pain.

Ulrian's rage had been a palpable thing, floating through the air, and Arthur breathed it in, feeling it settle in the back of his throat. He'd been thrown through the front door, shoved down the hallway and into the main hall, dragged across the room and pushed to his knees before the altar, the Witchfinder lingering in the background.

'You pray,' his father had demanded. 'You pray until I tell you to stop.'

'No.'

The words had left Arthur's mouth on their own. His head was spinning, his heart... his heart broken, shattered, left behind on that beach as Jalen was taken from him, as Jalen – vanished.

The demon of storms.

It wasn't possible. Jalen was human, as flesh and blood and *real* as Arthur was. He had held him, felt the heat of his skin, the feeling of his lips on his, the strength in his fingers and the firm line of his body.

His *human* body.

Ulrian's fist had connected with the back of Arthur's head, and then, Arthur exploded.

He couldn't really remember what happened, except his mind went blank and smooth as glass. There was heat and wind and light – bright, blinding light – and he was running. He ran out of the house, out of the town, diving into the trees, slipping over sand and stone, running until he was deep in the trees, panting and sweating and staring at his hands, hands that had just unleashed a wave of magic.

Magic Arthur had no idea he had.

He hadn't had time to gather himself, to slow down. He heard them coming, heard the dogs, so he'd run again. And he'd kept on running.

Now, he pulled his arms around himself. Dawn was approaching, and it was freezing. Mist swirled from the surface of the water, the waves lapping gently at the piers. There was a ship moored at the end of the long jetty. He was too far away to read the name of the vessel, but it was large enough to be important. Large enough that he could hopefully hide and not be seen, at least until they stopped at some other village where he could slip away. Hopefully, the ship was heading north, like he was; although, at the moment, anywhere would be better than here.

Arthur needed to go to Cruithea. There, the Old Ways held firm. He had questions – so many questions that needed answers for. He could feel his magic, like a living thing, sliding through his blood, pushing and pulsing and begging to be let out again.

But he wouldn't. Not because he didn't want to, but because he didn't know how. Jalen had said once that magic was instinct, that all he had to do was want something to happen, and it did. Arthur swallowed, thinking about his father, and about the Witchfinder. Had he wanted to hurt them? He had been so angry, so hurt, and so broken by what had happened on the beach. Perhaps it was instinct. Perhaps not.

And Jalen. The smallest breath of wind, the tiniest darkening of a cloud, and Arthur was looking over his shoulder, holding his breath, waiting and waiting for a demon, a demi-god, who might not show up at all.

The harsh cry of a gull pulled Arthur back to the present. Not long until sunrise. Swallowing his fear, he crept from behind the crates. There were a few men on the wharf, but they were busy with sacks and boxes at the far end. The jetty was clear of people. Arthur stood, forcing himself to breathe steadily, to be calm, to look like he belonged here. He made himself walk at a normal pace towards the ship, hands in his pockets, his stride casual.

No one called out. No one stopped him. The ship was close, so close, giant sails catching the sun as it climbed into the sky. The gangplank was lowered, waiting there like an invitation, and Arthur darted across it and onto the ship. He paused for a moment, then hurried across the deck and buried himself behind a stack of wooden crates.

He tucked his knees up to his chin, closed his eyes, and waited.

Arthur wasn't sure how much time passed, but soon, there were voices, female voices. On the ship.

Shit.

He was on *The Night Queen*.

Arthur shifted his position, peering out from behind the crates. Three women stood near the railing, one with her hands on her hips. She said something that made the other two laugh; their laughter ceased as a man's voice shouted up at them from the jetty. Arthur froze, his blood turning to ice. He knew that voice. A dog howled and he stopped breathing altogether.

'We're coming aboard,' the man called. Alric. One of the Konsel.

'Oh you are, are you?' one of the women sneered in response. 'Do I need to remind you whose ship this is?'

'The One God will protect me from the sorcery of Katarin Le Fey,' Alric called back. 'Now let me board. We're searching for a dangerous fugitive.'

'Pull the anchor,' one of the women demanded of another, her voice low, before she turned back to Alric, spitting in his direction. 'The One God has no power here, little man.'

Arthur heard running feet. Alric's voice was lost amongst those of the sailors, the women who ran this ship. From where he was hidden, Arthur could see the helm. He watched as a tall woman with long, dark hair loose around her shoulders positioned herself behind the wheel. She held her hands together at her breast; golden light began to glow between her palms and, when she placed them on the wheel, the ship groaned, the sails filled with a wind that came from nowhere and *The Night Queen* was moving – faster than she should have been.

The ship ploughed through the water, turning towards the open sea, and freedom.

Arthur had fallen asleep where he sat, still wedged between the stack of crates. When he opened his eyes, he found himself looking down the barrel of a pistol. Swallowing, he held up his hands.

'A stowaway,' the pistol holder said. Her voice was low, and her dark hair was swept back from her face, bright brown eyes glinting in the sun. She was dressed in man's trousers, a simple linen shirt and a brown vest. Silver rings adorned her fingers and ears. She smiled, teeth white in her sun-kissed face, and he realised she was the woman he had seen at the helm.

'Don't shoot me,' he said quietly. 'Please.'

'What are you doing here?' The question came from a second woman, shorter than the first, all curves and flesh where the other was lean muscle. She dropped to one knee to peer into his face, blonde hair tumbling over her shoulders. 'You got a name, boy?'

'Jonas,' Arthur said quickly.

The woman laughed, blue eyes dancing. 'I meant a real name, but it'll do. Get up,' she added.

'What are you doing, Tahnet?' the taller woman snapped.

Tahnet shrugged, flicking a length of blonde hair over her shoulder. 'The Captain wants to see him.'

'She knows I'm here?' Arthur stammered.

'It's her ship, little man,' the pistol holder replied. 'She knows everything. Up.'

Arthur climbed to his feet, legs stiff from sitting so long. He was still chilled to the bone, but he pushed his hair from his face and forced his legs to move. He followed Tahnet, the woman with the pistol walking behind him. He didn't have to look to know she had the weapon pointed at the back of his head.

He was marched to the stern of the ship, to the Captain's cabin. Tahnet knocked once, then opened the door, and Arthur was shoved hard between the shoulder blades. He tripped over his feet, falling on his face on a carpet as lush as the ones that decorated his father's home. A boot nudged him in the ribs, and he scrambled upright, red-faced, wiping at his clothes, before lifting his gaze.

Katarin Le Fey was the most beautiful woman he had ever seen.

Brown eyes surveyed him, her brows thin slashes that remained steady as she looked him over, head to toe. Her red lips did not smile, did not twitch as she leant forward in her seat, resting her elbows on the top of the grand desk she sat behind. He couldn't take his eyes off her – magic leached from every part of her, so strong he could almost see it. Sunlight slanted through the window behind her, haloing her head in fire. Arthur could see beads of bone and precious stones in the length of her dark red hair.

Katarin tapped her narrow chin with a long, pale finger. She sat back, her posture casual, relaxed, but Arthur remained tense. She sighed gracefully, picking up a letter opener and twirling it between her fingers, not taking her eyes from Arthur's.

'Do you know what I do with stowaways?' she asked.

He nodded.

'Cat got your tongue, little man?' Katarin said, her voice low. She stroked the tip of the letter opener along the sharp line of her jaw, before pointing it at him. 'What made you think you could hide on my ship?'

'I didn't know it was your ship,' he stuttered.

'That isn't an answer,' she told him. 'Who are you running from? Just who has frightened you so badly you've taken refuge on my ship?'

'No one,' Arthur said quickly.

'More lies,' Tahnet sighed. Arthur glanced at her worriedly; she flashed him a dangerous grin. 'It's my gift, little man. I can smell lies, especially on men. You can't keep anything from me, so you may as well tell the Captain the truth.'

Arthur swallowed. 'I'm looking for someone.'

Katarin waved the letter opener around. 'Lost your lover? Your girl runs off on you and you think she's here?'

'No,' he said, shaking his head.

The woman with the pistol stepped closer, taking his chin between strong fingers, turning his face in her direction. She had magic as well, he could feel it when she touched him, though it was nowhere near as strong as Katarin's. She stared into his face for a long time and he felt something brushing against the corners of his mind.

'Anything worth noting, Aelle?' the Captain asked, her tone bored.

Aelle released Arthur's chin, going to bend her face to Katarin's to whisper in her ear. The Captain's lips curled. 'At least I don't have to worry about you around my girls,' she said simply. 'There are no men on this ship, stowaway. Your boyfriend isn't here.'

Arthur said nothing. Katarin smiled and twirled that letter opener again.

'You can either tell me the truth, or I could simply find out for myself,' she added. 'But I'm tired and couldn't be bothered.' She tossed the letter opener carelessly onto the table, scattering pieces of paper and an extinguished candle. 'Your shielding is non-existent, your magic is depleted, and you're a mess.'

'I didn't even know I had magic until...'

'Until what?' she asked.

'Until I nearly killed someone,' Arthur mumbled, heart thundering, palms sweaty. He peeked up at her, finding her watching him curiously. 'I mean, I don't know if I killed him or not – I mean them – I might have, but...' He swallowed, and took a deep breath. 'What are you going to do with me?'

Katarin tapped her chin again. 'I'm going to feed you, give you some fresh clothes, let you bathe and rest.'

'And then?' he asked quietly.

'I'll let you know.'

CHAPTER 26

By the time Ordes sought his bed on the second night Jenyfer was onboard, she was already sound asleep, curled on her side.

Right in the middle of the bed.

He removed his boots and shirt and pushed the clothing that had somehow made it back to the armchair aside. It would do. Ordes shuffled around, slinging his legs over the side, feet crossed at the ankles. He glanced at the bed. The mound that was Jenyfer sighed and rolled over, then rolled again.

A bed hog and a restless sleeper. He closed his eyes and settled back into the chair but, no matter how hard he tried, he could not get comfortable. With a sigh, he uncurled himself from the chair and padded across the cabin. Only a few hours – that was all he needed. She didn't even have to know he was there. He'd been nursing a stiff neck all day, although that was probably less due to a single night on the armchair and more to do with the tension he'd been carrying in his shoulders since the night she didn't show up at the cave – the night he'd failed to help her.

He should have gone into that town and found her long before he was ordered to – by an Old One, no less – and long before he saw her fighting her way towards her sister on that beach.

Something had happened to her, something more than the Witchfinder. She hadn't said anything, but he knew, could feel it in his gut. Jenyfer rolled over again, mumbling to herself. He held his breath, one corner of the bedding clutched tight; when she didn't wake, he slipped quickly beneath the covers. His head had barely touched the pillow when Jenyfer sighed and rolled again, tucking herself against his side, her legs tangling with his, one arm draped over his torso.

She made a whimpering sound and her fingernails dug into his flesh, making him wince.

'Jen,' he whispered.

A mumble, completely incoherent. Gently, he nudged her shoulder, but she didn't shift over. As the heat from her arm sunk inside him, he relaxed. So did she. She sighed deeply and all the tension fled her body. Ordes closed his eyes, and, with her head tucked into his side and her arm clutching him, he fell asleep.

He woke when daylight was streaming into the cabin.

Jenyfer's head was still resting close to his arm, her face hidden by a mountain of hair. She was sleeping on her side again, her back to him, and the heat from her skin was like a burning brand. Above them, he could hear the crew going about their morning chores, could hear Iouen giving instructions for the day. Ordes should go up there, but he was afraid to move.

Jenyfer mumbled in her sleep. He held his breath, waiting as her breathing changed from gentle and relaxed to tight. He yawned dramatically, stretching his arms over his head to let her know he was awake, and in the time it took him to blink, she had moved, and there was a dagger pressed against his throat.

She didn't say a word, just looked at him, her eyes wide, a storm swirling in their depths.

'Where did you find that?' he asked. 'That's my dagger isn't it? From the table?'

She swallowed but still did not move the blade from his skin. 'Yes.'

Ordes chuckled. 'It's blunt, Jen.'

She blinked. 'What?'

'It's a paperweight,' Ordes told her, sliding his hand beneath his pillow. 'The sharp objects are here.' Quick as a flash, he pressed the point of his dagger into her ribs. 'One decent shove,' he mumbled. 'I should show you how to use one of these things.'

Jenyfer swallowed; fear flashed through her eyes. 'Why?'

'Because the next person whose throat you hold a blade to first thing in the morning might not be so nice about it.' Ordes let his gaze travel over her face, settling on her mouth. The sound of her breath catching in her throat made his pulse surge. Slowly, he withdrew the dagger, letting it rest on the mattress beside him.

'Do you always keep a dagger under your pillow?' she whispered.

'Do you?' he whispered back.

'I've never had to before,' she said.

He reached up with his spare hand to push stray strands of hair from her face. She didn't move as he traced the curve of her cheek, barely able to hear himself think over the pounding of his heart. His body was burning in all the places she was pressed against him. 'Why didn't you come to the cave?'

'I couldn't,' Jenyfer whispered. She withdrew her weapon and pulled away, sitting with her back to him.

'What happened?' he asked, sliding the dagger beneath his pillow once more and sitting up. When he reached out and touched her arm, she shrank away from his hand, making him frown. 'Jenyfer—'

'It doesn't matter,' she mumbled, then threw back the bedclothes and scurried from the mattress. She returned the blunt dagger to the desk with a sigh. 'I wouldn't have hurt you,' she said. 'I just... I'm on a *pirate ship*, Ordes. Forgive me if I'm a little nervous.'

'I get it,' he said, watching her avoid looking at him. He got up, searching for a clean shirt and pulling it on, then plonked himself in the armchair to slide his boots on. 'Stay in here today,' he told her. She glanced at him over her shoulder. 'If you want,' he added.

She nodded, and he left her to go above deck to face the morning. He was greeted by Iouen, half-way up the rigging, lowering his spyglass and calling out, 'Ship approaching.'

'One of ours?' Ordes called back, shaking sleep from his head.

Iouen shook his head. 'Don't think so. A sloop.'

'Merchant ship then,' Ordes said with a frown. They were in the open ocean, no land in sight. What was a merchant ship doing all the way out here? It was well off the trade routes – Teyath lay to the east of them, somewhere behind the horizon. Ordes chewed his lip, then went to find his father.

Tymis met him at the door. 'I heard. Shall we go take a look?'

Ordes shrugged. 'It might be worth seeing what they're carrying. It's been a while since we claimed a prize. I'm sure the men wouldn't mind lining their pockets again,' he said, and Tymis nodded, leading the way to the railing, removing a spyglass from his pocket.

'Too far away to tell, but she seems to be coming straight for us,' he murmured, before calling, 'Kayrus.' The helmsman acknowledged the Captain with a nod but did not take his hands from the wheel. 'Bring us in.'

Kayrus nodded, and spun the wheel. *The Excalibur* began to turn eastwards, slicing through the water as Jenyfer appeared on deck, still rumpled from sleep. Her hair was a mad tangle. She looked like she'd spent the night on her back; Ordes glanced around at the crew quickly, but their attention was on the approaching ship. Jenyfer spotted him and hurried over.

'We just changed direction, didn't we?' she asked and he nodded. 'Why?'

Ordes gestured to the east. 'We're approaching another ship. Probably just a merchant ship but we can't be sure,' he added. One of the men rolled a barrel past them. Jenyfer's eyes widened as she realised what was happening. The cannons were being loaded. 'It's just a precaution,' Ordes told her reassuringly. He turned from her to catch Iouen's arm. 'Hoist the false flag,' he said.

Iouen nodded, and hurried away.

'False flag?' Jenyfer asked.

'We want to appear like we're a merchant ship, until we're close enough.'

'Close enough for what?'

'This is a pirate ship, Jen,' he reminded her. 'You didn't think everything just appeared magically in the hold, did you? Below deck, back to my cabin. You'll be safe there.'

'What about you?' she said. Wind whipped their hair around their faces as *The Excalibur's* sails filled and they surged towards the other ship.

Ordes winked. 'I'm a pirate, love. I'll be fine.'

'Chain-shot.' The Captain's voice rang out across the deck. 'We don't want to sink her until we know what she's carrying. Let's give them the chance to surrender.'

The Excalibur turned sharply again as Kayrus brought them broadside of the merchant ship; Jenyfer watched the false flag run into the sky. It was blue, with three thick bands of white crossing it. 'I've seen that before,' she said.

'It's the flag of the Portsmouth Trading Company. Now go,' Ordes told her, giving her a nudge. He waited until she had vanished below deck, before turning back to his father. 'What do you think?'

The Captain lowered his spyglass. 'She's from the capital, but she's armed, Ordes.'

'Not a merchant ship then?'

'I'm afraid not.'

There was nothing to do but wait until *The Excalibur* had drawn level with the other ship. With the wind behind them, they were soon within firing range. The men hovered near the cannons, waiting for instruction. Their faces were alive with the thrill of what might come next and Ordes found himself grinning.

It was dangerous, hardly glamorous, but there was nowhere else he'd rather be.

As *The Excalibur* closed on the other ship, Ordes caught the flash of a red cloak. His stomach clenched. They had a Witchfinder onboard. 'Captain,' he called.

'I see him,' his father called back. 'Get ready to do your thing. This is your show now. I want him in one piece, Ordes. I have some questions for our red-cloaked friend.'

If it was magic the Witchfinder was looking for, Ordes would give it to him. It was rude to leave someone wanting, after all. The crew surrounding him stepped back; they had their weapons drawn, faces tight, but they were still smiling with the type of savage glee that gave them their reputation as the enemy ship swung herself around and came at them from the side.

There was still so much Ordes did not know about his magic, but what he'd told Jen was true – it was instinct. At this moment, his instinct was survival – his, and the crew's. He took a deep breath, calling his magic in his palms; silver light shone from his hands. Anticipation danced along his spine as the enemy ship came steadily closer.

'Hold us steady,' Tymis called to Kayrus.

There was a flurry of movement around the cannons – the chain-shot was quickly swapped for round-shot. They carried carcass ammunition but Tymis would never use it unless it was absolutely necessary. He always hoped *The Excalibur's* mere presence was enough to convince surrender.

From where he stood, Ordes could see the name of the ship painted proudly across the bow – *The Sea Serpent*. He could also see the

Witchfinder. The man was standing near the railing, red cloak billowing, a cruel smile on his lips.

'Tymis Merlyni,' the Witchfinder called, his voice reaching across the space between the two ships. There was no fear in his voice, only authority and purpose. The sea below was churning, the water cut to pieces, the waves choppy. Kayrus held the ship steady as she rocked beneath their feet.

Tymis strode to the railing, withdrawing his pistol from the holster at his hip. 'And who might you be?'

'I am here on the One God's orders,' the Witchfinder replied. 'I am His arm, His sword, and His will shall be carried out this day.'

Tymis laughed. 'That's ambitious,' he said, then raised his voice, addressing the rest of the crew and the ship's Captain. 'This is your chance to surrender. You know who I am. No one has to get hurt. All you have to do is turn around and head back the way you came.'

The Witchfinder shook his head. 'These men are loyal to the One God. They are His servants, and they do His work. Hand over the witch you have on board. We shall not surrender,' he added. 'The One God is on our side.'

'Have it your way,' Tymis said, tossing Ordes a meaningful look.

Jenyfer, Ordes thought, his stomach twisting.

Ordes drew his hands together at his chest, feeling his magic swirling through the air around him. He thrust his hands out and a wall of water rose between the two ships, arching over the *The Sea Serpent*. He could hear shouts of panic from her crew as the wave smashed into the ship, sweeping men off their feet; a mast cracked and tumbled towards the deck. Another wave of Ordes' hand and a mist rolled in, cloaking *The Excalibur* in a thick grey curtain, cutting off the brilliant shine of the sun. The Witchfinder was desperately barking orders .

Torn and water-logged, their sails dangled uselessly and *The Sea Serpent* was soon encased in mist and ocean spray as Ordes manipulated the winds, turning them into a weapon. The wind tore across the deck of the enemy ship, knocking over barrels and men and anything not nailed down.

The Sea Serpent lurched under the wind's violent assault.

'Easy,' Tymis called, his voice lost somewhere amongst the cries and curses from the enemy crew. 'Kayrus, bring us in, as close as you can.'

Slowly, *The Excalibur* moved towards the enemy ship as Ordes climbed onto the railing, using the rigging to steady himself, then hurled himself overboard. He was still too far away from *The Sea Serpent* to make the jump, so the sea rose to meet him instead, catching him in mid-air, propelling him through the mist and onto the deck of the enemy ship. He landed lightly, and was greeted with a sword swinging from the mist. The blade narrowly missed Ordes' shoulder. His opponent stepped into view. A grin spread across his face as he realised Ordes was unarmed.

'You're either a fool, boy, or—'

Silver light danced over Ordes' knuckles. 'Or?'

The man swore, taking a step back, before he changed his mind and attacked. He hadn't even raised his weapon again before he was left lying on the deck, silver light curled around him, binding his ankles and wrists.

Ordes never killed. It was a deal he made with his father many years ago – he'd give Tymis his magic, he'd help, he'd do whatever his Captain asked, but he wouldn't kill. It was a deal he'd made with himself as well, but no one else had made such a bargain; there would be loss of life today. It had been a long time between skirmishes and, after being marooned in the Bay of Calledun for so long, the crew were edgy and needed to blow off some steam.

The Sea Serpent shuddered as *The Excalibur* made contact; shouts and cheers of excitement rent the air and, moments later, Iouen was at Ordes' side, followed by a dozen others. *The Sea Serpent's* crew had regained their feet; there was a moment, a brief pause, where Ordes thought they'd surrender, but someone gave the order to engage and everything exploded. All was chaos and smoke from pistols, the smell of gunpowder overwhelming the salty scent of the ocean. Ordes fought his way through with fists, dagger and magic, his eyes locked on to a red cloak. The Witchfinder was standing against the railing on the starboard side and his expression was conflicted, as if contemplating whether to throw himself overboard or not. He clutched a dagger tightly in one hand; in the other, he held a battered leather-bound book.

'Abomination,' the Witchfinder hissed, as Ordes approached him, a rope of silver light curled around his arm like a snake. 'The One God—'

Ordes released his magic and the Witchfinder started shrieking and crying out to his god as the silver rope wrapped itself around his body, pinning his arms to his sides. The dagger fell to clatter on the deck but the man kept his hold on the book. Ordes strode forward and took it from him.

'Get your filthy hands off the Word,' the Witchfinder snapped.

Ordes ignored him and flipped the book open, reading aloud from the tiny, handwritten script that ran in perfect lines across the page. 'I come to you with a heavy heart, for I have not spread the Word as well as I could. Free me from my sins so that I cannot fail you again. Punish me as you see fit and I will not complain, for in the spilling of my blood shall I bask in your glory.' He paused, eyebrows raised, as the Witchfinder cursed and muttered under his breath. 'Fuck me. This is what you lot truly believe in?' Ordes asked, snapping the Decalogue closed and tucking it under his arm.

The Witchfinder sneered at him. 'My master will soon wipe the earth clean of your foul blood, Magic Wielder.'

'Is that a promise?'

'It has been written,' the man said piously, lifting his chin as much as he could.

'Ordes!' Iouen's voice cut through the smoke.

'Here,' Ordes called back. The Witchfinder was glaring at him with a mixture of fear and zealous bravery. Iouen clapped a hand on Ordes' shoulder. 'All secure?'

The boatswain nodded. Iouen had a gash across his cheek, a new scar to match his old, and his shirt was torn, but he appeared otherwise unharmed. 'You're coming with us,' he told the Witchfinder. Two of *The Excalibur's* crew came forward and took the Witchfinder by the arms, dragging the man across the deck. Ordes rubbed his face and looked around. The enemy crew were either out cold, dead, or sitting together on the deck, staring down the barrel of a pistol. With the Decalogue securely tucked under his arm, Ordes returned to *The Excalibur*.

The more Ordes read, the more convinced he was that Katarin's fears about Magic Wielders disappearing was something to seriously worry about. They had known for some time that the Sacellum in Malist had been sending Witchfinders into every corner of the continent, seeking out Magic Wielders, but usually those poor souls were burnt in their town squares in a great public spectacle. Knowing the Shaleitari were taking Magic Wielders to the Sacellum was deeply concerning.

Rescuing those accused of witchcraft was Katarin's thing but, now, Ordes was wondering if it should be theirs as well. Witchfinder ranks had swelled, according to the High Priestess's spies. Maybe it was time to fight fire with fire. Or, he thought with a shiver, magic with magic.

He shut the Decalogue and fixed his gaze on the Witchfinder.

'Read anything you like?' the man asked.

Ordes considered the Decalogue for a moment, then tossed it overboard. The Witchfinder cried out as it landed with an audible plop in the water. 'Nope,' Ordes said. 'But I have a question for you.' He strode forward, dropping to one knee so he could peer up into the Witchfinder's face. The man had been stripped of his red cloak and was bound to a chair on the deck. The sun beat down without mercy; the Witchfinder's skin was mottled, deep red patches standing out in brutal contrast to his pale flesh.

'What does the Sacellum want with Magic Wielders?'

The man smiled. 'It will be your filthy magic that will see your end, boy.'

'Care to elaborate?' Ordes asked quietly. The Witchfinder clamped his lips shut in a superior smirk. Tymis emerged from his cabin, coming to smack the man on the back of the head.

'My son asked you a question,' he said.

The Witchfinder glanced up. 'I know what you are, Tymis Merlyni.'

'Right now, I'm pissed-off that you're making my deck look untidy. So, tell us what we want to know and this will all be over with,' Tymis replied. He gave Ordes a quick look. 'You can either talk of your own free will, or we can make you.'

It was a bluff. Ordes had no idea how to use his magic to make someone talk, or even if he could, but the Witchfinder didn't know that. The man gave Ordes a wary look.

'And if magic doesn't work, we have other ways,' Tymis added, withdrawing his dagger and running the tip of it down the Witchfinder's cheek. The man shrank away from the blade as much as he could. 'So, let's try this again. What does the Sacellum want with Magic Wielders?'

'That is knowledge the One God has, not me.'

'So you're just following orders?'

A nod.

'How many have the Shaleitari taken to Malist?' Ordes asked. The Witchfinder jerked at the term. 'You've heard that word before?'

'Spoken from the lips of your cursed kind.'

Ordes and Tymis exchanged a look. If the Sacellum knew the Cruithean name for Witchfinder's, it meant they had managed to steal Cruithean Magic Wielder's from their country, a feat that, while impressive, was also terrifying.

'How many Shaleitari are there?' Tymis asked.

'More than you could ever know, *Captain*.' The Witchfinder spat the last word venomously, then closed his eyes and began to recite a prayer.

'You're a Magic Wielder yourself, aren't you?' Ordes asked. The Witchfinder's eyes flew open in alarm, but before he could confirm or deny it, there was a commotion behind them.

'I don't think....' Iouen was saying.

Ordes turned to watch as Jenyfer appeared on deck, pushing Iouen out of the way. Her face was pale, but her expression hardened as she caught sight of the Witchfinder. Her fists curled. Iouen was saying something to her quietly, but she shook her head and made her way to Ordes' side.

'Is this the one from Kernou?' he asked her; she nodded.

The Witchfinder's eyes locked on Jenyfer. 'There she is.'

'Here I am,' she said, her voice low, fierce. 'If you've come to get me, I think you can conclude you've made a mistake.'

The Witchfinder just smiled. 'The One God does not make mistakes.'

'But you're not a god, are you?' Jenyfer said. 'You're just a man, and like any man, you can bleed and you can feel pain. And you can die,' she added in a whisper.

'And are you going to be the one to kill me, witch?' the Shaleitari asked.

'No,' she said. 'But I'll watch.'

Ordes looked at her in surprise. She was strong, tough, he already knew that, but to willingly stand there and watch a man die, even someone like a Witchfinder, took a type of courage he realised he hadn't thought she possessed. Her chin was lifted, eyes hard as she stared at the Witchfinder. An eerie silence drifted over the deck until, eventually, Tymis sighed.

'Anything else to say?' he asked. The Witchfinder clamped his dry lips closed and shook his head. 'Run out of the Word? I didn't think that was possible,' Tymis mused, then sighed. 'It's a shame you can't be more useful.'

Jenyfer took a step forward, moving towards the Witchfinder. Ordes reached out and caught her wrist, but she pulled herself free. 'Jen,' he hissed. 'What are you doing?'

She didn't answer him. Tymis stood behind the bound Shaleitari, dagger drawn. He said nothing, watching Jenyfer with keen eyes as she approached. Her head tipped to one side as she studied the man and suddenly, Ordes could hear music. He shook his head, but the sound persisted, digging gently into his brain, into his blood. He felt calm, peaceful. Jenyfer moved closer to the Witchfinder and all he wanted to do was pull her back, but he couldn't move. The Witchfinder was watching her, a strange sort of triumph in his eyes. Ordes met his father's eyes; Tymis shook his head and mouthed, 'Watch.'

Swallowing, Ordes kept his eyes on Jenyfer. Slowly, she reached towards the Witchfinder, resting her palm on the man's forehead. His eyes were wide and wild and his head thrashed side to side. Tymis grasped the man's chin in one hand, the other resting on the back of his head, holding him steady.

'Sleep,' Jenyfer whispered, her voice low, strangely melodic. 'And then, die.'

The Witchfinder's eyes closed and he breathed a sigh. Ordes felt light as air, as if he was floating away as Jenyfer's words settled inside him and with it, a surge of power, of magic, that made his blood tingle.

The sound of cracking bone echoed across the deck as Tymis snapped the man's neck. The music in Ordes' head screeched to a stop. His temples were pounding fiercely. Groans from behind him told him he wasn't the only one who felt like their head was about to explode.

Jenyfer suddenly reeled backwards, gasping, stumbling over her feet and crashing against Ordes. 'It's alright,' he told her, closing one arm around her middle, holding her against him.

Her body shook but she shrugged off his hands and stood there, looking at the body of the dead Witchfinder, until she turned and vanished below deck without a word.

CHAPTER 27

Jenyfer had been on board *The Excalibur* for just over a week and, in that time, she'd already lived through one sea battle, thought she was going to die, and learnt that she knew absolutely nothing about pirates. She'd studied the crew as much as she dared, learning who smiled more, who was quick with their laughter, and who bothered to look at her at all. The navigator, Kayrus, she liked. He had a pleasant smile and kind eyes. She was yet to form opinions on the rest of the crew and still didn't know any of their names, but they were all high on their victory, the smiles and laughter having lasted days.

A victory where no one except some of the enemy crew lost their lives. And the Witchfinder.

The sound of his neck snapping like a piece of timber had haunted Jenyfer's sleep. She should have been pleased – one less Witchfinder in the world – but she wasn't. She couldn't help but feel responsible for his death, even though it had been the Captain that had killed him. Ordes had tried to calm her afterwards, telling her the man was going to die regardless, but it hadn't helped.

Her magic had played a role in his death and ever since she'd done whatever it was she did to the Witchfinder, Jenyfer's magic has felt more alive, more insistent. It was becoming harder to push it away. Her inner song woke her up by screaming at her most mornings.

She'd also moved out of Ordes' cabin. She'd needed to be alone, so he had some of the men organise the medic's cabin for her. It was small, furnished with nothing but a narrow bed and a small wash stand, but she didn't care. It was hers, for now.

And it was more than that - she needed to be away from him, from the temptation of him, from the way he looked at her, the way his eyes would catch hers and hold them. From the questions she could sense brimming on his tongue, and the answers she didn't want to give him. She needed to keep her distance, as hard as that would be on a ship, but she'd try, until she'd found some way to move beyond what had happened with Bryn, from what had been taken from her.

Breakfast was fruit and hard bread, as it usually was. Those of the crew not topside were in the galley with Jenyfer; she avoided looking at them as she collected her meal and took a seat at the end of a long bench. Most of them had seen what she'd done to the Witchfinder – she didn't blame them for staying away from her. There had been whispers, things she had half heard, but the crew were good at stopping their tongues at the right moment.

One word had stuck in her brain, one whispered word, spoken in fear and wonder.

Syhren.

Tymis Merlyni strode into the galley, coat tails flapping behind him dramatically. Everything about the Captain was dramatic, Jenyfer had decided, from the way he held a mug to how he threw himself into a chair, or how he stalked around the deck, lord of his watery domain. He stood no watch, came and went as he pleased, and was to be obeyed in all things. The men respected him, she'd been able to discern that much.

The Captain glanced around, spotting her easily; his lips curled into a half-smile that had her twitching in her seat. He headed straight for her and Jenyfer held her breath as Tymis took a seat opposite her.

'Where do you think we are?' he asked her.

The question took her by surprise. Jenyfer shook her head. The coastline she was most familiar with was long behind them. The wind had been kind, the great sails never failing to catch the currents of air.

Tymis fixed her in his unnerving grey eyes. She had no idea how old he was, how old any of the crew were. She knew a life on the water would have aged these men beyond their mortal years – she'd seen it on Bryn's face, the premature lines around his eyes from squinting into the brightness of the sun or half-closing his eyes against the oceanic winds.

Only Ordes was smooth-skinned; his faery heritage, she supposed. She'd never met a faery before, not even a half-faery, and she had so many questions running around her head.

The Captain reached across and stole the apple from Jenyfer's plate. She said nothing and kept her hands in her lap.

'You're quiet, for a woman, when you're not casting spells on Witchfinders.' It wasn't a question, so she didn't bother entertaining him with a response. Her heart thudded violently as he sat back, casually tossing the apple from one large brown hand to the other.

Tymis Merlyni wore a silver ring on nearly every tattooed finger. She'd never seen him without his dark blue long coat, brass buttons running from neck to thigh. Beneath it, he wore a simple linen shirt, the colour of bone, and the same dark grey trousers as the rest of the men. The only difference was the Captain decorated his middle with a scarlet sash of silk. Jenyfer swallowed, her mind immediately shifting to the Witchfinder – the man's body had been given to the sea and, although Ordes told her not to look, she did. The sight of his red cloak, so vivid, against the blue of the ocean had dug its claws into her brain and refused to let go.

'Do you know what you are?' the Captain asked her.

'No,' Jenyfer managed. Beneath the table, her fingers tightened on her thighs; water seeped through the fabric of her pants to kiss her skin. She shuddered and pushed her magic away. 'I have no idea. Do you? Do you know what I am? The men—'

'Sailors are superstitious,' Tymis said. 'When you live your life out here, with the sea as your mistress, you develop a certain sense for things. Let them talk. They'll get tired of the mystery of you eventually.'

Jenyfer swallowed. 'What do you mean, a certain sense for things?'

'These men see the world through different eyes. They see you through different eyes. Women don't sail with men, under usual circumstances. Sailors believe they are bad luck, because they distract the men, which angers the sea and, as revenge, the sea gives nothing but wild waves and treachery in return. While they're out here, sailors must only have one woman in their life, understand?' Tymis said. He held the apple between long fingers, studying it with interest, before his gaze returned to her face. 'But since you've been on board, the sea has been more cooperative than usual, and they've noticed that.'

Jenyfer frowned. 'Why would—'

'I don't know. Like I said, they're superstitious. I've got a job for you. You'll at least get a new wardrobe. Men's clothing doesn't do much for you, I'm afraid.' He leant forward. 'And you'll get a wash. To be honest, lass, you smell.'

Jenyfer opened her mouth but he just chuckled.

'New clothes, a wash, a brush for that hair. You'll be looking smart in no time.'

'And what, exactly, am I looking smart for?'

'Not what, who,' Tymis said. Before she could ask what he meant, he twisted in his seat and beckoned his son, who had just stepped into the galley. With a look somewhere between sufferance and amusement, Ordes crossed the room, his body perfectly balanced as the ship suddenly pitched sideways.

'Calm your shit, woman,' Tymis muttered and Jenyfer frowned, before realising he was talking to the ship. Tymis shot her a look as Ordes slipped into the seat beside his father. 'When you go ashore next, take her with you.'

'Why?' Jenyfer asked.

'My son here is my best source of information on the land,' Tymis explained quietly. 'No one else is keen to go and mix with polite society. There's a reason they're pirates. Ordes is rather skilled at procuring information, like where the rum is stored and how many crates of food we can get away with, schedules of the merchant fleet, getting us the best price for anything we want to sell, and he is rather skilled with his fists and his weapons. Ordes is also blood-bound to me, as is everyone on this ship, so he will do as I say.'

'Ordes is sitting right here and isn't sure this is a good idea,' Ordes muttered.

Tymis sighed. 'She can go places you can't, and you know it.'

'Where can I go?' Jenyfer asked. The idea of leaving the ship both thrilled and terrified her. She might actually get to see some of the world, some of the places she had heard about and dreamt of visiting. She might learn something about how to get to Avalon. No one on the ship wanted to talk about the island. The one man she had asked had looked at her like she was crazy. Pirates were more superstitious than fishermen, it seemed.

'You can move in women's circles, talk, gossip, do whatever it is women do. Ask questions men can't,' Tymis said simply, waving his hand dismissively through the air. She stared at him.

'You do know my town was going to burn me for witchcraft?'

'Your point?'

She said nothing, not knowing what to say, looking imploringly at Ordes.

He was frowning. 'Can you use a weapon?'

'I'll have you know, I'm rather handy with a kitchen knife,' Jenyfer said sweetly. 'A sharp one,' she added, folding her arms. She was going to get off the ship! She was going to *see* things!

A smile tugged at the corners of Ordes' mouth as Tymis burst out laughing. He took a huge bite out of the apple, tossing it back to Jenyfer and climbing to his feet. He ruffled Ordes' hair like he was a little kid.

'Teach her what she needs to know. We'll be at Skulls Rest in a week.'

Skulls Rest – a pirate town. If they were headed to Skulls Rest, that meant they'd gone south, around the headland from Kernou. A little thrill danced down Jenyfer's spine.

'Where are we going after that?' she asked boldly, holding the Captain's eyes.

'The Vale.'

The Vale! 'Will we go all the way around the continent?' Jenyfer breathed.

Tymis flashed her a quick smile. 'You ever seen a map?'

'No. Can I?'

'Sure,' he said, tapping his son on the back of the head. 'Show her one.'

Ordes flashed her a grin. 'Come on, then.'

'Where are we going?' Jenyfer asked, scrambling to her feet.

'To show you a map.'

Jenyfer stood before the books, running her fingers gently over the spines, as she had done countless times already in the days she'd been on the ship. Though she hadn't yet dared take one from the shelf.

'You like books?'

'My father used to read to me all the time – stories about the sea.' She glanced at Ordes over her shoulder. 'You offered me a book, that first night in the cave. One of these?'

He nodded and waved his hand. A book floated free of the small shelf, coming to rest in the air in front of her. 'Take it, if you want.'

Jenyfer closed her hands around the book. It was old, heavy, the leather cover worn, the pages dry and yellowing. '*The Magic of the Isle*,' she read, running her fingers gently over the embossed title. 'It looks important.' Holding the book to her chest, she took a seat on the edge of his bed. 'Do you miss it?'

'Avalon?'

'Yes.'

'You can't miss what you don't remember,' Ordes said. 'I was born there, but it isn't my home. I've been on this ship since I was six months old.' He ran a hand through his hair and sighed lightly. 'When my father left the Isle – and my mother – he took two things: this ship, and me.' Ordes was studying the tattoos on his knuckles. 'I don't remember my mother, but sometimes I think I do. Sometimes I think I hear her voice, in my dreams.'

Jenyfer bit her lip. 'You haven't seen her since you were a baby? That must be hard.'

He shrugged. 'It is what it is. Now, come here and look at this.' He motioned her over to the table, selecting a scroll of parchment from a pile, pushing the rest aside. He unrolled the parchment and spread it across the desk, weighing each corner with whatever was in reach – an ink pot, a mug, an apple, and the blunt dagger, then stepped back, inviting her to look.

Jenyfer swallowed, moving closer to the table, and the world laid before her. Her eyes found Kernou first; the village seemed so small, tucked into the Bay of Calledun. She stared at the neat script that marked her home, then let her eyes move over the map. The moor beyond her town became hills, then swept upwards to form a mountain range that stretched from one side of the continent to the other. She noted the forests and the rivers, the grasslands east of the mountains, and the towns and villages, all meticulously labelled.

Her gaze traced the coastline, returning eventually to Kernou. 'I thought I'd spend my whole life in that place,' she said quietly. Ordes said nothing. She swallowed the lump in her throat. 'Did you draw this?'

'Parts of it,' he replied, his voice soft.

'Avalon and Lyonesse are on here!'

'Yes, but it's a guess as to where they really are. Magical islands have a way of not being where you expect to find them,' Ordes said.

'So, where are we now?' Jenyfer asked.

He tapped the wide expanse of ocean at the southern end of the continent. 'Somewhere here. We passed Port Leore a few days ago.'

'And we're going there,' Jenyfer said, pointing to Skulls Rest. 'Why?'

'A rest. But it's also the perfect place for you to practise your new skills,' Ordes added. 'Skulls Rest is full of pirates and smugglers. Most of the crew will go ashore there. They don't usually leave the ship, but Skulls Rest is a safe place.'

Jenyfer's eyes returned once more to Kernou. 'I'm glad to be gone. I don't ever want to go back.' She took a deep breath, turning to look at Ordes. 'What is it you want? Surely it can't be to spend your life on this ship?'

'Why not? I don't know what else I'd do with myself,' he answered.

'But you must want something?' she pressed.

'What's to want? I'm free,' he said softly.

Jenyfer could understand that. 'And now I'm free as well, I guess.'

Ordes reached for another of the scrolls of parchment. 'Take a look at this,' he said, excitement colouring his tone as he unrolled the parchment with a touch of drama, obviously inherited from his father. He placed the new map over the other, securing the corners, then stepping back. 'Look.'

There were three land masses etched on the map, a large stretch of open water separating the larger two, Teyath, and two places Jenyfer had never heard of – Aileryan, and Ruritoris.

'What is this?' she whispered.

Ordes grinned. 'This is what we know of the world.' He placed a finger on the Bay of Calledun, then slowly moved it westwards, between the islands of Lyonesse and Avalon, across the Nyanian Ocean, coming to land on the continent of Ruritoris. Above it was a larger land mass, Aileryan, a place divided into five countries, all labelled.

'There is more than just Teyath,' Jenyfer murmured in astonishment. 'Have you been to these places?'

Ordes shook his head. 'One day, perhaps, but no, not yet.'

'Is there more than this?' Jenyfer breathed.

'I don't know,' Ordes replied. 'Maybe.'

'Maybe one day you'll find out,' Jenyfer said. She was still looking at the map, her eyes tracing the names of places she hadn't ever imagined existed, places like Eshlune and Tiquia, and deserts! There were deserts in these places!

Ordes carefully rolled the maps up and placed them back in the pile. 'So...' he began.

Jenyfer cleared her throat, lifting her eyes from the rolls of parchment to his face. 'So what are these skills I'm going to learn?'

'Normal pirate stuff,' he said, laughing when she gave him a blank look. 'Things that would make the One God turn over in his grave.'

Jenyfer's gaze returned to the maps. 'I need to find my sister.'

'I can't take you to Lyonesse, Jenyfer.'

'But—'

'I told your aunt I'd keep you safe, and I mean to do that. What you're about to learn will put you in danger, but much less danger than if you went anywhere near Melodias.' Ordes frowned, drumming his fingers on the table-top. 'After Skulls Rest, we will sail to The Vale, and then, who knows? If you're going to come with me, you will need to know how to use a weapon. You'll need to know how to defend yourself.'

Her stomach twisted. 'What will we do in The Vale?'

'Ask questions. Steal.'

'Steal?'

Ordes' face shifted into a broad grin. 'You're going to learn to be a pirate.'

CHAPTER 28

Arthur had never been on a ship before. While the scent of the sea was familiar, the shifting beneath his feet was not, nor were the groans and creaks *The Night Queen* made as she ploughed through the water.

He'd been given a cabin; it was small and dark, but he didn't mind. At least it wasn't the brig. He'd fallen into the narrow cot without complaint, grateful to sleep on something that was not hard stone or cold earth. He'd woken to find a platter of fruit and hard cheese, fruit juice as well as a change of clothes, and a large tub of water. The woman who'd found him, crouched behind the crates in the frigid air that swirled around the deck, had run her finger through the water in the tub. Steam rose from the surface and she stepped back, her eyes challenging him to say something, but he didn't.

Thankfully, she'd left him to bathe and dress in private, but he could sense her outside his door, waiting, so he hurried through his wash, tossing his travel-worn filthy clothes into the corner of the cabin. They'd given him woollen trousers and a linen shirt, a woollen vest and short coat, but no shoes – so he brushed the worst of the dirt off his other pair and pulled them on.

Before he opened the door to face Aelle again, Arthur ran his hands quickly through his hair, smoothing it down, working out the tangles. His father had cropped his own hair severely short, and had wanted Arthur to do the same, but he'd managed to avoid it. It was only a small thing, a vain thing, but he liked his hair. It was as brown as bark, thick and wavy, and now, even after fussing with it, it stuck up all over the place.

He sighed, pretty certain Katarin Le Fey didn't care about his hair.

He had no idea what to say to her, how much truth to tell. She'd said Aelle could read the truth from his mind, and Arthur suspected Katarin herself would be able to do the same, and much more. Aelle didn't speak to him as she led him up the ladder and onto the deck. He had a moment to register they were in the open ocean, no land mass in sight, before he was ordered to follow the pirate to see her Captain.

His Captain now, too, he supposed. Or maybe not. Katarin could still throw him overboard.

Arthur decided quickly to tell the truth. He didn't want any of them rifling through his head. There were things there he hadn't yet reconciled, things he was still trying to piece together, and they were private, those things. He would hold onto them as tightly as he could.

Katarin was standing with her back to the door, hands on her hips as she watched the water from the wide window of her cabin. A breeze sauntered into the room through the open window. She turned to face him, her face fresh and eyes bright, her red hair glowing.

'Sleep well, stowaway?'

'Yes,' Arthur said. 'Thank you.'

She crossed the room to fling herself gracefully into a seat on one side of the grand desk she'd been perched behind last night. Arthur let his gaze slide around the room – a large bed sat in one corner, the bedding ruffled and half-hanging on the floor. He saw a wardrobe, the doors open, clothes spilling out, and a dresser covered in small bottles and ceramic jars. He had no idea what was in any of them. There was a stack of books on the floor, a screen in the other corner, which he guessed hid a bathing area. The faint scent of soap and flowers drifted around the room.

The desk was dark timber, the top thick and heavy looking, and covered in maps and parchment, that letter opener, candles in holders, quill and ink, and several glasses and a bottle of what he guessed was rum.

'See anything you like?' Katarin asked him, her voice low, purring, her smile cat-like.

He swallowed and shook his head.

She leant forward in her seat. 'You're a nervous little creature, aren't you? But you intrigue me. Sit.' It wasn't an invitation, but a command, so he did what he was told. 'Where have you come from?'

'I've come from Kernou,' he answered softly.

Aelle was standing behind her Captain and the two women exchanged a glance.

'Are you a spy?' Aelle demanded, hands on her hips, fingers coming to rest on the weapons at her belt – a dagger and the pistol she had pointed at Arthur's head the previous night. 'We know what goes on there,' she added.

'No,' Arthur replied emphatically. They were watching him, two pairs of shrewd eyes crawling over his face, so he took a deep breath, and let it out. 'My father is Ulrian Tregarthen.'

They didn't react like he expected. He was ready for knives, pistols, a bullet through his brain, a dagger through his heart, or to be smashed to pieces by magic, but Katarin Le Fey just threw back her head and laughed.

'Bullshit. Arthur Tregarthen is a weakling. He'd never have the guts to run away from his father.'

'What if I told you I left my father bleeding on the stones before his beloved altar?' Arthur snapped. 'That I let my magic – magic that I didn't know I had – attack him and the Witchfinder he had with him, and that I liked it?' Arthur halted. He'd not realised this, not until he spoke the words. Katarin was watching him closely. He swallowed, fidgeting with the hem of his shirt. 'I mean... I didn't want to kill either of them, but it felt good, you know?'

'Oh I do know,' she said smoothly. 'Why did you run?'

Arthur's legs shook and if he wasn't sitting he'd have fallen into a heap on the carpet, as weak as Katarin thought he was – as everyone seemed to think he was. He pulled a hand through his hair again, and then it all came pouring out. He didn't know why he told her, why he let all his secrets spill into the space between them. He couldn't sense any magic at work.

He spoke because he needed to. Because he'd been carrying it for too long.

He spoke about the hours at prayer, voicing his love and obedience to a god he did not believe in. He told her about the whip, that hated, horrible thing. He spoke about the lies. And he spoke about Jalen.

Silence settled in the cabin as Katarin just looked at him. She opened her mouth, then closed it again, and he was left with the feeling she was about to say something important, but her face snapped closed.

'Will your father continue to look for you?' Aelle asked.

Arthur started. He'd almost forgotten the other woman was there. 'I don't know.'

Katarin's expression shifted; her smile became feral, eyes glinting with the promise of violence. He was amazed to see her skin shimmering – her magic, he realised. 'Let him come. I welcome the chance to have a little chat with your dear father, Arthur Tregarthen.'

'Why?' he breathed.

The Captain of *The Night Queen* leant forward in her seat, elbows resting on the desk. That smile did not leave her face. 'We have history, Ulrian and I. We're old friends.'

Arthur's head was spinning. 'You are?'

Katarin nodded, then waved him away. 'Aelle will show you around.'

'So, I can stay?'

The Captain nodded. 'For now.'

Aelle scowled, but did as she was asked, gesturing for Arthur to stand. He followed her out, pausing in the doorway, glancing at Katarin Le Fey over his shoulder. She was watching him. He gulped, and stepped out into the blazing light of the day.

CHAPTER 29

The best thing about learning to be a pirate was that Jenyfer had been able to change her clothes. The navigator, Kayrus, had led her deeper into the belly of the ship – the hold, she learnt it was called – than Ordes had on her first night, where she was dumbfounded at the cargo held down there. Crates of weapons, barrels of food and rum and fresh water, plus numerous chests containing clothing and jewellery. But no gold. When she mentioned that, the sailor laughed heartily.

'You've got the wrong idea about pirates, girl.'

There were large crates of textiles, smaller ones of spices and tea, tobacco, and a strange red powder. Kayrus waited patiently while she hunted through a crate of women's clothing, finding several simple dresses made of dark wool. At the bottom of the crate was a fine gown, more beautiful than anything she had ever seen before. Jenyfer ran her fingers over the material; it was silky, like cool sand, and was the colour of the ocean under sunlight. She could feel Kayrus watching her fondle the material and let it drop from her hands, stepping away from the crate.

'Go on, love. Take it,' Kayrus said.

'Oh no, I can't.'

'It's not like any of us will be wearing it,' the pirate said simply.

Jenyfer swallowed. She knew what her sister would think about the dress – impractical, possibly immodest, and, while thinking about Lamorna caused something to pinch in her chest, Jenyfer let herself imagine the disapproval her sister would dish out. Let herself imagine for just a moment that Lamorna had decided to run away with her and was standing there with her hands planted on her hips. Jenyfer smiled, and gathered the dress into her arms. 'Alright.'

Kayrus dug through another crate, muttering to himself. 'Ah ha! And this, lass.' He passed her a small mirror with a long brass handle. The glass was cracked in one corner, a fractured line travelling from one side to the other. Heart pounding, Jenyfer raised the mirror to her face and looked at her reflection for the first time since she was a child.

The old sailor said nothing as she simply stared. Her skin was darker than she remembered, splattered with freckles, and her eyes were bright and shining, her lips the colour of freshly picked berries, the bottom plumper than the top. Her nose was pert, and her eyes – they were like sea-glass, a swirling mix of blues and greens and greys. The colour of the sky over the ocean before a storm crashed across the sky.

'This is what I look like,' she mumbled. 'I'd almost forgotten.'

Kayrus flashed her a smile, but his eyes were sympathetic. Jenyfer lowered the mirror and went to hand it back. 'Keep it,' was all the man said, so she did. On Kayrus' suggestion, she took another coat, socks, and a pair of sturdy leather boots that actually fit.

In one crate, Jenyfer was delighted to find a stack of washcloths and towels, but also soap, and a hairbrush. Cradling her new things, she turned towards the ladder, then stopped, glancing at Kayrus over her shoulder. 'Thank you,' she said softly.

The sailor looked at the ground. 'No bother, lass.'

Jenyfer swallowed. 'That day, with the Witchfinder...'

Kayrus' head snapped up.

'I didn't know what I was doing,' she said quickly. 'I just want you to know that. All of you. Whatever happened that day, I didn't mean it.'

The navigator cleared his throat, then rubbed at his cheek, whatever he was going to say vanishing as he settled on a nod instead.

Jenyfer returned to her cabin to unload her treasures. Tymis was right. She stank, but she had no water for a wash. Fresh water was for drinking, not bathing. Jenyfer stared longingly at the soap, then sighed. Leaving her feet bare and the clothes on her bunk, she tied her hair back with a strip of leather, then made her way to the deck.

Ordes was waiting for her, arms folded, leaning against the main mast, his unearthly smooth face clear of emotion. His eyes swept over her quickly and he nodded in approval. 'Let's begin,' he said simply.

'What, just like that?'

'Sure. Everything has to start somewhere. Here.' He tossed something at her; it was a dagger, hilt and blade tumbling over one another smoothly. Jenyfer shrieked and jumped out of the way. The weapon clattered on the deck near her feet. 'You could have killed me!'

'It's blunt, Jen,' Ordes said, smothering a laugh. 'Pick it up.'

She did, recognising it as the dagger he used for a paperweight, the one she had held to his throat. Jenyfer swallowed, running the tip of her finger over the blade, squaring her shoulders and lifting her eyes to Ordes'. 'I want you to promise me one thing.'

'And what is that?'

'Treat me like you would anyone else. Don't go easy or try to be nice because I'm a woman,' she said, tossing the dagger back at him; he snatched it out of the air, looking at her curiously. 'Give me something sharp.'

Ordes grinned. 'Alright,' he concurred, setting the blunt dagger on top of a nearby barrel, withdrawing another two from the sheaths at each of his hips. He gave her a quick look and for a moment, she thought he'd toss one at her, but he held it out, hilt first.

Jenyfer could feel the men on deck watching her every move as she approached Ordes and closed her fingers around the hilt of the dagger. He didn't let it go.

'A dagger is a close-quarters weapon,' he told her softly. 'To use it, you have to be close to someone, unless you've got a good throwing arm.'

'I could hit my sister with a rock if I tried hard enough,' Jenyfer said. 'Have you ever stabbed anyone with this dagger?'

'What do you think?' he asked.

'I think you haven't,' she said softly. 'I think it takes a certain type of man to be violent, to want to hurt others, and I don't think you're that sort of person.' Her resolve wavered as she thought of Bryn. 'I could be wrong,' she added. 'But I don't think I am.'

Ordes still hadn't let go of the blade of the dagger. He hadn't looked away from her face; she felt his thumb brush the tip of her finger, making her shiver. He must have seen something in her expression, because he whispered, 'What happened to you? Why didn't you come to the cave?'

'I don't want to talk about it,' Jenyfer said firmly. She tugged on the dagger; Ordes let his hand drop and nodded. He took a step back, indicating the daggers they both held.

'The blade has a double-edge,' he said. 'So it cuts in both directions. The trick is to get close enough to be able to use it, but to stay far enough away that one can't be used on you. There are two ways to hold it. Like this.' He flipped the dagger so his fingers were wrapped completely around the grip, the blade facing away from him, pointing towards the sky. 'Or like this.' He shifted his grip so the blade was facing towards the deck.

Jenyfer copied both grips, earning a nod. 'Now what?' she said. Around them, the men continued their work and the sun beat down. Jenyfer could feel her skin burning, but she would deal with it later. She could hear the mast creaking gently, the sails flapping in the wind, and the soft chatter of the men, the occasional grunt and groan.

'You need to keep your body behind the blade,' Ordes told her. 'And protect yourself with your other arm. Your knife hand is always out in front, Jen.'

He motioned her forward; Jenyfer did as she was instructed, stepping within range of Ordes' hands. She kept her eyes on his dagger, feeling the firm timbers of the deck beneath her feet, feeling the sun on her face. The muscles in her arms and shoulders were pulled tight.

'Relax your shoulders; be fluid, like the water, Jen,' Ordes murmured. 'And don't focus just on the dagger – focus on my face as well. You have to learn to read my expression, work out what I'm going to do, how I'm going to move, before I do it.'

She nodded, lifting her eyes from the dagger to his face. 'How do I do that?'

Ordes winked. 'That would be telling. Now, I'm going to show you how to move, but slowly,' he added, a smile playing on his lips. 'Don't stab me, Jen.'

She swallowed and nodded again, deciding now was not the time to like the way he called her 'Jen'.

'I'm going to attack you—'

'What?' she practically shouted; a trickle of sweat began the journey down the side of her face. She wanted to wipe it away, but didn't, too scared to move in case he lunged at her.

'I won't hurt you. It's simple – if I move towards you, move away, stay out of my reach. If you can grab my knife arm – my wrist, for instance – do it. Then you can strike with your blade. Your aim is to get me to drop my weapon,' he said. 'Ready?'

Jenyfer took a shaky breath. 'No!'

'You'll be fine. Feel free to punch me,' he said, then stepped towards her.

She stepped back, heart pounding, staying out of his reach, like he said. Again and again. They moved around one another like dancers, Jenyfer keeping her eyes on Ordes' face, looking for something that would let her know what he was about to do, how he would move.

Sweat had gathered in Jenyfer's armpits and on the back of her neck. She could feel it sliding between her breasts and trickling down her forehead.

Without any warning, Ordes's movements became faster, his strikes more accurate as he closed the space between them, forcing Jenyfer to move, to keep her weight on the balls of her feet. He struck, she deflected. Saw the praise in his eyes. Again and again, until Jenyfer's song, which had been unusually quiet, like it knew she needed to concentrate, burst into life inside her. There was an urgent tone to it – it wanted her to move, to thrust the blade.

It wanted her to attack, not defend.

She side-stepped, then she lunged, slipping easily beneath Ordes' arm. She was smaller, shorter, and it gave her an advantage. She saw the surprise on his face; she moved, lunged again, and it was him deflecting her, blocking her, moving back, out of her way. Jenyfer struck out with her spare hand, struck out at his chest with her fist, then lunged again.

He spun out of her way, as swift and agile as a bird. She darted forward, lunged, swept the dagger upwards; he moved again, slipped out of her reach. Frustrated, she pulled her bottom lip between her teeth. One step forward, hand steady. Wrist loose. A feint to one side, then her dagger connected with something firm, but slightly soft.

Frowning, she glanced down at the same time Ordes gasped.

'I told you not to stab me!'

'I'm sorry!' Jenyfer said. She still had hold of her dagger. With a cry of dismay, she dropped it, the weapon clattering to the deck at her feet, narrowly missing her toes. The blade was decorated with bright red blood. Her stomach turned over. 'Shit!'

'I'm okay,' Ordes told her, pressing his hand to his ribs. 'You didn't hit anything important.'

'I stabbed you,' Jenyfer whispered. 'I can't believe I stabbed you.'

'Well,' he said, ignoring the crew, who had realised what had happened and who were laughing. Hard. She wasn't sure how she felt about that. 'You'd better patch me up then.'

By the time they'd made it below deck and into her cabin, Jenyfer had apologised twenty-five times. 'I'm fine,' Ordes told her, letting her take him by the arm and lead him across the small room. She made him sit on the edge of the bed while she muttered to herself, rummaging through the top drawer of the dresser, a triumphant little sound escaping her as she turned to him.

'Show me,' she demanded. Ordes noticed she held a needle and thread.

'You know what, I think it's fine,' he said.

Jenyfer's eyebrows rose. 'I stabbed you. With a very sharp dagger. You will need stitches.'

'Have you ever stitched anyone?' he challenged.

'Yes,' she answered. 'Myself.' She patted her thigh. 'Accident with a sharp object. Fish filleting knife. I slipped. Now, show me.'

He ran his eyes over her, taking in the tight lines of her face, the wild hair and her bottom lip, swollen and ripe. She'd been chewing on it the whole way down here, muttering and cursing to herself in between apologising. 'You stitched yourself?'

'My aunt was out and my sister wasn't going to do it – Lamorna doesn't like blood,' Jenyfer explained, setting the needle and thread down on top of the dresser and reaching for a cloth instead, dipping it into a bowl of water he hadn't noticed her preparing. She wrung the cloth out and turned to him, her face firm. 'Now, are you going to let me fix my mistake?'

With a sigh, Ordes removed his hand and lifted his shirt, exposing his ribs, and the wound, to Jenyfer's eyes. She crouched before him, a frown on her face as she examined him.

'It's not deep,' she said eventually. 'You won't need stitches.'

Ordes let out a breath; she chuckled.

'You were scared.'

'I wasn't.'

'Never been stitched before?'

'I've never been stabbed before,' he shot back.

Jenyfer sat back on her heels. 'I didn't mean to stab you.'

He nodded. 'I know.' He kept his eyes on her face as she leant forward and gently cleaned around the wound with the cloth. 'What happened?'

She didn't look at him, but her hand stilled against his ribs. 'What do you mean?'

'One moment you were defending yourself, the next... something changed. I saw it in your eyes,' Ordes said softly.

She stood, keeping her face turned away from him as she opened the top drawer of the dresser again and found a bandage. 'Isn't the point of a knife fight to win it?'

'I suppose,' he said.

'Well then,' Jenyfer said, returning to kneel before him. 'I won, didn't I? Lift your arm,' she commanded. He did what he was told; she didn't look at him until she'd tucked the end of the bandage in securely.

'Jen—'

The ship pitched suddenly and she lost her footing, falling into him and sending him tumbling backwards onto her bed. She fell with him, crushing his ribs and sending a bolt of searing heat through him. He sucked in a pained breath; Jenyfer scrambled off him, face pinched.

'You need to keep that clean,' she told him, busying herself with the cloth and the bowl. She was skittish, her eyes darting around, brushing against everything but never settling, hands shaking slightly where they rested on the bowl, and he knew instinctively it had nothing to do with the fact she'd just stabbed him. Whatever had happened to her was more than her magic being released. She held her shoulders differently – tighter, bunched up.

Ordes sat up. 'Jenyfer,' he said. 'Why didn't you—'

'Keep that clean,' she ordered, and swept from the cabin, taking the bowl and bloodied cloth with her.

CHAPTER 30

Jenyfer's body *hurt*. Her shoulders were stiff, thighs burning with each step, and her fingers were sore from holding weapons, from making fists that she threw at Ordes' face. Since the stabbing incident, he'd decided she was not allowed to have a weapon, either sharp or blunt, so he was teaching her to use her fists instead. So far, all she'd hit was air. He was too fast, too swift on his feet. Her backside was sore from where he'd swept her legs out from under her and put her on her arse, leaving her blinking up at the brightness of the sky and wanting to cry.

But she'd told him not to take it easy on her and, even though she sensed he wasn't being as severe as he'd be on someone else, she was grateful he wasn't treating her like she was made of glass.

She rolled her shoulders to loosen her muscles, curling her fists, ready for the next round. She'd hit him this time – she was determined. She'd hit him right in the mouth, the one that kept asking her questions she didn't want to answer. He couldn't talk if he had no teeth, could he? Before she could try, the Captain approached them, and Ordes relaxed his stance and stepped back, joining his father.

Father and son assumed identical poses – arms folded, feet shoulder-width apart, faces slightly creased as they worked through whatever was churning around in their individual heads. They had the same smile, Jenyfer noted, watching as the corner of Tymis' lips curled up and Ordes' copied him.

Tymis' voice broke the silence. 'Is she ready?'

Ordes hesitated before replying. 'She can stab things.'

'So I heard,' Tymis mumbled, smothering a chuckle.

Jenyfer planted her hands on her hips, her temper springing to life before she could stop it. She was hungry and tired and sore and didn't like them talking about her like she wasn't standing right in front of them. 'I don't think I want to be a pirate. Let me off at the nearest port.'

'You said you wanted to be useful,' Tymis reminded her.

Jenyfer glared at them both. 'How is any of this helping? I'm tired and sore and I really want to find my sister. She might be a pain, but she's my sister, and it's my fault she's wherever she is right now. So if you won't help me find her, let me off this ship.'

Neither Tymis nor Ordes spoke.

Jenyfer closed her eyes, pinching the bridge of her nose. She thought of Lamorna's calm, her capacity to remain poised no matter what the situation. When she opened her eyes, it was to see Ordes, arms folded, that one corner of his mouth still tilted upwards. The Captain had moved away and was engaged in conversation with one of the men, but Jenyfer could sense him half-watching and listening.

'Alright,' Ordes said eventually. 'No more fighting. You aren't very good at it anyway.'

'Thanks,' Jenyfer responded sourly.

'You're not in Kernou anymore. You have nothing to fear out here, so, let's teach you to use your magic,' he said.

'No.' The response was automatic.

'Why not?'

'Because I said so.'

'You know that isn't a reason.'

'It's reason enough. You're as annoying as my sister,' Jenyfer said, rubbing at her temples. A droplet of water hit her in the face. She looked up, startled. A sphere of water hovered in the air beside Ordes' head. Casually, he flicked his fingers. Droplets shot from the sphere to hit Jenyfer on the cheek.

'Stop,' she demanded.

He didn't. 'Make me. It's instinct, Jen. Think about what you want to happen, and make it happen.' Another droplet, this one landing on her nose; she wiped it away furiously. 'Your aunt bound you before, but now you can use it. No one will stop you. Show me what you've got.'

'I've got a headache,' she snapped.

Another droplet. Another. One more.

Jenyfer's anger shot through her and her inner song surged. She took a deep breath, feeling something tugging inside her. She closed her eyes, concentrating on the feeling and when she opened them, Ordes was watching her. His sphere of water still hung in the air near his head. Jenyfer's fingers tingled. She curled them into fists, then let them go.

Ordes' sphere exploded, drenching him.

'Well,' he murmured. He was dripping wet, his dark hair plastered to his head, his clothes streaming with it and she noted, scowling as she did so, clinging to his body and accentuating every detail of what was beneath his clothes.

He took a step towards her, and then stopped, frowning. 'What—'

Hundreds of spheres of water suddenly rose from the ocean, hanging in the air. Jenyfer watched them, the way they caught the sunlight and sparkled like jewels. Her blood was thrumming, her song alive, twisting and dancing as she realised she could *feel* all that water.

The crew had stopped what they were doing and were watching the spheres as well.

'Jenyfer,' Ordes said. 'Put them down.'

'It isn't me,' she whispered.

'Well, it isn't me.'

The spheres rose higher, until they hung directly above the deck.

'What do I do?' she said tightly. The spheres began to wobble, then they joined together, merging to become one very large ball of water. 'Ordes... what do I do?'

'Let go,' he told her. 'Let go of the water.'

'I'm not holding it,' she cried, but then realised he was right. She was holding it. She could still feel it, like it was part of her. She took a deep breath. Instinct, he'd said. As she exhaled, Jenyfer imagined all that water was back in the ocean. The ball of water fell from the sky, heading right for the deck. Ordes lifted his hands; the sphere halted, then, he waved his hands lazily and the water flung itself back into the sea.

Silence rang out across the deck.

Before anyone could speak, Jenyfer rushed below deck, her feet stumbling on the ladder. She hurried down the passageway towards her room, mouth dry, heart thundering, her song singing triumphantly. Footsteps followed her.

Ordes caught her at the door, taking hold of her arm. 'How did you do that?'

'Do what, exactly?'

'You took control of my water.'

'Your water? It belongs to the sea,' Jenyfer answered, pulling her arm free and flinging her door open. She hurried inside; he followed.

'And then—'

'I don't have any answers, so don't bother asking any questions,' Jenyfer said quickly.

Ordes shut the door behind him. 'It's okay to be scared.'

'I'm not scared,' she responded. Her knees gave out suddenly and she pitched towards the floor as a wave of exhaustion washed over her. Ordes moved quickly, his arms closing around her before her face met the floor. He hauled her up, holding her against him. The wetness from his shirt soaked into her clothes as she lifted her head to look at him through hazy eyes.

He was so close she could see every individual eyelash. The warmth of his breath fanned her face. She licked her lips as he met her eyes, shifting against her. She realised one of his hands was pressed into her lower back and a shiver passed through her. Jenyfer swallowed; heat spread its way through her body, starting in her belly, then dropping deeper, until it coiled like a spring between her legs. Unconsciously, she clenched her thighs together. She couldn't speak.

'We need to teach you how to control what's inside you,' Ordes said.

'If not Lyonesse, then I need to go to Avalon,' Jenyfer managed. 'My aunt said...'

Ordes' face tightened. 'You can't.'

'What do you mean?'

'While you're on this ship, you won't be going to the Isle.'

'You said you'd get me there!'

'I said I would try, but I never said it would be this ship that took you,' he said.

'Then let me off this ship.' Her song suddenly flared to life and a strange surge of power crept through her, settling in her throat, coating her tongue. Power that she had only ever felt once before, the night Lamorna vanished beneath the waves. Jenyfer licked her lips again, and repeated the request, this time with conviction, her words an order. 'Let me off this ship or take me to Avalon.'

Ordes held her eyes; his breath hitched and his mouth dropped open a fraction, those full lips parting. She had the overwhelming desire to kiss him, to feel those lips on hers, to taste him again. The heat in her belly became a roaring flame, a glorious rush of it. The sound came from deep within her throat, warm and strong and tingling with power as she began to hum, her whole body vibrating with the depth of the sound. Something compelled her to reach out and touch Ordes' face, so she did, her fingers stroking his cheek as his arms tightened around her.

'Take me to Avalon,' Jenyfer whispered. She could hear her heart, its thundering rhythm, beating in time with her song. She trailed her fingers down Ordes' cheek again.

His face spasmed. Beneath the melody of her song she heard him swallow. He moved closer to her and her breathing quickened at the thought he was going to kiss her. But he didn't. Her knees gave out as another wave of exhaustion swept over her, threatening to wash her away.

Ordes scooped her off the ground, carried her to the bed and put her down as the music in her head shifted; it became soft and gentle, a lullaby, promising sleep and rest. Her heart was beating so fast she thought it would explode as he stood over her, nothing but a silhouette against the light pouring in through the porthole. Slowly, he leant forward, one hand braced either side of her head. She swallowed as panic seized her and would have flung herself from the bed but her limbs were heavy and her head spun.

'Stop,' she managed instead, her voice a croak, dry and frightened.

Ordes pulled away, his eyes roaming over her features. 'What happened to the woman I met in the stone circle? The woman who showed such fire when she spoke in the sea caves?' He paused. 'What happened to her? Where did she go?'

Jenyfer's vision was hazy, darkness closing in at the edges. Ordes sighed, pulling his hand through his hair in a gesture she'd learnt meant he was conflicted, before he moved away. He was at the door before he spoke again. 'I don't know what's happened to you, but all I can tell you is you're safe here. No one will hurt you.'

'You want to know what happened to me?' Jenyfer yawned. Her limbs were heavy, eyelids sliding closed. All she wanted was to let the motion of the ship send her to sleep. As her eyes fell closed, she wasn't sure if she spoke the next words, or simply thought them.

'I got married.'

CHAPTER 31

Married. She was married. So what the fuck was she doing locked in a cage in the town square? Where was her husband?

Ordes paced his cabin, as he had been most of the night. He could barely hear himself think and his magic was roaring beneath his skin. Had she been married when they met? Or had that... he froze.

If there was ever a time for you to take me with you, it's right now.

She hadn't come to the cave.

She'd basically told him she had no rights, no power of choice. She'd told him and he...

Ordes let his head fall into his hands and groaned. He had never stabbed anyone before but, if he ever laid eyes on the Chif of Kernou again, he imagined it wouldn't be too difficult to drive a blade into that man's chest.

The sun was high – golden light cut through the windows, unapologetic in its brightness. The sea was calm and *The Excalibur*'s passage through the water was smooth. Ordes padded across the floor to hunt through the pile of clothes on the armchair. He frowned. He'd given Jenyfer at least one shirt, so where were the rest? Still frowning, he opened the wardrobe. There they were. Hanging. On hangers. Neatly.

He was unable to stop the grin creeping across his face as he wondered when she'd done that, and why. Still smiling, he changed his clothes, then splashed his face with water from the basin on the washstand, before going in search of food. The galley was empty, but he found some bread and an apple, devouring the bread and pocketing the apple before heading topside to find Jenyfer.

She was standing at the starboard side of the deck, hands resting on the railing. Ordes stared at her fingers, remembering what they felt like on his cheek, the strange tingle that had carried from her skin to his. He chewed on his apple, not taking his eyes off her. That mass of hair was tied back with a strap of leather, and she was barefoot, dressed in dark trousers and a loose linen shirt.

Married... did she miss him, her husband? Ordes wondered, chewing on his apple. She didn't object to leaving her town, didn't tell him to wait, so what did that mean? Jenyfer's words had made a permanent home in his head, tumbling over and over, everything she had told him about Kernou and her family. Her desire to hide her magic. Her *fear* of what was inside her. And then, beneath all of that, there was the request, the *demand*, that he take her to Avalon; it beat through his blood, echoed in the rhythm of his heart. What had she done to him when she touched him?

She was no ordinary Magic Wielder, he was certain of that. He knew that, once, there had been many different fey creatures in the world and, according to his father's stories, children had been born to fey and humans. It was those children who became the first Magic Wielders. Perhaps Jenyfer carried some old magic in her blood, something not common anymore.

All he knew was her magic was different to his, and she had no control over it. Whatever she was, he'd promised he'd help her, as much as he could. Finishing the apple, he tossed the core into the water; it sailed past Jenyfer's head to land with a plop. Alarmed, she spun around, saw him standing there, and blushed.

Ordes took a deep breath and went to stand at her side, keeping his hands in his pockets. All he wanted to do was put his arms around her, tell her he was sorry, that he should have listened. He should have helped her when she first asked. Her face was closed, so he pushed everything aside and forced himself to focus.

'Magic today,' he told her quietly.

'I don't want to.'

He turned to face her, keeping his voice even. 'I know, but think about yesterday. A Magic Wielder not in control of their power is dangerous, Jenyfer.'

Her face fell, and then screwed up in a scowl. He went on before she could speak. 'Whatever you did to me yesterday... that was something I've never seen before, and I'm not talking about the water. I can't get your words, your voice, out of my head. I dreamt of Avalon, of a place I can't even remember.'

'I didn't mean it,' Jenyfer whispered, stricken. 'I have no idea how... I've never done anything like that before. I wish my aunt had told me more, told me something, *anything*. I couldn't control what happened yesterday, both with the water, and then... with you.'

'And that is the problem,' Ordes said gently. 'All Magic Wielders seem to share the basic traits. I told you our magic comes from the Old Ones, and while we are not the same as them, we share that magic. I can teach you enough that you can control the base of your power; or, at least, not hurt yourself or anyone else. Understand?'

'Yes.' Her voice was small, nothing like the sound that had left her mouth yesterday.

He indicated the deck. 'Sit down.'

She looked around. 'Here?'

'Yes, here. Our cabins are too small – we might need space.'

The look Jenyfer gave him was alarmed, but she did as she was told, dropping to the hard timber of the deck to sit cross-legged. He sat facing her, mirroring her pose, aware those of the crew who were topside were watching them.

'Magic is simple and strange at the same time. Touch and taste, for example, smell, sight – our senses are heightened. We can see between worlds, Jenyfer, if we know what we're doing.'

'Can you do that?' she asked, eyes wide.

'No, but the Old Ones can,' Ordes answered.

'What are they? I mean, I know they're Gods, but...' Jenyfer's voice trailed off. 'My aunt told my sister and I stories when we were children, about the Old Ones and the realms, about magic. I had always wished the things she said were true, and now... I guess they were.'

'The Old Ones aren't the only immortal beings with magic. There are also the demi-gods, those given the name demons,' Ordes explained. 'There aren't many of them left, as far as I understand, but demi-gods give their allegiance to the Old Ones.'

'What happened to them?' Jenyfer asked quietly. 'The other demi-gods?'

Ordes shrugged. 'My father once said that they disappeared as people stopped believing in them. They might be immortal, but they aren't true gods. Think of them as existing between the realms I guess. They are usually connected to places and things.'

'Like storms?'

He nodded. 'Like storms. Your town still believes in the storm demon?'

'Some people do. I think it's been harder than the Chif imagined to get fishermen to stop believing in the bringer of storms,' Jenyfer answered. She took a deep breath. 'Alright. Teach me about magic.'

Ordes flexed his fingers and silver light shifted lazily over his knuckles. 'We will start with touch. Touch magic is easy, it's intuitive. The skin carries the emotions and thoughts of its owner – a simple touch can speak of many things. Objects can do this as well, but it's more like a whisper. The skin shouts at you.'

She was frowning. 'So how do you do it?'

Ordes shifted a little closer to her. 'Give me your hands.' He held out his hands, palms up, and slowly, cautiously, Jenyfer placed her hands in his. He opened his senses, his magic slipping beneath her skin. He was assaulted with emotion, waves of fear and longing and despair washing over him. It was enough to make him suck in a breath as another wave of guilt washed through him. He concentrated, keeping his magic just below the surface of her. She had no shield, and her mind was wide open.

'You have to learn to close your mind,' he murmured. 'I could read your thoughts, if I wanted to.'

Jenyfer ripped her hands free, giving him a terrified glance.

'I didn't, and I won't,' he assured her softly. He held out his hands again; cautiously she placed her palms in his, but this time, he kept the barrier between their minds firm. 'What I want you to do is reach out with your magic and try and tell me what I'm feeling.'

Her face screwed up. 'How do I do that?'

'Your power lives inside you – it's part of you, so imagine it like an extension of your body – say, an arm. Imagine that arm reaching beneath my skin. Then, you need to concentrate on what you want to know – in this case, what I'm feeling,' he said.

'Alright.'

She closed her eyes; immediately, he felt her magic brushing against his flesh. He let the mental barrier between them dissolve, and her magic rushed inside him, pushing and probing and ripping its way through his body.

Ordes grit his teeth. 'Slow down.'

'Sorry!' Jenyfer pulled her hands free of his and tucked them in her lap. Her eyes were wide, expression terrified.

'I'm fine,' he lied; his head was spinning and he felt light as air. He could hear music, so faint it was a whisper. 'What did you feel?'

Colour rushed into her cheeks. 'I...' She swallowed and dropped her eyes. 'I felt... it's hard to describe.' She sighed and rubbed at her neck. 'It was like a heaviness, warm and smooth and aching. You want something, more than one thing, and it's confusing you.'

Ordes inhaled sharply. Everything she described was what he had felt when she'd used that strange compulsion on him, stirring a longing to return to the place of his birth. But it was more than that, he realised, his frown deepening. It was more than Avalon and his mother. Whatever Jenyfer had done to him had stirred a deep longing for *her*, one that now rushed back to swallow him. His hands were shaking. He wanted to lean over and kiss her, crush her to his chest and bury his fingers in the mass of her hair.

It was too much. She was too close to him. Jenyfer was still looking at her hands but she glanced up in surprise when he stood quickly, dusting off his backside.

'Enough for now,' he said. 'I don't want to push you. It can be draining and it's a lot to take in, especially after what happened yesterday. You should rest.'

It was bullshit, and she knew it. A frown crossed her features. 'I feel fine.'

But I don't.

She was watching him, those sharp eyes trying to see inside him. Her magic felt deep and dark, like a wave. *She called a fucking syhren to the beach, for the sea's sake,* he reminded himself. *What did you expect?*

Maybe he should take her to the Isle.

Ordes shook his head. Beneath the sound of the waves and the blaring heat of the sun, beneath the pounding of his heart, he could still hear Jenyfer's voice, low and sweet and tinged with power. It thrummed through him, settling behind his ribcage.

'What do you know about your magic?' he asked.

She blinked up at him. 'Nothing. I mean, nothing really. I've always felt... things.' She paused, and he waited for her to go on. 'The sea. I've always felt the sea. I could hear it, even when I wasn't near it. The waves, the pull of the water. And sometimes, especially if I was upset or nervous, water would leak from my skin.'

He held out his hand; droplets of water crept from his skin to dangle like translucent jewels from the tips of his fingers. 'I've always assumed it's because I'm always on the water, like it's now a part of me.' He caught her eye. 'What else?'

'Dreams,' she whispered. 'Of the sea, mostly, and a song—'

'A song?' His tone was sharp. His heartbeat sped up. 'What song?'

She shrugged. 'I don't know. It's just always been in my head.'

'Can you sing it for me?' he asked. The back of his neck tingled with premonition but he shoved it away, focusing on the terrified woman. She stared back at him, defiance and shame mingled on her face.

'I can't sing,' she said simply. 'I've never been able to sing.'

Before he could say anything else, she climbed swiftly to her feet and walked away from him, going to lean against the railing again, her face turned to the ocean. Ordes jumped when Kayrus appeared beside him.

'There's something different about her,' the old man mumbled. 'The men all sense it – it's as if they all want to be near her, but they know she's dangerous, like a fire.'

'A fire?'

Kayrus nodded thoughtfully. 'You hold your hands out to the flame, knowing that if you got too close, it would burn you, but you still do it. Jenyfer is like that.'

CHAPTER 32

Arthur placed trembling hands either side of the stone vessel. He could feel the magic rolling from it, ancient and powerful, borne of the land and the sea and everything that shaped the world around him. In the air he could smell sunshine and water, salt and burning sand, the damp of the forest, mist and soil. The vessel was warm to touch, humming and tingling beneath Arthur's skin.

The Grail. He knew what it was, instinctively, just like he could understand the stream of whispered words that flowed from the Grail in a language he had never spoken.

The King that shalt be.

King.

Arthur shuddered, trying to withdraw his hands, but they were stuck to the stone. Panicked, he tugged, but the ancient vessel clung tighter to him, the skin on his fingers flecked with granite and quartz and mica. A weight pressed down on his head but he couldn't lift his hands to feel what it was.

'Why do you fight it?'

Jalen's voice came from behind him. Arthur closed his eyes as Jalen's footsteps echoed off the floor of the main Hall in his father's house. The altar to the One God was gone, as were the seventy candles. Instead, a simple stone table sat in its place, the Grail resting on its top.

'Arthur.'

He opened his eyes. Jalen was standing before him, his hair haloed in gold from the sunlight beaming into the room through the ornate windows at his back. His eyes shone with reflected light and all the colours of a storm-kissed sky rippled over his face.

'You're not real,' Arthur said, his voice low, his heart breaking all over again.

'I'm as real as you,' Jalen replied. He ran the tip of one long finger along the edge of the Grail - the stone beneath Arthur's hands thrummed harder in response. 'Why do you fight it?'

'Fight what?'

'What you are destined to become.'

'I don't understand,' Arthur whispered. 'I'm not a King. There is no King.'

'There was, once, and there will be again,' Jalen replied quietly.

Arthur swallowed, his throat tight. 'Where are you?'

Jalen smiled, a gentle curving of generous lips. Arthur wanted to kiss him. He wanted to lift his hands and cup Jalen's face between his palms but his skin belonged to the Grail. Jalen touched Arthur's cheek; his skin was cool, like water, and when he withdrew his hand, Arthur could feel droplets of liquid slowly slide down his face.

'What are you?' he asked. The weight on his head grew heavier.

'You know what I am,' Jalen responded. The room fell into unnatural darkness; outside, clouds rushed across the sky and lightning lit up the world. The rumble of thunder reached through the house, slamming through the floor to curl into Arthur's bones.

He closed his eyes.

'Say it, Arthur.'

'I can't.'

'You can. Say it, and then look at me.'

The Grail was still thrumming beneath Arthur's skin, still whispering things he shouldn't be able to understand, but could. 'You're the bringer of storms. A demon. A demi-god.'

'Yes.'

Arthur opened his eyes.

Storm clouds were wrapped around Jalen's body. As Arthur watched, the blonde of Jalen's hair melted into a soft brown, the colour of seaweed. It lengthened and curled, until it tumbled over his shoulders, and his skin darkened, becoming smooth brown. Jalen's eyes, usually a sparkling blue, were a windswept grey, his pupils large and black.

He smiled.

Arthur smiled back. Jalen was still beautiful.

'Find the Grail, Arthur, and be what you were born to be,' Jalen instructed, before the clouds above his head swooped to cover his body. Thunder rippled across the world, and Jalen was gone.

Outside the small window of his cabin, there were no clouds covering the sky. The blueness of it was never-ending, as was the sheet of water that stretched to every corner of the horizon. Arthur sighed. Above him, he could hear the women of *The Night Queen* – voices reached his ears, too faint for him to make out what they were saying, but the ship was moving through the water, cutting a graceful path across the face of this new world Arthur found himself in.

His linen shirt and rough trousers – the clothes of a sailor – didn't fit properly but he didn't care. They were clean, and he was well-rested, despite the strange dream that still lingered in his head. He examined his fingers – his skin was its normal colour, no fleck of stone to be seen.

Arthur had no idea what time it was, what day it was, how long it had been since he had fled his home and left his father and the Witchfinder unconscious before the altar of the One God. He glanced at his hands again – his fingers were long, pale, the skin soft. No callouses marked his flesh. Hands that had never worked a day in their life, hands that had been schooled to hold a quill, to gently turn the crisp pages of a book as he scribed the Word, over and over again, each volume he copied distributed to the people of the village.

He hadn't lied to the Captain. He *had* enjoyed what he'd done to his father. Letting his magic free like that had been liberating – the look on Ulrian's face as Arthur's magic had wrapped around him and Arthur had thrown him to the floor with barely a thought... Ulrian had looked at him like he was a monster, and maybe he was; because Arthur had learnt that monsters wore different skins and different faces, and were as real as he was.

Then the Witchfinder had done something. Arthur had felt the man inside his head, and the realisation struck him like a slap. The Witchfinder was a Magic Wielder. The shock of it had given Arthur a strange surge of power as his magic rebelled against the force that tried to take hold of him. He didn't know what happened, or how, but the Witchfinder had crumpled to the ground, unconscious. So, Arthur had run.

His stomach grumbled. No one had left any food, so he supposed he was meant to go and find it himself. Aelle had shown him where the kitchen – the galley – was, so he left the cabin and made his way there, following the scent of bread and stewed apples. He'd been given a tour of the ship but could barely remember anything.

The galley was empty. 'Hello?' Arthur called.

Something shifted in the corner of his eye. He glanced at the table beside him to find a bowl of stewed fruit and a glass of water that wasn't there before. He swallowed, turning to face the table and the mysterious food.

'The ship has her own magic,' a voice said, making him jump.

Katarin Le Fey strode into the room, red hair swinging around her shoulders. She was wearing her weapons and he couldn't help but let his eyes linger on the cutlass and dagger at her hip. She smiled and let her hand drop to caress them, one at a time. He gulped, making her chuckle.

'You don't have to be afraid of me,' she said simply, gesturing to the table. 'Sit and eat. We have no cook – we don't need one. Whenever you're hungry, just come here and *The Night Queen* will provide. Although,' she added with a grin. 'We don't get a say in what she gives us. I hope you like apples. They seem to be the *Queen's* favourite.'

Arthur eyed the bowl again. It smelt delicious, so he sat, picked up the spoon and took a mouthful. Colours and sparks burst behind his eyelids. He might have moaned in appreciation.

'The fruit of Avalon,' Katarin said, slipping into the seat opposite him. 'The best apples anywhere in the world.'

Arthur gulped down another mouthful. 'Is that where we're going?'

'Not yet, but eventually. Niniane will call us home.'

'Your crew – where are they from?' Arthur asked.

'You would have to ask them,' Katarin replied. 'Some are human, some are faery, some are something between the two, but all have magic. They are skilled witches with different strengths.'

'Like Tahnet?'

'Yes.' The Captain waved her hand and his bowl vanished. He'd finished the stewed apples and not even realised. 'Come with me.'

Wordlessly, Arthur followed Katarin out of the galley, through the dark and up the ladder into the blinding sunlight. She led him to the starboard side, resting her hands on the railing and gazing out to sea. 'You know what we do?'

He swallowed. 'I have heard rumours.'

'If those rumours tell about how we save Magic Wielders across the continent from the pyre, or how we go into towns and villages and rescue women accused of witchcraft before they can be dragged naked through the streets and strung up for everyone to stare at before being carted away to die, then yes, the rumours are all true.'

The Captain of *The Night Queen* was not what Arthur had expected. For starters, he'd assumed she'd gut him like a fish and toss him overboard, or torture him for information. Katarin Le Fey carried herself with authority but, beneath it, Arthur could sense vulnerability, and pain. He swallowed, feeling around the edges of her mind with his shaky magic, encountering a wall that shimmered and quivered when he brushed against it, like water.

She turned a smug smile on him. 'You won't get in there. Better people than you have tried.' Katarin leant one hip against the railing, folding her arms over her chest. She was dressed much as the rest of the crew were in a simple shirt and vest, men's trousers and a coat with glimmering gold buttons. She considered him with interest. 'You don't know how to use your magic at all, do you?'

'I know a bit,' he retorted, then fidgeted under the doubtful look she gave him. 'I knew someone who was a Magic Wielder. He told me things.'

'Theory is vastly different to practise,' Katarin said, but not unkindly. She turned back to face the water. 'What was it like in Kernou?'

'Depends what you're asking about,' Arthur mumbled.

'Belief in the One God has spread, Arthur. The Sacellum's influence has grown considerably, and quickly,' Katarin said. 'People are turning from the Old Ones and the Old Ways in droves, and no one knows why. You lived it. What makes people believe in a god like that? What makes them turn their backs on the beliefs of their ancestors and follow a nameless, faceless god?'

Arthur swallowed. 'I don't know. Maybe they're looking for answers.'

'Answers to what?'

'The same things everyone wants answers to,' Arthur said softly.

Katarin was quiet, considering his words, and she didn't speak again. They stood and watched the water together until, eventually, she left, returning to her cabin. Arthur stayed where he was. No land was visible from the deck of the ship, nothing but water, still and calm, reflecting the clouds that were bunched on the horizon. He smiled as a brisk breeze skimmed across the ocean, fingers of it curling over the railing of the ship and caressing his cheek.

A storm demon indeed.

And Arthur was a Magic Wielder.

His smile deepened as something clicked into place inside him.

CHAPTER 33

Tomorrow night, *The Excalibur's* crew would be going ashore in Skulls Rest. Ordes would have to go below deck and double check the goods were ready for sale, and double check the list of things they needed to buy. The textiles they'd been carrying around for over a month would fetch a good price. There was no point in trying to sell spices in Skulls Rest – the spice groves and clove plantations stretched over the flat lands behind the town.

They needed food, rum and sail cloth, sewing supplies. Ordes finished his list and slid it into his pocket as someone knocked on his door.

Jenyfer, wearing an expression somewhere between pleading and scowling. Iouen was lingering in the background, a broad grin on his face.

'Skulls Rest,' she said.

'Yes?'

'Am I going ashore?' she asked simply.

'Yes.'

She frowned at his single word answers. 'Okay, then I need a bath.'
'A bath?'

'Yes, Ordes. That thing where you fill a tub with warm water and wash yourself, with soap preferably.' Sarcasm dripped from every syllable. Iouen was barely containing his laughter. Jenyfer folded her arms. 'I need a proper bath, not a wash in chilly water from a bucket,' she added, her scowl deepening. Ordes wanted to smooth it away with his fingertips. He shoved his hands in his pockets instead.

'Right. There are two bathing tubs on this ship. One is in the Captain's cabin, and the other...'

'Is here, in yours, yes,' Jenyfer declared. 'I know. Why do you get a bathing tub?'

'I'm second in command,' Ordes reminded her.

'So, can I use it? If I'm going ashore I need a bath, Ordes. I stink and my skin feels disgusting. I need to be clean,' she added, holding his gaze.

You hold your hands out to the flame, knowing that if you got too close, it would burn you, but you still do it. Kayrus was right, Ordes thought. This woman was like a fucking fire and he wanted nothing more than to touch her, even if she melted his flesh. His insides were burning. He ran his hand through his hair, and then stepped aside, motioning her into his cabin. Before he closed the door, he caught Iouen's eye – his friend raised his eyebrows suggestively. Ordes gave him the finger, mouthing a 'fuck off.' Jenyfer was standing in the middle of his cabin, her eyes crawling over the room, from the mess that littered the floor to the clothes draped all over the armchair once more.

'If I'd known I'd be entertaining again, I'd have cleaned up,' Ordes quipped.

She laughed. 'I just want to bathe, Ordes. No entertainment is necessary.'

'Behind the screen,' he said, pointing to the far corner of the cabin.

Jenyfer just nodded and disappeared behind the bathing screen. 'How do I fill it?' she called a moment later.

THE CALL OF THE SEA

'Right. Sorry.' Ordes clicked his fingers and soon, the sound of the tub filling echoed around the cabin. Jenyfer sighed in delight.

'Now that is a good use of magic,' she declared when the tub stopped filling. She muttered to herself as she stripped, while he made himself look out the porthole at the sparkling sea. He heard her get into the tub, heard her grateful sigh. 'Oh, gods, that's better. If this was my tub, I'd be in it all the time. Do you have soap? I forgot to bring some.'

'On the shelf near the tub.' Ordes grit his teeth, tried to think about anything except the very naked woman in his bathtub. Behind his bathing screen. Two metres away. The cabin wasn't large enough – there wasn't anywhere he could go where he couldn't hear her, couldn't imagine what—

'I'm going to check on something,' he called, keeping his voice light, completely nonplussed.

'Take your time – I'm fine here,' Jenyfer replied with a sigh. 'You have no idea how amazing this is.'

He did.

He really did.

Ordes ripped open his door so forcefully he almost pulled it off the hinges, and found Iouen leaning against the bulkhead examining his fingernails.

'Not a word,' Ordes mumbled, closing the door behind him.

'You're looking a little flushed.' Iouen laughed. 'Need someone to stand watch while you cool off somewhere? Or maybe you'd like me to bring you a bucket of cold water, Ordes?'

'Was this your idea?' he demanded, keeping his voice low.

'The lady wanted a wash, what was I supposed to do?' Iouen replied innocently.

'Tell her she smelt fine!'

'She does, but come on, you left yourself wide open, mate.'

Ordes pinched the bridge of his nose between his forefinger and thumb.

289

'There's a naked woman in your cabin,' Iouen added, most unhelpfully.

'Yes, thank you. Now fuck off and do something useful. Check over this,' Ordes ordered, pulling the list of needed supplies from his pocket and thrusting it at his friend. Iouen took the list, whistling as he sauntered down the passageway. Ordes counted to ten, and went back into his cabin. Jenyfer was still in the tub – he could hear her splashing around happily, the scent of soap floating through the air. He flung himself into his armchair, lip pulled between his teeth.

'Oh. I forgot a towel,' Jenyfer called from behind the screen.

Of course she did.

'And my clothes.'

Fuck.

'Ordes?'

'Yep sure. One towel and one shirt coming up. My pants won't fit you.'

The sound of water sloshing against the edge of the tub carried across the cabin. 'I'm not walking out of here practically naked. Get me a belt.'

'Sure thing boss,' he managed.

The thought of her wearing his clothes, again... Ordes swallowed, gathered what she needed, and held them out around the edge of the screen. Wet fingertips brushed his. He jumped.

'Thank you,' Jenyfer said quietly.

All he could manage was a nod. He returned to the armchair and waited. When she appeared, it was with a towel bundled around her head. His shirt hung to her knees, which, he realised, were bare. His pants and the belt were hanging over her arm.

'You were right. Your pants don't fit, even with a belt,' she said, tossing his pants onto the bed. The belt followed it, then she sighed and sat down, unwinding the towel and beginning to dry her hair. She hummed to herself, a lazy, happy sound.

'You're stealing all my shirts. I have a theory,' he said suddenly.

She paused, glancing at him between strands of damp hair. 'Oh?'

'You want me to be shirtless forever.'

She laughed, but to him, it sounded shaky. 'You've seen through my plans. Whatever will I do now,' she said, continuing to dry her hair.

'If you want me naked, all you have to do is ask,' he answered.

Jenyfer stopped what she was doing, straightening and pushing her hair back from her face. Her eyes moved over him so slowly he wondered if it was possible to burst into flames. 'I'll let you know.'

It was his turn to laugh.

Jenyfer strode past him to retrieve her dirty clothes from the bathing area. With them tucked beneath her arm, she came to stand in front of him. 'I'm taking the towel,' she told him. He nodded, and stood, not realising how close they'd be. He couldn't back away without falling over the chair and she didn't move either, but he didn't miss her quick intake of breath.

The towel dangled over her shoulders, and her hair was still slicked with water. 'Your hair is still wet,' Ordes commented.

'It's impossible to dry,' Jenyfer said, her eyes pinned to his. 'My aunt used to complain about it all the time.'

Slowly, tentatively, he reached out and unwound the towel from her neck and shoulders. 'Turn around,' he said. He caught the hint of a smile before she did what she was told. His shirt slipped off one of her shoulders, exposing milk-pale skin. No freckles littered her flesh, although they were scattered across the bridge of her nose. Gently, he scooped her hair from her neck, and bundled it in the towel.

'You're supposed to squeeze it, not rub,' Jenyfer mumbled.

He did what he was told, squeezing the length of her hair gently.

'I liked having a roommate,' he told her quietly, the words out of his mouth before he could stop them.

Jenyfer chuckled. 'Even one who hogs the bed?'

'Especially one who hogs the bed,' he said.

She turned to look at him; her hair slid free of his hands to tumble over one shoulder. 'Do you want me to come back, Ordes?'

Her voice was low, thick and heavy. He swallowed, and made himself speak.

'Now that you know where I keep the sharp objects, I'm a little frightened.'

She rolled her eyes. 'You know I didn't mean to stab you.'

'Liar,' he whispered. 'I think you stabbed me because you wanted to see me with my shirt off.'

'Is that what you think?' Her voice was low, and her eyes dropped to his mouth.

'Like I said, you only have to ask.' Ordes could barely hear his own words over the pounding of his heart. She was so close.

Jenyfer smiled. 'There's still water in the tub. It'll be cold now, though,' she added.

Ordes swallowed. He slid his finger beneath her chin, tilting her head up to his. 'Are you offering to wash my back for me, Jenyfer?'

She pulled her bottom lip between her teeth, then pushed herself onto her toes so her mouth grazed his, so lightly he wondered did he imagine the touch. 'I think you can manage.'

'Jen,' he murmured. 'What is this? Between us?'

She swallowed. 'I don't know.'

'I need to ask,' Ordes said softly. 'Your—'

Jenyfer stepped away from him suddenly, the spell broken as she backed towards the door. 'I don't want to talk about it.'

'Did you—'

She flung the door open, and left.

Chapter 34

Skulls Rest was a sprawling village clinging to the coast at the southernmost tip of Teyath. Jenyfer was surprised to learn it was a fortified town, complete with stone walls, gates, and watch towers. Iouen had explained that this was a trading port where pirates could gather to sell and buy wares plundered from captured ships. Whatever you wanted, he'd said, you could find in Skulls Rest.

The Excalibur had moored in the bay, along with at least five other ships, with Skulls Rest on one side and Arcdon, another trading port, on the other side of Skovers Bay. The area was known as the Pearl Coast and, from the deck of the ship, Jenyfer could see why. Under the moon, the water glimmered like a bed of pearls underwater, fractured light dancing over everything and, in the distance, the thin strip of sand twinkling like fallen stars.

It was beautiful. Her inner song hummed in delight, and then stopped abruptly when she remembered that Ordes had told her they were going to the tavern to unwind, put their feet up, and let the men have a night off – and Jenyfer would be joining them. She was exceptionally nervous. Apart from the ship, Kernou was the only place she had ever been, and she had no idea what to expect of a self-proclaimed pirate town.

Tymis would remain onboard – the Captain rarely left the ship, she'd learnt.

Apart from the crew of *The Excalibur,* these would be the first people Jenyfer had seen or talked to since leaving Kernou. Her belly swooped low as they climbed into the row boats and made their way across the water, then along the water-worn jetty and into the town itself.

The buildings in Skulls Rest were tall and narrow, built right to the edge of the water, with only a thin strip of sand visible between the stone foundations and the sea. From the short jetty, they stepped onto a cobbled street. The moon was bright above them, and lanterns hung outside most buildings. She'd learnt that behind the town were plantations of cloves, spices, and coconut palms.

Jenyfer smoothed her hands over her skirts. She was wearing the dress she had found in the cargo hold. In this light, it shimmered like the water. She'd never worn something with stays before, and had struggled her way through dressing herself. They still weren't as tight as they probably should be, but she could breathe and nothing was falling out into the night, so she was happy enough with her efforts. And, best of all, she was clean, her hair washed.

She thought the men would laugh at her, tell her to take the dress off and be sensible, but what she'd discovered when she appeared on deck ready for the journey to Skulls Rest was a crew dressed to impress. Gone were the ragged woollen pants, rolled to the knee, and the rough linen shirts and shabby vests. She'd encountered a collection of clean-shaven faces, the men wearing coats in bright colours, trousers that looked like they were made from velvet, polished boots and billowing silk shirts.

They looked proud, excited, and it had made her smile to see them that way. If there was one thing she could say for *The Excalibur's* crew, it was they worked darn hard – no one was ever idle – and their attitude towards her had begun to change, which she was grateful for. They flashed her little smiles now and then, and someone had even told her she looked nice.

As they were preparing to leave, there had been no sign of Ordes; Jenyfer had glanced around, fearful at the idea that he had changed his mind and wouldn't be coming with them. She swallowed, fingering the dagger at her hip. There was another one strapped to her thigh – something she'd not considered doing until the last moment. Her dress didn't have any pockets, or anywhere, really, to conceal another weapon and she could feel the cold bite of the steel against her skin.

Maybe Ordes was avoiding her? Her face burnt as she thought about her bath and, more so, what happened afterwards. She was astonished at her bravery, at the words that had left her mouth, at the implication of them, but there had been something inside her that day that wanted her to say those things, some wicked part of her that made her belly burn.

But then he'd asked about Bryn, and all the fire and courage that had sparked inside her dissolved and there was nothing but her fear. Fear that had clung to her ever since she'd hurried out of Ordes' cabin.

One of the sailors, Carbey, nudged her. 'Don't worry, lass. He'll be here. Just making himself pretty.'

'I wasn't worried,' she muttered, her comment drowned out by the men's laughter – at Ordes' expense, not hers. When he did finally appear, she couldn't stop looking at him.

He was beyond pretty. Dressed in a flowing black shirt, his dark, long coat and black trousers, his calf-high boots shining, skin silver under the moonlight, hair loose around his shoulders... that fire kick-started in her belly as his eyes found hers, and his lips curled in a smile.

Ignoring the men and their jibes about the pretty faery, Ordes stepped up and offered Jenyfer his arm, and he stuck close to her side during the short journey across the water – and was still close to her now.

It made her hot and cold at the same time. She concentrated on not tripping over her feet as they made their way into the narrow, winding streets of Skulls Rest, passing men stumbling along, others sitting on the ground sharing a bottle, singing off-key and at the top of their lungs. Jenyfer turned away from the couple enjoying what each other had to offer – in full view of everyone; her stomach twisted.

The crew cheered as the tavern came into view, their pace quickening.

From the outside, the *Cat's Claw* looked inviting. It was a large building tucked tight between a bakery and an apothecary, yellow light pouring through the windows into the world outside. A little thrill shot along Jenyfer's spine. She had never been in a tavern, only snuck glances through the windows in Kernou. She expected tables arranged in neat rows, music playing gently in the background; a bard, perhaps, singing ballads from far away places. She expected the smell of roasting meat, conversation and camaraderie.

She did not expect the front door to be violently flung open and a body tossed outside to land at her feet. She took a hasty step back as the man peered up at her. He blinked red-rimmed eyes, then climbed to his feet, giving her a bow of apology and tipping an imaginary hat, before staggering back inside.

Ordes gave her a smile. 'Ready to become acquainted with some real pirates?'

'What are we then?' someone grumbled from behind them.

'Dignified,' Ordes shot over his shoulder, still grinning. 'Although, tonight, be whatever you like.' He slipped his arm around Jenyfer's waist, lowering his head so he could whisper in her ear. 'Trust me – this is for your own good.' He gave her waist a quick squeeze; she jolted, and the look he flashed her was concerned, but he kept his smile in place. 'That dress...'

Jenyfer dropped her eyes. She shouldn't have worn it. Maybe she could get someone to take her back to the ship to change. 'What's wrong with it?' she whispered, cheeks hot.

'That dress was made for you,' he said, his breath tickling the skin on her neck. 'It clings to every part of you but shows nothing – meaning men, possibly some women, will want to see what's beneath.'

Jenyfer recoiled. 'I don't want people to think that.' Her heart was pounding; sweat broke out on her forehead and the back of her neck and her mouth felt like sand. She swallowed, then swallowed again, pulling a gulp of air into her lungs and feeling close to tears. She'd glanced at herself in the broken hand mirror Kayrus had found for her before she left the ship, her eyes sweeping over her face – the high cheekbones and slightly pointed chin, the sharp line of her jaw, lips that were always the red of fresh apples, and her sea-blue eyes. Jenyfer didn't know if she was pretty or not. No one had ever said she was, not that she expected them to, not in Kernou, where any sign of vanity was considered a sin in the eyes of the One God.

Ordes steered her away from the main doors. 'Jenyfer—'

She pulled out of his grip. 'I'm fine.'

'You're not.'

Fear made her angry. 'Don't tell me what I'm feeling.'

'Then talk to me,' he said.

She shook her head. 'No. Let's go.'

Jenyfer didn't know what she had expected – but it wasn't the chaos they encountered beyond the main doors. Tables and chairs were scattered about the cavernous room in no particular order; some were tipped on their sides and most of those that remained upright were occupied.

The air was thick and hot, the smell of bodies, rum, and food mingling to the point of overwhelm. She hesitated in the doorway, but not for long. Ordes tugged her inside, drawing her into the room. Great wooden beams held up the ceiling, lanterns dangling at equal intervals, throwing warm light over everything. Someone was playing a fiddle – the sound rushed across the room to plunge inside Jenyfer's chest. Her skin tingled and her heart raced as she let Ordes lead her, weaving through bodies and tables like water between pebbles. Men glanced up at them as they passed, and Jenyfer could feel their eyes on her back; her fingers brushed the hilt of the dagger at her hip.

They found a table unoccupied and sat. A pretty girl with dark hair and glowing eyes appeared almost instantly with drinks. She plonked a mug in front of them both and left, throwing a wink over her shoulder that Jenyfer knew wasn't for her.

The rum was warm, the spices sinking onto her tongue and making her sigh. Alcohol was another thing women had been denied in Kernou and Jenyfer drank carefully. It wouldn't take much for it to go to her head, and a tavern in Skulls Rest was probably not the place for her to get drunk for the first time.

The music continued; men were singing off-key and out of time, their voices falling over each other, clashing with the hum of conversation and the tell-tale tinkling of gambling as coins were scattered on tables. The discordant melodies made her head hurt but she ignored it, determined to enjoy the evening.

Jenyfer cradled her drink while Ordes had another. After a long sip, he set his mug down, resting an elbow on the table and plonking his chin onto it, angling his body towards her. His eyes walked her face.

'What?' Jenyfer asked nervously. She could feel other eyes on her but didn't dare look around to see who might be watching her.

'Most beautiful women know they're beautiful but you...'

'You think I'm beautiful?' Jenyfer whispered. Something inside her started to crack and unfold, something she hadn't even known was there.

'Why does that surprise you?'

She swallowed, squeezing her hands together in her lap. 'No one has ever said anything like that to me before. Most people never looked at me long enough to notice anything, except for the things they didn't like.'

'You want me to tell you what I like the most?' Ordes said softly. Jenyfer's stomach tightened, but she nodded, ignoring the whispered lecture about vanity in her sister's voice that started swirling through her head. 'Your eyes. There is something about them. I could look at your eyes all day, Jenyfer,' he added, but *his* eyes had fallen to her mouth.

A rush of heat speared through her, followed quickly by fear. She tried to summon up some of the bravery she'd felt in his cabin, with his towel dangling over her shoulders and nothing but his shirt separating their flesh, but she couldn't. The fire inside her had gone out, leaving her chilled.

Ordes lowered his voice. 'See that woman over there?' He nodded discreetly at a woman with dazzling blonde curls. She was across the room from them, perched on the lap of a man who appeared old enough to be her father. She was striking, dressed in a deep red gown, her breasts spilling out of the corset, lips painted the same shade as her dress. She tossed back her head and laughed, and every man within earshot turned to look at her.

'What about her?'

Ordes sat back, picking up his drink again. 'What those men fail to realise is that, while she is entertaining them, her friend is picking their pockets.'

It was only once he said it that Jenyfer could see, through the murky air and dim lights, the slender figure moving unnoticed throughout the group of men gathered around the blonde-haired woman.

'Man, or woman?' Ordes asked in a low voice.

Jenyfer chewed her bottom lip. 'Woman, but she's dressed like a man. I can tell she's a woman by how she moves.' The thief was young, her hair cropped short, and she was dressed in dark clothing. Jenyfer watched as she slipped her hand in and then out of a man's pocket, stashing whatever she had pinched in the pocket of her trousers. 'They don't notice her?'

'No, they're too distracted. Misdirection,' Ordes added. His eyes shifted around the room. 'And that is what we're about to do.'

Jenyfer's head whipped around so quickly she gave herself a crick in her neck. 'What?'

Ordes drummed his fingers on the table-top, his expression thoughtful. 'There's more to being a pirate than being able to stab things.'

'You didn't tell me I was going to be *stealing* from people,' she hissed, keeping her voice low, as his words sunk in.

'It's the perfect cover,' Ordes argued.

'Are you serious?'

'What we're going to do is this – I'm going to go to the bar for more drinks, and you are going to follow me. There's a group of men sitting at the table closest to the bar. You're going to take a fall, Jen. Hit the ground, pretend you've hurt your ankle. And, while you've got their attention, I'm going to rob them,' Ordes said simply. 'Of course, when one of them offers you a hand up, maybe puts his arm around you—'

Jenyfer shuddered.

'—because he won't be able to help himself, you're going to see if you can relieve him of the contents of his pockets,' Ordes finished. She gaped at him, then shook her head.

'I can't.'

'Why not? They're pirates. Whatever is in their pockets has probably been stolen already,' he added.

'No, I mean, I don't know how to do what she's doing.' Jenyfer nodded at the blonde woman. 'I can't hold the attention of a group of men like that.'

'Every man in this tavern has looked at you at least once, some more than once. And I can bet they're all thinking about driving a knife in my belly when we leave here. They're wondering what they have to do to have you all to themselves because, as far as they can tell, I'm your lover,' Ordes said casually.

Jenyfer felt the blood drain from her face. 'They don't think that.'

'They do. Watch the men at that table near the bar.' Before she could stop him, Ordes moved his chair closer to hers, until his legs were either side of her, one behind her and one pressed against her knees. Jenyfer's breath hitched as he shifted the length of her hair away from her neck, exposing her throat. He ran the tip of his nose along her skin, from collarbone to ear. She made to move away, unable to bear the shivers that were racing through her, but his arm slid around her middle. 'Watch them, Jenyfer,' he commanded.

She took a deep breath, then did what she was told.

As Ordes' lips touched her throat, she watched that group of men, took note of how their eyes seemed drawn to her, how they followed the movement of Ordes' mouth along her skin. Her body was burning again, her breathing thick. Unconsciously, Jenyfer tilted her head back, not taking her eyes from the men at the table, a fire smouldering in her belly, in her blood, inside her bones, as the fear dissolved and something else took hold of her, something powerful that thrummed through her veins.

Ordes' arm tightened around her, his lips brushing the shell of her ear. Jenyfer felt something shift inside her as she realised she liked it. She liked knowing people were watching her, that they couldn't look away. She liked how it made her feel; instead of vulnerable and exposed, she felt powerful, in control. And she liked the way Ordes' mouth was making her feel – like liquid, warm and heavy. She liked the feeling of his arm around her, how his fingers dug into her flesh.

A hum wandered lazily up her throat, sliding over her tongue. She smiled, her inner melody sneaking into the air, low and vibrating inside her mouth. She wound her fingers through Ordes' hair, pulling his head back so she could see his face. She wanted to kiss him, and by the fire burning in his silver eyes and the way his lips parted a fraction, he wanted to kiss her as well.

She wanted him to melt beneath her mouth.

She wanted control and, in that moment, she wanted him. She wanted to taste him, to crawl inside him, to delve into the very heart of what made him who he was.

The hum was a gentle vibration in the back of her throat. Ordes' hand rose to cup her cheek, sliding into her hair, fingers digging against her scalp. Jenyfer's head spun and as he moved closer to her, his lips grazing her cheek.

She felt his breath against her ear before he slowly sat back, keeping one arm around her. Her stomach was in knots, her body heavy, and there was music in her ears. She swallowed, shifting away from Ordes a fraction and rearranging her dress. When she was done, she glanced at him, her cheeks hot.

He wasn't watching her. His eyes were moving around the room, the lines of his face tight. He slipped his hand beneath the table to squeeze her leg, just above her knee. She opened her mouth to object, but he spoke instead, his voice low.

'What we're going to do is get up very slowly, and leave.'

'What?'

'Trust me,' he whispered. 'Take my hand, and don't let it go until we reach the boats.'

Jenyfer swallowed tightly. She didn't know what was going on, but Ordes' tone – and the tightness to his face – had her heart thundering, her pulse rapid. She couldn't sense anything wrong – music was still playing, men were still singing, people were drinking... but there was something she couldn't put her finger on. Something had changed in that room and, whatever it was, Ordes had sensed it and she hadn't.

He stood; she followed, gripping his hand tightly. She tried not to look at anyone, keeping her eyes on her feet as they made their way towards the door, where Ordes seemed to have a minor disagreement with himself, his face pulled into a frown. So quickly Jenyfer barely saw him move, he stuck his head out the door then back in, gesturing she should go first.

'What—'

'Come on.' Ordes led her through the cobblestoned streets, glancing over his shoulder as they went. He didn't slow his pace until they'd reached the jetty.

'What is going on?' Jenyfer whispered.

'What did you do back there?'

'Me?'

His eyes cut to her, silver and burning. 'There's magic in your voice,' he stated. 'I felt it. Every man within two metres of us felt it. That's why we're here.' He ran his spare hand through his hair, his expression conflicted. 'You didn't feel it, did you?'

'Feel what?' Jenyfer asked. Her head was spinning, the fire that Ordes' touch had lit inside her still burning and blazing.

He looked at her again, his eyes full of shadows. 'Their intent – towards you. And none of it was good, Jenyfer. I didn't need to touch any of them to know what was in their thoughts because I could see it. I could hear it. They may as well have screamed it.'

She felt dizzy as the meaning of his words smashed their way into her skull.

'So I'll ask you again – what did you do? How did you do it?'

'I don't...' Jenyfer shook her head. She pulled her hand free and wrapped her arms around herself, and didn't speak. She didn't know what to say, hardly able to believe what he was saying, hardly able to think clearly.

'Okay. We'll wait for the others here. You're safe, Jenyfer,' Ordes added. 'I won't let anyone hurt you.' His hand lifted towards her, hesitated, then he brushed her cheek with the back of his knuckles, his touch gentle.

She nodded, and let him lead her to the end of the jetty. She sat. 'I'm sorry,' she said eventually. Ordes sat beside her, close enough that their shoulders were touching. Jenyfer wanted to crawl into his arms, to feel his lips on her skin again. Instead, she tucked her knees beneath her chin and wrapped her arms around her legs as the sun finally gave in and night swallowed the landscape.

'Can you do it again?' Ordes asked her. 'Whatever you did with your voice?'

'I don't know,' she whispered. 'I don't understand what I did, or how I did it.'

'There is only one faery I can think of that could do what you just did, but you couldn't be,' he mumbled. He shifted so he could see her face clearly, his eyes flickering over her, as if trying to see something in her. 'Maybe,' he continued. 'It's not unusual – not so common though. This is all speculation and I could be completely wrong. You're obviously partly human, but I've never met one before.'

Jenyfer swallowed. She wasn't sure she wanted to hear what he was going to say next. He'd said her magic was different. 'Never met what?'

'A part-syhren.'

Chapter 35

Katarin and Arthur were sitting opposite one another in her cabin. It was early morning and she had been trying for the better part of an hour to teach Arthur to reach his magic, but everytime he tried, he couldn't find it. He could feel it there, but it was slippery, sliding from his grasp whenever he attempted to pull it to the surface and into his fingers.

'Imagine it as something alive; a part of you,' Katarin said.

Arthur closed his eyes. He tried to do what Katarin had said – sink inside himself and find his power, call it to him. He took a deep, steady breath, held it, then let it out, trying to still his mind, to pause the kaleidoscope of images barreling through his head for just a moment, just long enough that he could grab hold of that kernel of power.

All he could see was his father, face-down on the stones before the altar, blood leaking from his head, the smell of singed flesh permeating the air – and the Witchfinder, flung across the room.

Arthur felt his magic stir. He reached for that warmth, the golden light he could feel shifting through him.

Ulrian's face flashed into his mind like a solid wall – Arthur's magic withered and slipped away.

'I can't,' he said, defeated.

Katarin threw her hands in the air. 'You're too...'

'Too what?'

'Self-conscious, Arthur. You need to let go,' Katarin commanded, stomping away from him to plonk herself into her chair and put her feet up on the desk with a sigh.

'The last time I let go I almost killed my father and the Witchfinder,' he snapped.

She gave him a look that told him she didn't consider that to be a problem.

'I'm scared,' he admitted, dropping his gaze to his hands. He examined his fingers – long, pale, slender. He still found it hard to reconcile what had come from his hands that day before the altar of the One God.

'I know,' she said simply, her voice softening a little. 'But if you let fear control you, Arthur, you will never be able to master your gift.'

'Is it really a gift?' he asked, still looking at his hands.

'Yes,' Katarin said firmly. 'It is. What do you remember about that day? With your father?'

'Heat, and light, pouring through me – I couldn't control it. It was like it burst out of me,' Arthur said. 'I was so angry, at my father, at the One God, at what had just happened with Jalen. It was like an explosion.' He frowned. 'I'd been feeling something for weeks leading up to that moment, though, like there was something beneath my skin that wanted to get out – but I thought I was just worried. I'm always worried,' he added, scowling.

'You had reason to be, but you can toss those worries out the window now,' Katarin said softly. The way she said it sounded like she wasn't finished but she paused and, when Arthur looked up at her, she was looking at him, her eyes pensive. 'I want to tell you a story,' she said finally, smiling at the surprised look on Arthur's face.

'You know so little of the world of magic, Arthur, and that's not your fault, but it's your world now.' Her smile widened. 'I'm going to tell you about the Gods.'

Before the world existed there was only darkness, a void of emptiness devoid of life. But, within that black untamed, shadows were the seeds of magic; from that magic came the light. It was from this magical light that Danu, the Creator, brought forth the first of the Old Ones – Niniane, the Green Knight, and Melodias. They belonged to the world and the world belonged to them.

Danu gave the Old Ones four Treasures: a stone that would sing the truths of the world; a bow from which arrows always flew true; a sword that, once drawn, would not be stopped; and a cauldron, which contained the power of all three and held within it the power to shape the land. This cauldron was known as the Grail, and it was with this that the Old Ones crafted the world that the Creator had left them to tend – Teyath.

The Old Ones saw that the world was divided – the land, the sea, and an empty space they had no name for. Magic was woven through all these realms, which the Old Ones decided needed ruling over; for they knew that, soon, the people of the world would come forth. The people, their children, and their children's children, would need guidance.

Niniane became the Goddess of Magic. The realm of the Earth was given to the Green Knight, and the Sea to Melodias. The Old Ones waited and soon, from the Earth and the Sea and through the Magic of the world, others appeared.

First, it was the fey creatures, who flocked to Niniane's side. Then the people, who rose from the Earth, and were given to the Green Knight to watch over and protect. Melodias, jealous, created his own creatures with their own magic of the seas – the syhrens. He called them his children, and brought them to live with him on a rocky island.

The first people were created through magic, and so the Old Ones taught them to use that magic, which could be found in every rock and tree and speck of dust in existence. But the Old Ones are forever, and people are not. As people faded from the world, the Old Ones named the empty, black space the Otherworld; Ankou was born, and the souls of the dead were given into his keeping.

Other Old Ones appeared as the people's quest for knowledge and understanding grew. Morrigna, the Goddess of Fate; the Sisters, Inanna, who ruled over love, fertility and war; and Ereshki, the Red One, she who embodies the shadow self. But, like the shadows that lurk in the hearts of men, Ereshki grew to be filled with greed and envy, and she desired power over the others. The Old Ones could not be ruled by one of their own, so Ereshki turned to the humans, those whose minds were easily swayed—

'Wait, why would people listen to Ereshki?' Arthur asked.

'Why do people do anything?' Katarin replied. 'She offered them something they wanted – power. Through worship, she would grant them power.'

'And did she?' Arthur asked.

Katarin shrugged. 'I don't know. Her name isn't spoken anymore. It's like she's been forgotten.'

Something was beating against Arthur's skin. 'What happened to the Treasures?'

'Some say they never existed, some say they vanished.'

'Have you ever seen them?'

'No one that lives has, except for an Old One.' Katarin glanced over her shoulder, out the porthole at the ocean. 'There is a prophecy that says one day, someone will heal the wounds of the past and unite the land. A fairytale,' she added. 'I'm yet to meet a man who thinks about more than himself.'

CHAPTER 36

Water stretched to all corners of the horizon and while Jenyfer was usually calmed by the sight of the sea, today it was an unasked for participant in her inner torment.

Ordes thought she was part-syhren, but she didn't know how that could be possible. Her parents were human... weren't they? She didn't have many memories of her parents. She had been going over every moment of her life up until that tavern in Skull's Rest, combing through memory after memory until her head was screaming at her to stop.

To distract herself, Jenyfer had resumed her magic training with Ordes, when he wasn't in Skulls Rest on pirate business. They were here primarily to trade, she'd learnt, watching the men load crates of textiles and tea into the boats to be rowed into the harbour. Often, they returned with things as well – food and a crate of rum, sail cloth, and sewing supplies. She hadn't realised sailors could sew until she'd seen the men mending clothing and the sails. Lamorna would be impressed with their needle-work, Jenyfer decided.

Thinking about her sister made Jenyfer's stomach clench uncomfortably. She was no closer to getting off this ship and finding her way to Lyonesse or Avalon than she had been weeks ago. But she hadn't worked up the courage to ask anyone. She hadn't dared ask Ordes again, not after her magic had rattled him so much. Jenyfer looked at her hands. She didn't understand anything about herself. The only thing she knew was that, if she was a syhren, she was dangerous.

Maybe it was Lyonesse she should find, not the Isle of Mists – but her aunt's warning rang in her ears.

Then there was whatever was happening between her and Ordes. Ever since she'd met him, there had been something pulling her towards him. She thought it was magic, that common thing they shared, and her desire to understand the thing that lived inside her; but, now, she wasn't so sure.

What had happened in that tavern didn't make sense, but she hadn't been able to stop thinking about what it felt like to have him touch her like that – how it made her warm inside, how it pushed some of the hurt at what had happened with Bryn away. But those nights would never leave her, she knew that, no matter how much she wanted to forget them. She didn't know how to start trying to free herself from the weight of Bryn's body, the touch of his hands, his mouth on hers, his fingers...

Jenyfer shook the thoughts out of her head, concentrating on Ordes, who stood before her juggling balls of water like a circus performer.

She was drenched to the bone, her clothes clinging to her, the sun slamming into her skull. Whenever she failed, whenever the water lost whatever form Ordes had shaped it into and she dropped it, drenching the deck, he simply found more of it, and more and more, until she wanted to scream. He had the whole seas-damned ocean at his command and she couldn't manage to hold a sphere of water.

'Your turn.' With a wave of his hand, he flicked a ball of water at her; it floated through the space between them, hovering in the air. She could feel his magic wrapped around it. She lifted her hands, silently pleading with the water to obey her, to do what she wanted, only for a moment, as Ordes withdrew his magic.

The sphere wobbled dangerously above Jenyfer's hands.

'Control it,' Ordes said, then sighed as his carefully formed ball crashed to the deck to splash over their toes. They'd been at it for hours. Jenyfer was hungry and tired, her head pounded and she just wanted to rest, but he wouldn't stop.

'I can't,' she snapped. The sun beat down on them mercilessly, sinking into Jenyfer's skull and melting her brain. Her skin was burning and her tongue was thick in her mouth. 'I can't do this.'

'You can. You've done it before, Jen. Let's try again.' Ordes waved his hand at the side of the ship and a stream of water sailed over the railing to coil itself around his arm, like the snake she had once seen curled around a piece of driftwood on the beach.

Jenyfer watched the water moving around his arm like it was alive. 'If I'm really a syhren, shouldn't I be able to control the water?' She went on before he could speak. 'But I can't, so you must be wrong. You have to be wrong.'

Please be wrong.

Of all the things she imagined, of all the places she thought her magic might have come from, it wasn't from the Master of Songs and Death.

But her song had been singing all morning and it *hurt*. The melody was disjointed and warped, off-key, the pitch all wrong. Her stomach rolled and her limbs felt heavy. Jenyfer felt... different, more than frustrated. Her magic prowled beneath her skin like a discontented beast, and she was terrified of letting it out. She swallowed, tasting sand and salt and seawater. The song became louder, the melody threatening to drown her. It curled around every space in her brain, in her body, and continued to sing.

It was too much.

What had happened in Skulls Rest swam around her head, sinking into her blood and bones, a deep, gnawing hunger she didn't understand surging around her like waves. But worst of all was what she seemed to have done to herself.

She wanted Ordes, and it was driving her mad.

Having to stand on the deck within reach of his arms was driving her mad.

She couldn't sleep, couldn't think, the past and the present a tangled mess in her head. The shadows under Ordes' eyes had her wondering if he was having his nights tormented by dreams like the ones she was having – flesh and fire; the warm, sticky heat of breath on the neck; the gentle press of fingers; the pressure of a hand in the small of the back; the tingling of the scalp; and the incessant thundering of the heart.

A droplet of water touched her face, then another. Jenyfer opened her eyes. Ordes was flicking water at her again, one drop at a time, each one finding their mark – her cheeks, her forehead, the tip of her nose.

Something crackled inside her head, in her veins, in the marrow of her bones.

'Stop.'

He didn't. As another droplet of water touched her face, Jenyfer flung her head back and screamed as her song surged and roared into the light.

A wall of water rose from the ocean. It arched over the side of the ship, white tips foaming, as furious and distraught as she was. She heard shouts as those of the crew nearby scurried away, but she didn't care about them. *They* hadn't gotten under her skin.

The water rushed towards Ordes – it circled him, predator and prey, before it spread out like a blanket and wrapped itself around his body.

Through the swirling water, Jenyfer could see his face. It was calm, peaceful, and she smiled. Her body was tingling, water beading on her skin. Her hands shimmered silver in the sunlight. She closed one fist, and that cocoon of water wrapped around Ordes became still.

He was looking at her; slowly, a smile crawled across his face.

Jenyfer smiled back, her song bubbling up from her throat. As she opened her mouth, someone gripped her arm, hard, the pain of it enough to make her gasp, her control slipping, her song fading away.

The Captain had a hold of her. 'Let the water go, Jenyfer,' he commanded.

She swallowed and, as quickly as it had arrived, the wave vanished. Tymis released her; her knees wobbled and she stumbled, hitting the deck, a wave of dizziness flowing over her. She blinked, taking a deep breath. She knew this feeling. This was how she'd felt on the beach, when Lamorna...

Silence rang out across the ship. Jenyfer took another shuddering breath. Footsteps approached her and then Ordes was kneeling at her side. He was dripping wet, dark hair hanging in his face, but he was unhurt. A strangled sob erupted from her throat as he smoothed the hair back from her forehead.

'How—you should be dead,' she managed, her eyes racing over his features, tracing that honeyed skin, the sculpted cheekbones and strong brows. In the sunlight, his eyes were golden.

His lips curled into a bleak smile. 'I was born with a caul on my head. I can't drown,' he explained simply. His voice was low, yet it seemed to echo around them. The deck was silent as a graveyard, the men frozen in their tasks, one sailor paused half-way up the rigging, dangling from the ropes like bait on a hook.

The Captain was standing close by. He didn't say anything. He just watched her, before he shot his son a pointed glance and turned for his cabin. Ordes helped her to stand.

A prickle of unease skittered down her spine and her breath hitched – she was being watched.

'It's not like Skulls Rest,' Ordes whispered even as his arm tightened around her. 'You're fine.'

A shudder racked Jenyfer's body. 'I need to sit. I need...' The world spun and, just before blackness closed over her head, Ordes swept her into his arms.

Tymis was sitting behind the grand desk, his head in his hands, dark strands wrapped tightly around strong fingers; fingers that had patched up Ordes' skinned knees, his cuts and bruises. Hands that had held his smaller ones as Tymis led his son around the ship, teaching him how she worked, what was what, his voice low and warm.

Ordes bit his lip. Sunlight filtered through the ornate windows at his father's back, casting him in a golden outline. Tymis glanced up sharply as Ordes shut the door, crossed the room, and took a seat opposite his father. The desk was crowded with maps and pieces of parchment. Absently, Ordes picked up the nearest map, running his eyes over it, a distraction while he worked out what to say.

Tymis sat back in his seat, watching his son closely. 'Have you worked out what she is?'

Ordes' fingers tightened on the map. 'I think so. And she's fine, thanks for asking.'

'Did she know?'

Ordes tossed the map back onto the desk. 'She didn't.'

Tymis drummed his fingers on the top of the desk. 'Are you sure about that? Syhrens don't always tell the truth, Ordes. She survived years in a place that would have killed her for what she was – that nearly did kill her. She's either an accomplished liar, or very lucky.' He paused. 'Are my crew in danger?'

'No.'

'You're sure of that?'

Ordes couldn't answer. The Green Knight's words swirled around his head, mixing with everything Jenyfer had told him, and everything he'd begun to put together – a piece snapped quickly into place. 'She's part of the prophecy, isn't she?'

'Perhaps.'

'Do I tell her?'

Tymis shook his head. 'She's a syhren, who has been raised as a human. She's had her magic bound her whole life. She has no idea what she can do. It's best if you don't tell her, for now. Let her come to terms with what she is first.' He sat back, his face thoughtful. 'There aren't many syhren half-breeds, and most spend their life on Lyonesse, with their own kind. They learn their songs there, learn how to control their magic. Learn how to use their voices.'

'Are you suggesting I take her to Melodias?'

'No.'

Ordes rubbed at his face. 'Then what can I do? The Old One said to help her. How do I do that? I don't know anything about syhren magic.'

'You help her learn how to survive in this world. Keep her in your sights at all times. Keep her away from the crew, for now, until she can control herself. When we dock at The Vale, you're to take her with you,' Tymis ordered. 'I want her off my ship for a while. The men are nervous, and I don't need a nervous crew. Have you noticed how many ships are anchored off the Pearl Coast?'

Ordes sighed.

'We're protected here, remember, but once we leave the safety of these waters, the rules don't apply. If any of those ships and their crews learn we have a syhren on board...' Tymis said.

'They'll come for her,' Ordes finished.

'And even you can't defend us against the bulk of Teyath's pirate fleet, son.'

CHAPTER 37

Jenyfer slept until after dawn the following day. Her head was
spinning, her stomach empty and aching. She watched the sunrise
over the ocean through the tiny window cut into the bulkhead.
Ordes brought her food, and waited while she ate the bread and fruit she
could barely taste. Silence drenched the space between them.

'I'm sorry,' she said eventually. 'For the water.'

His expression remained neutral. 'What was that?'

'I don't know,' Jenyfer whispered. 'I just... it was me, I'm not saying it
wasn't, but it was like it was only part of me, and that part was stronger
than the rest of me at that moment.' She shook her head furiously. When
she spoke again, it was through her teeth. 'I just want to find my sister.
That's all I want. I just want to find Lamorna... I don't care about the
bloody magic.'

Ordes rubbed at his face, his silver eyes conflicted. 'I was told to rescue
you from Kernou, by the God of the Earth. He appeared on the deck of
this ship and gave me an order.'

'What?' Jenyfer breathed, her stomach turning over. 'Why?'

'I have no idea. Look, I'm as lost in all this – whatever it is – as you are. My life is usually very boring, Jenyfer, but since I met you...' Ordes shook his head, frustrated with himself. 'I want to help you, but I don't know how. If you really are a syhren, I don't know what to do. I don't know a thing about your magic, or how to help you wield it – or control it,' he added softly.

Jenyfer's mouth was gritty, like she'd swallowed sand, and her eyes stung. Her breath hitched. She was going to cry, she knew it, and she put her hand over her eyes, not wanting him to see her tears while she struggled to get her emotions under control.

It was too much. Her aunt left behind in Kernou, her sister gone – possibly dead – and she was a syhren, or a half one, and no one could help her. Jenyfer rammed the heels of her hands into her eyes, rubbing until spots popped behind her closed lids. Water leaked onto her wrists, or maybe it was tears. She couldn't tell.

She had never felt so hopelessly lost before, not even when she was living her life looking over her shoulder.

Ordes crossed the floor, sat on the bed next to her and closed his arms around her. A moment of panic rushed through her, but then Jenyfer relaxed into his embrace. He kept her tucked against his chest, one large hand pressed in her lower back, the other around her shoulders, his fingers resting on the back of her neck. She buried her face against his shirt, determined not to let him see her cry.

'You're allowed to be upset, Jen,' he murmured.

She shook her head reflexively. She was so used to keeping the fear hidden, keeping her emotions tightly under control – she didn't know how to let them out. Lamorna was the strong one, Jenyfer thought sadly, realising she'd never acknowledged it before. It took strength to believe as firmly as her sister did. Lamorna was so sure of herself. She knew who she was, what she wanted.

With a sigh, she pulled away from Ordes, wiping her hands on her shirt. She caught his eyes – fear, nerves and wonder – and then he smiled.

'Do you want to try your magic again?'

Jenyfer gaped at him. 'You've got to be kidding. No. I won't do that again. I wouldn't be able to live with myself if I hurt you. You say you can't drown, but what if you're wrong? Then I'd have killed you and... and... then what? Your father will throw me to the sea, or cut me into tiny pieces and *then* throw me to the sea!'

Ordes quirked a brow and a smile tugged at the corners of his mouth again. 'I think you might be overestimating how much he actually likes me.'

Jenyfer couldn't return his smile. She hated that she allowed her mind to linger on how it had felt to be held against the firmness of his chest and she hated, absolutely hated, how she noticed that, when he smiled at her, one side of his mouth lifted higher than the other. She hated that she could still feel his mouth on her throat, his fingers digging into her waist.

She hated that she *liked* him, that she'd liked him since that first night in the cave, where he answered her questions without judgement, and just allowed her to talk, to empty her brain into the air around them.

He was watching her, those silvery-blue eyes fixed on her face. Her cheeks heated; her hands itched to touch him, to run her fingers along the nape of his neck and slide them into his hair, to press her lips to his and...

Jenyfer huffed a breath between her teeth. 'I need to get out of here.' Before Ordes could speak, she hurried to the door, flinging it open and rushing down the passageway, up the ladder and into the sunlight. On deck, the men had paused in their work, their eyes combing her, their fear of her obvious.

Kayrus was at the helm, and Jenyfer decided the old sailor was good company for her mood. Kayrus was quiet, and there was a gentleness to him that she liked. She prayed silently that he wouldn't send her away.

He didn't spare her a glance, his attention on the horizon, his large, scarred hand resting casually on the wheel. Jenyfer stood beside him for a while, before she turned her attention to the ship's wheel. There were markings engraved in the timber. They looked like words but were in no language she knew.

'What do they mean?' she asked.

'What does what mean, girl?' Kayrus replied.

Jenyfer reached out her hand. 'These.'

When her fingers touched the wheel, the world suddenly seemed to shrink and grow dark. A wicked wind rose from nowhere, tearing across the face of the ocean and filling the sails. Clouds raced across the horizon, blocking the sun as lightning shot through the blanket of silvery-black above them. She could hear shouts, could hear the pounding of waves on a far-off shore. Could smell salt and blood and feel the throbbing heart of the ocean beneath her feet.

She could hear music – beautiful, deadly music.

The ship began to change her bearing.

Trembling, Jenyfer tried to rip her hand free, but her flesh was stuck to the wheel by some terrible magic she did not understand. Water dribbled from her fingers to trickle down the spokes of the wheel and the music! It was so loud and forceful. It hurt her ears, caused her head to spin and pound and her bones to ache, like they were being pulled from her body, like she was being pulled somewhere else.

A face flashed into her mind – a man, his features partially cloaked in blackness, with a crown that gleamed white. Bones.

He wore a crown of bones. His lips curled as lightning flashed again. The wind faded and the clouds dissolved and Jenyfer was blinking at the brightness of an unforgiving sky, the man and the crown gone.

Kayrus was gaping at her. The old man opened his mouth but nothing came out. He took a step back. She could sense his fear, could smell it in the air.

Jenyfer could still not let go of the wheel and the timber beneath her skin pulsed with life, with magic. Her blood sang and danced and her head whirled as the sun glared down on them as her song screamed and pulsed through the core of her. The scream crept up her throat.

She grit her teeth, and pushed it back down.

The Captain strode onto the bridge. 'Get her away from the wheel,' he barked.

Ordes followed his father, pushing past him to stand at Jenyfer's side. He closed his hands around hers and, magic shimmering in the air around them, gently prised her fingers free. She gulped and blinked back tears as the song in her head faded away and there was nothing but the sound of the wind in the sails and the lapping of the waves against the hull.

Ordes was still clutching her wrist; Jenyfer went to pull her hand back but he held tight, and when she looked he was frowning, but not at her.

At the black lines that were slowly stretching up her arm.

'What the fuck?' she whispered.

'Now you sound like a sailor,' Ordes quipped, but his tone was wrong. It was puzzled, and she caught a hint of fear in his voice. They both watched the inky lines spread further up her forearm to disappear beneath the sleeve of her shirt. Jenyfer swallowed, too horrified, too fascinated by the marks and by what had just happened with the ship to be scared.

Ordes traced one of the shadowy lines with the tip of his finger. A jolt shot through her as something sparked within her chest and, suddenly, she could hear a heart beating alongside hers as the lines on her skin changed from black to ocean blue.

She pulled her wrist free and scrabbled at her chest, at the unfamiliar feeling. A sob clawed its way free of her throat as she scratched at her chest, her heartbeat irregular, loud, but not loud enough to drown out the one that was not hers.

Ordes took her hands and held them. 'It's okay,' he murmured. 'I feel it as well.'

Jenyfer gulped, blinking furiously, trying desperately to hold on to something, to not be swept away. 'It's your heart? You can feel mine?'

He nodded. He appeared calm, but his face was pale, his eyes tight. Magic was more familiar to him, she realised, but this... this was something different. Ordes squeezed her hands. She took a deep breath, trying to be steady, focusing on the markings on her arm.

What was happening to her?

Tymis pulled her other sleeve as high as it would go.

'Hey!' she protested, squirming away from his touch.

Tymis shot his son a look; something passed between them in that look and Jenyfer was certain they were hiding something from her. She ripped her arm free, tucking it against her chest protectively.

Kayrus was peering over Ordes' shoulder. 'It's a map.'

They all looked at him.

He shrugged. 'Looks like a map to me.'

'Right. You,' Tymis demanded, pointing at Jenyfer. 'Where does it lead?'

'How should I know? I've never seen it before... I have no idea what's going on.' Her voice was tiny, lacking substance, and she hated how it sounded. Panic was rising again, a wave of it. Her breath trembled.

'It's the ship,' Ordes said quietly. '*The Excalibur* is trying to tell us something, show us something. Where we need to go. She's already turned herself around.'

Tymis looked at his son, then at Jenyfer. 'I want a copy of that map.'

Jenyfer shuddered as the meaning of the Captain's words sank into her skull. 'If you think I'm just going to strip and let you all look then—'

Tymis shook his head. 'You'll show him,' he said, pointing at Ordes, before he turned and stomped his way down the ladder and across the deck to disappear into the Captain's quarters.

'Come on,' Ordes said softly.

'No.'

He sighed and ran a hand through his hair, his eyes troubled. 'Jen...'

'He wouldn't dare,' Jenyfer hissed. 'I'd rather he toss me overboard and if he won't, I'll throw myself into the sea.'

'Go with Ordes, love,' Kayrus said gently. 'He'll behave himself. And if he doesn't, you come and let me know.'

The grandfatherly note in the older man's voice soothed the rough edges of her panic. Throat tight, Jenyfer nodded. Despite what had just happened, despite how afraid the old sailor was, Kayrus was being kind to her. She turned to Ordes, realising she had no other choice. 'I swear, if you so much as look at anything other than this mysterious map I'll...'

That lopsided grin was shaky. 'You'll what?'

She scowled. 'I'll find some way to make sure you do drown.'

CHAPTER 38

'Stay still.'

'Easy for you to say,' Jenyfer snapped. 'You're not the one half-naked.'

Ordes lent forward so his breath touched the shell of her ear; she shivered. 'I can always remedy that. In fact, I could be fully naked if you like.'

'You're a pig.'

'I'm trying to lighten the mood here, Jen. Help me out.'

'Well, don't.'

'Sorry.' All he wanted was to put his mouth on her skin again. He was tied up in knots, burning from the inside out, and being this close to her like this was torture. The creamy skin of her back puckered to gooseflesh under his hands. She shrugged away from him and he sighed, rubbing at his face as she crossed her arms tighter over her bare breasts. Her spine was so stiff he thought she'd snap in two and he could almost see her discomfort rising from her like a cloud of mist. The 'map' had made its way up both her arms, curling over her shoulders and down half of her back.

He could feel how uncomfortable she was when he rested his fingers on her flesh and he pushed his magic away, reinforcing the shield he had wrapped around his mind. She was overwhelming him with her emotions; they danced beneath her skin, shattering and reforming and breaking apart again. Her control was paper thin. He could feel her magic as well, swirling and pushing against the cage of her body. Music lingered in his ears whenever he touched her. He didn't understand syhren magic one bit, only that it was powerful – and dangerous. His father was right. If the other Captains found out Tymis had a syhren onboard, there would be trouble.

And, now, this map. Another thing that made Jenyfer valuable to others, even if no one knew where it led. Ordes bit his lip. *The Excalibur's* crew were loyal to his father, but ply a man with enough rum...

He knew Tymis would keep the crew ship-bound until they worked out what to do.

Then, there was the heartbeat that echoed softly in his ears, that Ordes could feel in his chest. The heartbeat that was not his. He moved away from Jenyfer to lean over the wooden desk tucked against the wall of his cabin. Picking up the quill, he dipped it gently in the pot of ink, holding the piece of parchment steady with his other hand. He'd copied the lines on her arms and shoulders already – they stared back at him, doing absolutely nothing to help him figure out what he was supposed to be looking at.

Ordes glanced up. Jenyfer was watching him over the curve of one pale shoulder. He held her eyes just long enough to see her cheeks colour. She turned back to face the window, muttering curses to herself. It would make this easier on both of them if she'd just relax, but he had no idea what to say to her to calm the heart he could hear, that he could *feel*, racing.

'Are we done?' she asked, her tone clipped. A shiver passed through her again as she tucked her hands into her armpits. It was cold below deck without the warm glow of the sun.

They were in his cabin; more than once, his eyes had floated to his bed, with its rumpled sheets and soft mattress. More than once, his belly had tightened as the memory of what had happened between them – or nearly happened – in that tavern in Skulls Rest ploughed through his head. He worked hard to keep his mind steady, to not let her realise where his thoughts kept straying. If he could hear her heart, he had no doubt she could hear his.

'Almost,' Ordes replied, dragging the stool across the floor and settling behind her again. He traced the curve of her waist, the gentle flare of her hips, with his eyes, biting his lip. She jumped as one of his hands came to rest on her waist. 'Be still,' he murmured.

She swallowed but did as he asked. The warmth from her skin spread inside him; she made a little noise and jerked away from his touch. He let his hands drop.

Jenyfer cleared her throat. 'When you... touched me, the map...'

Frowning, Ordes stood and moved to stand in front of her. His eyes shifted over her skinny arms, the swell of her breasts rising from behind them. 'What happened? Did it change colour again?'

This mysterious map scared the shit out of him, but not as much as how it had changed from inky black to ocean blue when he'd prised her fingers free of the ship's wheel. The lines were black once more now, though, so dark against her pale skin.

Jenyfer shook her head. 'No. It became hot.'

His eyebrows lifted. 'Hot?'

'Yes, hot.' Her frown was deep, worried. 'What does it mean?'

Ordes pinched the bridge of his nose. 'I don't know.' He sighed again, rubbing at the back of his neck. Jenyfer gasped. She reached for his forearm, exposing one milk-pale breast as she did so.

'Was this there before?' she asked, shoving his sleeve roughly up his arm.

'Was what...' Ordes glanced at his arm, at the black lines that were slowly spreading over his skin. 'What the...'

'... fuck,' they breathed together.

Her eyes were wide when he looked at her again. They stared at one another, both caught by whatever this was unfolding on their skin. Ordes stripped his shirt off, tossing it on the bed.

He winked. 'Now we're even.'

Jenyfer couldn't even muster a scowl. Her eyes moved over his chest, lower, slowly carving a path of blazing heat across his flesh while he made himself breathe, steady and calm. He could feel her heartbeat, its quick, unsteady rhythm, and warmth spread through his body.

'My face is up here,' he whispered. He was definitely going to be shirtless from now on.

She quickly lifted her eyes, crossing her arms tightly over her chest again. Her cheeks were flushed, lips slightly parted. She looked like she wanted to kiss him, or perhaps kill him. He shouldn't tease, but she was absolutely stunning when she looked like she'd strangle him with her bare hands.

Hands he really wanted her to put on his skin.

Ordes tore his eyes from hers, focusing on his arm, on the marks that crept along his flesh towards his shoulder. As they both watched, the lines began to spread across his chest. He felt *The Excalibur* pause, then slowly shift to the east. 'The ship has changed her bearing again,' he murmured.

'Where is she taking us?'

Ordes was studying the map, trying not to panic. 'I don't know.'

'This doesn't scare you?'

He looked up sharply and their eyes met again. 'Of course it does.'

Jenyfer hesitated, then reached out and touched the tip of her finger to his skin, setting the fire that was simmering under his flesh to blazing and tearing through him. Without thinking, he cupped her face and rested his forehead against hers.

'You want to know something?' he asked, his voice low. Jenyfer's breathing was thick and heavy, shaking. 'I wanted you that night in Skulls Rest,' Ordes said. 'But the question is, did you want me? Did you really want me, or was it your magic?' He pulled back so he could see her face, could see every eyelash and faded freckle splattered across her nose. Her eyes dropped to his mouth; a spasm walked her face, quashing the desire he'd seen there before she pushed him away roughly.

'Don't.'

'Jen—'

'Don't do that,' she said tightly.

'Do what?'

'Say things like that! It's confusing, alright? It's confusing because I want you to touch me but I don't want you to touch me at the same time! And I shouldn't want you to touch me, not after...' She was red-faced and trembling, eyes glimmering, arms wrapped tightly around herself.

Ordes felt like someone had doused him with icy water. The flame that had been burning inside him went out, replaced with a crawling anger that burnt with its own, cold heat. 'What did he do to you?'

'Who?' Her voice shook.

'The man you married.'

Jenyfer swallowed audibly but held his eyes. 'He did what he was told to do. What was expected of him.'

'And you? What was expected of you?' Ordes asked quietly.

This time, she turned away from him. He saw her shoulders shake as she took a deep breath, then another, and her voice when she spoke was low, controlled. 'I had to do what I was told. It didn't matter that it wasn't something I wanted. It didn't matter that I didn't like it.' She scooped her shirt from the floor and pulled it on, glancing at him quickly. He caught the shimmer in her eyes, but not one tear fell.

Ordes stepped aside, giving her access to the door. His mind was spinning, his insides turned to soup. He wanted to know who. He wanted a name, so he could find them and smash their faces in.

Jenyfer didn't move. 'What about the map?'

'What about it?' he asked quietly.

She ran her eyes over his chest, her gaze burning a hole through his skin. 'I think... it looks like it joins up.' She crossed to the table and snatched up the parchment he'd copied her part of the map onto. Frowning, Jenyfer approached him, her eyes on the parchment. 'See? Here.'

'Jenyfer,' Ordes began.

Her eyes jumped to his and then away again. 'I need to think about something else, Ordes. Even magical maps and whether I'm a syhren or not is better than...' she shook her head, and held the parchment next to his arm. 'Look.'

Where the parchment met his skin, the lines of the 'map' blended together perfectly.

'It's a coastline,' Ordes said in wonder. 'But I don't recognise it.'

They stood in silence, until she busied herself with returning the map to the table, weighing down the edges carefully. Before she left, she met his eyes.

'I didn't want you to know,' she said.

'I've never killed a man,' Ordes said quietly. 'But I would make an exception.'

'It wasn't his fault,' Jenyfer whispered. 'I'm not defending him – I hate him for what he did to me – but it was my fault we were in that situation in the first place. Because I lied that night the Chif found me on the beach – with you. I lied to protect you, Ordes,' she added.

He felt like she'd punched him.

'I also lied to protect myself. But I was naive. I knew what would happen but, somehow, I didn't think it would happen to me,' she said, those sea-storm eyes sweeping his face. 'It's not your fault, so please don't look at me like that. It's not even Bryn's fault.'

'It isn't yours either,' Ordes began furiously, but she held up her hand and he fell silent.

'I know. I'd spent my life being careful, so careful, and maybe it was knowing that freedom was so close that made me careless. I should have thought, because in Kernou, under the eyes of the One God, everything is always a woman's fault.'

CHAPTER 39

Katarin and Arthur were sitting in front of the open window in her cabin. Dinner had not long finished when Katarin had invited him for a drink, and Arthur hadn't dared refuse. He was still fiercely aware of his unimportance on the ship. He had no idea what he was doing, something he was reminded of through the frequent glances and muttering of the crew. There were over thirty women on the ship, most of whose names he didn't know, but he couldn't help but admire them. They were tough and strong – he'd watched the muscles in their arms shifting as they hauled on the rigging or swabbed the deck. Magical ship or not, *The Night Queen* still required maintenance like a regular ship.

He'd offered to help, but they'd just looked at him – and didn't bother trying to hide their amusement. He'd had two drinks, out of nerves more than anything, and now the rum had loosened him; he felt light, floating, his head wrapped in clouds as he realised he'd never been drunk before. Katarin just smiled and topped up his glass before he could stop her.

Katarin was smoking a pipe. Arthur watched, fascinated. She handed the device over, explained what to do, and he followed her instructions, pulling smoke into his lungs.

He broke into a violent coughing fit that left her laughing in delight. 'That's foul,' he managed.

'I know, but it relaxes me,' she said, puffing away, blowing a stream of smoke out the window. She sighed and put her feet up on the window ledge. The stars were strewn across the sky from one corner to the next. Arthur could spend all night watching them. They glittered like promises yet to be fulfilled, but he'd barely allowed himself a moment of hope since fleeing his father.

'What will you do now you're free of your father's yoke?' Katarin asked.

'I thought I'd become a pirate,' he said, and she laughed again. He liked being able to make her laugh. If he could continue to do that, perhaps she wouldn't change her mind and throw him to the water. He shrugged. 'I'm not sure. My father had been preparing me to be Chif, but I knew that, deep down, he didn't think I was cut out for the job – and it seems he was right, doesn't it?'

She said nothing.

'I want to know what happened to Jalen,' Arthur said softly. He reached across and snatched the bottle of rum from Katarin, drinking straight from the neck. In a rushed voice, he told Katarin of the day Jalen had been taken. 'He's not human.'

'Does it matter?' Katarin asked him.

Arthur blinked. 'No, I suppose it doesn't.'

Katarin chuckled. 'In any case, he's reasonable, for a demi-god. They can be unusually annoying and arrogant, gods but not quite gods.'

'You know him?'

'We've met.'

'What was a demi-god doing living in a town, pretending to be a fisherman?' Arthur said. 'What was he doing with me?'

'Perhaps he liked you,' she said, tossing him a wink. When he said nothing, she set the pipe aside. 'Do you love him?'

Arthur sighed. 'I don't know. I don't know what it means to love someone. Did my father love me? Maybe, in his way, but I think he loved his God more than me.'

Katarin was quiet for a moment, then, 'What about your mother?'

'She died birthing me,' Arthur said, his heart pinching as he thought about the woman he had never known, the woman who had died so that he could live.

'You don't know who I am, do you?' The lantern light from behind them cast deep shadows over Katarin's features. The curves of her face became all angles and sharpness.

'Is that a trick question?' Arthur asked warily.

'Do you miss your home?' Katarin asked him. Her expression was smooth, composed, giving nothing away.

Arthur quickly shook his head.

'I was born in Cruithea—' she began.

'Wait, aren't you a faery?' he interrupted.

'I am – now – but once, I was human, like you, Arthur Tregarthen. I was just a normal girl,' she said, turning her gaze to the night sky. 'When I was young, maybe six, my father died. I don't remember how, but my mother had many suitors after he was gone. Perhaps one of them had killed him in the hope of getting close to her. She was very beautiful.' Katarin sighed sadly. 'She soon met a man. He arrived in our village – he'd been travelling the continent, and had come from Malist, but was not from there. He was sick. He had a terrible fever and was ranting about gods and curses and the moon. My mother was a healer, so the man was brought to her.'

'She healed him?' Arthur asked gently.

'And then they fell in love,' Katarin said with heavy bitterness. 'We left our village, our home, to be with him in his own land.'

Arthur swallowed another mouthful of rum. 'My mother was Cruithean,' he volunteered. 'That's all I know. I've never met her family. I was hoping to find them one day.'

'But you found me instead,' Katarin finished. 'Your mother?'

'She married my father and settled with him in Kernou.'

Katarin's face changed; it became tight, her eyes hard. 'They never married.'

'What?'

'Igraine never married him,' the Captain said in a low voice.

Arthur dropped his glass. Rum spread across his lap, but he didn't move. He only knew his mother's name through constantly pestering his father when he was younger, until eventually, no doubt to shut him up, Ulrian had given him a name, but nothing more – *Igraine*.

Katarin turned to him, her dark gaze sweeping his face. 'You have her eyes, but you wear your father's face.'

Arthur's blood was burning. 'How do you know my mother?'

'He never spoke of me, did he?'

Arthur blinked. 'I don't—'

'Igraine was my mother. Ulrian Tregarthen was the young man who, fever-struck, fell in love with her and managed to woo her back to his world.'

'Why didn't I know this?' Arthur gaped. 'Why were... what... what happened, Katarin?' he said in a rush, then, quietly, 'You're my sister?'

Katarin held his eyes but didn't speak while his heart pounded painfully and he forgot how to breathe. She poured another glass of rum and drank the lot in one go. When she looked at him again, her eyes were glistening.

'Igraine fell pregnant with you, but it was a hard pregnancy. The healers in Kernou didn't think she would survive the birth. If she'd been allowed to return to Cruithea, she might have stood a chance. The magic of her people could have saved her, but your father had begun his turning to the

One God before they even met, and the One God had been whispering poison to him.'

Arthur went very still. There was a roaring in his ears. 'What did he do?'

'The One God told him if he really loved Igraine, he would do anything to save her,' Katarin said. 'I overheard him at prayer – heard him speaking to himself, heard him raving.' She pinned Arthur to his seat with the sharpness, the weight, of her gaze. 'His god told him to sacrifice a child, so that his would live. If he did this, Igraine would be saved.' She laughed, deep and bitter, making Arthur jump. 'But Ulrian was a coward. He wouldn't wield the knife himself, not even to save her, so he tied me to that stake and left me to die. He didn't even stay to watch me drown.'

Arthur opened his mouth but no words left his tongue. A million of them were stuck in his throat but none of them would be right, none of them would convey the horror he was feeling.

Katarin sighed and rubbed at her face. 'It didn't matter. Igraine died anyway. Rather than blame the One God, Ulrian became convinced that magic was at fault, especially when it was reported to him that the child he had left to die didn't die at all. She was rescued by the Queen of the Isle.'

'Niniane saved you?'

'She sent a faery for me. He parted the waters, stepped up to where I was tied, and rescued me,' Katarin said simply. 'It is my understanding that, since then, your father's hatred of magic and Magic Wielders – like me, like our mother, like you – has only gotten worse the deeper he fell under the One God's spell.' Katarin rubbed at her face again, as though she could wipe the truth from her mind if she just scrubbed enough. Eventually, she said, 'I don't blame you, Arthur, for what happened to our mother, or to me – but I blame him. And whether you like it or not, I will have my revenge.'

Arthur swallowed. 'I won't stop you,' he said. 'I won't stand in the way, Katarin.'

She was watching him closely.

'He beat me, had me torture myself, tried to wash away the sins I carried – things I cannot control anymore than he could,' Arthur said, then added, '"Man shall not lie with man as he does with woman."'

They stared at one another. Arthur's brain was spinning, his thoughts tripping over themselves until they were a tangled mess resting in his head while, all around, storm clouds swirled and the stars winked at him. Slowly, Katarin smiled, lifting her glass in a toast. Arthur lifted his. 'Well, little brother, it looks like we have quite a lot to discuss.'

'It looks like it,' he replied. He frowned as he recalled being pisky-led through the darkness of his father's house, of finding that list of names in the desk drawer – the names of all the women and girls that had been gifted to the sea by his father. One name pushed its way free of the others – the first name on that list. 'Your name isn't Katarin, is it?'

'No. It's the name I gave myself,' she answered. 'It became my shield, my protection against the memories of what happened, but nothing can truly wipe away the past. My real name is—'

'Morgaine,' Arthur answered.

She nodded.

Arthur groaned, slowly sitting up and cradling his head in his hands. His temples were throbbing, his tongue dry and thick in his mouth. All he could taste was rum, or was it vomit? He was fairly certain he'd thrown up somewhere, but couldn't remember where.

After Katarin's – *Morgaine's* – revelation, he'd polished off the rest of the bottle of rum, and didn't object when another was placed in his hand. The rest of the evening after that was a blur, but he had a vague recollection of someone – Tahnet, perhaps? – helping him down the ladder and into his cabin where he had fallen face-first onto the narrow bed and not moved again. All was blackness and tortured dreams from there. He'd seen Jalen, and the Grail, and an island covered in trees and shrouded in mist. Avalon, he guessed, but if it was, he had no idea why he was dreaming of the Isle of Mists.

The fact that he had *magic* was still a shock, and most mornings, when he woke, Arthur would flex his fingers and feel once again that strange current running through him, pushing at the cage that was his body, twining itself around his bones, threading through his blood.

But all the magic in the world wasn't going to help him now. The light that shone through the small window speared into Arthur's head with all the force of a weapon. He blinked, then shut his eyes, his stomach rolling with each wave *The Night Queen* crested. The sea felt rougher than usual; the ship rocked and swayed, but the day was clear.

Groaning again, Arthur burrowed back into his bed, pulling the blankets over his head, one hand on his churning belly, the other over his eyes.

The door crashed open. 'Up. The Captain wants to see you.'

'I'm dying,' he moaned.

A laugh, too loud and too bright. 'You're not dying, little man. Come on.'

The blankets were ripped away from him and his arm was grabbed in a strong hand as he was hauled to sitting, blinking and gasping for air. Tahnet knelt before him, staring up into his face.

'You look like shit,' she declared bluntly.

'I feel it.'

She smiled. 'You need fresh air and food.'

'No food.'

'Trust me, Arthur. Come on. Your sister is waiting.'

Sister.

Katarin was his *sister*. His father had tried to kill her. Ulrian had tried to murder a child.

His father was many things, and Arthur would never dispute any claim that Ulrian Tregarthen was a hard man, but he never imagined his father to be so callous, even in his grief, to do what he tried to do to Katarin. Arthur's stomach heaved again as he imagined a tiny, red-haired girl bound to the stake on the beach in Kernou. How frightened she must have been! He swallowed, standing on shaky legs and taking a deep breath. He rubbed at his face, pulled a hand through his hair, and hunted around for his shirt, turning his back on Tahnet.

She sucked in a sudden breath and he knew what she'd seen.

The whip marks.

While they no longer hurt, he knew he'd carry the evidence of what he'd been forced to do to himself for the rest of his life. Tahnet said nothing as he pulled on his shirt and attempted to tidy himself. When he turned to face her, she had arranged her expression into the one she normally wore, but there was a tightness to her eyes that wasn't usually there.

'We won't judge you on your appearance,' she said airily; an attempt to seem like everything was normal. 'Not after last night anyway.'

'Oh gods, what did I do?'

She snickered and shook her head. 'It's better you don't know. She's waiting and, family or not, the Captain doesn't like to be kept waiting.'

Arthur nodded and followed Tahnet above deck, where the sun plucked at his eyes with fingers of fire and slammed inside his head. Before she knocked on the door of Katarin's cabin, Tahnet caught his arm.

'When we get to Avalon, Niniane can remove them for you,' she said softly.

He swallowed, but shook his head. He wanted to keep them. He wanted them to always remind him of what his father had become, and what he had managed to escape. Tahnet nodded in understanding, and reached up to undo the top two buttons of her shirt. Before Arthur could look away, he saw them. Slashes across her skin, the scars faded to silvery pink but still visible.

'My husband tried to kill me,' Tahnet explained softly. 'He accused me of using my magic to make another man fall in love with me, and he stabbed me and left me for dead. I was found by Aelle and brought to Katarin. That was over a year ago.'

Arthur made himself speak. 'Your husband?'

Tahnet's lips curled into a sly grin. 'Seems he didn't like being visited by a ghost. He threw himself from his boat in terror and, unfortunately, drowned,' she said. Her expression shifted again. 'Men like him are the men we target – those who harm women like us. I know why you want to keep your scars, because I chose to keep mine.'

She turned and pushed open the door and when they went in Katarin was sitting with her feet up on the desk, face fresh, eyes bright and alert. A jug of water, two mugs, and a platter of sliced apple and cheese sat before her. She grinned when she saw Arthur's face.

'It gets easier,' she commented, motioning for him to sit and demanding he drink the water and eat some fruit. Hands shaking, Arthur poured himself a drink, and his mouth sighed in relief when he took a sip. Katarin didn't speak until he'd finished his water and eaten two slices of apple.

'You remember what I told you?'

'How could I forget?' Arthur mumbled. 'What do I call you?'

'Katarin,' she said softly. 'I left my other name behind when I was reborn.'

'What do you mean, reborn?' he asked.

'Niniane's magic not only saved my life, it changed it – it changed me. She bathed me in the waters of Avalon and when I emerged, I was this,' she said, gesturing to herself. 'A faery, I suppose. I had a small amount of magic as a human child that I had only begun learning to use.'

Arthur studied his hands. 'What do you want me to do?'

'Do?'

339

'Yes,' he affirmed. 'I told you last night I wouldn't stand in your way when it came to my father, and I meant it, but,' he said, lifting his eyes to Katarin's. 'I want something in return.'

Her eyebrows lifted. 'Do you, now? What?'

He felt his cheeks heat. 'I need to find Jalen and I need your help to do it.'

'That won't be too difficult. When we go to Avalon, Niniane can find him for you,' Katarin said simply.

'So, we're going to Avalon?'

'We are, but I can't say when.'

Arthur drummed his fingers on the desk. 'Will Niniane be able to help me understand my dreams?'

Katarin narrowed her eyes. 'What have you dreamt?'

'Just about the Grail.' And about being a King, Arthur thought, his belly twisting again. They lapsed into thoughtful silence, and thoughts of the Grail and Jalen inevitably led him back to one, single, burning truth. 'I hate him,' he whispered forcefully. 'I hate what he allowed himself to become.'

Katarin said nothing, turning her face to glance out the window at the brightness of the sun that poured across the world. The ship rocked, creaking rhythmically in time with the gentle splashes against the hull. Her face shifted suddenly, eyes swinging back to his. 'Do you hate him enough to kill him?'

'I...'

'Do you hate him enough to tell Niniane what you know?'

'I don't know anything.'

'About the One God,' Katarin confirmed. She leant forward, quick as a striking snake, and speared a piece of cheese with a dagger Arthur hadn't seen her reach for. He watched her closely as she popped the cheese into her mouth, tapping the tip of the knife on her smooth cheek. 'Niniane will want to find the Grail.'

'She can keep it when she does,' Arthur mumbled. He wasn't a King. He didn't want to be a King; he didn't want to be a Chif either. Whatever Jalen thought he was destined for, he was wrong, Arthur decided.

He was wrong.

Katarin was watching him with interest. 'Our mother was a powerful Magic Wielder, Arthur.'

'You said she was a healer.'

'She was. She used her magic to heal the sick, to help the dying pass into the Otherworld, but it was not all she was.' Katarin sighed. 'My earliest memory of her was waking before dawn to find her tending to an elderly man. It was still dark, and I couldn't find her, but I knew where she would be. I wasn't supposed to go into the kibitka where she treated people, but I was a child who wanted her mother, so I snuck in. I think she knew I was there, but she said nothing. The man was lying on the floor, in a nest of blankets. I could hear his breathing – a gurgling, rattling sound as he pulled air into dying lungs. Mother was sitting with him, her hand on his forehead. Her lips were moving but I couldn't make out what she was saying. The man heaved one last breath, and then, he was gone.' Katarin paused and flicked her fingers; her mug slid across the table to her hand. She took a long drink, wiping her mouth with the back of her hand. 'She told me later she helped him leave this world. That it was her gift, and her burden.'

'She killed him?' Arthur whispered.

'No, she helped him pass over. There is a difference, Arthur,' Katarin said, drumming her fingers against her mug. 'Death is not the end. That man knew that. He knew that, in the next realm, he would be greeted by family who had passed long before. He would meet with his ancestors. Death is a part of life. We should not fear it.'

'The Decalogue teaches that death is something to be scared of; not dying itself, but what comes after – the Pit and the Beast, or a place of wonder and light,' Arthur said.

'The Decalogue is wrong,' Katarin said firmly. 'The Otherworld does not judge the dead. That's not Ankou's role.'

'Then what happens when we die?'

'I can't say,' she said, a wry smile twisting her mouth. 'I haven't died. Yet.'

'Can you die?' Arthur asked slowly. 'You're a faery now.'

'I'm not immortal. Only the Old Ones are forever, in some form,' Katarin answered.

CHAPTER 40

There was music on the ship. When Jenyfer was young, there was often music in Kernou. Bards and minstrels would perform in the tavern, their voices floating into the street outside where the children would gather to listen, or in the market square, serenading the villagers as they shopped under a cloud-streaked sky. Sometimes, people would dance, their faces alight with the joy of moving their bodies to the music. The fishermen would sing as they hauled in their catches and Jenyfer's aunt was always humming.

But the One God was not a musical god.

Jenyfer sat on an upturned crate, cradling a mug of rum, and listened to the crew sing – a sailor's song, full of cheek, that would make her sister's hair curl.

Thinking of Lamorna caused her heart to pinch, a painful ache spearing itself through her body. Jenyfer pushed aside the horrible twisting of her belly. She needed to find her sister, but had no idea where to begin. Her aunt had told her to stay away from Lyonesse but, now, something was urging her to find the Master of Songs and Death. *If* she was a syhren, didn't it make sense? She still thought Ordes had it wrong. She couldn't sing, and syhrens were known for their voices, voices so beautiful and alluring that sailors threw themselves from the decks and let their vessels smash into the rocks when they heard a syhren's song.

Then, there was the map. Jenyfer lifted her arm, letting her sleeve slip back, examining the mysterious map in the weak light. Gently, she touched it; something thrummed beneath her skin, tingling and twitching. Alarmed, she let her arm drop, hastily tugging her sleeve back down. She'd stared at the map Ordes had drawn, her head filled with questions that had no answers. Since leaving Kernou, her life had been tipped upside down, everything she thought she knew shaken from her head and shoved back in, so it sat there in a churning, burning mess that no one could explain.

Her aunt's face flashed into her mind, Tamora's confession about binding Jenyfer's magic making her muscles tighten. Jenyfer believed her aunt when she'd said she'd wanted to protect her, but Jenyfer could not stop the flash of anger that speared through her. Binding her magic might have protected her, but it had also left her ignorant – and now vulnerable.

It kept you alive, a little voice whispered.

Jenyfer sighed and rubbed at her eyes with the heel of her hand. There was nothing she could do, so she pushed her aunt and all the mysteries and cryptic clues out of her mind for the moment and opened her ears to the music, unable to help the smile that pulled at her mouth. Despite having a voice that crawled from the throat of a dying whale, Jenyfer loved music. She loved dancing. While the ship's crew might not have the same charm and finesse as the bards and minstrels, their enthusiasm was infectious as they performed reels and jigs and shantys, their singing loud and bawdy, their voices drowning out the wheel-fiddle and pipes. The sound of the fiddle echoed across the deck, sinking into Jenyfer's blood, and the drums vibrated through the timbers of the ship, rattling her bones as that prickling sensation beneath her skin increased.

'Enough of this,' Tymis called, and Jenyfer felt a stab of dismay at it all ending so soon, but the Captain strode from the port side rail to stand mid-deck. An expectant silence fell over the ship and the air became still and heavy. She let her gaze wander over the faces of the men – all eyes were on their Captain.

At a nod from Tymis, the wheel-fiddle began again but instead of the rolling, foot-tapping rhythm of a shanty, the music was slow and steady, the notes pulling and bending. Jenyfer held her breath as the sound floated over her, and the lilting voice of the pipes joined in, followed by the drum.

Then Tymis opened his mouth, and sang.

The hair stood to attention on the back of Jenyfer's neck as his voice, so rich and pure, made of starlight and the power of the ocean, reached inside her. It wrapped around her heart and squeezed, and a hot rush of emotion spread through her.

She gasped, dropping her mug as tears sprung to her eyes and every hair on her body stood on end. It fell to smash at her feet, but no one turned to look and the music did not stop.

The song was a ballad, the language one Jenyfer had never heard before. She could *feel* the music in the very marrow of her bones. It flowed through the air with all the force of a storm, the melody swirling and pulling on Jenyfer's insides. Tymis' song was delicate and soft, yet strong and powerful at the same time. It swept her up, up, into the night sky where she lingered between the stars, caught in the space between worlds. The melody called to her, stirring the magic in her blood, plunging into the deepest recesses of who she was, parts of her that were new and freshly awakened by the unbinding of her powers. She was enchanted by the sound, by the notes that bent and slid over her to slip beneath her skin and call, *call*, to her, an invitation she didn't understand.

By the time Tymis finished the song she was crying but, in her blood, her magic felt different – as if all the unknown parts of her had started to come together. Sniffing, she wiped at her face roughly, cheeks slick with tears, but she wasn't alone in her emotion. There were many pairs of glistening eyes on deck and the men all found their toes to be the most interesting thing around.

Someone pressed another mug into her hands; Ordes' fingers brushed hers and she jolted, then blushed, her cheeks heating. They'd not spoken much over the last few days. She hadn't meant to tell him anything, especially not that she'd lied because she was worried about him, but there was no way she could take the words back.

'He has that effect,' Ordes mumbled, nodding towards his father.

'It was beautiful,' Jenyfer said, her voice low and husky. She played with the mug, twisting it between her fingers, her heart still singing and swirling with the song, with the melody that continued to flow through her, rushing through her veins, her bones, her heart. She swallowed, and forced herself to speak. 'What language was that?'

'The language of Avalon,' Ordes answered softly. He glanced down at his tattooed knuckles, running his fingers over them. A piece of hair had fallen to brush his forehead and Jenyfer wanted to reach up and push it away, but she kept her hands tightly on her mug.

'What do they mean?' She nodded at the tattoos. 'You said you'd tell me.'

Ordes gave her a little smile, sinking to the smooth timber of the deck beside her. 'I did, didn't I?' He pointed to the mark on his left index finger – a spiral, the lines seemingly without beginning or end. 'Loyalty.' Then the second finger, two lines crossed over another. 'Sacrifice.' The thumb on his right hand, then the index finger – three concentric circles, and what looked like a spindly tree. 'Love, and hope.'

He looked at her quickly, then away again. She found it hard not to watch him. One side of his face was painted golden with lantern light, the other silver with the moon, the contrast of cool and warm on his skin strangely mesmerising. The lines of his face were sharpened by the light, highlighting the shape of the high cheekbones and strong jaw, the full lips and the slightly pointed tips of his ears. She'd never noticed that before.

His eyes slid to hers again and she cleared her throat, feeling her cheeks warm, embarrassed to be caught staring at him. 'Was it magic?' she asked, nodding at the Captain as the men began a simple folk song, one she had hazy memories of hearing.

'His voice? No, the bastard is just talented,' Ordes said with a chuckle.

Jenyfer sighed. 'Singing and music wasn't allowed in Kernou, not since the One God. I love music! I've missed it,' she added wistfully, then frowned. 'We weren't allowed to dance either.'

They fell silent, listening to the singing. Ordes smiled, a slow smile, one that Jenyfer thought made him even more beautiful than he usually was. 'They did this for you,' he said.

'What?'

'The men. They thought you might like it. They thought you might need cheering up. It's their way of saying sorry, for being stand-offish when you first arrived on board,' Ordes replied. 'You scare them – what you are scares them – but they still did this. Maybe they think that, if they're nice to you, you won't try and drown them or cause the ship to sink to the bottom of the ocean.'

Jenyfer opened her mouth to object, then realised he was making a joke. She didn't know what to say. Her face was burning, but not with embarrassment, or shame, or anger – or any of the things she was used to feeling. She swallowed, pulling a steady breath into her lungs as she collected herself.

Above them, the stars twinkled, tiny, silver-white gems.

'What do you think they are?' she asked, glancing up.

'The stars?' Ordes said, then shrugged. 'Some say they're the lost souls that didn't make it to the Otherworld, others say they're the eyes of the dead, or gods... on normal ships, sailors use them to navigate, reading them like a map.'

'But not this ship.'

'No, not this ship.'

'Ordes,' she said as he turned to leave; he paused, twisting his head to look at her over his shoulder. 'Thank you.'

'For what?'

'For not judging me.'

He stared at her for a long moment; the deck had fallen quiet, the men all sitting back, drinks in hand, their postures relaxed. Ordes held out his hand.

'Dance with me.'

Jenyfer nearly dropped her mug again. 'What?'

'Come on.' Before she could object, he took her mug, set it away, and reached for her hand. 'Kayrus,' he called. The navigator looked up, bow dangling from one large, scarred hand, the fiddle held gently in the other. 'Something the lady can actually dance to, if you please.'

'Ordes,' Jenyfer hissed.

His eyes sparkled with captured stars. 'I dare you.' The words were low, for her ears only, his lips curled in a challenge. 'Come on. Show them how brave you are.'

'I'm not brave,' she objected quietly.

'You most certainly are.' His tone left no space to argue, so she nodded, a tiny movement of her head no one else would see or understand. She could feel the eyes of the crew on her and remembered what Ordes had told her, only moments ago.

They did this for you.

Jenyfer pushed a breath from her lungs and stood, shaking back her hair.

'Am I allowed to touch you?' Ordes asked quietly. 'To dance, nothing more.'

She swallowed, remembering that moment in his cabin, her consuming fear, the overwhelming panic and the look in his eyes. 'Yes.'

'Then try not to step on my toes,' he whispered, slipping one arm around her middle.

'Do faeries even know how to dance?' Her skin tingled where he touched her.

He put his mouth close to her ear. 'I'll have you know I'm an excellent dancer, faery or not,' he murmured, his breath tickling her flesh. She shivered, her stomach tightening; Kayrus drew the bow across the fiddle strings and Jenyfer was suddenly flying, spun around the deck in Ordes' arms as the faces around them became a blur and the stars whirled overhead.

Ordes was like water, so fluid and graceful on his feet. He was sure of himself, leading her expertly; she kept her eyes on her feet, terrified she would step on his toes.

'Don't watch your feet,' he instructed in a whisper. 'Pick something else to look at and focus on that.'

'What should I look at?'

'Me, if you want,' he said, the words rushing from his mouth. The look on his face told her he hadn't meant to say them.

She smiled. 'The last time you told me to do that, I stabbed you.'

He gave her a rueful smile, then spun her out of his arms and back again.

As they danced, Jenyfer felt like an unfolding flower. The music was inside her, crooning and calling, almost begging for something. Her chest was tight, her body an extension of the sound that bloomed in and around her. Her body tingled, from the toes in her boots to the tips of her fingers. Music scurried across the back of her neck and she could hear each individual note, picking them from the layers of sound that swirled around her. She could *see* the notes in the air, wisps of gold and silver and ocean blue, and they danced around her, around Ordes and the musicians of the crew, swooping and swirling but never touching them.

Ordes was smiling, his eyes on her face. 'You look...'

'What?' she managed to whisper.

'Different.' His hands tightened where he held her, one arm around her lower back, her fingers woven through his. 'You look happy, Jen.' With the next step in the dance, she shifted closer to him, winding her arm around his neck, her fingers moving into his hair. She felt his surprise, but his steps didn't stumble, not until she rested her cheek on his neck, and he stepped on her toes, making her pull back with a gasp.

'Sorry,' he whispered. His cheeks were flushed, hair teased by the breeze. His eyes sparkled as he flashed her a grin. 'Do you want a new partner?'

Jenyfer shook her head. That grin widened, making her heart skip a beat. She swallowed and dropped her eyes, hiding the colour she could feel racing across her cheeks.

The music changed. It became slower, deeper, a pulsing sound that echoed the pulse of her blood.

Something cracked and crackled inside her, something she had felt before, in the tavern in Skulls Rest. A sound bubbled up in her throat, crawling its way into her mouth to sit on her tongue. It was warm, soothing, a comfort she hadn't known was possible. She let go of Ordes' hand, sliding both arms around his neck, pressing her face to the curve of his neck again. The heat of his skin was a brand against her cheek. He smelt like the water, the wind, sunlight and sand.

Her inner song was dancing beneath her flesh, shifting along her veins, drowning out the voice of the fiddle. The words came from somewhere deep inside. 'Hold me.'

His breath hitched, and he moved, one hand reaching up to curl around the back of her neck, the other pressing against the base of her spine as he pulled her into his body. Jenyfer started to hum, her inner song brought to life, the sound vibrating through her. They had stopped dancing, but Ordes didn't let her go, holding her even tighter against him. She closed her eyes; still humming softly, a sound only he could hear, she pressed her lips to the underside of his jaw.

Ordes slid his finger under her chin, tilting her face up to his.

So close. His lips were so close they shared breath. His eyes were glazed, locked with hers. She moved a fraction closer.

The music faltered, the wrong note ringing across the deck.

Jenyfer stopped humming; Ordes shook his head slightly as she stepped away, heart pounding, skin tingling, that song echoing through her ears. Her cheeks were hot, her belly tight, body burning. The deck was silent, no more music floating through the air. Jenyfer couldn't look at anyone.

She turned and hurried below deck, music etched on the core of her and echoing through her ears as, beneath her skin, her magic roared with all the power of the ocean, smashing apart whatever barriers still remained from Tamora's binding spell.

CHAPTER 41

Kat had given the crew three hours – three whole hours to explore Carinya. Arthur's heart was in his throat as he followed Tahnet down the gangplank and onto the jetty. The sun had climbed over the horizon and the water around them blazed with golden fire, forcing him to shield his eyes.

Carinya's harbour was tucked deep in against the coast, the landscape long eaten away by the never-ending slap of the waves. In the middle of the harbour was a rocky islet, the passage between it and the rugged coastline so narrow Arthur was surprised the *Queen* had managed to sail through. There were no other large ships docked close to the shore and, with a wry smile, Arthur realised the magic of the *Queen* let her go wherever she, or Katarin, wished.

'No one will bother us here,' Tahnet said over her shoulder, answering Arthur's unasked question. 'Kat is respected here, for what she does but also for what she is.'

'What do you mean?' Arthur asked, catching up to Tahnet and slowing his stride to match hers. Up ahead, Carinya was scattered around the shoreline, a series of mismatched buildings clustering for the best view of the water. Close to the beach were dozens of small wooden boats, but, unlike the boats in Kernou, these were painted bright colours – some were green and blue, some red. Seagulls perched on the prows of the boats, their harsh cries echoing into the morning air.

Tahnet flashed a grin. 'That god of your father's holds no meaning here. Cruithea is just around the headland,' she added, gesturing to their left where the landscape curved away, the deep green of Celivale Grove bleeding into the distance. Beyond the Grove, just visible, were the first of the teeth of the Nemhain mountains, which stretched like a jagged spine almost all the way to the southern tip of the continent. Those mountains formed a barrier between Kernou and Malist, the capital lying on the eastern coast of Teyath. Arthur wondered how long the journey across the mountains – and then the barren waste that was the Camlann Plains – would have taken him, had he let his father bundle him into a carriage and send him away.

Arthur let his eyes linger on the gentle sweep of the coast to the east of him. Cruithea, and his family, Avalon and Jalen, or—

'What will you do with your hours of freedom?' Tahnet asked him, snapping him out of his thoughts. She nodded towards Carinya.

Arthur knew almost nothing about the town he was about to enter. He knew fishing was the main industry, as it was in most coastal towns. He knew Tahnet was correct – the One God had not made his presence known here. Arthur recalled his father muttering about it to himself more than once. Shrugging, he shoved his father and the One God from his mind. 'What can I do here?'

Tahnet's smile was broad. 'Whatever you like, little man.'

Arthur managed a grin at the nickname, knowing now that it was not an insult. 'What will you do?'

'I'm going shopping,' she announced, linking her arm through his and drawing him along from the end of the jetty and towards the town. The sand spread beneath them; inside his boots, Arthur wriggled his toes.

He had rarely been on the beach in Kernou and suddenly he wanted to strip his shoes off and feel the silken grit on his skin.

'Shoes, a new dress, some jewels.' Tahnet patted the pouch at her hip while Arthur just stared at her. She burst out laughing at the look on his face. 'Clothes and pretty things are my weakness.' She slowed her pace. 'Do what your heart tells you. If all you want is to wander the streets, do it. If you want to sit here and watch the water, do it. This time is for us, Arthur.'

He nodded and they resumed walking, Tahnet leading him down a lane so narrow their shoulders touched as they were forced close together to avoid the granite walls of the buildings. The laneway widened into a wide street bordered by guild houses – there was a tanners, bakery, butchery, and blacksmith. Brightly coloured fruit and vegetables in wooden crates decorated the cobblestones outside the grocers.

Tahnet squeezed Arthur's arm, pointing to a small shop at the far side of the street. 'Come on,' she said, dragging him along in her excitement. As they neared the shop, *Rosa's Dresses and All Things*, Arthur laughed, untangling his arm from Tahnet's.

'Yes, this is you, but definitely not me. I'll... I don't know.' He glanced around, eyes scanning the street, passing over the guild houses, the bakery, a cobbler, until he paused, heart surging.

A book shop.

'I'll be in there,' Arthur announced.

Tahnet pinched his arm gently, and vanished into the dress shop. Arthur hoped Rosa, whoever she was, was ready. Swallowing, he turned towards the book shop, his feet moving without having to think about it.

In his old life, books were forbidden, the knowledge contained within their pages deemed too dangerous. Arthur had been denied the simple pleasure of a book since childhood and now it was as if all the knowledge, the power and the secrets of the world were about to spread themselves before him without judgement, without asking anything in return except for him to promise to take it all in, to hold the words he was about to consume inside him and never forget them.

The book shop did not have a fancy name like Rosa's dress shop. The sign was simple, a scrawling of white letters over a thin slab of dark timber dangling like a fish on a hook from the awning.

To Arthur, that sign said welcome.

He took a deep breath and pushed open the unassuming wooden door. No squeal or whine rose from the hinges, the door swinging wide for him, the space beyond dark and mysterious.

'Hello?' Arthur said. His voice echoed, too loud, and he gulped down a breath and then another. As his eyes adjusted, he saw them – rows upon rows of books, leather-bound spines lined up invitingly. He took a step further into the shop.

'Hello.' The voice came from his left, causing Arthur to jump and clutch at his chest. He turned to face an old man, white hair glowing in the dim light, his lined face partially hidden in the shadows. 'I've not seen you before, boy.'

'No, no,' Arthur stammered. 'I'm with Katarin. On her ship.'

The man chuckled. 'Where else would she be? How is the good Captain?'

'You know her?'

'Everyone knows her here,' the man declared. 'What can I do for you?'

'Oh,' Arthur began. 'Are you not open? I can come back...'

The man stepped closer, sliding his arm around Arthur's shoulders. Arthur tensed involuntarily, sucking in a sharp breath, but the man simply nudged him deeper into the shop, until all corners of Arthur's vision were filled with books and his nostrils were filled with the smell of old paper and dust, of words he had not yet read, and he was filled with a hunger that gnawed at his insides, making him gasp. The man gave Arthur's shoulder a squeeze and then he was gone; Arthur was alone with the towers of books as tall as trees, the wisdom contained within their pages planted as seeds and long grown into something that Arthur felt he could harvest and consume. It was a banquet of knowledge laid out before him.

Arthur's stomach was tight. His blood was tight, burning, and a little voice – his father's voice – was in his ears, reminding him of his sins, of this new sin he was about to commit.

The One God sees all, Arthur. He knows all. He sees what you do. He sees the inside of you and He knows, Arthur. He knows what you are. Heathen. Blasphemer. Sinner. Stained and corrupted. He knows.

Arthur shut his ears to the words, closing his eyes until they had faded to nothing more than echoes of a past he was determined to... forget? No. He would not forget, for in forgetting he would be denying the things that had happened to him, to the people he knew. He would be denying, shaming, his memories.

Katarin had told him his magic was inside him. Opening his eyes and turning to the books, Arthur sought a different magic, a magic that was written in ink.

The One God—

'Can kiss my arse,' Arthur mumbled, reaching for the nearest book and sliding it free of its companions. He did not bother looking at the title, not yet. He didn't care what it was about. The book could be about fish and he would still read it. He would still open his mind and fill it to the brim with words. Glancing around, he spied a simple table set beneath a window, its panes coated in a layer of dust. Arthur turned back to the shelves and grabbed as many books as he could carry, making his way to the table and setting the volumes down gently, with the sort of reverence his father showed at the altar of the One God.

Ulrian's face flashed into Arthur's mind. His bleeding, broken face.

Arthur shook his head, pulling out the wooden chair and sitting himself at the table, the books waiting patiently. He took up the one from the top of the pile and ran his fingers over the cover, reading the title with both eyes and skin – *A Guide to Fungi*. Arthur grinned. He was going to learn about mushrooms.

He didn't care, but as he opened the book, he glanced at the stack before him, taking a sneak peek at the titles.

Avalon.

Swallowing, Arthur shoved the book about mushrooms to the side, sliding the book on Avalon out from beneath one about trees, but he stopped before he opened it. He would soon see the magical island for himself; would reading someone else's words, someone else's opinion, alter whatever perception he would have of the place? He didn't know, and couldn't be sure. Hands hovering over the book, Arthur chewed on his lip, deciding quickly not to let anyone sway him, to keep his mind open and ready to form its own opinions on the Isle of Mists.

He pushed the book aside, then took the next one from the pile.

The Old Ones.

Eagerly, he dove into it, careful with the pages, which were thin and crisp beneath his fingers. He read the same information and stories Katarin had told him already, almost word for word. Disappointed, Arthur turned to the next page, and found himself confronted with an illustration of a man that was unmistakably Jalen. Heart in his throat, Arthur read the inscription quickly, noting the date the picture was drawn – over one hundred years ago.

Arthur sat back, eyes on the drawing.

Jalen was a demi-god. Ageless. Part of the landscape, part of the fabric of the world. Powerful. Once considered so important that people worshipped him, like they would an Old One.

Arthur rubbed at his face, then pressed the heels of his hands against his eyes, his heart swelling and clenching at the same time. The atmosphere in the room suddenly shifted. A breeze tickled the back of Arthur's neck and the temperature slid away, causing the skin on Arthur's arms to tighten. Something touched his cheek – fingers, warm and strong. They stroked once, twice, then withdrew.

'Open your eyes, Arthur.'

He swallowed, and did as he was told.

Perched on the edge of the small table, one hand tracing the title of the book about Avalon, was Jalen.

'Am I dreaming?' Arthur whispered. He did not move, not wanting to break whatever spell it was that had been woven around him, scared to even breathe in case Jalen vanished again.

'Do you want to be dreaming?' Jalen asked, withdrawing his hand from the book and running it through his sandy-coloured hair. It was a gesture Arthur knew so well, one that he had watched numerous times and wished it was his fingers tangled in Jalen's locks.

Arthur smiled. 'No,' then, quietly, 'where are you?'

'Not far.'

'Come to the *Queen*,' Arthur said quickly, forgetting his fears and taking Jalen's hands in his. 'Kat won't mind.'

Jalen chuckled. 'She would. No men, not even demi-gods, are allowed on her ship. A brother, though...'

'You know about that?' Arthur breathed.

'I've always known,' Jalen said softly. 'Are you happy? You're discovering your family. I remember you telling me once how much you longed to meet your mother's kin, to know them, and to have them know you – the real you.'

'That isn't what I said,' Arthur replied, frowning. 'Is it?'

'No, but it's what you meant.'

'You know my thoughts do you?'

Jalen smiled, and nodded. Feeling bold, Arthur pushed back his chair and stood, slipping his arm around Jalen's middle and leaning into his body. 'Now what am I thinking?' he murmured, leaning forward and pressing his mouth to the place just beneath Jalen's ear, smirking as Jalen's fingers dug into his arms and his legs shifted apart so that Arthur could nestle between them.

'I miss you,' Arthur whispered. 'I miss just being able to talk to you, to see you, even if it's just for a moment.'

Jalen's hands found the small of Arthur's back. 'I'm here now.'

'But you're not really, are you?'

'Does it matter?' Jalen asked softly. One of his hands untucked Arthur's shirt and slipped beneath it. The moment his fingers touched Arthur's bare skin, Arthur sucked in a breath, pulling back quickly, sliding his hand up to grip Jalen's throat. He caught a glimpse of Jalen's eyes, a flash of his smile, before their lips drew together like the needle of a compass is always drawn north.

It was a gentle kiss to begin with, a soft meeting of their lips, but something changed and Arthur wasn't sure if it was him or Jalen who pressed harder, who opened their mouth and swept their tongue out to claim the warmth of the other, to suck and taste and drink them down, driven by simmering desire and the passionate flame that had been steadily burning since the moment they spent in the cave.

Arthur pulled back only long enough to yank at his shirt, ripping it over his head and tossing it to the floor. Jalen copied his movements, eyes gleaming, and then he reached for Arthur's hands, placing them on the broad expanse of his chest as he lay back on the table, an invitation for Arthur to touch, to explore, to take all the time he wished.

Only Arthur did not want to take time. He dug his nails into Jalen's chest, making him gasp and arch his back, then leant forward so he could catch the bead of sweat that trickled down Jalen's throat, their chests pressed together, their skin slick. Arthur was on fire, his body tingling as Jalen's hands moved over his flesh, down the curve of his spine, over the sharp line of his hips until they reached the buttons on Arthur's trousers.

And stopped.

'I want you,' Arthur murmured, his teeth grazing against Jalen's nipple. He kissed his way up Jalen's chest, over his collarbone, along the strong column of his throat, closed his teeth over the soft lobe of Jalen's ear, one hand fumbling between their bodies, the other moving into Jalen's hair.

Arthur frowned as his fingers brushed something firm. He took hold of it – it was small, sharp, slightly rough to touch. He pulled it free and rested his weight on his elbows, examining the object in the muted light.

It was a piece of coral.

He showed it to Jalen, who nudged him gently. Arthur pushed himself upright, still holding the coral between his fingers. Jalen sat up and kissed him gently. He took the coral, placing it in Arthur's palm, and, as Arthur watched, the coral grew and changed until Arthur was holding a crown.

'Why don't you try it on?' Jalen suggested, his voice husky from kissing. 'See if it fits.'

Arthur shook his head. He didn't want to think about crowns. He wanted more kissing, more touching, *more*. But he could not take his eyes from the crown. It was neither silver nor gold, but something in between. There were no jewels. No ornamentation. It was a simple crown.

'It's heavy,' Arthur declared. 'It feels like it will snap my head from my shoulders. I can't wear this.'

'You can, Arthur. It isn't too heavy for you.'

With a sigh, Arthur returned to his seat and set the crown on the table before him. The fire that had been burning inside him had gone out, and he was aware of the sweat drying on his skin, on the cool crispness of the air around them. He drummed his fingers on the table-top in time to the music that was suddenly pulsing through his brain. 'Why does it sing?'

'I don't hear a song,' Jalen told him. He climbed off the table and stood behind Arthur; his fingers fluttered over Arthur's hair, down the sides of his neck, until his hands were resting on Arthur's shoulders. 'It only sings for you. That means it is yours.'

'But how?' Arthur whispered. He could not take his eyes off the crown. 'How is this meant for me? I don't know how to be a king. I'm not....'

'Not worthy?' Jalen said softly.

'Yes,' Arthur said.

'Try it on,' Jalen suggested again. 'Humour me. I want to see what it looks like.'

Arthur hesitated, then reached for the crown. His fingers tingled. The song inside him surged into life.

'Let me help,' Jalen said, his mouth near Arthur's ear. He reached around Arthur and lifted the crown from the table. Arthur watched it rise in Jalen's hand from the table, watched it travel into the air and then vanish above his brow before it was placed gently on his head.

Heat raced through him so forcefully he gasped and then it was gone; but Arthur could still feel it lingering there, caught somewhere between his blood and bones.

'It suits you,' Jalen said, and Arthur twisted in his seat so he could wind his arms around Jalen's naked torso. Jalen's fingers trickled like water over Arthur's cheeks, before he cupped Arthur's face between strong hands and kissed him again.

Desire rose like a great snake in Arthur's belly, twisting and swirling through him, merging with the music that seemed part of him now. He went to stand up, wanting to go back to the moment where he had Jalen on his back amongst the books, or maybe it could be the other way around, but Jalen's hands were on his shoulders and his mouth pulled free of Arthur's.

Arthur closed his eyes.

'Wake up, Arthur,' Jalen whispered, his lips brushing Arthur's ear. 'I'll see you in Avalon.'

Arthur jolted upright, his cheek tingling from where it had been pressed against the pages. The book was still clutched between his fingers. Gasping, he dropped it, reaching up, his fingers trembling. He found nothing except his hair, slightly tussled, in need of washing.

He was fully dressed.

There was no crown. There was no Jalen.

But inside him, a song was singing.

Chapter 42

Compared to Skulls Rest, The Vale was an ordered town. Jenyfer and Ordes had been dropped on the beach, *The Excalibur* anchored far out to sea, a silhouette of tall masts and loose sails against the setting sun. Ordes had led them through the short, cobblestoned streets towards the inn – a neat, two-storey building fronted by what Jenyfer assumed was a market square. Shops and guild houses bordered the square on the other sides and, beyond the inn, she imagined there were cottages with neat roofs and pretty gardens.

The inn, *The Forest Rose*, was aptly named; thorny vines climbed the face of the building, delicate pink roses dotted throughout, a sweet perfume hanging in the air. Trees that sported bright bursts of purple blossoms lay behind the building, branches stretching into the sky and arching almost protectively over the freshly thatched roof. Ordes organised their room while Jenyfer tried not to gape at what she found inside the main door.

It was the most beautiful place she had ever seen. The carpet was lush cream and she wanted to drop to her knees and run her hands over it.

The walls were a deep mahogany colour, the curtains the gold of a rising sun. Lamorna would have called it 'garish', but Jenyfer was too awed to care what the One God would make of such a place. A fire burnt in a hearth on one side of the foyer, the air warm and dripping with the scent of roses; a vase of the blossoms was arranged perfectly on a small table in one corner, while two inviting armchairs embroidered with a pattern of tiny rosebuds sat either side.

The innkeeper was a shapely woman with a generous smile, her hair gold ringlets that were beginning to fade to grey. Her dress was buttoned to the throat, the tiny specks of pearl glimmering against the dark grey fabric.

'Newly wedded, are we?' she asked.

Jenyfer abandoned her admiration of the room, opening her mouth to object, but Ordes cut across her, his voice smooth. 'Just this week.'

'Well,' the innkeeper said, her smile dropping a fraction. 'Our best room is already booked, but if you're happy to take the second-best...'

Ordes withdrew a leather pouch from his coat pocket. 'I'm sure your second-best is as good as your first,' he said, glancing at Jenyfer over his shoulder. 'The wife won't mind, will you, love?'

Jenyfer swallowed, face burning. 'No, I don't mind.'

Ordes paid for two nights and the innkeeper passed him a shining golden key. 'Enjoy your stay at *The Forest Rose*. Breakfast is included. The dining room is to your right, unless you were wanting your meal left at the door?' Her eyebrows lifted with the tiniest hint of suggestion.

'Room service won't be necessary,' Jenyfer said firmly, stepping up to the counter and taking the key from Ordes' hand. A jolt went through her as her fingers brushed his. She ignored it, turning and heading for the stairs, following the innkeeper's directions. Ordes sauntered along behind her, whistling to himself. She could feel him grinning. When they found their room, Jenyfer unlocked the door, grabbed him by the sleeve of his coat and hauled him inside.

'You're keen.' His chuckle made her bones rattle. He was so close to her – too close – making her stomach knot and her muscles liquify.

'Newly married?' she hissed, shoving him away.

He shrugged. 'What else could I say? This is a respectable place, and a respectable inn. I could hardly tell her we were here on pirate business, could I?'

Jenyfer ground her teeth and huffed a sigh, before turning her attention to their room. She didn't notice the curtains or the carpets. She didn't notice the colour of the walls or the wash stand and dressing screen. Her eyes fell on the bed.

The one bed.

Slowly, she turned to face Ordes.

He held up his hands, then crossed the room to the window, pulling back the curtains and peering out. The sky was dark gold shot through with lurid pink and purple. 'I'll take the floor, Jen. The market is in the morning.'

'And?'

'In Skulls Rest, I was about to teach you how to steal.'

Her blood warmed at the memory of what had happened between them in that tavern; whatever Tymis' song had recently awoken inside of her purred and sighed in longing. She ignored it as well, like she'd been ignoring it ever since she and Ordes had danced to the music on the deck of *The Excalibur*. 'You're going to teach me tomorrow, aren't you?'

He nodded, still looking out the window. His hair was knotted at the base of his skull; her traitorous eyes moved over the broad sweep of his shoulders and the nape of his neck, with its extremely soft skin. Her fingers tingled. Jenyfer bit her lip and clenched her thighs together.

'It's not as hard as you think,' Ordes said, turning to face her. 'Most people are fixed on what they are doing – it all comes down to picking the right mark. You want someone who is distracted, who won't notice someone standing a bit too close to them, and who won't notice when you slide your hand into their pocket.'

In Kernou, the punishment for stealing was severe. 'What happens to thieves here?'

Ordes shrugged. 'The same as anywhere.'

'You want me to risk my *hand* so you can... what? Why exactly are we doing this? Why is it important that I can do this?' She wanted to kiss him, and that bed was watching her, as if it knew every thought that dwelt in her brain. Her teeth snapped together so tightly her jaw twinged in protest.

'Number one – magical map or not, you'll be more valuable to my father if you can do something he considers useful, and two,' Ordes said, going on before she could object. 'This could save you from hunger. It could save you from spending night after night sleeping rough. If you've got some coin in your pocket, you can always pay for a room and a hot meal somewhere.'

'If I end up somewhere on my own, you mean,' Jenyfer concluded in a small voice.

Ordes said nothing.

'Well, then,' she said, shaking back her hair. 'You'd better hope you can teach me to be useful, so I don't end up left behind in some shady port town while *The Excalibur* sails off into the sunset.'

'I'd hardly call this place shady,' Ordes answered playfully.

She put her hands on her hips.

'I don't make the rules,' he said gently. 'But I'm as bound by them as anyone else.' He sighed, moving away from the window, shedding his coat as he went and tossing it on the armchair in the corner of the room. His shirt followed and Jenyfer turned away, listening to him hunting around the cupboard tucked against the far wall; but the image of what he looked like without half of his clothing had branded itself on her brain weeks ago.

She shouldn't want him at all. It felt wrong, to desire his touch, to want him close to her, after Bryn and what had happened, but part of her couldn't help it.

'Did you mean it?' she blurted, keeping her back to him.

'Mean what?'

She swallowed tightly, then turned so she could see his face. 'You'd kill him for me?'

Ordes' expression darkened. 'Yes.'

'Why? Why would you offer to do something like that?' she asked.

His hands tightened on the blanket he held. 'Because what happened to you was wrong, Jenyfer. I know you said he had no choice, but he did. He didn't have to... what sort of man behaves like that? I'd have let them tie me up to that stupid stake before I'd ever hurt someone like that,' he added softly. 'Before I'd hurt you like that. It wouldn't matter what I wanted, how much I wanted you, I'd never...' Ordes stopped, shook his head. He glanced at her again. 'So yes. I'd kill him. If you asked it.'

Jenyfer could only nod and turn away, hunting through the small bag they'd brought for something to sleep in. When she next looked, Ordes was lying on the carpet, the pillow under his head, a blanket spread across his long legs. His eyes were closed, but she knew he was not sleeping.

Jenyfer had never enjoyed the market in Kernou, where unseen eyes watched her every move, noted who she talked to, how long she looked at someone. She'd felt safer walking the market with Bryn, when they were friends and nothing more. His presence had made her relax, knowing that he was there, a barrier between her and those who watched her, as they watched all the young women in the village. It was well known and accepted that women must be observed, contained and restrained.

She missed Bryn. She missed her friend; but the man she'd glimpsed when he took the title of her husband was not the man she knew. She was still incredibly angry with him – for hurting her, for allowing himself to be manipulated and for allowing himself to fall under the One God's spell.

Jenyfer's throat tightened. Ordes touched her arm, jolting her back to the present. He'd spent the hours since dawn instructing her on how she should move through the crowd, throwing instructions at her from his place on the floor while she ground her teeth, panic rising to coat her tongue.

He was dressed in what she thought were probably his most respectable clothes – a tidy white shirt, dark vest, and trousers that were too tight to be respectable. She'd decided that when he'd emerged from behind the dressing screen in their room in *The Forest Rose*; but she'd said nothing, and she'd made sure her eyes didn't linger on any part of him. His boots were polished and his hair was tied at the base of his neck again, arranged so it covered the pointed tips of his ears.

Jenyfer had learnt The Vale was a trading port, and that ships from all over Teyath stopped here. It was the largest settlement in the south of the continent, sweeping from the beach and up the gently rising hills behind it. Security was tight here, owing to the close proximity of Skulls Rest, but Ordes had told her it was not a place frequented by pirates which, he said, worked in their favour.

'No one will be expecting a beautiful woman to pick their pockets in broad daylight,' he'd said with a grin that Jenyfer thought was nervous.

He wasn't sure she could do this, and for that, she'd decided, she would.

Wearing the same dress she'd worn in Skulls Rest, but topped with a long lady's coat of soft velvet she'd found in *The Excalibur's* hold, Jenyfer squared her shoulders, reaching up to make sure her hair was tucked in its neat bun. Her sister would be impressed that she'd managed her hair by herself.

Jenyfer swallowed, resisting the urge to look out to sea, to imagine where Lamorna was at this moment – and whether she was even alive.

Pushing thoughts of Lamorna aside, Jenyfer focused on the people around her, not making eye contact for more than a moment, like Ordes had told her. *You don't want them remembering the woman who looked at them a little too long,* he'd said, so she kept her glances brief and polite. She walked slowly, her arm linked through Ordes', the two of them looking for all the world like they really were a couple, her flesh burning where he touched her. She knew he'd be able to feel her thundering heart rate and tried to pull a layer of calm over herself. He pretended to show her things at some of the stalls – a brooch, a pair of earrings that he pretended he would buy for her. When she played the game and objected, he bent his head to hers, whispering in her ear.

'I'll come back for them later.'

The morning wore on. Jenyfer wasn't sure how much time had passed since they'd stepped from the inn and into the ordered bustle of the market, but the sun was warm on her face, climbing higher into the sky. The air was thick with moisture, and she was sweating under the heavy dress and coat. She tugged on her sleeves, making sure the magical ink of the map was hidden. Ordes was scanning the crowd, one hand resting in the small of her back. Everytime he touched her, her head spun. She'd barely eaten breakfast, picking at a few pieces of fruit while Ordes crammed his mouth with pancakes and strawberries. She had tried not to watch him eat, tried not to watch those lips wrap themselves around a plump strawberry, and tried really hard not to think about what those lips would feel like on other parts of her body.

Jenyfer cleared her throat. 'I'm ready.'

His eyes passed over her, then moved through the crowd. 'The elderly gentleman near the jewellery stand.'

'I can pick my own mark,' she said in a low voice.

'Alright,' Ordes concurred softly. 'Off you go then.'

'You'll be right here, won't you?' Jenyfer asked as nerves clawed their way through her chest; a quick glance at the crowd told her he'd chosen the best person, so the elderly gentleman at the jewellery stand it would be.

Ordes nodded, and she took a deep, steady breath, smoothed her hands over her dress and moved into the crowd, keeping her eyes on her mark even as she smiled and feigned interest in the furry peaches and smooth-skinned pears displayed in a basket.

She'd been given instructions before they left the inn on how to approach a mark, how to remain unnoticed, but as she neared the man near the jewellery stall, all of those commands fled her mind and she was suddenly filled with music. It swam beneath her skin, as smooth and powerful as a cresting wave, and her magic shifted in response. It calmed her, made her steps slow and her smile coy as, deep within, a voice urged her to touch the man's arm.

She did, her hand snaking out before she could stop it. He started, and then, when he saw a young woman resting her hand on his forearm, he smiled. He was not as old as Ordes had suggested, hardly elderly. His hair was faded and the skin around his eyes was gently creased, but his smile was kind.

Jenyfer motioned to the jewellery. 'It's all so beautiful,' she breathed in a voice that was not hers. It was low and sultry, purring, and she smiled at the man.

'It is, yes,' he agreed, not taking his eyes off her face.

'I do like those earrings,' she whispered. 'The pearls.'

The humming started low in her throat, spilling into the air, loud enough for only her mark to hear. It was Tymis' song she hummed, the melody that had been caught in her blood since she'd first heard it.

The man's eyes became glassy, his face slack. 'The pearls, you say?'

'Yes,' Jenyfer said. She stroked his arm, staring up into his face. 'Will you get them for me?' The humming continued, low and deep in her throat, and she could almost see the music in the air between them, the way it bent and flexed and crept over the man's face until it eased itself into his ears.

He didn't take his eyes off her. 'Of course.'

Jenyfer smiled as he withdrew a fancy pouch from the pocket of his coat, and held her breath as he paid for the pearl earrings. She willed the stall holder to hurry, not sure how long the magic would last, amazed that it had worked in the first place, *terrified* that it had worked. When the man placed the wrapped earrings in her open palm, Jenyfer pushed herself onto her tiptoes and kissed his cheek gently. Then, heart thundering, she turned and walked calmly back across the square.

Ordes was frowning, and she knew he'd been watching. 'Did you—'

She grabbed his arm and led him swiftly away, not daring to look over her shoulder as she hurried him back to the inn and into the foyer. He looked at her in puzzlement but she shook her head and dashed up the stairs, waiting, waiting for the man from the jewellery stall to come crashing through the door.

He didn't, and Jenyfer opened the door to their room with trembling fingers, her magic dancing and swirling in triumph beneath her skin. Ordes followed her in, shutting the door behind him, turning to her.

Before he could speak, she reached into her coat pocket and withdrew the tiny parcel. Still frowning, he took it from her and unwrapped it gently.

His eyes shot to hers in shock.

'I didn't have to steal a thing. Your elderly gentleman purchased them for me,' she said simply, shrugging out of her coat with a sigh. Her heartbeat was slowly returning to normal, but Ordes' had increased in tempo, beating out of sync with hers.

'How?'

She grinned. 'I asked very nicely. Now, if you don't mind, I'm going to get out of this dress.'

She left him gaping after her, stepping behind the dressing screen to change her clothes.

CHAPTER 43

That night, after sharing a meal downstairs, Jenyfer's eyes jumping to the door every five seconds, Ordes made up his bed on the floor and fell asleep the moment he'd tucked himself under his blanket. He'd asked her over and over how she did it, but Jenyfer just smiled. Beneath her casual facade, she was terrified. Since that moment in the market, music had been swirling beneath her skin, echoing through her ears, its tempo matching the rhythm of her heart and the pounding of her blood. She was restless, and had to force herself to be still, to spend the rest of the day in their room, avoiding Ordes' eyes and staring out the window, chewing on her lip, tension digging its claws deep into her muscles.

It wasn't until night fell that she allowed herself to relax. If the man hadn't come for her yet, he wouldn't. Now that the adrenaline had worn off, Jenyfer was tired, but sleep would not come. She lay in the large bed, her skin itching. Her body would not be still. She could not get comfortable. Even in this unfamiliar place, at the far end of the continent, she could hear the sea, the same sound that had been in her ears every night for as long as she could remember. That never-ending melody of waves lapping the sand pulsed through her blood, making her twitch and ache with a longing she couldn't name.

Ordes was snoring. She made a mental note to tell him.

Jenyfer sat up and tossed back the bedclothes. Slipping from the bed, she tiptoed to the window, pulling back the curtains to peer out at the night. Stars littered the sky and the moon was almost full. The sand would be silver and the foaming peaks of the waves would glitter in the moonlight. She bit her lip and clenched her fists; water beaded on her skin.

She shifted her weight from one foot to the other, her movements a dance, in time with the music that beat in her chest, in her ears, in her blood, and in her bones. Pulling her bottom lip between her teeth again, she bit down, until the warm, salty tang of her blood slid onto her tongue.

Salt. She moaned, then clamped a damp hand over her mouth.

Jenyfer cast a glance at Ordes. He hadn't stirred.

Unable to stand it any longer, she held her breath and crept across the room, making sure she didn't accidentally step on any part of him. She kept her eyes on him as she hunted through their bag for a spare pair of trousers and pulled them on, stealing one of Ordes' shirts. She backed towards the door, easing it open like she had so many times in her aunt's house in Kernou as, in her head, swimming alongside the music, was the sound of the sea.

It was calling, and she couldn't ignore it for a moment more.

The innkeeper was in bed, the foyer empty. Almost crying with need, Jenyfer unlatched the front door of the inn and stepped into the night.

She paused, waiting for someone to call out, but there was nothing. No sound except for the sea. The Vale was sleeping, calm and peaceful. Jenyfer ran, bare feet slapping against the cobblestones, and she was almost sobbing by the time she hit the powdery sand. It was as cool and smooth as silk beneath her feet, but she kept running until the sand became firm and her footprints marked the beach.

Where the water left patterns of white lace on the sand, she stopped, sighing with relief, with gratitude, as the ocean kissed her skin. Weeks on a ship, surrounded by water, and it was not the same as actually touching it, feeling it lap gently over her flesh.

Jenyfer's legs gave out and she sank to the ground. The water swelled and surged around her, and she could hear music, louder than before. She closed her eyes and just sat, her legs tucked up, her chin resting on her knees, the music of the ocean washing over her.

The sand beneath her vibrated gently, like it was humming. Jenyfer heard herself begin to hum in response and her eyes flew open, the sound dying in her throat, but she could still hear it. Frowning, she narrowed her eyes.

Out to sea, something moved and a fin broke through the silver-kissed face of the ocean. Jenyfer held her breath, waiting, as the sea seemed to pause, before it rushed forward, surging up and around her middle. She scrambled to her feet, then froze in shock as the water receded.

Standing before her, naked limbs glistening, the moonlight captured in the delicate scales that covered her skin, was a syhren. The faery cocked her head to one side, then opened her mouth.

The most beautiful music Jenyfer had ever heard erupted from the faery's throat. It washed over her, powerful and alluring, and she felt the magic inside her swell in response to the sound. Slowly, the syhren approached, each footstep as light as air, no imprints left in the sand to show where she had been.

Jenyfer swallowed, unable to take her eyes off the faery.

The syhren smiled, revealing rows of sharp teeth. Her hand shot out and closed around Jenyfer's wrist; she threw her head back involuntarily, a song bursting from her lips, the same song the syhren was still singing.

Gently but firmly, the faery began walking backwards, pulling Jenyfer with her. The water closed around their calves, their thighs, their waists and, all the while, they sang, their voices melding together, weaving in and around one another like ribbons made of starlight and crystal.

As the water reached Jenyfer's throat, she faltered; the syhren pulled on her wrist.

'No...'

The faery lunged, throwing her arms around Jenyfer's neck, and pulled her under.

The world beneath the surface of the water was dark and cold. Jenyfer thrashed in the syhren's grip. She kicked and scratched at the lightly scaled arms, at that unearthly face, hitting out at that mouth that, somehow, was still singing.

Jenyfer's lungs were burning; her body became heavy. Her inner song was so loud. Everything hurt, inside and out, and, not knowing what else to do, Jenyfer opened her mouth and screamed.

The syhren released her. Before she shot off into the depths of the ocean, Jenyfer thought the faery looked startled. Cheeks bulging, her vision dancing with black spots, Jenyfer kicked for the surface, but she was so far under and it was so dark, she couldn't tell which way to go.

I'm going to drown, she thought. Everything hurt. Her eyes burnt, her lungs... her lungs felt strange. Desperate, Jenyfer clamped her lips shut. Everything inside her was urging her to open her mouth, to suck the sea into her body, to be one with the water.

She closed her eyes, her limbs heavy.

Something grabbed her around the middle, but she had no energy left to fight. She was dragged through the water swiftly, her hair streaming past her face, and then Jenyfer was gasping and spluttering, pulling air into her lungs while her head pounded and throbbed and saltwater licked at her throat. Sobbing, she put her face on the wet sand. Seafoam kissed her cheeks.

A hand on her back, a thump between her shoulder blades, and she vomited, head spinning, eyes burning, her chest tight. Strong arms closed around her, lifting her gently.

'You're okay, Jen,' Ordes whispered.

With a sob, Jenyfer flung her arms around him and buried her face in his neck. He carried her up the beach, onto dry sand, where he set her down gently, kneeling in front of her, taking her face between his hands. He brushed away her tears with his thumbs, his eyes scanning her face.

'She tried to kill me,' Jenyfer managed, then burst into a fit of coughing. Her clothes clung to her and she was starting to shiver, despite the warmth of the air around them.

'Who did?'

'A syhren. She...' She took a deep, shuddering breath. 'I just wanted to see the sea. This isn't my village, my home, but it's the same sea, isn't it? It was calling me. I couldn't sleep, couldn't rest... I don't know how it happened. I was just there, watching the water, and then, a syhren... I've seen one before, in Kernou, and she didn't try to hurt me.'

'This time?'

'She tried to drown me,' Jenyfer whispered. 'She pulled me into the water and tried to drown me. I screamed at her and she let me go. And then I was lost in the water, until you...'

He didn't smile; his fingers stroked her cheek, then he leant forward and kissed her.

Jenyfer froze.

He pulled back. 'I'm sorry. I thought... you should be dead, Jenyfer. You were under a long time. I woke up—' Ordes paused, breath fanning her face. 'I woke up and you were gone. There was music in my ears, and your heartbeat, it was so loud. I don't know how I knew where you were – I left the inn and just ran. When I got here, you were already under, but I could still hear your heart, so I—'

'Ordes...' There was a small frown between Ordes' eyes and she wanted to smooth it away. She licked her lips; his eyes followed the movement of her tongue.

'You're safe, that's all that matters.' His voice was low, warm. It washed over her, making her shiver. Jenyfer remained still as he brushed the back of his knuckles down her cheek, fingers trailing along the line of her jaw, down her throat. He never looked away from her face, eyes shining in the moonlight.

She tried to tell herself the trembling in her fingers was from almost being pulled under the water to her death. It had nothing to do with the way he was looking at her; he had nothing to do with the way her heart was racing and her skin was tingling.

Her song was singing again, low and soothing. It moved through her veins, filling her with music, with melody and harmony. With a longing she didn't understand.

The fire that blazed in Ordes' eyes rattled something loose inside her and she sucked in a breath; the fear that had gripped her for as long as she could remember started to dissolve. Jenyfer stared at him, watching the way he watched her, watching the emotions that crossed his face.

Ordes sighed and made to pull away, but she wound her fingers through his sodden hair and pulled him back to her, pressing her lips to his. His arms closed around her, his hands against the small of her back, and she closed her mouth over his bottom lip and sucked. A rush of something hot and powerful speared through her as he made a noise in the back of his throat, fingers digging into her back. He kissed her fiercely, guiding her backwards, until she was pressed against the sand, his body resting over hers.

Jenyfer's heartbeat thundered in her ears alongside his. She was hot and cold and fragile and strong at the same time. She was burning and boiling and coming apart at the seams. His hands were in her hair, on her face, her arms. Her body responded, moving on instinct as heat pooled in her belly, lower, her muscles coiled so tight she thought they would snap as Ordes grazed his teeth over her jaw, down the column of her throat. Jenyfer sighed and tipped her head back; his teeth nipped at her collarbone while his hands moved beneath her shirt.

'Jen—' he whispered.

'Don't stop,' she heard herself say, her voice nothing more than a breath sliding into the heated air between them. She pushed her body closer as his hand slid along her rib cage to brush the underside of her breast. Sparks shot through her, and she trembled, arching her body towards his touch, but he withdrew his hand, leaving her writhing on the sand as his head came to rest in the curve of her neck.

Ordes' breathing was ragged, his blood thundering in her ear. She ran her hands along his spine, feeling his skin shiver and twitch beneath her fingers. He pulled back; his eyes roamed her face, his expression wild, tortured. 'Not like this. Not here.'

A shiver shot through her at his words. 'I have wanted this since Skulls Rest. Since before then, actually.' She ran her hand up his arm, over his shoulder; her fingers drifted lower, over his hip. He caught her hand, and held it steady.

'You could have died, Jenyfer.'

She shivered as a chilly breeze swept over them.

Ordes kissed her again, then pulled away and helped her to her feet. 'Come on. Let's go back to the inn. You need to get warm and dry.'

His head was swimming with her scent, her taste, the heat of her skin, her fingers on his skin. Every muscle was so tense Ordes thought he'd snap. She stood near the dressing screen, clothes clinging to her, hair a wet slick over her shoulders. He stood leaning against the small table for two in the centre of the room, hands gripping the edge to stop him closing the space between them and taking her then and there.

'I haven't got any more clothes,' she said softly, digging through their small bag.

'Me either,' he said. 'You're wearing my shirt.'

'Oh.' Jenyfer glanced down at herself, colour painting her cheeks. 'You can see through this, can't you?' She asked, tugging the shirt away from her chest.

Ordes swallowed. 'I can.'

She met his gaze, a smile crawling slowly over her lips. 'Well then,' she said huskily; and, before he could stop her, she pulled the shirt over her head. 'Now we're even.'

Ordes bit his lip and clenched his fists, tried not to think about what it was like to touch her. Tried not to think about what she smelt like, what she tasted like, the tremors he'd felt race through her body when he'd pressed her against the sand. Tried not to think about what it would be like to taste the rest of her.

Her fingers moved to the buttons on her trousers and his mouth went dry. Three steps. That was all it would take to be able to wrap his arms around her. She wasn't ready, he told himself, even though all he wanted was to bury his face between her thighs.

'We should sleep,' he managed.

'I'm not tired.'

He gestured at her naked flesh. 'You should get warm.'

'I'm not cold.'

He closed his eyes. 'Jen—'

In the space of a heartbeat, she was standing in front of him. 'Maybe I am a little bit cold,' she whispered, but he could feel the heat from her flesh while beneath his skin, a fire was raging. She trailed the tip of her finger down his chest. 'Ordes, open your eyes.'

'I don't want to,' he said.

'Why?'

'Because if I keep them closed, I can't see you. I can't look at your mouth and want to kiss it. If I can't see you, I won't touch you before you're ready,' he whispered.

She stepped closer and placed both hands on his chest, running them down his body, over his hips, and slipping her fingers beneath the waistband of his trousers. His breath caught in his throat; his fingers twitched.

'What if I want you to touch me?' Jenyfer whispered. 'What if I want you to kiss me?' She slid her hands around to his front, fingers fiddling with the top button of his trousers. 'Ordes, open your eyes.'

He did, only to find her staring at him, her lips parted and plump. In the moonlight, slanting through the window, her eyes were silver. The air around them crackled, like it did before a storm crashed over the horizon. Jenyfer smiled, a hesitant, nervous smile, pushed herself onto her toes, and kissed him.

Chapter 44

The song that lived inside Jenyfer was awake and alive. It flowed through her like a river, running from her toes to the top of her head and back again, shimmering and glorious. It had never felt so powerful, not even when she'd used her magic in the tavern in Skulls Rest.

Jenyfer had been taught that desire was a thing only men experienced; but if the burning in her belly and the tingling that pricked across her flesh wasn't desire, then what was it?

Maybe it was nearly dying. Maybe it was what had happened with Bryn. That had not been her choice, but this, this would be, because surely the pounding of her blood, the rhythmic pulsing that beat between her legs had a purpose. A reason for being.

'Jenyfer...' Her name was a breath in the darkness, low and laced with longing, making her chest tighten and her belly flop. Her pulse was thrumming as Ordes held her eyes, his hands coming to rest on her hips. He squeezed, just hard enough to pull a gasp from her mouth.

'Stop looking at me like that,' he murmured. 'It isn't helping.'

'What's not helping?'

'That look,' he said. 'That one right there – the one that makes me want to touch you.'

Jenyfer swallowed, looping her arms around his neck, trailing her fingers along the curve of his shoulders, feeling him shiver beneath her touch. She was on fire, her insides a tight, knotted mess. She wanted him so badly she couldn't think. She wanted – needed – to feel his skin against hers.

'Then touch me.'

He hesitated, then his arms closed around her; she could feel how every muscle in his body was taut, and she was filled with a need to *know*. His hand slid along her ribs to close over her breast.

Jenyfer gasped, her back arching, pushing herself into his touch.

'Jen,' Ordes whispered, 'tell me to stop.'

She shook her head. 'I don't want you to stop.' She kissed her way along the line of his jaw, his throat. 'I want you.'

'Then you can have me,' he murmured. 'As much or as little as you like.'

'I want to touch you,' she said softly.

A shiver passed through him. 'Please do, because I'm afraid that if you don't I'm going to go mad.'

She could hear the furious beating of his heart, could feel it through his skin and the strange connection they had. She swallowed and stepped back so she could see him. Every line of his body was tense, but he stood still, letting her look, letting her run her eyes over the shape of him, the broad shoulders and gentle curves of the muscles on his arms. The expanse of his chest, the lines of the map barely visible in the darkness. The ridges of muscle on his abdomen, the slight dip of his waist and the sharp lines of his hips.

Jenyfer reached out and grazed her hands against sharp bone and firm muscle, trailing her fingers across his belly from one hip to the other, up his chest and back down again, her touch light, feather-soft, delicate. She'd never touched Bryn like this – it hadn't occurred to her, or him. It hadn't been like this, then. The thing that surprised her the most was how much she liked it, how she liked the goosebumps that sprang to life as her fingers brushed Ordes' skin, the sharp intake of his breath, the little noise that rose from the back of his throat that he tried to hide from her, and the rise and fall of his chest as he breathed, deep and ragged.

'When I was with Bryn,' Jenyfer began, her voice soft. 'Everything happened so fast. I mean, it was all over so quickly, and I didn't like it. I'm not even sure he did, to be honest, but we did what was expected of us.' She swallowed the memory, the pain of Bryn's betrayal, away. 'And now, I don't know what's expected of me.'

'Nothing – what you do with your body is up to you,' Ordes said.

'I know,' she said quietly, 'which is why I want you to touch me. I want to know what it's like.' She could feel him studying her in the darkness and couldn't look at him, fixing her eyes on her finger as it traced the outline of his nipple. It tightened under her touch and his breathing hitched. 'I want to know,' she repeated firmly.

'You've never touched yourself?' he asked, the question making her cheeks flame, but there was no mockery in his tone, only curiosity.

'No. It's a sin. *Was* a sin,' Jenyfer said. 'Plus, I shared a room with my sister.'

Ordes chuckled lightly. 'I can't tell you what you'll like, Jen. I can tell you what I like —'

'Then do that,' she cut in. 'Tell me what you like and I'll do it.'

'How is it any different to Bryn and the rules of the One God?'

Jenyfer took a deep breath. 'Because I'm choosing this. There wasn't much I could choose for myself, Ordes. Everything in that town was so strictly monitored. There were eyes everywhere, watching everything, and none of us were free to simply be ourselves or feel what we wanted, with whom we wanted.' She glanced up at him briefly. 'But now I have the freedom to choose, so I am. And, right now, I'm choosing you.'

Jenyfer stopped, her fingers hesitating over his skin. She lowered her eyes, focusing on the centre of his chest, nervous again. 'That is, if you want me...'

'I want you,' he declared roughly. 'By the Gods I want you. But why me?'

'For some reason, I trust you,' she whispered, remembering the last time he'd asked that question. 'And I like you.'

'You probably shouldn't; I'm a pirate.' It was an attempt at a joke, but his voice cracked around the edges. 'Well, you can tell me to kiss you.'

'You've already kissed me.'

His lips twitched. 'Trust me, I haven't.'

'Okay,' Jenyfer said quietly. 'Kiss me.'

He moved closer to her, so slowly it was like time stood still. One hand cupped her cheek, the other pressed against her lower back as he nudged her forward, until her chest was pressed against his. Gently, he lifted her hair off her neck, leaning over to press his lips to the sensitive skin below her ear; she clenched her thighs together.

His lips trailed down her neck, over her collarbone, making her tremble and tip her head back, a reflex action she didn't even think about, like before. Her body moved on its own. Her hips shifted and her spine turned to liquid. She dug her fingernails into his flesh. His lips were everywhere except where she wanted them.

When Ordes finally claimed her mouth, she melted against him. Her hands moved into his hair as his tongue swept the inside of her mouth; the fingers resting on her lower spine tightened. Jenyfer's insides were burning, her head spinning, everything she was washed away in the searing heat of his kiss. He kissed her until she was panting and squirming against him. Her belly swooped low as she realised the effect all the kissing had had on him.

She trailed her hand down his chest.

He rested his forehead against the curve of her neck, while her body tingled and burnt.

Jenyfer hesitated. She'd been so bold before but, now, she was filled with nerves. 'What if I do it wrong?'

'You won't,' he said simply. Still, she hesitated. He gently took her hand and guided it to his lower belly, placing the flat of her palm against his skin. Slowly, he slid their hands lower, until she could slip her fingers beneath the edge of his trousers again. Mouth suddenly dry, she undid the buttons and eased his trousers over his hips, realising she'd never seen a naked man before, let alone touched one so intimately. Without taking his hands off her, Ordes managed to step out of his trousers and kick them away.

'What do I do?' Jenyfer asked, her voice trembling.

Ordes closed his hand over hers. 'I'll get you started.'

His voice was watery, tight, on the edge.

It was exhilarating; power surged through her. Not magic, but something else.

With his hand over hers, Jenyfer touched. Silk stretched tight, that's what it felt like, she decided. She forgot Ordes' hand was guiding her until he let go and left her to explore, to discover what made him groan, what made his breathing change. To feel him twitch and shudder beneath her hand made her grin, biting her lip again to suppress a moan as that fire that burnt in her belly moved lower, coiling in the deepest part of her.

Jenyfer was powerful, glorious, in control for the first time ever.

And trusted, she realised. She held the most sensitive part of Ordes' body in her hand and he trusted her with it. His face was still buried in her neck, but he shifted away a fraction.

'Look down,' he whispered.

She took a deep breath and looked.

And looked.

'When you're done with me,' Ordes whispered, 'it'll be time to find out what you like.'

The way he said it made her clench her thighs together again. Her belly was tight and burning with need. She couldn't get enough air into her lungs. There had to be more than the quick thrusting and grunting she'd experienced.

She had no idea if she was doing any of it right, but he didn't complain, didn't tell her to stop until he whispered her name, then pulled swiftly out of her reach, his expression tight, almost pained as he put his back to her. She watched the muscles in his back tense and relax as he exhaled on a sigh.

She frowned, then, 'Oh!'

His laugh was strangled and weak.

Jenyfer was amazed at how her hands, her ordinary, simple hands had turned him into a mess. How his hips had shifted, his fingers dug into her skin. And the way her name had sounded when he whispered it – like she was special, revered.

Powerful.

And she liked it. More than anything else, she liked it.

When he'd recovered, Ordes took her face between his hands and kissed her, long and deep, until she was clinging to him, her whole body thrumming and burning, her muscles liquefied as she became as light as air, as heavy as water.

'Now,' he said against her mouth. 'Your turn.'

She trembled as he guided her onto the bed, and she didn't stop trembling as he eased off her already loosened trousers. Her instinct was to cover herself, but he pressed his lips to hers and began to explore her body. Her breathing deepened as his fingers dipped into curves and hollows, tracing a path he followed with his tongue and lips, down the line of her throat, over each breast, so gently. Her fingers wove through his hair as he closed his mouth over her nipple.

A low moan escaped her. Her cheeks heated at the sound and she wanted to tell him to stop, embarrassed at the noises she was making, noises that didn't sound like her but that were coming from her mouth, her throat. His fingers trailed over her stomach, dipping into her belly button – she gasped, her back lifting off the mattress as she felt his teeth graze her nipple.

'I'll assume that's something you like,' Ordes murmured, lips brushing the soft flesh of her breast. She couldn't speak, only whimper her agreement. He ran the flat of his hand gently over the curve of her hip, moving back up her body to cup her breast, his palm so hot she thought it would melt her.

Jenyfer could barely breathe. She was outside her body but so deeply inside it at the same time it was overwhelming. Receiving pleasure, she decided, was wholly different than giving it. She felt like she was balancing on the very edge of her control, teetering there, ready to tumble off into something she didn't know.

She was panting, her hips shifting on their own.

'You want me to stop?'

'No,' she breathed.

Ordes dropped a kiss on her lips; a light kiss, but her hands gripped the back of his head, wanting more of him. When he pulled away, she was almost sobbing with need, with a want she didn't understand, the pressure between her legs heavy and burning. He watched her face, reading everything there. She felt the tremble in his hands as he ran them over the shape of her, over her thighs, the muscles flexing and shifting beneath her skin, until he paused, glancing at her again.

'Please,' she whispered, not knowing what she was asking for. When his fingers found the warm, swollen centre of her, she sighed in relief; but, soon, it wasn't enough, and her hips rolled against his hand.

'Jen...'

'More,' she managed. 'I want more.'

He stopped for a brief second while she writhed and squirmed, then his fingers filled her again, his thumb pressing down on the spot at the apex of her thighs that had been burning and aching for days. His movements were slow and smooth, his fingers plunging in deeply and withdrawing, again and again. Without slowing his pace, he kissed her lower belly as she mumbled nonsense, any control over her mouth long gone.

Ordes was looking up at her and she should have felt embarrassed at being so exposed, so bare before him, but she wasn't. His expression was shattered, as if he'd been ripped to pieces and put back together wrong. His fingers were still moving and, with each press of his thumb, sparks danced behind her eyes. At the first touch of his tongue against the thrumming core of her body Jenyfer gasped and fisted her hands in the bedding.

Alive. She had never felt so alive before, her every breath caught up in the movement of his mouth. Heat rippled through her, and something, something deep within her released, ripping through her almost violently. He didn't stop until she had gone quiet, her body still and boneless, legs splayed, chest heaving. Sweat littered her skin, the night air on her naked body making her shiver.

Words didn't exist and Jenyfer didn't have any anyway. She was nothing but water and feeling and flesh and an empty ache inside. She squeezed her eyes tight; sparks continued to dance behind her lids and there were tears on her cheeks.

'Jen, look at me,' Ordes whispered.

She took a deep, steady breath and wiped at her face, opening her eyes, not knowing what she'd find, but his face was soft.

'I think I understand why the One God considers pleasure a sin. Nothing should feel that good - *nothing*,' she said.

Ordes burst out laughing, then lay down beside her, pulling the blankets up around them. Jenyfer closed her eyes, curling against his chest, cocooned in his arms, and was asleep in seconds.

CHAPTER 45

Aelle had been lecturing Arthur in magic while she kept her eyes on the horizon and one hand on the ship's wheel. She was as bad a teacher as Katarin – neither of them having the patience for his blundering and lack of confidence. He'd tried to shake it off, like Katarin had suggested, and let go of fear, but that was not so easy to do when he'd spent his life being stalked by the threat of discovery. Keeping things hidden was what Arthur was good at.

How was he supposed to be a King when he hadn't cultivated the courage to be himself? The Kings from stories were fearless, fearsome, men who became legends. They were fierce leaders, pragmatic politicians, and they inspired others to follow them, to bend their knee and pledge their lives, to bleed, to *die* for them.

A King was a rock in the centre of crisis and chaos which others could fall against and find support on. Kings stood tall and did not waver, buoyed by the strength of their convictions.

Arthur rubbed at his chin. He couldn't decide what to have for breakfast. Having the freedom to suddenly make choices about his own existence was both liberating and utterly terrifying. Jalen, or the vision of Jalen that appeared in his dreams, told him he would be King.

If that was to be his destiny, Arthur needed to start making changes.

He glanced at Aelle from the corner of his eye. He would start with her, with this woman whose magic and strength left him weak in the knees. Aelle was shrewd and canny, a straight-talker who suffered no nonsense from anyone. But she was loyal. She would die for Katarin, Arthur knew that without having to ask. He had seen it in her eyes, in the way she looked at her Captain – with reverence, with devotion, with admiration.

Arthur needed to become the sort of person that others would look to.

'The ship responds to the will of the Captain,' Aelle was saying. 'Katarin is tied to this ship – the core of who she is, her magic, is bound to *The Night Queen*.'

'What does that mean, exactly?' Arthur asked.

The faery woman shot him a look. 'It means we go where she wants.'

'Why do you follow her?'

Aelle shot him a surprised look. 'Have you met your sister?'

He said nothing, just waited, and eventually, she sighed.

'Katarin saved my life. I was the first to join her. I was raised as a Priestess of the Goddess, on Avalon, but I wanted to see the world. Niniane granted me leave, and I travelled to the mainland. Humans fascinate me. They also disgust me. I found myself in Kunis, just north of Malist, and it took me less than a day to realise I was a long way from home. They were going to burn a girl in the town square for simply being what she was, and I spoke out against it.'

'What happened?' Arthur asked.

Aelle was silent for so long he didn't think she would answer him. 'They burnt the girl, and threw me in a cell. I was so scared I wasn't thinking – I could have easily escaped but, then, I had not learnt to use my magic to harm, only to heal, as is the job of a Priestess of the

Goddess,' she explained. 'The dead girl's bones weren't even cold when they tied me to the stake. By the time Katarin exploded into that square, the fire had been lit and the soles of my feet were burning. She was incredible. I had never seen anything like it and, at first, I thought I was dreaming, that pain had made me delirious. I knew her, of course, being Niniane's foster child, but I had never spoken to her. She left the men of Kunis dead and bleeding, and took me with her.' Aelle rubbed at her face. 'I could have healed myself, but I carry those burn scars on my feet still, as a reminder. Every step is pain, but I choose to live with it.' She turned her gaze on Arthur, and her face was proud. 'As to why I follow your sister – it's my duty, and not just because she saved me, but because of what she represents – hope, Arthur. In Katarin, there is hope. I just wish more could be like her.'

Arthur swallowed. Slowly, tentatively, he reached out and lay his hand over Aelle's. She jolted at his touch, but did not pull her hand away. 'Thank you for telling me,' he said simply.

'When we get to Avalon, you will see a different world, Arthur,' Aelle murmured. 'I know your life has not been easy, but hopefully, on the Isle, you will learn who you are.' She saw his look and smiled sadly. 'There are many different types of suffering. You know that already. Do not measure your own pain against that of others.'

Aelle fell silent, so Arthur let his thoughts shift, storing what she had told him away to think about later.

Avalon. He was going to see Avalon. After his dream in Carinya, he'd come back to the ship and practically demanded they go to Avalon; he needed answers. To his surprise, Katarin had agreed.

Like anyone from the mainland, he'd heard tales of the Isle of Mists – a floating island with no fixed location, shrouded in mist and magic. And he'd heard the stories of Niniane as well. That she was ruthless and powerful, capable of causing the seas to rise and swallow the land. That she craved dominion over men.

Kat had told him differently, and Arthur wasn't sure what to believe, but he'd come to understand a lot of the things he thought he knew were simply not true. He sighed, staring out at a world of water that had no beginning or end, before returning to his cabin, his mind churning with everything Aelle had said and with his dreams of the Grail. The ship rocked beneath him. Peering out the small porthole in his cabin, Arthur saw a sky coated in clouds, their undersides grey shot through with yellow.

Over the course of the day, those clouds merged, their bellies full of water, and by sunset it was raining lightly. He threw on a coat and headed onto the deck to realise *The Night Queen* was headed straight for the approaching storm. Arthur swallowed nervously. It was one thing to stand on the beach or the headland and watch the storms roll over the ocean; he imagined it was another thing entirely to be in the middle of it on a ship, getting tossed from one wave to the next.

He returned to the helm, where Aelle was still standing, and indicated the clouds. 'Will it be bad?'

Aelle looked up at the sky. 'Probably. The closer we get to Avalon, the fiercer the storms become. Although the Queen of the Isle doesn't usually welcome visitors, the storms are not her doing. It's the island – Avalon itself does not wish to be found. But,' she added, 'was a ship to wash up on her beach, Niniane would tend its crew, have the ship repaired and send them on their way again.'

'I've never heard that before,' Arthur murmured.

Aelle laughed. 'Of course not. The crews of those ships find their memory muddled, and find they cannot speak of where they have been or what has happened to them.'

The storm hit them that night. Arthur was ordered below deck, practically shoved down the stairs and into his cabin. The ship rocked violently. He watched the ocean through his porthole. The waves rose as tall as mountains, and seafoam flecked the glass before being washed away as a wave crashed over them. The wind was a raging, living thing, grabbing at the ship with angry claws, pulling and tugging and shoving *The Night Queen* around like a child's toy.

Arthur gripped the window sill, his heart in his throat. He could swim, but he knew instinctively the ocean would swallow him, pull him down into the depths to meet the King of the Otherworld.

The ship groaned; the door to Arthur's cabin was flung open as *The Night Queen* pitched sideways. He scrambled off the bed and stumbled across the floor, reaching for the door, and froze. Above deck, it was chaos – he could hear shouting, the voices of the crew snatched by the wicked wind and thrown to the waves. A barrel rolled down the passageway towards him, smashing into his door before he could close it.

Forgetting what he'd been ordered to do, Arthur braced himself and pushed into the passageway, his steps lurching, his legs wobbly. The floor beneath him rocked and rolled and the ship groaned again, sounding like she was in pain. He remembered what Aelle had said about Katarin being connected to the ship. Swallowing, Arthur dug deep for a piece of courage, and pulled himself up the water-slicked ladder and into a sodden world.

The deck was saturated – water sloshed over every side of the ship, washing over his boots. Lightning streaked across the sky, followed by a boom of thunder loud enough to give *The Night Queen* a jolt. Aelle was at the helm. Arthur could see the strain on her face as she used both physical strength and magic to try and hold the ship steady. Aelle's skin glowed in the darkness, a pulsing light emanating from her body as the sea spat spray at her.

Two of the crew hurried past him, rolling a barrel between them. As Arthur watched, they popped the lid, rain lashing their faces, and poured the contents of the barrel over the side. Oil. Where the oil and water met, the sea calmed briefly; wind rippled across it but could not pick up the water and throw it back at them.

Katarin was on deck, hair plastered to her scalp, clothes dripping. 'Shorten the sails!' she shouted. Arthur watched, amazed, as a woman scaled the rigging, climbing swiftly up the main mast. Two others followed her up the smaller masts.

The ship pitched and he lost his footing, falling to his knees, rain smashing against his back as his stomach heaved.

'What are you doing up here?' Katarin pulled him to his feet. 'Get—.'

'No. You need help,' he shouted over the roaring wind.

'You're not a sailor, Arthur,' she retorted, shoving him towards the hole that led below deck. *The Night Queen* rolled again; Katarin fell into him and, on the contact, his magic leapt into life. She felt it too and her eyes widened. She looked exhausted and he figured she'd been using her magic to try and keep the ship – to keep them all – safe.

'Let me help,' he said. 'You're tired, Kat.'

'No.' She pushed at him again.

'Katarin – *Morgaine*,' Arthur shouted, grabbing her by the shoulders. They stared at one another, wind and rain lashing their faces, and he realised in that moment that they shared the shape of their eyes.

'Fine,' Katarin shouted. 'You need to let me draw on your magic.'

'How?'

'Open your mind and let me in. Don't fight me,' Katarin added. Arthur slipped his arm around her, holding her against him. She was smaller than she appeared. He hadn't realised he was actually taller than her. Katarin's skin glowed. 'We need to get midship,' she called as the storm continued to throw the ship around. Arthur nodded, and they scrambled across the deck.

'Now what?' he asked, clinging to the main mast.

'Give me your hand,' Katarin commanded, and he did so without hesitation. The moment their bare skin touched, he felt her inside his head, beneath his skin, her magic pulling at his, drawing it to the surface. It hurt. As his magic flowed from him and into his sister, Arthur grit his teeth, holding tight to the mast, the other hand gripping Katarin's.

All the light fled her skin and then, Katarin flung her head back, tilting her face to the storm. Her lips were moving but the words rushing from her mouth were in a language Arthur could not understand. He could feel his magic draining from him, and wondered how much she would take, how much there was to take.

He closed his eyes and waited, letting it all flow out of him as the rain continued to slam into his face. He felt heavy, weighed down, like he had been wrapped in a thick blanket. It grew cold and he started shivering, his teeth chattering so violently he could hear nothing but the grating sound of teeth as they rattled in his skull.

Before he fainted, he opened his eyes. Katarin's smile was a slash of white in the rain-soaked world, and then darkness closed over his head.

Arthur was dreaming of the Grail again, but this time, he was not in his father's house. He was in a cave, dark and damp, the sea lapping at the entrance. The Grail rested on a stone altar in the middle of the cave. It was bathed in a light that shone from nowhere.

A woman sat near the Grail. Her eyes were closed, and her skin was slick with water, her sodden hair hanging over slender shoulders. In one hand she held a staff, the end decorated with feathers. Her other hand rested on the edge of the Grail. Arthur could hear its song.

He took a step forward. The woman opened her eyes.

'Not yet,' she told him, her voice as powerful as the storms that lashed the ocean.

'Who are you?' he asked.

'I am the Fisher Queen, and you are the King that shalt be.'

Arthur went to shake his head, but she snapped her fingers and he was alone in the cave. He could hear music. Singing. The hair stood up on the back of his neck. He followed the sound, leaving the cave, drawn to the magic he could sense in that voice.

Sitting on the rocks outside, facing the ocean, was a woman. She was naked, and delicate scales glinted on her flesh, shining mother of pearl and aquamarine under the cloudy sky. He moved closer to her, stumbling over the rocks while that song dove inside him, swirling and tugging on his magic. She turned to him, still singing, and he stepped back in shock.

He knew her.

Before he could say anything, she stood, her dark hair covering her like a cape. She dove into the water and vanished while overhead, lightning split the sky and a fierce wind rose from nowhere, wrapping around Arthur's body. He shielded his eyes with his hand and when the wind died, Jalen was standing before him. He smiled, and when he leant over to press his mouth to Arthur's, the world shifted and Arthur was suddenly sitting up, gulping for air.

He was in his cabin on *The Night Queen*. The storm was gone – no wind tore at the ship and, outside his window, the waves were calm. Arthur patted his body; he was warm and dry, but something was different.

'It'll come back, don't worry.'

Katarin was sitting on a chair near his bed. There were deep shadows under her eyes, but her skin still shone with magic. His, he realised. Arthur swallowed, shifting so he could face her.

'The ship?'

'In one piece,' she replied, leaning forward so she could stare into his face. 'You're powerful, Arthur. Your magic... it's warmth and darkness and light all at once. It's life and death, damp soil and leaves, and water.' She sat back, while he stared at her.

'So it worked?'

'It worked. You passed out before the best bit though – the clouds above us parted and then peeled away like the skin of a fruit,' Katarin explained with a small smile. 'It was amazing.'

Arthur rubbed at his face. 'Where are we now?'

'Getting closer to Avalon.' She paused, glanced out the window briefly, before fixing him in a curious look. 'You were dreaming. What about?'

'The Grail,' he answered softly. 'It was in a cave. There was a woman there. She called herself the Fisher Queen. Does that mean anything to you?'

Katarin was frowning. 'She is the guardian of the Grail, the shade of an ancient Queen. The Grail was given to her to protect. I'll tell you a bedtime story, little brother,' she said softly, stretching her legs out and resting her boots on his bed. 'Once upon a time, magic ruled the world. Teyath was once ruled by a brother and sister, Enyon and Eseld, who lived in their castle built into the mountains near the Camlann Plains. Their house was known as the House of the Serpent and their sigil was a red serpent eating its tail. Enyon and Eseld worshipped the Old Ones, like everyone did, but they were seduced by the promises of Ereshki, the Red One. Some say she appeared as a serpent, who whispered poison into the ears of the siblings. The Serpent convinced Enyon to kill his sister but, unable to do it – even for the power he was promised – he wounded her in the thigh with a poisoned blade instead. When she died, she cursed the land around Camlann, which has remained barren and withered ever since. The Old Ones banished the Red One and barred Enyon from his home. He was left to wander the world.'

'Camlann is deserted,' Arthur murmured. 'The castle a ruin. My father told me.'

Katarin made a noise of agreement. 'What Enyon did not know was that Eseld had begun to resist the whispers of the Red One and, when she died, she did not truly die. The Old Ones let her linger in the space between the realms, and the Grail was given into her keeping. It is said that the one who can find the Grail will heal the land with magic.' She sighed, pulling her legs free of Arthur's bed. 'But it's just a story. The Grail has been missing for centuries, along with the other Treasures of the Gods. No one will ever find them, not even Niniane.'

Arthur's eyes were heavy. Sleep was pulling him under again. 'I've seen it,' he said, smoothing a yawn. 'The Grail.'

'What, in a book?' Katarin asked.

'In my dreams,' he whispered, before blackness claimed him again.

CHAPTER 46

The shoreline of the Pearl Coast was visible in the distance, the sand sparkling in the setting sun. The ship had barely moved since they had returned from The Vale, *The Excalibur* was idle on the water, the sails limp even though a warm, sub-tropical breeze blew around them. The crew went about their tasks as usual, but the mood was strangely sombre.

Ordes and Jenyfer were sitting on the ladder leading to the helm. Not touching her the way he wanted to was torture. He kept his hands in his lap, kept his breathing steady. She glanced at him quickly, then looked away again, and he wondered did she hear the furious pounding of his heart, or feel the press of his lips in her sleep. They sat with their shoulders touching, legs pressed close; Jenyfer rested her head against his upper arm.

His gaze moved to her bare arms, to the map that was inked there. It hadn't changed since it first appeared, neither had his, and they still had no idea where it led. Kayrus hadn't recognised the coastline either – none of the crew had – which filled Ordes with a combination of nerves and wonder.

He sighed, dropping a kiss on Jenyfer's forehead. She tilted her head so she could see his face, and her smile was content. 'Hungry?' he asked her.

'No. Tired.'

'Come on,' he said, standing and offering her his hand. 'Bed.'

She smiled and placed her hand in his; his skin tingled like it always did when she touched him. She let him lead her to her cabin. He wanted nothing more than to curl up under the blankets with her, but his magic was restless, his skin itching still. He knelt at her feet instead, resting his hands on her legs. She ran her fingers through his hair, tucking it behind his ear. She traced the pointed tip, sending a shiver through him.

'If I'm a syhren, even a half-syhren, that means I'm a faery, doesn't it?' Jenyfer asked, continuing to run her fingers over his ear. 'Why aren't my ears like yours?'

'Maybe they are. I'd have to check,' Ordes told her, standing so he could slide his fingers over her cheeks and tuck her hair behind her ears. She waited as he pretended to inspect her ears; he felt her tremble as he explored the curve of her right ear, then giggled when he bent and kissed it, that giggle switching to a low moan as he pulled her lobe into his mouth. 'No,' he murmured, pulling away. 'They're just normal ears.'

Her breathing was deep, her lips curled into a playful smirk. 'I'm not really tired.'

'Oh?'

Jenyfer patted the mattress. 'There's plenty of room.'

Ordes felt his stomach tighten. 'There is, yes, but I need to see my father. I still have a job on this ship, you know.'

'Are you saying I'm distracting you from your job?' She shook her head in mock disappointment. 'Well then, you'd better go.' She shuffled back on the mattress, reaching down to remove her boots one at a time. They hit the floor with a gentle thud. Her fingers went to work on the buttons on her trousers and she lay back, lifting her hips so she could slide them off and toss them on the floor.

Their eyes met. 'Good night,' Jenyfer said simply, rolling over and putting her back to him. Ordes bit his lip, then reached out to trail his fingers along her bare leg, from ankle to thigh.

She shivered; her breathing changed and her heart increased its pace.

'Sweet dreams,' he whispered, leaning over to press a kiss to her thigh, before forcing himself to turn around and leave. He returned to the deck, where he watched the water while trying to get his heart rate, and his twitchy magic, under control. When the egg-yolk yellow sun slunk beyond the horizon and flames kissed the sea, his father joined him.

'No dinner?'

'Not hungry,' Ordes said. Then, 'Why is the ship responding to her?'

'No idea. Don't let her out of your sight – shouldn't be difficult,' Tymis added in a murmur, his gaze dropping to the hands he rested on the railing; he drummed his fingers against the timber.

Ordes stiffened. There, not far from them, a small boat glided, hanging low in the water, as if weighed down. Empty, save one – the helmsman. Ordes shivered, wondering how many souls were in that boat on the way to the Otherworld.

Tymis followed his gaze. 'What do you see?'

'The Bag Noz,' Ordes mumbled, not taking his eyes from the vessel, or the figure that stood there, draped in dark cloth, his face hidden. No one had ever seen the face of the helmsman of the Night Boat and Ordes hadn't laid eyes on the vessel since before Jenyfer was brought on board. He wasn't sure why he could see it and no one else could, and why he was seeing it now, out here, in the middle of nowhere.

When the Bag Noz had gone, Ordes left his father on deck, retreating to his cabin, his brain flying, his body on fire as he climbed into bed. His magic was restless, more than usual. Jenyfer was on the level below him, curled in her bed. He rolled over onto his stomach, shoving his head under the pillow.

What was she thinking at this moment? Ordes bit his lip, fighting off the waves of desire, of the memory of how her flesh felt beneath his hands. How she tasted. He'd thought about her almost every moment since they'd woken up curled around one another in The Vale. His belly tightened and he clenched his fists, nails biting into his palms, forcing himself to breathe, in and out, steady and deep, until he eventually fell asleep, the taste of her on his tongue.

When he woke, the sky was grey, the wind biting.

He found Jenyfer above deck, staring out to sea. He went to stand by her side, close enough to satisfy the craving in his blood, just for a moment. He rested his hip on the railing, taking in her face and the scowl that resided there. The wind teased strands of her hair free of her braid; they danced across her cheek and he wanted to push them away. He folded his arms tight, fingers digging into the fabric of his shirt so he didn't crush her to his chest like he wanted to. He couldn't stop looking at her and he knew, instinctively, where she was at every moment of the day.

She gave him a tiny smile, one corner of her mouth twisting, and he couldn't help it – he reached over and ran the tip of his finger along her bare forearm, watching her skin pucker.

'All my life, I've felt off balance,' Jenyfer told him. 'The ground seemed to shift beneath my feet and my stomach always rolled but out here, on the water, it doesn't. My aunt used to make teas for me, to help with the nausea. Probably magic teas,' she added, the scowl returning. 'I know something strange is going on, but I need to find my sister, Ordes.'

'I already told—'

'I need her back,' Jenyfer said, her voice low and firm, deep and powerful, her fingers tightening on the railing. Her voice washed over him, making him shiver. It wasn't only him who was caught up in the magic in her voice. He'd seen the way the crew looked at her when she spoke, their faces slightly vacant, eyes glistening.

'I don't think we can help.'

She turned her vivid blue gaze on him, her eyes furious. 'Why?'

'The Captain won't take you to Lyonesse, not for anything,' Ordes said quietly. 'And your aunt told you not to go to the island, to stay away from Melodias.'

'I know that, but I can't just forget about Lamorna,' Jenyfer fumed. 'We haven't had the best relationship, but she's still my sister. I can't abandon her. It's my fault she ended up in Lyonesse. I was the one who called that syhren to the beach. I'm the reason she is with Melodias in the first place. And, if I am a syhren, isn't that where I should be? Isn't Lyonesse the best place to learn about my magic?'

'Tell me what you know about Melodias? About the Master of Songs and Death,' Ordes asked, keeping his voice low. The thought of her going there made him sick to the stomach. 'If you're so insistent on marching into Lyonesse, you need to know what, *who*, you're going to face.'

Jenyfer swallowed. 'I know what everyone knows – Lyonesse contains the portal to the Otherworld, and Melodias controls that portal.'

'That isn't exactly correct,' Ordes told her. 'Melodias is the God of the Seas, but he is also a master of tricks and illusions. He is the King of the syhrens, who answer to him and him only. The portal to the Otherworld is not his to control. Souls do pass through there on their way to Ankou – the Bag Noz travels the river that runs through Lyonesse. Melodias built his castle over the river so he can watch over the souls of the dead, but he has no power over them.'

'Then why did he do that?'

Ordes shrugged. 'I don't know. My father once said that when the Old Ones were created, they were given the chance to choose which realm they ruled over. Melodias wanted the Otherworld, but he was too mercurial, too fickle and volatile, ever-changing – like the sea. So he was given dominion over the waters and all they contain instead.' Ordes looked out over the ocean. 'He's dangerous, Jenyfer. He's a God with a bad temper and a grudge.'

She was silent for a long moment. 'But he's the only one who can teach me to use my magic, isn't he?' She lowered her voice. 'I need to go to Lyonesse, Ordes.'

'We don't know for sure if you're a syhren,' he argued.

Jenyfer took a deep breath. 'Regardless, I need to rescue my sister, if she's truly there. I don't know if she's dead or alive, but I need to know.' She glanced at him. 'I'm asking for your help.'

'I can't help you,' Ordes answered. Jenyfer jammed her hands on her hips, eyes pinned to his face. Her lips were a thin line and every part of her body was tense. He wanted to kiss her. He unfolded his arms and rubbed at the back of his neck as something in his chest caved in, a gaping wound emerging. 'I'm sorry.'

'Then take me to Avalon,' Jenyfer said as she moved closer to him and her fingers curled around his wrist. 'Come with me. I want you to come with me.'

Ordes took a breath that tasted of apples and regret. 'I can't.'

'Why not?'

His eyes drifted towards his father's cabin. 'I can't leave him.'

In her dreams there was a voice. It was deep and soothing, melodic and powerful. It spoke of nothing and everything at the same time, flowing over her and diving inside her. Music drifted through the air, wrapping her up and holding her in its embrace, as loving and tender as a mother with her child.

Jenyfer floated in a space that was neither here nor there. She was weightless. She was heavy, light, hot and cold at the same time. Her blood burnt and sang and her skin felt like it was splitting apart. It felt like it would swell and cover the world.

She was naked. Ashamed, she put her hands over her breasts, trying to cover herself from whoever might see, but it was only her, and then it was Ordes, standing before her. He gently removed her hands, exposing her to his eyes, before he bent and took her nipple in his mouth.

Sparks shot through her, whorls of heat and light dancing through her blood as music swirled around them, the notes plump and ripe like sweet fruit she could pluck from the air. She did just that, catching them as they floated past her and putting them in her mouth, where they exploded on her tongue. Bright, white light pierced her vision and water lapped at her toes like Ordes' tongue on her breast.

Jenyfer closed her eyes and when she opened them she was alone, sitting on the rocks with the ocean spread before her. Music bubbled up her throat, so she opened her mouth and sang. She didn't care that she was naked. She didn't care that her skin glimmered with scales. There was only the sea and the music that speared through her, painful and pleasurable at the same time and so she sang and sang until her throat was raw and she could taste blood.

Something moved behind her. She glanced over her shoulder to find a man staring at her.

She knew him.

Recognition flashed across his face as he looked at her and she wanted to speak, to ask why he was there, in her dream, but she was still singing, notes suspended in the air around her. The man took a step forward and, for a moment, Jenyfer saw a crown atop his head; then it was gone, leaving his wavy brown hair free for the wind to tease.

He opened his mouth to speak to her but the ocean called, so she jumped to her feet and vanished beneath the waves.

CHAPTER 47

It was late evening on *The Night Queen*. The sun had slunk beneath the horizon hours ago, and the stars were hidden with a layer of cloud. Arthur glanced up, unable to help thinking of Jalen – of the demon of storms and the winds. After being on the ocean in bad weather, sailors would speak of hearing the voice of the demon on the wind. Before the One God, people would leave offerings on the beach to placate him – usually fish – in exchange for clear skies and calm seas.

What did it mean that Jalen had been in Kernou, pretending to be nothing more than a simple fisherman? Arthur glanced at his hands, seeing again his flesh speckled with stone as he held the Grail and, for a moment, he could feel the weight of that crown, the one that Jalen had placed on his head.

Arthur thought he might lose his mind if he kept thinking about it over and over and over again, so, to distract himself, he tried to fit in on the ship. He knew Tahnet's story, and he'd learnt that Aelle was fey, born and bred on the Isle of Mists. Some of the other women – the quiet boatswain, Avery, was beaten for refusing to sell her body on the streets of Skulls Rest. The other women had similar stories, with one common theme – mistreatment at the hands of men.

All Arthur had to do was think about Kernou and the rules of the One God to see that a great injustice was being done to the women in his village, and had been done to women all over Teyath for a long time. It made him sick. Katarin's story alone was enough to turn his stomach. It was only in Cruithea, Tahnet had told him, that women held power. She was going to go there, after they had finished their work.

Arthur made his way to the galley, finding a bowl of stew waiting for him, and, to his delight, a small plate of fresh apples, sliced so fine the fruit was like a wafer, melting on his tongue and exploding through his blood, making his magic sing.

That's where Tahnet found him and hurried him through his food. When he was done, she linked her arm through his and led him above deck, then to the Captain's cabin. Arthur swallowed, stopping and pulling back on Tahnet's arm.

'What's going on?'

She shrugged. 'We're working out where to go next.'

'I thought we were going to Avalon.'

'We were, but... just come in. It will make sense,' she said softly. When he didn't move, she rolled her eyes. 'You're not intruding. Your sister asked me to get you.'

Sister. It still felt so strange to have a sister. For so long, he'd thought he was all alone, had longed for his Kin in Cruithea in the hopes they might understand him in a way that his father did not – but he had never imagined a sister, a sibling. He had to keep reminding himself it wasn't a dream.

He followed Tahnet into the cabin. The setting sun streamed through the window, the generous room warm and golden, candles burning in sconces around the room. Katarin was sitting with her feet up on the desk, a glass of rum in one hand. She waved the bottle at Arthur, but he shook his head.

Aelle was standing near the window, arms folded, a deep frown on her face. 'There are at least four ships following *The Excalibur*,' she said. 'Two of ours – pirates,' she added, glancing at Arthur, 'and two others.'

'The pirate ships?' Katarin asked.

'*The Black Rose* and *The Crimson Shadow*,' Aelle answered.

Katarin sighed. 'What has Tymis done to piss off Marsh and Booth?'

'Who are they?' Arthur asked.

'Captains of the other ships. Bastards, the pair of them. Bloodthirsty and ruthless. Tymis must have something they want,' Tahnet said, sitting back in her chair.

Aelle chewed on her lip. '*The Excalibur* feels different. She's... singing to me, words I cannot understand but it makes me want to follow her.'

Arthur bent his head in Tahnet's direction. 'She can feel the ship?'

Tahnet nodded. 'It's often how we find it. Sometimes it's just chance but mostly it's Aelle – her magic – that guides us.'

Arthur drew his attention back to the conversation in time to see Kat reach up to rub at her temples.

'Ordes?'

'No, not his magic,' Aelle said.

'Who's Ordes?' Arthur whispered to Tahnet, who shushed him. Aelle continued talking, saying that the magic on *The Excalibur* was different. He gasped as something fell into place so quickly it hurt his brain; three sets of eyes jumped to his face, making him blush.

Aelle put her hands on her hips, glaring down at him. 'What?'

Arthur rubbed at the back of his neck. 'There was a woman from Kernou – a Magic Wielder. Her sister was declared a witch by my father and the Witchfinder, but it was a ploy to draw out Jenyfer. That's her name, was her name, sorry I don't know if she's dead or alive, but I've been dreaming of her.'

Aelle smirked. 'What will your boyfriend think?'

Arthur's cheeks burnt but he ignored the comment. 'She called a syhren to the beach to save her sister.'

Tahnet's mouth dropped. 'No one should be able to do that. Syhrens are Melodias' creatures. They answer to no one but the Master of Songs and Death. Are you positive it was a syhren?'

Arthur told them about Lamorna's rescue.

'We have to find her,' Aelle muttered, beginning to pace. 'No one can command a syhren but the Master of Songs and Death. Where is this woman?' she asked, turning her burning gaze on Arthur.

'That's what I'm trying to say.' He sat up a bit taller, squared his shoulders. 'I think she is on *The Excalibur*. The ship had been in the Bay of Calledun for weeks. Jenyfer vanished before they could burn her, and rumour was a pirate rescued her.'

'Pirate?' Katarin's voice was sharp. 'So that was what he was so distracted about,' she added in a low voice, then sighed. 'If Tymis has a syhren on board, and Marsh and Booth know about her...'

Aelle continued to pace, Tahnet gnawed on her fingernails, and Kat was very still, her gaze unfocused. Arthur squirmed, an unfamiliar flare of impatience rushing through him.

'Why does it matter if Tymis has a syhren on his ship?' he asked eventually.

'Power,' Katarin said. 'Your syhren friend is a tool, a potential weapon. With the power of a syhren at their command, men like Marsh and Booth would seek to rule the seas. Who would challenge them, besides the Master of Songs and Death?'

'And would he?' Arthur asked.

'He would,' Katarin answered.

'And then what?'

Aelle stopped pacing. 'Then we go to war, little man.'

'War?' Arthur squeaked.

Aelle chuckled. 'Scared?'

'Of course I'm scared,' Arthur said quickly.

Aelle opened her mouth but Katarin held up her hand. 'Will you let Aelle into your head?'

Arthur tensed, shooting Aelle a sideways glance. 'Why?'

'I need to know if the girl is where you think she is,' Kat replied smoothly. 'You cannot put too much trust in dreams, Arthur. For those of us with magic, sometimes they are true tellings of things that have, or that will, happen; but sometimes they are tricks. But your memories are real, and Aelle will get a true sense of her that way.'

Aelle was scowling, probably as enthused about having to dig through his head as he was. The fey flexed her fingers, her scowl shifting into a wicked grin when she realised he was watching her.

Arthur swallowed. 'Fine.'

Aelle moved so she was standing behind Arthur. The hair stood up on the back of his neck as her hands came to rest on his head. Immediately, he could feel her, like flames and ice combined. His scalp was covered in pin-pricks and a headache assaulted him, a pounding in his temples that increased until he thought he would scream. He grit his teeth as Aelle shifted through pieces of his mind like they were things she could pick up and toss away and he hoped she knew what she was doing, that she wasn't looking at things she shouldn't be.

Just as he was about to vomit, she released him, the cool heat of her magic withdrawing and leaving him blinking back tears and gasping.

'He's telling the truth,' she said simply.

'Of course I am,' Arthur snapped, rubbing at his temples.

Katarin sighed, twirling a piece of blood-red hair around her index finger. Her eyes found Arthur's. 'We need to change course.'

'What? No.'

'I need to see the girl,' she said softly, her voice calm, measured. 'And we need to warn them about the other ships.'

'No,' Arthur said again. 'We need to go to Avalon now. What difference does it make if Jenyfer is on that ship?'

Katarin's expression hardened. 'Because this is what we do, Arthur. We rescue those who need rescuing, and at the moment, it's Tymis and his crew. He might be a shit most of the time, but he's just like me, like you – a Magic Wielder, but unlike you and me, Tymis is without his power. Ordes can't defend that ship against those others on his own, not without killing himself in the process.'

Arthur clenched his jaw so hard he felt it twinge. The need to go to the Isle of Mists burnt in his blood, a fire that mingled with the song that hadn't left him ever since Jalen put that crown on his head, even if it was in a dream. Somehow, Arthur knew that Avalon was where the answers to all the questions he hadn't even voiced yet were to be had.

'You want Aelle to toss you overboard?' Katarin said.

'You want to throw me off your ship, do it yourself,' Arthur challenged. He didn't know where the words came from. He held his sister's eyes, his heart thundering painfully. 'But you won't,' he went on before Aelle could indeed grab him. 'Because you're not callous, Katarin.'

She lent forward, and it was like they were the only people in the room. 'You don't know a thing about me, Arthur Tregarthen.'

'I know more than you think,' he said. 'I know your revenge only runs so deep. I know you do what you do because you don't know what else to do to heal the wounds of your past. I know you're not heartless – you've just proven it, and you showed it when you let me stay. You didn't have to, but you did, even knowing where I had come from.'

Silence spread through the cabin. Arthur did not break eye contact with his sister. Katarin's cheeks coloured; her lips were a thin line, eyes as hard as stones. Eventually, she sat back. 'I was wondering how long it would take you, little brother.'

'To do what?'

'Stand up for yourself,' she said casually. 'Listen, the two other ships are from Malist. They have a Witchfinder with them.'

'How do you know?'

Katarin motioned to Aelle. 'She can sense them as well. How do you think we manage to save so many women? The truth is, Magic Wielders are disappearing, Arthur, and I don't just mean they're being tied to stakes or burning on the pyre. Something is happening. I want a closer look at those ships because I'm very interested to see where they are headed.'

'Where do you think they are headed?' Arthur asked.

'You said your friend escaped a Witchfinder in Kernou? I would bet those ships are tracking *The Excalibur* as well and if they find it...'

'They find Jenyfer,' Arthur finished.

'Tymis won't go down without a fight,' Tahnet said softly.

Katarin's smile was feral and dark. 'Two against one doesn't seem like very fair odds, does it?'

Aelle's answering smile was wide. 'No, it does not.'

'Marsh and Booth?' Tahnet asked, frowning.

'Won't get involved until after, if they do at all,' Aelle said with certainty.

'Then we have our bearing,' Katarin declared. 'Go save Tymis and his crew and *never* let him live it down, see if the girl is onboard, catch us a Witchfinder, and then we go to Avalon.'

The cabin slowly emptied. Arthur stood up to leave, but Katarin stopped him.

'Not many people challenge me like that,' she said, her voice low.

He swallowed, but lifted his chin.

His sister smiled, raised her glass in a toast. 'It will be a big day tomorrow. And Arthur,' she added; he paused with his hand on the door knob. 'This time, you stay below deck. I don't want the Witchfinder to know you're onboard, understand?'

Arthur nodded.

CHAPTER 48

The sky was free of clouds, the water as still as a mirror, reflecting nothing but the blue expanse above them. The crew weren't idle, but even Jenyfer could see there was a lack of general enthusiasm for the daily tasks. The singing had stopped, but her inner song had been blasting at her ears since that almost fateful moment with a syhren in The Vale.

Their passage north was slow, *The Excalibur* crawling through the water, as if unsure, hesitant, of her destination. The ship had changed direction several times, turning southwards, then west again, before she switched her heading to north-east, then, infuriatingly, west once more, until she seemed to settle on a northern bearing.

Jenyfer could not stand still, as agitated as *The Excalibur*. Her brain was churning. Restless energy had dug in deep, pulling and tugging and ripping at her insides. Her magic was still so strange, so alien and mysterious, but it felt calm, strangely soothed, especially when she was near Ordes. All of her was calm when he was near her but she hadn't seen him this morning and her skin threatened to crawl from her limbs in anticipation. She imagined it peeling back until she could see what truly lay at the inside of her.

Making her way to the starboard railing and resting her arms on it, Jenyfer looked out to sea. The sultry, sub-tropical breeze caressed her face and the sun beat down, the sticky warmth of the day sinking beneath her flesh. Heat was smeared across the world, a heavy haze that lingered over the horizon. Something moved in the depths. Jenyfer glanced down to watch as Ordes surfaced from beneath the water along with a surge of need in her chest, pushing his hair from his face. He turned and floated on his back, eyes closed. He looked so peaceful, so free, that she considered throwing herself overboard and joining him. If she truly was a syhren, shouldn't she be able to swim? What had happened in The Vale thrust itself into her mind, but she pushed it aside.

It was time to be brave.

Quickly, before she could change her mind, Jenyfer climbed onto the railing. Someone called out behind her, but she took a deep breath and let herself tumble into the blue water below her.

There was nothing graceful about the way she hit the water, and it stung, like something had slapped every inch of her flesh, even through her clothes. As the water closed over her head, she realised her mistake.

Syhren or not, Jenyfer couldn't swim.

Her shoulders and neck tensed up, legs kicking uselessly as she began to sink, like something was pulling her towards the ocean floor. The water was tugging on her body, urging her down, down, down to the sandy bottom of the sea. She opened her eyes; they stung, the salt sharp and stabbing.

Something changed, like something inside her kicked into life. Jenyfer blinked and the world beneath the waves swum into focus, everything becoming clear and crisp. She could see the layers of water moving around her, and could *feel* the currents pressing gently against her body.

But her lungs were burning. She struck out for the fractured light twinkling on the surface above her. It seemed so far away. The muscles in her arms were aching and no matter how fast she moved them, she didn't seem to be going anywhere.

An arm hooked around her middle, and she was being pulled towards the surface, bursting through with a gasp, blinking at the brightness of the sun. She was held against a firm chest, an arm still wrapped around her waist.

'That's twice now,' Ordes breathed in her ear. 'What were you thinking?'

Jenyfer spat out a mouthful of water. 'I thought... I thought that maybe I could swim. If I'm actually a syhren, I should be able to swim, shouldn't I?'

Gently, Ordes let her go; she panicked and spun around, grabbing for him. He caught her arms, holding her effortlessly, her head free of the ocean as the blood-warm waters lapped at her throat. He frowned, peering at her face. 'Your eyes...'

'What about them?' She blinked furiously; water clung to her lashes, refusing to let go.

'I thought... they looked different,' he said. Then, 'Alright. Despite nearly drowning twice, you want to swim, so I'll teach you.'

'Really?'

'Sure.'

'You make it look so easy,' she commented, experiencing a stab of jealousy at the way he held himself effortlessly in the water.

Ordes gave her a smile, then leant over to plant a light kiss on her nose. 'You'll get the hang of it but, for now, let's get back on deck and get dry.' He guided her to the hull of the ship, to the rope ladder that dangled over the side, holding her until she had managed to haul herself free of the water. She tumbled over the railing, landing on her knees, then stood and wrung the water from her shirt as best she could while waiting for him.

As fluid as shifting sand, Ordes climbed onboard and Jenyfer followed him across the deck to where a bundle of clothing waited. He glanced at her quickly, and her mouth was suddenly flooded with the taste of him, her fingers tingling, heartbeat flying. She took a deep, steady breath, trying to calm herself as he used his shirt to dry off his hair and torso.

She didn't bother trying to hide it – she let herself look at him, at the sweep of muscle that flowed from one shoulder to the other, at the way the muscles of his back shifted beneath his flesh and the way his torso tapered to narrow hips and strong thighs. The lines of the map that decorated his flesh seemed to shimmer like they were alive with every movement he made.

Jenyfer wanted to kiss him, to feel his lips against hers, to feel his hands travel over the curve of her body again.

'We should train today,' he announced, slinging his shirt around his neck and scooping his coat and boots from the deck. He would have felt her eyes on him; the smile he gave her suggested he knew exactly where her thoughts had been straying.

'With magic?' Jenyfer asked.

Ordes shook his head. 'You need to learn how to fight, Jen.'

She couldn't hide her irritation. 'Ordes, my magic—'

'I don't know if I can help you with that,' he said, heading below deck towards his cabin, wet trousers dripping water everywhere. She followed, chewing her lip.

'You're scared,' she stated, halting in her tracks as the thought, the realisation, barrelled into her mind; her inner song seemed to agree. It settled into a low hum that vibrated through her. 'You're all scared of me. I can sense it.'

'I'm not scared,' Ordes retorted, then pushed a frustrated breath between his teeth. 'Alright, I'm scared. I'm fucking terrified, but not for the reasons you think. I'm terrified at how quickly I'm falling,' he murmured. His coat and boots dropped from his hands to land near his feet. 'I'm scared at how deeply consuming you are. I'm scared by how much I want you, and I'm scared at what I'd do for you. If you asked me to kill for you, Jenyfer, I would. If you asked me to throw myself to the sharks, I would.'

Something deep inside her purred at his words, at the meaning they held. She wanted to wrap herself up in them, and brand them on her body. The light of the whole world seemed to shine in the silver of his eyes and, when he looked at her, Jenyfer was weightless, floating away; the only thing holding her steady was his eyes, his arms. She was like fresh shoots on a branch, finally unfolding after being kept curled in on herself for too long.

She couldn't explain it, couldn't justify her feelings, and didn't know where they came from. There was something that drove her to look for him, to want to touch him, to want to see him smile or hear him speak.

Jenyfer took a deep breath and stepped closer, trapping him between his door and her body. She caught the motion of his throat as he swallowed and his arms folded around her. He scooped her off the ground; her legs wrapped around his middle as he spun them around, his breathing sharp and hot on her face as he pushed her against the bulkhead.

She could feel the tension in his body throbbing beneath his skin as her hands slid up the back of his neck, and she couldn't tell which was his heartbeat and which was hers – they were both so strong, thundering and drumming against her ribcage and hammering in her ears so loudly it was almost unbearable.

The burning knot inside of her, all her fear and worry, started to unravel as she pushed herself closer to him, so close that not a breath of air existed between them.

'I need to touch you,' Ordes managed.

'You're touching me right now,' she breathed.

'That isn't what I meant and you know it,' he growled. 'I saw the way you were looking at me up there. I expected you to pull out a plate and arrange me on it for breakfast.'

'That does sound appetising.' She kissed him, her hands threaded through his hair so tightly it must have hurt, but he didn't seem to care. He kissed her back, hard enough to bruise her mouth; there was nothing gentle about this kiss – their teeth clashed and she bit his bottom lip, chuckling when he hissed against her mouth. Her fingernails dug into his scalp and he had one hand up the back of her shirt, the other gripping her arse as she rolled her hips against him once, then again and again, her body moving on its own, her actions controlled by some deep part of her. He groaned against her mouth as she deepened the kiss, wanting to crawl inside him, wondering if she could, if it was possible.

His palm found her breast; his lips closed over the tender skin on her throat as he pinched her nipple between his thumb and forefinger, making her suck in a breath, a spike of pleasure shooting through her to settle between her thighs.

'Your cabin or mine?' Ordes whispered against her burning skin.

'Yours is closer.'

He cupped his hands under her arse, lifting her higher up his body, walking them backwards, holding her with one hand while he fumbled for the door knob. Jenyfer giggled and he silenced her with a quick kiss, which became a long one, the door forgotten. She didn't want to stop kissing him, but he set her down, kicking the door open as she fumbled with the buttons on his pants, thrusting her hand inside, making him sigh in what she thought was relief.

Suddenly, the ship lurched sideways, throwing them off balance. They crashed through the door and landed in a heap on the floor, panting and half-undressed, staring at each other with wide eyes.

'What's going on?' Jenyfer whispered.

'I really don't give a fuck.' Ordes shook his head, cupping her face and kissing her as the ship shuddered again. He ignored it, rolling them over so he could undo her pants and tug them down her legs. He waved his hand at the door – it slammed closed and locked itself.

Someone was calling his name. He ignored that too, his fingers between Jenyfer's thighs as she melted beneath him; he kissed her fiercely, until she couldn't breathe. She rolled her hips against his fingers, wanting more, her hand down the front of his trousers again, her touch fast and desperate.

'I don't think we're going to make it to bed,' he managed to whisper.

Jenyfer's brain was mush and she was on fire, the music in her head crooning and swirling and *happy*.

Someone shouted down from the deck – a panicked sound.

Reluctantly, she pulled her mouth free. 'Ordes, something's wrong.'

'Fuck it!' he cursed, scrambling to his feet and helping her to stand, leaving her to fix her clothing while he flung the door open and hurried into the passageway. Heart pounding, Jenyfer followed him, rushing up the ladder into the bright light of the sun.

It was chaos on deck, men running everywhere, shouts of panic ringing through the air. Jenyfer skidded to a stop as a ship emerged from the waves, dripping with water. There was a bubble surrounding it – it shimmered before it vanished with an audible snap. She sucked in a breath of wonder.

'It's *The Night Queen*!' she breathed.

'She's coming broadside!' The Captain had his cutlass drawn, face like thunder. 'To the cannons. If this bitch thinks she can take my ship, I'll leave the *Queen* decorating the sea bed.'

Ordes hurried to his father's side as *The Excalibur* groaned, turning so sharply Jenyfer nearly lost her footing. Kayrus was at the helm, his face tight as he fought to bring the ship out of Katarin's reach. The crew hurried around the deck, shouting to each other, unsheathing weapons. Someone loosened the sails; others busied themselves at the cannons.

'We've been sitting ducks down here,' Tymis snapped. His eyes floated over Ordes, then Jenyfer; her cheeks heated. Tymis shook his head and turned to face Katarin Le Fey.

The Captain of *The Night Queen* was standing amidship, red hair blazing in the sun. 'Stand down, Tymis,' she called urgently. 'As fun as it would be, I'm not here to fight this time.'

He snorted. 'Bullshit. Your boss wants her ship back.'

Katarin shook her head, coming to stand at the railing. 'You've got a Witchfinder on your trail,' she announced. Jenyfer's heart froze, then surged so quickly it hurt.

'Two ships. They're around the headland and coming your way.' Katarin paused. 'You've either pissed someone off – which I'd believe – or you've got something they want.' Her eyes shifted over the crew, coming to rest on Jenyfer. 'Who do we have here, then?'

'She's not your concern,' Tymis replied quickly.

Katarin looked like she was going to argue, then shook her head again. 'Thirty minutes. They've got the wind at their back and you're practically dead in the water. How long?'

'Days,' Tymis said wearily. His eyes skittered to Jenyfer then away again. 'Alright, I'll trust you, but only because I don't have a choice. What's the plan?'

'One each,' she replied. Her crew were loading the *Queen's* cannons. 'But leave the Witchfinder to me.'

Tymis smiled. 'All yours. And Katarin,' he added. 'Betray me, and you're dead.'

Katarin smiled, leaning her hip against the railing to wait, as they all did. Soon, the enemy ships came around the headland, moving into open water. 'Here they come. Let's play, shall we?'

Tymis retreated to stand near the main mast. 'Cannons! Round-shot. No mucking around this time – let's send them to the depths.'

Ordes turned to Jenyfer, reaching for her hand. 'I might need your help,' he told her.

'With what?'

He gestured to the approaching ships. 'We can't outrun them, so we're going to have to fight, Jen.'

Jenyfer felt the blood drain from her face. 'What can I do?'

Ordes ran a hand through his hair. 'We've got Kat and her crew, but I might need your magic. When they get close, when I tell you, put your hand on my arm and let your magic go. Direct it into me, understand?'

'Ordes, I don't—'

'Remember when we practised touch magic? Just like that but, this time, you're not taking anything from me, you're giving it,' he explained quickly. He didn't wait to see if she nodded, releasing her and turning to face the water. *The Night Queen* had drawn up alongside them and both ships were now facing the approaching vessels.

'They're armed,' Tymis said, lowering a spyglass. 'A little more than last time, I might add. Seems they're ready for you,' he added, giving Ordes a feral grin.

Ordes grinned back.

Tymis tossed Jenyfer a quick smile. 'Ready to become a pirate?'

'No,' she said simply, making him laugh.

There was nothing to do but wait. Jenyfer stood beside Ordes. Every muscle in her body was tight enough to snap, and she was afraid to move in case she shattered. The enemy ships were closer now, coming fast, their huge sails cupping the wind. They looked so large but Jenyfer reminded herself where she was, and who she was with. *The Excalibur* was made for battle, and *The Night Queen* was renowned for it. It didn't do much to calm her nerves though, knowing there was another Witchfinder across the water.

The sound of snapping bones echoed in her ears for a moment.

Jenyfer did not take her eyes off the approaching ships. The sea around them was churned to soup, their great bows pushing through the water with ease. She could see their flags rippling in the wind – not the flags of merchant ships, she noted. This was something else.

Iouen handed Ordes a dagger as he hurried past, which he offered to Jenyfer.

'What about you?' she asked.

'I don't need it,' he said simply.

She nodded, not understanding what he meant, and they continued to wait, the sun beating down on them, the wind pulling at their hair and clothes. Jenyfer barely took a breath in the time it took for the enemy ships to reach them.

On *The Night Queen* Katarin was barking orders.

'Ordes, a little cover for the lady, if you please,' Tymis said. 'You might want to stand back, Jenyfer,' he added. She scuttled away as Ordes held his arms out by his side. The air around him rippled silver and blue, light shifting down his arms to gather in his palms. As he thrust his hands towards the oncoming ships, thousands of droplets of water rose from the ocean, hovering between the vessels. Ordes closed his fists and the droplets transformed into a thick fog that raced across the water and engulfed the enemy ships. Katarin called out a thanks as the magical bubble reformed around her ship and *The Night Queen* dropped beneath the waves.

Tymis had the spyglass to his eye again and Jenyfer wondered how he could see anything through the fog, but he cursed and let the glass fall. 'They're about to fire on us.'

Ordes, hands still held out before him, called out to Jenyfer.

She hurried to his side and rested her hand on his bare arm, her skin tingling with the contact, her magic straining against the confines of her body. She closed her eyes, imagining a hand reaching beneath her skin for her magic, not having any idea whether she could do what Ordes had asked.

Her magic rose like a serpent, dark and powerful, filled with music, melodies tumbling over one another. She felt it flowing from her hand; Ordes jolted beneath her touch. Jenyfer opened her eyes, expecting to see cannon balls barreling towards her, but a wall of water stretched between *The Excalibur* and the enemy ship.

'Keep going, Jen,' Ordes said from between clenched teeth. She did, pushing her magic out of her, letting it flow freely. Slowly, the water hanging in the air like a sheet started to freeze over, crystals of ice spreading from the edges until they joined in the middle in a mosaic of blues, white, and greys, shot through with veins of aquamarine.

The wall of ice trembled as cannon fire collided with it, once and then again. Three times. She wondered how long the magic would hold, and tightened her grip on the dagger clutched in her other hand.

Fog was all around them. Jenyfer couldn't see what was happening on the other side of the ice wall, but she could hear pistol fire and shouting, cries of pain, the splintering of timber, the firing of cannons, and music – beautiful, blissful music. It echoed through Jenyfer's ears as blasts of golden light shone through the wall of ice momentarily, like the sun peaking between the clouds after a storm.

Ordes' knees gave out and he pitched towards the deck.

'Ordes!' Tymis called.

The wall of ice suddenly collapsed back into the ocean and the fog vanished. Sweat dripped from Ordes' skin. Jenyfer crouched beside him. He was pale, his hair drenched. Shivers rippled over his skin. Alarmed, she looked up as shouts and the creaking of a ship carried across the water to them. Tymis came to stand beside them as the enemy ship collapsed, nothing but a carcass of timbers and cloth. There was no sign of the other ship, but *The Night Queen* bobbed gently in the middle of the carnage. Bodies floated face-down in the water, and Jenyfer swallowed her stomach.

Ordes tried to stand, staggering a little; Tymis caught him and held him upright.

'I'm alright,' Ordes whispered.

Tymis shook his head, looking at his son in concern. 'No, you're not. You need to rest.' His eyes moved to Jenyfer. 'Are you alright?'

'I feel fine,' she said. It was true. She did. She felt alive and energised and like she could swim the entire length of the ocean over and over again. 'What's wrong with him?'

Tymis shook his head. 'Burn out. My son isn't as powerful as he thinks he is.'

'Fuck off,' Ordes mumbled.

Tymis chuckled. 'Bed. Now.'

When Ordes woke, his head felt like something had trampled on it. He was in bed. He blinked; the world slowly swam into focus. Warm, golden light crept in through the small porthole near the bed and the water was calm, stroking the hull of the ship. Gentle clinking echoed through the cabin. Ordes swallowed – his throat was as dry as old paper.

'You're awake.' Jenyfer perched on the edge of the bed and handed him a mug of water.

He drank greedily, wiping his mouth with the back of a hand that trembled. 'How long was I out for?'

She shrugged. 'A few hours, maybe.' Her expression was calm, smooth, but spots of colour were painted on her cheeks. 'Your father came to check on you a million times but I told him to leave.'

'And he listened?'

She nodded, a faint smile tugging at her mouth. 'Does that always happen?'

Ordes shook his head, then groaned. He sat up fully, fidgeting with the mug. 'I use magic everyday, but for little things, like turning on the lights. I'm not usually—'

'Defending a ship,' Jenyfer finished softly. She glanced at him and then away, getting up to return the mug to the top of the dresser. 'That was incredible,' she added.

'The *Queen*?'

'In one piece and long gone. They took the Witchfinder with them. What will she do to him?'

'Probably better you don't know,' Ordes said.

Jenyfer nodded and came to sit by him again, running her fingers lightly over the back of his knuckles, tracing the inked markings there. His skin tingled. Ordes shuffled back down onto the pillow, shifting onto his side to make room for her. Jenyfer bit her lip, then lay down, curling against his chest, her head tucked beneath his chin, and he wanted to pause the world for just a while, so they could stay like this. Her arm was folded over his middle, fingers stroking his back lightly.

'What did you feel when you fed me your magic?' he asked. He could still feel it – cool and dark like the ocean, powerful and full of life. And there had been music tunnelling through his head, until it filled every part of him. He could still hear it, but only faintly. And his own magic had soared in response to hers, more powerful than he'd ever felt it.

Jenyfer shuffled a little closer to him. 'I felt... powerful. Even though I wasn't using my magic myself, I could still feel it, if that makes sense. I could feel what you were doing with it.'

'What did your magic feel like to you?'

'Like light,' she whispered. 'Like the calm after a storm, where the world is drenched and dripping and you can smell the dampness. Everything is glistening with rain and swept with wind, cleansed and renewed. It felt like that.'

Ordes said nothing, just tightened his grip on her, then a thought struck him. 'How did you get me into bed?'

She pressed a kiss to the underside of his jaw. 'Iouen and your father carried you. I was left with very stern instructions to look after you.'

He laughed, then rolled them over so she was pinned beneath him. The motion made his head spin but he ignored it. 'Is that so?' he murmured, his hand sliding down her side, over the curve of her, until he reached her thigh. Keeping his eyes on her face, he slowly, gently, gripped her knee, easing her leg free of his body so he could lift it and fold it around his hip.

Jenyfer's breathing deepened. 'You're supposed to be recovering,' she chided weakly.

'Well, this is the medic's cabin. What sort of medic are you if you don't help a man recuperate?'

She laughed. 'A bad one.'

'So you're going to deny me treatment?'

She rolled her eyes. 'You'll live, I'm certain of it.'

'That's your professional medical opinion, is it?' Ordes shifted against her, pressing himself closer, pulling a groan from her lips that she tried to swallow away. 'We were in the middle of something before we were rudely interrupted.'

Her laugh was shaky this time, but she wound her arms around him and kissed him until his head was spinning again, his breath stolen, body tingling, heart racing. The night a pisky led him through the dark streets of a foreboding town, he could never have predicted this would happen, and if it was up to him, they'd never leave this cabin. He'd happily drown in the smell and taste of her forever, but she pulled away, nudging him off her.

'You need to sleep.'

'Will you be here when I wake up?'

'If you're lucky,' she said. He let her up regretfully, and was asleep again in moments.

CHAPTER 49

The Fisher Queen was waiting. Wearing mist like a cloak, she was perched on the rocks outside her cave, hunched over, her face turned towards the water. Arthur approached cautiously, picking his way over the water-slick stones – pebbles scattered at his feet, and she turned. Seeing it was him, she beckoned. Today, a crown of coral sat on her head, its peaks chipped. Grey moss grew over what remained of the crown, the coral a bleached white that glowed in the misty dark of early morning.

She held a fishing rod between her slender hands.

'They're not biting,' she told him. He wasn't sure whether to sit at her side or not, so he remained standing, looking out at the sea. The waves were restless, tumbling over one another in a chaotic swirling of lacey foam and sharp peaks. The water at the Fisher Queen's feet was still, a mirror reflecting the moody sky above. She gestured to the water. 'What do you see in its face?'

Arthur crouched beside her, peering into the grey water. 'Nothing,' he said. 'I see nothing. What do you see?'

Her pale lips parted in a sigh. 'I see death. I see myself.'

He swallowed. She set the rod to one side, climbing awkwardly to her feet. Indicating he should follow, she turned towards the cave, its gaping mouth dark with shadows and mystery.

'You're injured,' Arthur said, noticing how she moved, the way she favoured one leg.

'Yes,' she said simply.

'Can I help?' he asked.

She shook her head; the crown of coral toppled to the rocks with the movement. Arthur bent and picked it up. It was light, like it was made of air. Another of the pointed tips had broken free. He picked it up as well, examining it with a frown. It reminded him of—

The Fisher Queen shook her head sadly. 'It cannot be mended, King that shalt be. It is as it should be.'

Carrying the crown gently, he followed her into the cave. It was dark and chilled; no fire burnt in the pit in the centre of the space. Arthur placed the crown on the ground near the dead fire and rubbed at his arms.

'Shall I light it?'

'If you wish. There is wood,' she said, glancing towards the back of the cave. 'Oh. You will have to fetch some,' she said, seeing it was empty.

He nodded and hurried out into the morning, glancing up at the sky. A storm was brewing. He could smell it. He could smell apples, their sweetness at odds with the briny scent of the ocean. Moving from the rocks to the pebbled beach, Arthur headed for the forest but, where the sand gave way to soil, there was nothing but blackness.

No grass. No leaves clinging to the branches of the trees that stretched far into the sky. No life.

This place was dead, a barren wasteland. His stomach clenched, but he did as she had asked and collected all the wood he could carry, ferrying it back to the cave, where he arranged them in the blackened pit. Soon, a fire was crackling and the cave was filled with warm light and golden shadows.

'Why is the forest dead?' he asked the Queen, who sat across from him. She stared at him, then slowly reached for the hem of her ragged dress, lifting the material to expose a milk-pale thigh. Arthur averted his eyes, but not quickly enough.

'Look,' she commanded, and so he did.

An open wound reached like the mark of a single claw, starting at her knee, stretching up and up, running the length of her thigh.

He gasped, leaping to his feet. There would be herbs in the forest he could use to help her but... then he remembered.

'It cannot be healed,' she said softly. 'Many have tried, but none have succeeded.'

'Can I help?'

'Perhaps,' she whispered. 'It shall depend.'

'On?'

The Fisher Queen snapped her fingers and in her lap rested the Grail. Arthur sucked in a breath. He could feel its power, and could hear it calling, *singing*, to him. She watched him closely. 'Do you desire it? The power the Grail could give you.'

'I don't know,' he answered honestly. He could not take his eyes off the stone and coral vessel. He lifted his eyes to her face. 'Who does the Grail serve?'

She smiled. 'You.' She snapped her fingers again and Arthur was tumbling through blackness. The cave was gone. The ocean was gone. He was in a forest, green with life and alive with music and sounds of... screaming.

Heart in his throat, Arthur pushed through the undergrowth, following the screams. He could smell smoke, its acrid, choking smell reaching through the forest to wrap around his throat. He could taste ash and the ground beneath him was hot. He ran, jumping nimbly over rock and root and in his hands he held a sword, the hilt decorated with a dragon; there were words in a language he did not know engraved on the blade.

He could feel the weight of the sword.

He could hear its song and feel its power.

The trees gave way to a grassland that blazed with fire, the air choked with smoke. He had stumbled onto a battle, but between who and for what reason, he did not know.

'Now you see,' said a soft voice at his elbow.

The Fisher Queen stood beside him. She carried no weapon. Her fishing rod dangled uselessly from a pale hand.

'Now you see,' she repeated, and then she was gone, and Arthur was sitting up and clutching at his chest, the taste of smoke in his mouth and the power of the Grail tugging at his insides as *The Night Queen* rocked gently beneath him and music floated through his brain.

CHAPTER 50

Jenyfer dreamt of war.

The sea rose to swallow the land, surging through villages. Buildings collapsed beneath the force of the water. The air was filled with screaming and crying. People clung to whatever they could manage to wrap their arms around while Jenyfer watched, floating somewhere above the chaos, helpless and powerless.

No, not powerless. Her song pulsed through her, forcing its way up her throat. She opened her mouth and sang and, as her song filled the air, the water continued to rise.

No, she thought. This isn't what I want, but she could not close her mouth, could not silence the song that flowed from her with a mind of its own.

She was standing on the beach while the water swirled around her waist. She was not alone.

Her voice was not the only one saturating the air. Magic threaded through the water around her as, from the waves, a syhren emerged, then another, more, until an army of the sea faeries stood on the beach.

Alarmed, Jenyfer could do nothing as they advanced on the village. She was drawn along with them, her legs moving without her consent. Glancing down, she noticed she was naked, her skin flecked with scales that glimmered silvery-blue while, all around, the air swelled with the syhren's song.

The world went dark and Jenyfer was thrust backwards, flying, tumbling head over heels, landing on her hands and knees on hard wood. The world rocked and rolled beneath her. She was on the deck of a ship, but it wasn't *The Excalibur*. This ship was different, but it still hummed with magic. She could feel it through the timber, could smell it, and her skin crawled.

Slowly, she climbed to her feet, relieved to see she was no longer naked. She was dressed as a sailor, in a linen shirt, vest, and knee-length loose trousers. It was night. The moon was a bloated disc above her, bathing the ship in milk-pale light.

Standing at the helm was Katarin Le Fey. Jenyfer's heart lurched. She waved her arms, but the Captain of *The Night Queen* looked right through her. Frowning, Jenyfer moved towards the helm, stopping when she noticed a man standing with Katarin.

'Arthur,' she breathed but, unlike Katarin, he looked straight at her. 'How are you here?'

'Where?' he asked her, his calm voice oddly disjointed.

Jenyfer remembered she was dreaming. 'Oh,' she said softly.

Arthur Tregarthen smiled at her, holding out his hand. He beckoned. Curious, Jenyfer joined him and Katarin at the helm. The Captain showed no sign she knew Jenyfer was there, but Arthur took her hand.

A jolt shot through her and she jumped.

'It gets easier,' he whispered.

'What does?'

He released her hand and a blinding light ripped across Jenyfer's eyes. She screwed her eyes closed against the light. Beneath her feet, the ship pulsed with magic and she could smell rain and damp earth and salt.

'Look,' Arthur commanded.

She did.

In his arms, he held a vessel of stone. Droplets of water hung in the air above it and within the bowl itself was rich, damp earth. A tiny tendril of green life pushed through the soil.

The Grail.

'You can touch it,' Arthur told her, holding it towards her. It must have been heavy, yet he held it like it weighed nothing at all. Jenyfer shook her head.

'I don't want to,' she whimpered, suddenly afraid. Music filled the air, a fierce wind ripping across the world, and she could hear it, the Grail, the song that it sang. She took a step back, shaking her head.

'Jenyfer, you must,' Arthur insisted.

She shook her head again, opened her mouth, and sang.

The world tilted. She was standing in the cavernous room again, the air tinged with blue and silver. Braziers sat on stone pillars along each side of the room and at the end of a stretch of dark carpet was an ornate chair, like a throne. A man sat on the throne, his face hidden in shadow but on his head, gleaming white in the darkness, was a crown made of bones.

Music was all around them, notes hanging in the air, falling towards the ground like snowflakes. Jenyfer reached out her hand and caught one.

The man uncrossed long legs and leant forward, his face slipping into the light. Jenyfer caught a flash of dark hair and pale skin, before she was falling, falling into the blackness while music swelled in a glorious crescendo around her.

Jenyfer woke with a start, sitting up and clutching at her chest, her breathing short and sharp, the light of the morning crashing through her window to spear into her eyes. Her heart was hammering, her mouth dry as sand, but water dribbled down the sides of her face. She yawned and stretched until her joints popped as her mind tried desperately to hold onto the last snatches of her dream.

Music, more beautiful than she had ever heard before. A man with dark hair. A crown. The details of her dream were expanding and while she could never remember them, she had the sense that the next time she dreamt of the man, she would finally see his face.

Jenyfer threw back the bedclothes, and froze.

Arthur Tregarthen was onboard *The Night Queen.*

She scrambled out of bed and tugged on the first clothes she could find. Racing from the room, she finger-combed her hair and ran her hands over her face, rubbing the sleep from her eyes as she flung herself up the ladder to the next level, hurrying down the dark passageway.

Chewing on her lip, she could barely see where she was going. Arthur's face rushed through her mind, and the Grail... he was holding the Grail. One of the Treasures of the Gods. She had never even seen a picture of it, but she knew it, like an instinct, as surely as she knew to breathe. It had been singing to her, she knew that as well.

Jenyfer raced out into the passageway, running headlong into Kayrus. The navigator caught her in his strong arms, holding her steady. 'Woah, lass. You look like you've seen a ghost.' He gave her a speculative look. 'You haven't, have you?'

'The Captain,' she managed to mumble. 'I need to see the Captain.'

She hurried away from Kayrus and scrambled up the ladder, her eyes darting around, searching for Ordes. Relieved when she didn't see him on deck, she knocked firmly on the door to the Captain's cabin. She didn't know why she was about to tell Tymis about her dreams, about the Grail, and for a moment, she paused, waiting, listening to her song. It was there, beneath her panic, and it thrummed away happily.

Tymis was sitting at his desk when she went in.

'The mysterious Jenyfer. What can I do for you?' he asked.

Swallowing, Jenyfer closed the door, turning back to face the Captain.

His eyebrows lifted. 'Should I be worried? Are you going to sing to me?'

'So you think I'm a syhren as well?'

'What do you think?'

Jenyfer took a seat opposite him, running her fingers along the edge of the desk; water beaded on the smooth timber. She wasn't sure what she thought. She held the Captain's eyes. 'I've dreamt about the Grail. More than once now, but at first, I didn't know what it was.'

Tymis' expression did not shift. 'What makes you so sure it was the Grail?'

'Because it sang to me,' she said simply. 'But it's not real. We were always told it wasn't real. My aunt used to tell stories about it, but that's all they were – stories.'

He laughed. 'It's real, lass. All the Treasures of the Gods are real, and so are the stories. You've heard of the Treasures I assume?'

Jenyfer nodded. 'There are four Treasures – the Sword, the Stone, the Bow...'

'And the Grail.' He sat back, looking at her with interest. 'What else have you dreamt?'

'Water and music. And darkness. Like I'm far under the surface of the sea in a cavernous space, with blue and silver light. A man with dark hair and pale eyes, but I don't ever see his face.' She paused, folding her arms. 'I have a question for you. Why am I on this ship?'

'Ordes didn't tell you?'

'I want you to tell me,' she said.

'We were asked – no, *told* – to rescue you by the God of the Earth,' Tymis answered.

'Why?'

He drummed his tattooed fingers on the desk. 'Because of a prophecy made a long time ago, one that foretold the coming of Teyath's King, a man who will shape the future of this world. A man who will protect magic from those who would see its end, and who will protect people like us, like you and me and Ordes, and who will find the Treasures of the Gods.' He paused, never looking away from her face.

Jenyfer frowned; though her brain was spinning, tumbling under the weight of his words, she latched onto one thing. 'What does this prophecy have to do with me?'

'The Treasures of the Gods need to be reclaimed and you are going to help that happen. Why else would an Old One decide you weren't to die yet?' Tymis asked.

'Can you tell me—'

'I can't, but only because I'm not allowed to, Jenyfer.' He tapped the map. 'Do you know where we are? We're directly between two islands, neither of which are marked on this map. Lyonesse lies to our south, Avalon to the north, and my ship is currently torn in both directions, which is why we're sailing in circles.' His silver eyes, so like his son's, bored into hers. 'You are tied to this ship because you are tied to the water and, right now, as your magic grows, as you start to claim it—'

'Are you saying I'm controlling the ship?'

'I'm saying you're influencing the ocean. You're a syhren and your powers are connected to the water, so while you're onboard, confused, we are stuck here, until you make up your mind about what you want. It also explains why you're dreaming the way you are – water is a mirror, but it is also a portal. We can see things in it, we can see through it. You are seeing things that have either happened, or are going to happen. Has no one told you syhrens are sometimes Seers? Blessed, or cursed, with knowledge of things that are yet to come to pass?'

There was something else, something he wasn't saying. Like the notes of music in her dream, Jenyfer could almost see the unsaid words hovering in the air above the Captain's head. 'What else?' she asked.

'There are two ships following us – *The Black Rose* and *The Crimson Shadow*. They've been on our trail since we left Skulls Rest,' Tymis said simply. 'They backed off during the fight with the Witchfinder's ships, but now they're back in our sights.'

'What do they want?' Jenyfer's song was silent and still, waiting.

'You,' the Captain said. 'Ordes told me what happened in that tavern in Skulls Rest, and what else has happened when you've used your magic on him. You're powerful. And the Captains of those ships know it. No doubt they or some of their crew were in the *Cat's Claw* that evening as well. They want you.'

'Why?'

'Because your magic is a weapon, Jenyfer, and a pirate ship can never have too many weapons,' Tymis explained.

'But I don't know how to use it!' she cried.

'They don't know that,' he said. 'For now, they'll simply follow. They'll watch, and when the time is right, they'll strike.' He paused, rubbing at his face. 'My son will do something stupid, to save you, and you can try to convince yourself otherwise all you like, but it's the truth.'

Jenyfer swallowed tightly. 'I have to get off this ship, don't I? And I know you don't mean a brief trip to shore.'

Tymis nodded. 'For now.'

'Where do I go?'

'You have two choices.'

She stared at the map, at the blank spaces north and south of their position.

'You would learn to use your magic on Lyonesse,' Tymis said softly. 'The island is nothing but rocks on the surface. Melodias' realm is beneath the island, under the water, but I won't take you there,' he added. 'You need to go to Avalon, to Niniane, but I can't take you there either.'

'Then who will?'

'Katarin.'

'She was just here!' Jenyfer shouted, then forced herself to be calm, rubbing at her temples as her song changed pace in time with her racing heartbeat. 'How do I find her?'

'In three days, she will be in Newlyn.'

'We're miles from there!'

'Swim there.'

'I can't swim.'

'You're a syhren,' Tymis stated. 'Of course you can swim, and that distance is nothing to you. But,' he added, while her brain was swirling at the idea she could *swim* not only that far, but at all, 'you go alone. Ordes is under your spell and isn't thinking straight. If you asked him to slit his own throat, he would.'

'He isn't under a spell!' she snapped.

'Isn't he?'

She opened her mouth to object, and then stopped.

'It isn't your fault,' Tymis said gently.

Jenyfer nodded, and was at the door when he spoke again.

'I know you have other questions, and the answers to those questions are not with the Master of Songs and Death, Jenyfer.'

She nodded, but hesitated, lingering with her fingers around the door knob.

'What else?'

'Arthur Tregarthen, the Chif's son, is on Katarin's ship.'

Tymis frowned. 'How do you know this?'

Rubbing at her face, Jenyfer returned to the seat, took a deep breath and recounted what she could remember about her dreams.

Ordes stepped inside the Captain's cabin and closed the door behind him.

His father was sitting behind the desk. A half-finished platter of food sat at his elbow, along with a bottle of rum and a glass. The desk was in its usual state of disarray, but Tymis had cleared everything off the map of the known lands. His eyes were on the lines scratched expertly across the parchment. The crew of *The Excalibur* had been slowly adding to the map over the years.

Tymis sighed, pushing his chair back. He stood, catching Ordes' eye before he moved to the window, where he opened the shutters and peered out into the night. 'Take Jenyfer to Port Leore, but make sure no one sees you leave the ship. We don't want the other crews knowing she's off the ship.'

'They're still following us, then?' Ordes asked.

'Yes. Kayrus seems to think this map of Jenyfer's'—he shot Ordes a look over his shoulder—'of yours as well, could be the coastline around Port Leore.'

Ordes frowned. 'But it's nothing like that coast.'

'Not now it isn't,' Tymis said. 'Kayrus remembers seeing a map as a young man that showed a completely different coastline. Teyath has changed over time – the seas have changed. The map Kayrus looked at was hundreds of years old, if not older. It was incomplete – ancient knowledge of the sea and the land was more limited than what it is now.'

'You think the Grail, or one of the Treasures, is somewhere close?'

'Maybe,' Tymis mumbled, flinging open the windows, beckoning Ordes to join him. 'Use your faery eyes, son, and tell me what you see?'

Ordes did as he was asked. Letting his magic free, he focused on the view outside the window. Slowly, the colours of the night shifted until they were grey rather than black. All he could see was the ocean, an endless expanse of it, but then...

'Mist,' he murmured; his stomach rolled and his magic exploded while he breathed deep and pushed it away. 'On the horizon. And I can smell... apples.'

Tymis nodded, before he shut the window firmly, giving Ordes a stern look. 'Take Jenyfer to Port Leore. Do some digging.'

CHAPTER 51

They arrived at Avalon just after dawn, the mists parting for them like a curtain, *The Night Queen* coming to a gentle stop beside a simple, wooden jetty. Arthur stood on the deck beside Katarin, his stomach in knots. He'd barely slept, tossing and turning most of the night, his magic restless the closer they sailed to the Isle, like something was pressing at the inside of him.

The Witchfinder they had captured had spent his time on *The Night Queen* lashed to the main mast. Stripped of his red cloak, he was just a man. Arthur had watched him curiously from the helm, wondering what it was that drove him to follow the path he had. What had caused him to take to the seas and risk his life. Surely it was more than just an escaped Magic Wielder. He had wanted to ask, but hadn't, leaving the man to the sun and the salt that had formed a crust around his lips. None of the crew had gone near the Witchfinder, which Arthur found surprising. He had expected some jibes, jeering, but none had come. Perhaps their silence was more powerful than vocalising their hatred? The Witchfinder seemed to understand this, but even so, he kept his chin lifted proudly.

'The others will stay on the ship,' Kat said softly as the gangplank was lowered. 'It's us Niniane wants to see.'

'And the Witchfinder?' Arthur asked, unable to resist glancing over his shoulder to where the man was still bound to the mast.

'Will be brought ashore later,' Katarin replied simply.

'And then what?'

'Niniane has questions for him.'

Arthur nodded, unsure of what to say to that. The very idea that he was about to meet the Witch of the Mists both thrilled and terrified him. His stomach tightened further. He'd still not told Katarin that the Grail seemed to think he'd be King, and he hoped Niniane didn't know and didn't reveal that finer detail, not until he'd had a chance to explain it. He wasn't sure why he was worried about Katarin's reaction.

It was chilly in the crisp air of the morning, with the mist stroking his skin. Arthur collected his coat and went to put it on.

'You won't need it,' Kat told him. 'You'll find the temperature on the island somehow perfect, exactly what you want.'

'Magic?' he guessed and she nodded. Katarin was quieter than usual, her energy still, nervous. She flashed him a ghost of a smile then led the way down the gangplank and onto the jetty, long red hair swinging behind her like a living thing, the tails of her long coat flapping behind her like raven's wings.

Mist clung to the world. It beaded on their skin and eyelashes; when Arthur blinked, a wet smudge was left on his cheek. The air grew thicker, warmer, as they neared the end of the jetty. He could hear nothing – even the sounds of the ocean were strangely muted. It was like they were in a bubble. There was nothing but the grey cloak of mist surrounding them, layered so thickly he hurried to catch up to his sister, who had become a slim silhouette ahead of him.

'We're nearly there,' she said.

'Nearly where?'

'Avalon.'

Arthur gestured around them. 'This isn't Avalon?'

Kat smiled. 'No.'

The silence around them was thick and eerily deep. Up ahead, the mist thinned and the air shimmered with light. Arthur could see the tops of trees, their dark green foliage almost black in the wan morning light. The sounds of the ocean came back to him suddenly – he could hear the lapping of the waves behind him and glanced towards the sound.

Crystal-clear water brushed a pebbled shore; the rocks glittered, shooting rays of iridescent blue into the air.

Kat quickened her pace and then the mist vanished and she sighed.

'Home.' The smile she gave him was wide. 'Welcome to Avalon, little brother.'

Trees towered above them, branches interlocking over their heads to form a tunnel. The trunks, gnarled and twisted with age, were decorated in pale-green lichen, artfully arranged. They stepped from the hard timber of the jetty. Instead of grass, they walked on a bed of spongy moss the colour of emeralds.

The air was sweet and Arthur breathed deep. He could almost taste the magic of this place, could feel it humming and churning beneath his feet as he followed Kat under the avenue of trees. Light shone up ahead, so bright he had to shield his eyes, and the trees suddenly gave way to fields of flowers, their colours so vibrant they didn't appear real.

They walked through golden grasses that nodded in the soft breeze. Butterflies, as big as birds, hovered in the air, wings flapping lazily. Arthur turned in circles, taking it in – Avalon rested beneath a cloudless sky and he got the impression the island had never been lashed by storms. He could feel eyes watching him and caught sight of a tiny creature with a humanoid face, her skin as brown as bark. Leaves were tangled through her hair. She winked at him, and was gone. As they walked, he saw other fey creatures. These were different to the piskies he had seen – there was a wild, untamed sense about them. They peeked at Arthur and Kat from behind stalks of grass or clumps of granite scattered across the ground.

On the other side of the almost endless ocean of flowers and gold-kissed grass was an orchard of apples, their skins as red as blood. Bees darted between the trees and there were birds in the branches.

'These apples grow all year,' Kat said. 'You can eat them. Here.' She waved a hand – an apple the size of his fist snapped free of a tree and floated to her hand. 'They're the same as the ones we have on the ship but here they're better.' She passed it to him, watching as he took a bite.

'Oh gods,' he moaned. She laughed and continued walking, Arthur trailing behind her as he demolished the apple – if any had been left in his mouth it would have fallen out as they left the orchard and his jaw dropped.

Rising from the earth, seeming part of it, was a castle of pale grey stone, stretching until it kissed the lingering mist that hovered above it. The stone sparkled in the morning light. Windows were cut into the sides, some small, some as large as a wall. Birds swooped through the expanse of growing blue above them, and ivy twined its way up the sides of the castle like veins.

'Who lives here?' he asked in wonder.

'We all do,' Kat answered. 'And you will as well, while you're here.'

Arthur nodded numbly, following her through a simple gate into a neat, cottage garden. Lavender nodded purple heads, fragrant herbs burst from their beds, and there were more fruit trees – pears and peaches, plums and more apples, these ones golden – and a grape vine that wound itself artfully over a trellis.

A gravel path that crunched under foot led to a sweeping stone staircase. Another path curled away from the steps, disappearing into the gardens. 'What's down there?' he asked.

'The House of the Priestesses,' Katarin told him. 'They are Avalon's healers, devoted to the Goddess, and to magic. They used to go to the mainland, but not anymore.'

Aelle, Arthur thought, but said nothing.

Kat rested one foot on the bottom step. 'Ready?' she asked.

'She knows I'm coming, right?'

'Yes.'

Arthur straightened. 'Then I'm ready.'

Kat swept up the stairs and pushed open the set of simple oak doors.

Arthur hadn't stopped gaping. He knew he should close his mouth, but he couldn't.

Beyond the main doors was a courtyard so beautiful he could do nothing but stare. A waterfall tumbled gracefully into a pool of crystal-clear water cut into the centre of the courtyard. Water lilies the size of tables floated on the surface, and bathing there were two of the most beautiful women he had ever seen. Their skin shone with golden light and they were naked, long limbs glistening, their hair like spun gold. They giggled when they spotted him, hiding their faces behind long fingers.

'Nymphs,' Kat whispered as they passed. She led him through an archway of stone, into another wide, open space. There were no walls in this room, only wide, white gauze curtains that shifted in the breeze. Arthur could smell flowers and water, apples and soil. Fresh bread and sweet wine.

The floor was carpeted in lush rugs in muted, earthy tones and coming across the floor towards them, her arms outstretched, was a woman.

She moved unlike any person Arthur had ever seen. Her bare feet barely seemed to touch the ground, and she was wearing a gown of white with delicate, lace trimmings. It trailed on the ground behind her. White flowers were caught in the length of dark hair that tumbled to her waist in perfect waves. Bright blue eyes, delicate brows, and high cheekbones sat above a hunter's bow mouth, as red as the apples in the orchard. Her skin looked like she'd never been touched by the sun.

The woman folded Katarin in her arms. 'I'm glad you're back,' she said, her voice low and husky, dripping with magic. She released Kat and turned to Arthur, those brilliant blue eyes coming to rest on his face. 'Arthur Tregarthen, the Grail Bearer.'

'The Queen of the Isle?' he guessed, his stomach tightening at the name she so casually bestowed on him.

She nodded. 'Come. Sit. I will have food brought.'

'You will conjure food more like,' Katarin said with a smile.

Niniane flashed her a grin. 'Yes, that too.'

Arthur stared. *This* was the Witch of the Mists? This tiny, floaty thing who was smiling and joking. At the far end of the room was a dias, thick comfortable looking cushions scattered around it. Lounging there, her eyes moving over him with interest, was a woman with long, dark hair. A raven was perched on her shoulder.

Kat groaned.

'What is it?' Arthur whispered, his mouth dry. He licked his lips.

'Morrigna, the Goddess of Fate.' Katarin nodded towards the dias. 'Whatever she tells you is likely to give you nightmares.'

'I've had enough of those,' Arthur murmured, while at the same time his head was spinning. He was in Avalon, in the company of not one, but two, goddesses. He wanted to pinch himself.

He could feel Morrigna's eyes on him as he crossed the room at Kat's side. His sister held herself tall and proud, while he just wanted to shrink beneath the stones of this wondrous place and disappear from sight.

The Goddess inclined her head. 'The King that shalt be.'

'King?' Katarin asked sharply, her face folding into a frown.

Morrigna nodded, her lips curling into a satisfied smile. The raven ruffled its feathers, staring at Arthur with liquid eyes. 'You didn't know, *Morgaine*. How interesting.'

'Don't call me that,' Kat snapped, then sunk onto a cushion as if her legs could no longer hold her. Arthur lowered himself to the ground beside her just as platters of food appeared from thin air – fruit and cheese, bread, olives and nuts, fresh berries – his mouth watered at the sight of the sliced apple. The platters hovered in the air before lowering themselves gracefully to the floor. Grumbling, Kat leant forward and snatched a handful of food. He could feel her hurt and wanted to explain, but the Goddess of Fate was watching him expectantly.

'What if I don't want to be King?' he said bluntly.

'It doesn't matter – it's already written,' Morrigna declared, as if it were the most simple thing in the world.

'I don't get a say in it?' Arthur asked.

The Goddess simply shook her head.

'Bullshit,' Katarin challenged, shoving grapes into her mouth. 'Everyone has a say in their fate. Don't lie to him.'

Morrigna dismissed the comment with a languid wave of her hand. 'Your fate is sealed, Arthur, but not by me – by prophecy, by one who has seen what is yet to pass. This is your path, whether you like it or not. What sort of King you shall be is up to you,' she added.

'The Grail cannot be found by you alone, Arthur,' Niniane said, seating herself beside Morrigna. 'It was made of ancient magic and, before it will reveal itself, the Treasures of the Gods must be recovered first.'

'So he has to find the Treasures as well?' Kat asked.

The Queen of the Mists shook her head. 'Not alone. The prophecy makes mention of three people – one of the earth, one of the sea, and one who stands between the worlds.'

'Any idea who these other two are?' Katarin asked.

'That, I do not know,' Niniane answered simply. She turned back to Arthur, her unearthly face curious. 'What do you know about the Treasures of the Gods?'

Arthur rubbed at his cheek. 'I read about them as a child, but my father said they weren't real.' He looked from one goddess to the other, noted the anger on Morrigna's face and the sorrow on Niniane's. 'I'm going to assume they are real.'

'They are very much real,' Niniane said simply. She shifted her position and a pair of gossamer wings unfolded from her back. Arthur gaped. 'Once, I could use these to fly. But when our Treasures were stolen—'

'By who?' Katarin demanded.

'Ever so keen for vengeance, Katarin, darling,' Niniane said. 'One of our brethren stole the Treasures. She betrayed us for power. She is a master of lies and deception,' Niniane explained softly. Her voice held no bitterness, no pain, just an acceptance of what had been, and a yearning, lying deep beneath the simple words. Beside Arthur, Katarin ground her teeth, her face fierce. 'When she stole our Treasures, she sought to steal our power, the essence of who we were,' the Witch of the Mists continued. 'But she should have known better, because our power is not in an object.'

'Then how did you lose the ability to fly?' Katarin asked, gesturing at the magnificent silvery wings rising above Niniane's shoulders.

It was Morrigna who spoke. 'As word spread amongst the humans who believed in us about the loss of our Treasures, they started to question the things they knew were true. They did not stop believing in us, but that belief began to waver, enough that it affected all the Old Ones, including the one who betrayed us to begin with.'

Arthur chewed his lip. He knew from Aelle that the magic of the Old Ones, their power, their very existence, was only as strong the belief in them was. If belief in the Old Ones vanished from the world, so would they. He swallowed tightly, his thoughts flying to Jalen. Was it the same for demi-gods?

Katarin was frowning. 'How do we find the Treasures, then?'

'Many have tried over the years, but all have failed to locate them,' Niniane said. Her gaze shifted to Arthur. 'But you won't.'

'How can you be so sure?' he challenged quietly.

'Because I have seen it,' Morrigna said. 'And the Myrddin prophesied it.'

'Myrddin?' Arthur asked, the unfamiliar word rolling around his mouth. A spark of power shot through him.

'You will meet him soon,' Niniane said with a soft, wistful smile. 'The Grail is the most powerful of the Treasures, because it can reshape and heal the land.' She waved her hand through the air and three objects appeared there – an illusion, but so real Arthur felt he could reach out and touch the Treasures. One was a bow and a quiver of arrows, the other a smooth, flat stone that would fit in his palm, and the third—

He gasped.

Niniane's eyes narrowed. 'You have seen the Treasures?'

'Just the sword, in a dream,' Arthur managed, unable to take his eyes off the vision.

'The Sword of Light, the Sword of the White Dragon,' Morrigna said. 'It is yours to find and yours to wield. Once drawn from its sheath, it cannot be stopped. No one can resist its power, so you should not draw it unless you intend to use it. It can kill a God,' she added softly.

Before Arthur could ask more questions, the atmosphere in the room shifted. Morrigna rolled her eyes as thunder rumbled through the stones beneath them, muttering about demons and their theatrics, while Niniane reminded her he wasn't a demon, but a demi-god. Arthur's heart stopped beating for a moment – lightning flashed outside, although the sky was free of clouds. Wind ripped through the room, a whirlwind that slowly came to rest not far from the dias.

Arthur swallowed his stomach – and turned to face the demon of storms.

CHAPTER 52

Jenyfer and Ordes made their way across the main square in Port Leore. The sun was sinking through the pale-blue sky. Fluffy clouds hung low on the horizon, their undersides painted with broad strokes of gold, orange, and pink. They couldn't see the ocean from the middle of the town, but Jenyfer could hear the waves crashing into the headland along the coast, the cries of sea birds fierce in the sultry air.

'When we get to the ale house, leave the talking to me,' Ordes told her.

Jenyfer tugged at the sleeves of her dress, making sure the map was covered. Ordes, she noticed, had his sleeves rolled up, the inky lines spread across his honeyed skin on full display. He could get away with it, she supposed. The map could easily pass as a tattoo; acceptable on his skin, not so on hers. Tymis' words echoed through her head, making her stomach churn uncomfortably. He'd obviously said something to Ordes – they'd left *The Excalibur* just on dark, their boat shrouded in magical mist.

She cleared her throat. 'And what will I be doing while you're talking?'

'Looking amazing.'

She shook her head at him. That morning he'd woken up grumpy; he'd grumbled the whole way to Port Leore but, now, he was full of cheek, full of smiles, and full of shit.

It's a mask, she realised suddenly, much like the one she used to pull onto her face whenever she had to go and mingle with the good people of Kernou.

'You don't have to pretend with me,' Jenyfer said softly.

Ordes gave her a startled look, then smiled, leaning over to press his lips to her temple. She kept her eyes on the ground. It was easier that way. If she didn't look at him too often, she didn't think about him and didn't have to think about what she needed to do.

At least, that was what she told herself.

The truth was, she'd thought about him almost everyday since the first night she met him. Those nights in the cave, just sitting and talking, or just sitting and saying nothing, had been some of the most tranquil moments in Jenyfer's life – even though it was dangerous, she couldn't deny how calm she'd felt. Her inner song, usually so demanding, so forceful, had been soothed, and it had crooned to her, as if it knew how important he would become to her, long before she knew it.

So how could she possibly leave him?

To distract herself, she lifted her eyes and focused on the town around them. Not shady, like Skulls Rest, and nowhere near as grand and important as The Vale, Port Leore was something in between. It was too large to be considered a village, but fishing appeared to be the main industry, if the small boats that lined the beach were anything to go by.

A shiver walked Jenyfer's spine as she recalled the map she'd glimpsed when first on board *The Excalibur*. They weren't far from Kernou; the Bay of Calledun was on the other side of the sweeping headland.

Port Leore's town square, like Kernou's, was bordered by shops – bakery, blacksmith, a food market that was still open as they passed, baskets filled with fruits and vegetables. There was an apothecary and Jenyfer breathed deep the familiar smell of herbs and tonics.

There was something about this place that made Jenyfer's skin crawl, something familiar that she couldn't put her finger on. Her song was humming in low tones that sounded very much like a warning. Their mission was to ask, as subtly as possible, about the Treasures of the Gods. Jenyfer wasn't sure how one asked about mystical – and possibly not real – ancient relics while remaining subtle. Jenyfer was glad to be doing something, even though it seemed fruitless. If the Treasures were indeed here, why hadn't anyone found them?

She suspected the whole thing was nothing more than a ploy, a distraction conjured by Tymis; but a distraction for her, or for Ordes, Jenyfer wasn't sure.

The ale house, a large, circular building with a low roof, was dark inside, the air heavy and thick from the dozen fire pits blazing at even intervals. Arranged around each pit were mountains of cushions. There wasn't a table in the place – drinks appeared to be served from a central station. A man with cropped hair was busily pouring ale into mugs and setting them on trays, which were scooped up by a younger man with a nervous face.

Slowly, Jenyfer looked around. Sweat had gathered in her armpits and on the back of her neck. A trickle of it made its way down the curve of her cheek and the shiver that danced along her spine switched from light feet to heavy as she realised there were hardly any women in the ale house.

Ordes scanned the room, then gripped her hand and led them to a fire pit, the cushions occupied by a group of younger men. They looked up in surprise as Ordes flashed a smile.

'Can we join you?'

Five sets of eyes crawled over Jenyfer's face. For a moment, none of the men moved, until one of them grunted in what she took as assent because Ordes directed her to a cushion and plonked himself beside her, immediately engaging the men in small talk about the weather, fishing, how much of the world they had seen – it was effortless for him. Jenyfer felt a spike of jealousy. She couldn't talk to people, and here he was, a pirate, and a *faery*, having a conversation with people he'd never seen before.

All Ordes' talking must have helped their new companions relax; either that, or the drinks he paid for. Conversation switched to Kernou, and the strange things that had been happening there.

'Missing their eyes?' Ordes said, his face the perfect imitation of shock and fear. 'Do they know who did it?'

One of the men, the oldest of the group, shrugged his shoulders and sipped at his ale. 'Probably that fey bitch and her nasty crew,' he said simply, the others nodding along with him. Ordes leant forward, lowering his voice to a conspiratorial whisper.

'You're talking about Katarin Le Fey?' Ordes said. 'Have any of you ever seen her? Or the *Queen*?'

A young man, with a shock of flame-red hair, nodded eagerly. 'I have! The ship came from beneath the water, pulling up right beside us!'

'Bullshit,' another man put in. 'You'd be dead if that really happened. We all know what Katarin Le Fey does to those she catches.'

The young man blushed and mumbled something Jenyfer didn't catch, but one of the older men with cropped, dark hair and a stern expression set his mug aside. He'd barely drunk a thing, she realised. His eyes swept over her before they moved slowly, deliberately, around the circle of men. He sat back, crossing his legs at the ankles. Around his neck, Jenyfer caught a glimpse of a gold chain. It disappeared beneath his shirt, so she couldn't see what, if anything, dangled from it.

'Women don't belong out there on the waves,' he said in a steady voice.

'Oh? Where do they belong then?' Jenyfer spoke without thought.

The man's eyes bored into hers. 'They belong in the home, with their husband, not out in the world without supervision. Everyone knows a woman alone cannot be trusted.'

Dread crept down Jenyfer's spine. She swallowed dryly, taking another sip of her ale, not even noticing the bitterness of the liquid as it slid down her throat to settle in her stomach. She did not look at the man again, setting her mug to the side, shifting closer to Ordes. She closed her eyes, listening as he continued to talk to the men. There was music in his voice as well; not like hers, but in the way Ordes could hold an audience, hold people captive with nothing but the power of his charm. She knew what it felt like to be on the receiving end of that charm, of the way he strung words together, the way he spoke.

Ordes touched her knee; a brief touch, but enough to send sparks shooting through her, setting a fire burning beneath the fear and worry that tugged on her.

How much of it was real? She wondered. Was he under a spell, *her* spell, or did he truly want her? She couldn't tell. She'd tried to keep her magic contained around him, but now that it was free, she could feel it at work, could see it in how people's eyes would glaze over, and she hated it, wishing her aunt had left the binding spells in place.

But how much would be different if Tamora hadn't released her? Jenyfer swallowed.

Everything, she realised. Everything, and nothing.

She wondered what would happen if she used the magic in her voice on the men sitting opposite them? Would their jaws slacken and their eyes go hazy?

The men were talking amongst themselves.

'You want to leave?' Ordes asked quietly, sensing her mood. His fingers found the back of her hand and he stroked her skin gently. 'Jen?'

'I'm fine,' she whispered, opening her eyes and smothering a yawn. 'But I am tired.'

He patted his thigh, an invitation. Jenyfer cast a quick look around the ale house. People were both sitting and lying on the cushions and some patrons looked like they were sleeping. After a moment's hesitation, she lay down, resting her head on Ordes' thigh, lying on her back so she didn't have to face their companions across the flames. She could feel their disapproval but Ordes had told the smooth lie about them being married. She jumped when he stroked her forehead lightly, then – when his fingers slid into her hair to run over her scalp – she relaxed, unable to resist.

He was mid-conversation with one of the men when she fell asleep.

It was dark when Jenyfer woke, and she was no longer in the ale house. She was moving. She blinked, letting her eyes adjust before she realised Ordes was carrying her.

'What are you doing?'

'What does it look like?'

She sighed. 'I can walk.'

'I know, but from here, I have a rather wonderful view down the front of your dress,' he said playfully. She hit him even as her belly warmed.

'You're going to carry me all the way to the boat?' she asked after adjusting her clothing.

He chuckled. 'Don't be silly – you're heavier than you look.'

Jenyfer smacked the side of his head again, making him grin and let her down. They walked in silence for a while, close together but not touching. She could feel the heat from his body and shifted a fraction closer, until she was able to press her arm against his. Without a word, he wrapped his hand around hers, their fingers weaving together as they entered the deserted town square. It was late, the moon high above them, splashing her pale light over the town.

'How long was I asleep in there?' Jenyfer asked softly.

Ordes shrugged. 'Not long.'

'Did you learn anything about the Grail or the Treasures?'

'Rumour, nothing more,' he said.

'Rumours have truth though,' Jenyfer mused, and he nodded, then stopped and pulled her into his body, slipping his arms around her. Her heart skipped a beat, or maybe it was his. She could hardly tell anymore. They had reached the other side of the square. The town was quiet and still, the only sounds were the soft breeze that danced between the buildings and their mingled breathing.

Ordes cupped her cheek, his thumb moving over her skin, looking at her intently, as if searching for something, his face more serious than she'd ever seen him. He smiled, then bent his head and kissed her; her whole body began to tingle, her inner song humming along in delight. His lips were soft, gentle. Jenyfer liked this kiss – it was slow and sensual, lazy almost. But it soon changed. Heat sped through her, the music in her head and the magic beneath her skin wanting more, even though she knew she should distance herself, but she couldn't.

She clutched him tightly, sucking his bottom lip into her mouth.

The look he gave her when he pulled back sent sparks exploding through her blood. They were both breathing heavily. She could feel the tension in his shoulders, could see it in the line of his jaw, so she reached up and trailed her fingers down his cheek. His hands moved over her and she sighed against his lips, her blood singing, her pulse surging like the tide.

Someone cleared their throat.

'I thought I recognised you,' said a gruff voice. Jenyfer froze, her whole body turning to ice. Ordes looked at her, his eyes telling her to let him deal with it and she was more than happy to leave this up to him. Slowly, with one arm around her middle, he turned to face the speaker.

'Have we met?' he asked cheerfully.

'Yeah, boy, we've met.'

'Ah,' Ordes said. His fingers tightened where they rested on Jenyfer's waist – a warning. Her mouth went dry.

'You were only there for the rum,' the speaker continued.

'That I was, and then, as you can plainly see, I left.'

'But not before strange things started happening in Kernou.'

Jenyfer's stomach twisted and she made sure her face was hidden.

'Strange things were happening there long before I arrived,' Ordes said. His heartbeat had steadied, until it was almost still, and Jenyfer could feel his magic shifting beneath his skin. His hand dropped casually to the dagger he wore at his hip. 'If that's all, we'll be going.'

'Who have you got there?' It was another voice, one that Jenyfer knew.

Her stomach dropped further and she could feel the ale she'd drunk creeping up her throat as footsteps approached them. Ordes chuckled.

'You can find your own girl, I'm sure.'

'I'm sure, but my interest is not the same as yours, pirate,' the Konsel man spat. 'The One God does not indulge in pleasures of the flesh as readily as some.'

'Maybe he should,' Ordes said. 'Maybe then he'd be less of a bastard. A good fuck does a man wonders, you know.'

'Shut up,' Jenyfer hissed. She felt Ordes look at her at the same time she felt the Konsel man's eyes on her body. Suddenly, she realised what she'd failed to see earlier, her head so caught up in everything else – the symbol of the One God on the outer wall of the bakery: the cross. And the old man's words in the ale house, the gold chain around his neck.

'Women should not be out after dark,' the Konsel man said firmly.

'I don't believe in your god,' Ordes shot back. Jenyfer squeezed his hand, trying to tell him to leave it, let it go, and take her back to the ship.

'It seems this woman needs to be taught her place; you as well.'

Jenyfer's head shot up. That voice was one she knew well, one she had heard for years. That she had laughed with, cried with, argued with and, most recently, woken up to.

Bryn.

Slowly, she turned her face to his.

He went white beneath his tan, his mouth opening and closing stupidly.

'Like you threatened to teach me my place before?' Jenyfer snapped. She completely forgot the danger they were in - she wanted to strangle him with her bare hands.

'Wait...' Ordes breathed. She nodded, not trusting her voice again.

That was when Ordes shoved her behind him and drew his dagger.

'Don't,' she implored, but he ignored her. He flipped the dagger expertly in one hand, while the air around his other hand shimmered and shifted as sparks danced across his knuckles.

'Witchcraft,' the Konsel man hissed.

'I'll even things up,' Ordes said. He handed Jenyfer the dagger. 'Fists only, if it makes you feel better boys, and no magic. One at a time?' he paused, and pointed at Bryn. 'You're first, arsehole.'

Bryn took a step back, then recovered himself and stood up straight. 'Fine.'

Jenyfer shook her head. 'Bryn, he'll knock your teeth out.'

'Don't speak to me, witch,' Bryn snarled at her, and she scowled, hoping he did indeed have his teeth removed from his mouth. He rolled up his sleeves and stepped forward and Jenyfer resisted the urge to sigh. Despite the situation, despite the danger they were in, she couldn't help but feel men were utterly stupid.

Ordes moved like smoke, like water, so fluid and light on his feet, like he had been when they danced. Jenyfer had never seen a fight so, to her, it looked like a dance; although Bryn was nowhere near as graceful as Ordes, who managed to punch him in the nose not once, but twice. His bones snapped with an audible crack.

Blood dribbling down his chin, Bryn held up his hands, stepping away. Jenyfer couldn't help the warm and heady satisfaction that flowed through her. Bryn looked at her through watery eyes and she grinned smugly.

Ordes and the older fisherman were dancing now. Ordes was smiling, utterly enjoying himself as he ducked beneath the man's arm and slammed his fist into his gut. The fisherman doubled over with a groan.

Wiping his hands on his shirt front, Ordes rolled his shoulders as the fisherman stumbled to his feet.

'Watch out!' Jenyfer yelled, but too late – Alric moved swifter than the dour, big-bellied Konsel man seemed capable of. His fist connected with the back of Ordes' head and he crumbled to the ground.

Alric turned to Jenyfer with a smile, wiping his hands on the front of his shirt.

Horrified, her eyes shot to Bryn, who was clutching his broken face. He looked away from her and she knew, at that moment, she was completely alone.

'Now to deal with you, witch,' Alric whispered, eyes shining with savage glee.

Not taking her eyes from Alric, Jenyfer dropped to her knees beside Ordes, shaking him roughly. 'Come on, come on,' she muttered as the Konsel man and the old fishermen from Kernou approached. Bryn lingered behind them, his expression torn. She held his eyes for as long as she could, before Alric rushed forward and grabbed her arm, hauling her to her feet.

'The Chif will be very pleased to see you, Miss Astolat,' he said.

Her body moved before her brain; her fingers curled and her fist barrelled into his gut. It wasn't a hard blow, but it surprised him enough to loosen his hold. She pulled herself free and darted out of his reach, brandishing the dagger, holding it firmly, like she'd been taught.

Alric snarled at her. 'The One God has plans for your kind.'

'Does he?' Jenyfer said, desperate to keep the man talking. She circled around Ordes' still form, keeping one eye on Alric and the other one on Bryn and the old fisherman. 'And what is that?'

Alric smiled. His eyes were burning, almost glowing in the darkness. 'You will all be eliminated. The One God is raising an army to wipe your kind from the face of the land. It has already begun.'

Jenyfer shifted closer to Ordes and gave him a hard kick. He groaned and rolled onto his side. She bit back a sigh of relief, not taking her eyes from Alric. 'Are you going to tell me how and when this will happen?'

Behind Alric, Bryn's expression shifted. Jenyfer glared at him. 'You're okay with all this I take it, Bryn?'

He mumbled something she didn't hear.

'You left me to die,' she reminded him. 'You're a coward.' Her emotions swelled, as the music in her head swelled, building and building, until it reached a crescendo, deafening her. Her magic surged beneath her skin.

'Enough,' Alric spat.

Jenyfer flexed her fingers, her song swimming beneath her skin, clamouring up her throat, begging to be let out.

Suddenly, Alric raced forward.

Jenyfer opened her mouth, and sang, her voice low, purposeful. She sang without thinking. She sang because she had to, because she couldn't not sing. Her voice was pulled from her mouth by something stronger than she was.

The Konsel man stopped. A peaceful expression crossed his face. Behind him, Bryn and the older fisherman were staring at her, mouths agape. Ordes groaned again and pushed himself onto all fours at her feet. She kept singing. Alric took a step closer, drawn to her song, to the magic that pulsed through the air between them, the notes that she could see suspended there, like leaves falling in slow motion. She watched his eyes shift, watched the fear and wonder crawl across his expression, and her song changed.

Slowly, he withdrew the dagger she didn't know he carried.

Jenyfer kept singing, letting the music sweep around them. She kept her eyes on Alric, never looking away, and, eyes wide and panicked, he lifted his arm, and plunged the dagger into his gut.

The shock of it made her stop. Alric looked at her, then slumped to his knees. Bryn and the fisherman raced forward but she held up her hand and they halted, fear scrawled across their faces.

'What have you done?' Bryn whispered.

'Leave,' she ordered, her voice low and hard. 'Now.'

Bryn didn't move. 'I was supposed to keep you in line,' he said. 'The Chif promised me, if I could keep you under control...'

'What did he promise you?' Jenyfer snapped.

'He said he would make me important. He told me the One God had plans for me,' Bryn answered swiftly. 'But you...'

'What happened to you?' Jenyfer asked as Ordes shifted onto his knees, rubbing at the back of his head. 'What happened to the man who was my friend, who could see past the bullshit of the One God? Whatever the Chif promised you... I hope it was worth it, Bryn.'

Bryn's face collapsed, but he said nothing.

'Leave,' Jenyfer repeated. 'Or I'll make you.'

Bryn nodded, the red of his blood smeared across his nose and chin. He and the fisherman grabbed Alric by the arms and dragged him backwards, the Konsel man groaning in pain. Jenyfer's heart was thundering, her magic thrumming through her, but she did not look away until they had vanished from sight.

Biting down on the sob that sat in her throat, she put her arm around Ordes' middle and pulled him awkwardly to his feet. 'Come on, come on,' she urged. 'I can't carry you and they might come back.'

'What—I heard music... a song...'

'Walk,' she commanded, and he did, his footsteps becoming steadier, Jenyfer shooting glances over her shoulder, but no one came after them. Supporting Ordes' weight with one arm, she dragged him through the streets, heading for the beach. 'You have to help me,' Jenyfer whispered, straining under Ordes' weight. 'You're heavier than you look.'

'I'll take that as a compliment,' he mumbled, but did as she asked, putting one foot in front of the other. 'What did that bastard hit me with?'

'His fist,' Jenyfer answered as the beach came into view. They staggered across the sand towards the boat. 'Come on, get in,' she ordered, helping him climb over the edge of the boat.

'Jen—'

'We need to get back to the ship,' she said, climbing in after him. Ordes reached for the oars, but she shook her head at him.

'You can't row, Jen,' he mumbled, rubbing at the back of his head and wincing.

'I'll manage,' she said. 'I watched you do it, I should be able to,' she added, chewing her lip. She turned on the wooden seat so she was facing the ocean, and held out her hands, closing her eyes and calling on her magic. Her fingertips tingled, but the boat didn't move.

'Come on, come on,' Jenyfer muttered. She tried again, but this time, pulled her inner song to the surface tentatively. It came willingly. Her whole body thrummed with magic.

'Did I break his nose?' Ordes whispered.

'Yes. Now shush, I'm concentrating,' Jenyfer scolded. Her song was swimming through her veins, her magic warm and alive, like lightning and storms. The boat shuddered.

'Are you pleased?'

Jenyfer smothered a laugh. 'Yes. Go to sleep, Ordes,' she commanded. She heard him sigh, and when she glanced over her shoulder, his eyes were closed.

When she was certain he was asleep, Jenyfer sang.

She was unable to stop from smiling as their boat shot free of the beach and headed through the first set of waves. Only when they were in open water and *The Excalibur* was lingering on the horizon, silhouetted by moonlight, did she let her smile fall.

What worried Jenyfer the most was not that the One God's poison had spread from Kernou, but that she had coerced a man into knifing himself with her voice.

And part of her liked it.

CHAPTER 53

Arthur had been given a room with a balcony. The sun was sinking as he pushed the sheer, white curtains aside, opened the frosted glass doors and stepped out. The view took his breath away.

Directly below him were the expansive orchards of Avalon, the trees growing in perfectly straight rows, their branches intertwined in places. He wondered how old they were as he let his gaze drift further, to the fields of golden grass in one direction, the dark foliage of the trees he and Kat had walked beneath reaching into the sky. In the other direction, granite mountains scraped low-hanging clouds. Birds bigger than any he had ever seen swooped in and out of the clouds, coming to rest occasionally on the side of the mountain. Nests, he realised, they must have nests there. A waterfall spilled lazily from between two of the peaks, tumbling into a mass of white foam that spread into a lake. Small trees clung to the base of the mountains, and the grass that rolled towards the castle was like a carpet of emeralds sparkling in the twilight.

He moved closer to the railing, gripping the stone tightly, and peered over the edge. So high. He hadn't recalled climbing that many stairs to reach his room, following a woman wearing a billowing, saffron-yellow dress through the wide halls, the walls hung with artworks so lifelike he wanted to stop and run his fingers over them.

Arthur straightened, closed his eyes, and took a deep breath. He could taste sunshine and grass, the sweet apples he had eaten earlier – and would probably crawl over broken glass for another bite – and freshwater. As he watched, the sun dropped further and the mist that shrouded the island on all sides seemed to thicken, until the light was completely swallowed and Avalon was plunged into darkness.

Avalon. He was in Avalon. Arthur pinched himself.

'No matter how often I see it, it never fails to amaze.'

Arthur spun around. Jalen was leaning casually against the doorframe. His hair was back to its golden-sand colour, and he was dressed in simple grey trousers and a loose, white shirt. He was barefoot, his gaze on the vista before them. Slowly, his eyes moved to Arthur's face.

Silence dripped between them until, eventually, Jalen sighed and rubbed at the back of his neck, such a human gesture, but—

'You're not human,' Arthur stated simply. He turned away, looking out over the island again. Lights winked in the darkness. He wanted to know what they were, but he couldn't ask, not yet, not now, not when this conversation had to happen.

'No, I'm not.'

'Was any of it real?' Arthur looked at his hands, hating the way his voice sounded – viscous, desperate, emotional.

'You think because I'm not human that I don't feel?' Jalen asked, his words nothing more than whispers in the misty darkness. 'You think I don't love, or feel desire?' He moved closer to Arthur, reaching hesitantly for Arthur's hand where it gripped the balcony railing, running his fingers along the back of Arthur's knuckles.

'It was real, Arthur,' Jalen murmured. 'All of it.'

Arthur shook his head. Kat's words echoed there, bouncing around the confines of his skull.

Does it matter?

'You're a demi-god,' he said softly, watching Jalen's face carefully. 'What do you want with me?'

'I was never supposed to care about you, Arthur, not the way I do,' Jalen replied. 'I was supposed to help you, monitor you, as the Old Ones wished, but the more time I spent with you, the more I saw, and I saw pain and uncertainty. I saw despair but, beneath it, I also saw a sliver of hope.'

Jalen slipped back into the room, going to perch on the edge of the grand bed. 'They didn't want me involved with you, not like... but I decided you needed a friend, someone who was like you, who could help you, and that was my intention to begin with, but then I actually met you. I talked to you. And I saw you – the man you are to become.'

Arthur drifted closer, stopping just inside the archway, gauzy curtains tickling his feet. 'And who is that?'

Jalen smiled. 'A leader. A King.'

Arthur laughed sadly. 'I'm no King. Kings are strong and fierce, like in the stories. They're wise, they're—'

'You would not have survived your father, and the One God, if you were not strong, Arthur,' Jalen interrupted. He stood again; the air around him shifted as a breeze rushed through the room. Arthur stood very still as Jalen approached him.

'What are you doing here now?' Arthur breathed.

Jalen's eyes sparkled in the darkness, the colour of storms and wind and the tempests of the sea. 'I'm here for you.'

Arthur's heart sped up. 'What does that mean, exactly?'

'It means,' Jalen replied, taking Arthur's hands, the warmth of his skin slipping beneath Arthur's flesh to mingle with the fire that was slowly building there. 'That I have a role to play in this saga as well. I am here to guide you, and protect you, until the Myrddin comes.'

'Who is that? Morrigna mentioned him as well,' Arthur asked.

'He will help you shape the world as it should be,' Jalen replied. Slowly, he took a step closer, until his body was pressed against Arthur's and, suddenly, Arthur was back in that cave on the beach, with his head spinning and his blood burning and his mouth wanting to touch, to suck, to taste. This was real. It was not a dream.

He took a deep, shuddering breath.

'I missed you,' Arthur whispered. 'I missed this.' He sighed and pulled away gently, releasing Jalen's face, his hands immediately aching with emptiness. Jalen wandered back into the room, the four-poster bed Arthur had barely looked at before behind him.

He looked at the bed now – curtains dangled from the mahogany framework, and the walls of his room were covered in beautiful tapestries of scenes so fantastical, so magical, he knew they were not of the world he had come from. There was so much he didn't know.

'This dance we are all now engaged in was written long before you were born. Long before your father and his allegiance with the One God. It is what was always destined to happen,' Jalen said.

Arthur curled his toes in the lush rug that covered the stone floor, then sighed heavily, letting his eyes move around the room. A timber wardrobe with an ornately carved face sat against one wall, a dressing screen close by, and a giant mirror hung from the wall. He approached it on hesitant feet, realising he had never truly seen his reflection, other than in the polished candlesticks on the One God's altar in his father's house.

He closed his eyes, and then he looked.

A tall and lanky man stared back at him, with bark-brown hair and irritated, green-gold eyes. He frowned. He didn't remember his eyes being that colour. He'd thought they were brown, like his father's. There were shadows beneath those eyes, and Arthur's face was pale and pinched. Worried. He watched in the mirror as Jalen stood and crossed the floor, coming to stand beside him.

'You know what I see?' the Storm Demon – the demi-god – asked.

'What?'

'I see a man who does not yet know what he is capable of,' Jalen answered gently. Keeping his eyes on their reflection, he reached up to touch Arthur's cheek with feather-light fingers, then rested his hands on Arthur's shoulders. 'I see a man unsure if his shoulders are strong enough to carry the weight of what is being asked. But they are. I can see that as well. Only, you don't. Not yet, but you will. I hope.'

Arthur was silent for a long time, watching his reflection, watching Jalen.

'I'm tired,' he said eventually, turning from the mirror. His feet were heavy as he trudged across the carpet to flop onto the bed, burying his head in a pillow as soft as clouds. 'Niniane said I can't wield the Grail alone, and that the other Treasures need to be found first,' he said softly. 'What do I do?'

'What *we* will do is go to Cruithea,' Jalen stated firmly. The bed dipped with his weight.

'Cruithea?'

'Yes. The Myrrdin may come to you there, he may not.'

'How do you know?'

'You need to trust me,' Jalen whispered. 'The world has waited a long time for you, Arthur Tregarthen – I've waited a long time,' he added. Arthur shifted onto his side as Jalen stretched out beside him. They were so close, so close, but neither made a move to touch the other. Desire and longing churned through Arthur's gut as Jalen's eyes moved over his face, waiting, giving him the time he needed.

'I don't know the first thing about being a King,' Arthur admitted.

'Which is why you will make an excellent King,' Jalen said, reaching out to stroke the side of Arthur's face and Arthur's eyes dropped closed. 'It's why the Grail chose you. There is no greed in your heart, no lust for power, no false pretences.' Jalen's hand moved over Arthur's arm, up and down, his fingers soothing and gentle.

Arthur opened his eyes. He wanted to see Jalen's face.

'I know you will be the King Teyath needs – that it must have if there is to be a future without fear and suffering.'

'No pressure, then,' Arthur joked – but Jalen didn't smile.

'There is blood yet to be shed,' he said regretfully.

Arthur swallowed tightly. 'Whose?'

'I can't say. But there will be blood, on the sand and in the sea, mingling with the soil and threaded through the air.' Jalen's voice had dropped, taking on a sing-song quality.

Arthur sighed and flopped onto his back. 'Cruithea, then.'

'Yes. You told me you wanted to visit your family. Morgause, the High Priestess, she will support you and she will help you,' Jalen said. He shifted closer, tucking his head against Arthur's shoulder. Arthur let him. 'She is your mother's sister.'

'What?'

'You didn't know?'

'I know nothing about my mother,' Arthur replied. 'Only what Katarin has shared.'

'In Cruithea, you will learn everything you need to know, about your family, and about the King you shall be,' Jalen said with certainty. 'Now, sleep. I will be here when you wake up.'

Arthur fell asleep, Jalen tucked in close beside him, and in the morning, as the sun slowly crawled over the island, he climbed from bed, leaving Jalen sleeping. He explored the wardrobe, finding clothes that somehow fit his body like they were made for it, and went to find his sister.

Katarin was sitting in the courtyard by the pool, fingers trailing through the water. There was no sign of the nymphs Arthur had seen when they first arrived. He frowned, taking a seat beside her, letting his feet dangle over the surface of the water.

'How long have we been here?'

She shrugged bare shoulders. 'No idea. Time moves differently here. It might have been two days, it might have been two weeks.' She sighed and ran her fingers over the skirt of the gown she was wearing. It was as green as moss; the material appeared light and floaty, and Kat's long red hair was brushed and arranged neatly around her face, held back with silver pins so that it flowed down her back like a waterfall of blood. She scowled at his expression. 'Shut up. I hate dresses but Niniane insists. I'm not a pirate while I'm here – I'm her daughter.'

'She calls you that?'

'She does,' Kat replied. Everything about her was softer here, including her voice. She flashed him a smile, but he could see the lingering hurt behind it and swallowed.

'I'm sorry,' he said softly. 'That I didn't tell you about the... King part of my dreams.'

Katarin's gaze was shrewd. 'Do you want to be a king?'

'I don't know,' Arthur answered. 'I mean, who actually wants that sort of thing?'

She laughed, shaking her head. 'You are unlike any man I have ever met.' She reached out to touch Arthur's hand. 'I sail at first light in search of the location of the Treasures. Are you coming? There is a place for you on *The Night Queen*, if you want it, which I know you don't, not now anyway,' she added with a cheeky smile.

'You're leaving?'

Katarin nodded. 'I'll see you again, Arthur. Sooner than you think. Things are happening, whether you want them to or not. Once the Treasures are found and you have the Grail, everything will change. While you are here, take the time to learn. Listen to your magic.'

He looked at his feet. A silver fish darted beneath them. 'Jalen says we have to go to Cruithea, that they will help me.'

'They will. You'll be safe there, Arthur. And well protected.'

'Have you been back, since...'

'Not for long, only to drop people off.' Katarin looked away from him briefly, then flashed him a smile. 'You can be yourself here, as you can in Cruithea. Remember that.'

'What if I don't know who I am?' Arthur mumbled.

'You will,' Katarin answered with certainty. 'Now, leave me alone. I don't like goodbyes, even if it's only for a short time.'

As he left the courtyard, Arthur glanced back. A large butterfly came to rest on his sister's hair. She scowled and brushed it away, then climbed to her feet and stalked off in the opposite direction.

CHAPTER 54

Since returning from Port Leore, Jenyfer had been sleeping in Ordes' cabin. It wasn't something they'd actually discussed, but something that just seemed to happen. She felt better when she was close to him. Safe. She was happy to curl up against him each night and just sleep, his heartbeat in her ears, her blood warm in her veins. What had happened with Alric and Bryn in Port Leore haunted her dreams. Seeing Bryn had been hard enough, but what she'd made Alric do haunted her. She saw the Konsel man's face every time she closed her eyes, and heard his shocked breath as he plunged that dagger into his own body.

Now, she was sitting above deck, the sun slowly sinking below the horizon. The ocean was coated with strokes of burning orange and deep pink, the colours dazzling against the growing darkness.

Jenyfer sighed and tucked her knees up to her chest, resting her chin on them. She watched the sun sink completely, giving one last burst of light, before darkness engulfed her. Most of the crew were below deck in their bunks, or in the galley. She could hear faint singing beneath her, and her skin tingled, that strange connection she had to music tugging at her, urging her to find the sound, to let it wrap itself around her.

To sing.

She didn't.

After Alric, Jenyfer never wanted to sing again. That she even could still stunned her. She didn't remember her voice, didn't remember what she had sung, both in reality and in her dreams. But she had no clue how to wield her magic, or if she even could. She couldn't control it – whenever she felt it creeping up her throat, it felt like the magic was in control of her, not the other way around.

Syhrens were dangerous. Deadly. And she was one of them.

The crew were right to fear her.

Tymis was right to suggest she leave. The two ships were still behind them, far enough back so that they didn't appear threatening, but how long would it be before they came a little closer? Jenyfer rubbed at her eyes. Tomorrow morning, she would go. She didn't want anyone else to get hurt because of what she was.

Jenyfer thought about her parents – her very human parents. Which one of them was not what they seemed? Had her mother been a syhren? Or was it her father? He was always out on the ocean, but her mother... she stayed away from the water, and she hadn't wanted Jenyfer to play in the surf either. Jenyfer frowned. Had her mother lived her life like she was now – at the mercy of a magic that was dark and deadly, that seemed to have its own purpose and intentions?

Tamora knew, Jenyfer realised. She knew what Jenyfer was and she'd never told her. Hot and bitter anger clawed its way up Jenyfer's throat and then faded just as quickly. She couldn't blame her aunt – Tamora had done everything she could to protect Jenyfer, from the dangers of her magic and the dangers of the Chif and the One God.

Lamorna's face flashed into her mind. *Please be alive*, Jenyfer prayed. *I'll never use magic again if you're alive. Let me find you, Lamorna.*

With a sigh, Jenyfer climbed to her feet and went back to the cabin, wanting to curl up in bed and sleep, despite knowing her dreams would be haunted by everything that was swirling around her head. When she went in, it was to find Ordes sitting at his desk with a frown on his face, the lantern beside him coating him golden. His hair was damp from a bath and he was studying the map he'd copied from both their bodies. Jenyfer drew closer, glancing over his shoulder, her eyes running over it. She knew which lines were his, and which were hers, and neither of them were any closer to understanding *why* it had appeared on their skin than they were weeks earlier.

She rested her hand on Ordes' shoulder; he jumped.

'Sorry,' she mumbled. He shook his head, twisting in his seat so he could wrap his arms around her middle, his head resting on her belly. She stroked his hair from his forehead gently. It had grown, she realised, tucking a loose curl behind his ear, her fingers tracing the delicate tip. 'I'm going to bed. My head is so full I can't think straight.'

Ordes leant over and blew out the lantern, then stood, sliding the chair out of the way with his foot. 'You need a distraction,' he murmured. He was so close that they breathed the same air, shared the same beating heart, driven and pulsing with the rhythm of the waves stroking the sides of the ships in the harbour, the coastline, the rocks that littered the beach.

Jenyfer swallowed. 'I do?'

'Hmmm,' he said. 'You do.'

'What sort of distraction do I need?' she breathed.

'You need to *feel*, not think, Jen,' he whispered, cupping her face between his hands. She sighed and flowed towards him like water, pressing herself so close her head was swimming with the smell of him. Sleeping beside him every night had been such sweet torture. Jenyfer wrapped her arms around him, holding as tight as she could. Her belly had not stopped burning, and the pulse that beat between her legs like something alive had been relentless in its intensity, not letting her forget what had already happened between them.

Jenyfer dragged her fingers down the side of his face, tracing the shape of it, committing it to memory as heat sparked and pulsed with all the force of a storm between them.

Dangerous. Powerful. Purposeful.

Terrifying.

Tymis' words echoed through her mind. It couldn't be a spell, she thought. It couldn't be. But maybe it was. Maybe this thing that burnt and crackled between them was magic. She sucked in a breath.

'What's wrong?' Ordes murmured, his lips on her throat. 'Your heart is racing.'

'Nothing,' she whispered. Would she be able to do it? Spend the night in his arms and then throw herself into the ocean before dawn? Tymis had assured her that was the quickest way to get to where she wanted to go – and that was something she hadn't decided yet. Lyonesse, or Avalon.

'If I was to leave, would you come with me?' she asked.

'Wherever you asked,' Ordes replied. 'I'd follow you to the Otherworld, Jenyfer.'

She took his face between her palms and stared into his eyes. They were glazed, that brilliant silver muted grey and her insides pinched.

He isn't thinking straight.

Choking back a sob, Jenyfer pressed her mouth to his.

'I could kiss you forever,' he murmured, grazing his lips over hers. His tongue flickered out, caressed the flesh of her bottom lip. 'You taste like the sea – salt, sun, and sand.'

Ordes closed his mouth over hers again; their lips parted. Jenyfer groaned as his tongue swept its way into her mouth, as if he could drink her in, swallow her whole. And he possibly could – her bones became water as she melted in his arms.

'Now what do I taste like?' she managed as his lips trailed down her jaw; she tilted her head back, gasping as he sunk his teeth into her flesh, branding her and sending a trembling burst of heat between her legs.

'Me,' he growled against her throat. 'You taste like me.'

The heat from Jenyfer's body set a fire under his skin.

Naked, they lay side by side in his bed, a light blanket covering them. Ordes wanted to toss it in the corner – he was on fire, hardly able to think straight for wanting to touch her.

Nerves had caught her. He could see it in her face, in her eyes as she lay there with her head resting on his arm. He could see it in the way she held her shoulders. Her breathing was deep and even, lips parted, skin shining. He cleared his throat, but before he could say anything, she moved forward and trailed her lips, then her bloody *tongue* over the line of his jaw.

'Jen...' he ground out. 'We don't have to do anything you don't want.'

She shifted closer until her body was pressed tightly against his again. 'Such a gentleman. You're a disgrace to pirates everywhere.' Her voice shook, and she ran trembling fingers over his shoulder, along his neck, tracing the shell of his ear and slowly but surely sending him crazy. She brushed her lips against his, so lightly it was like she wasn't touching him at all.

He ran his thumb over her ribs; she shivered and wriggled against him as his fingers stroked the soft curve of her breast. They kissed again, harder this time. He was fiercely aware of how desperate he was, how much he wanted to feel her skin on his, all of it, to feel every inch of her body. How he wanted to crawl inside her and never come out.

He saw stars as she pushed her hips against him, linking her arms around his neck and bringing his face close to hers. She brushed her lips gently against his, then kissed her way along his jaw.

Ordes dropped a kiss on her mouth, then rolled them over, settling his weight onto his elbows. Her head fell back onto the pillow as he dragged his teeth over her jaw, her throat, down lower, going under completely, drowning in her. Her skin was so warm, so smooth, so silken it didn't feel real.

The dark mass of her hair was spread across the pillow, eyes closed, lips stretched in a cat-like smile. He pulled back, wanting to take a moment to simply *look* at her. He trailed his fingers down her body, from the base of her throat, between her breasts, over her belly, lower, while her flesh rippled and shivered with snatches of silver light.

He wanted to take this slow, take his time touching her, like last time, because he didn't know how long he'd last once he was finally inside her. He wanted to hear her vocabulary of contented noises again. He wanted to hear his name on her lips. He wanted her to scream it, sigh it; he wanted to kiss her until she couldn't speak at all.

Ordes paused and her eyes fluttered open, pinning him where he sat, poised between her legs, one hand resting on her hip, the other hovering over the heart of her body.

She raised her eyebrows.

'I'm looking,' he managed, his voice deep, husky, unfamiliar to his own ears.

'At what?'

'At you.'

Her face shifted and he saw her throat bob as she swallowed, but she said nothing. She let him look, staying perfectly still, though her chest shifted with the force of her breathing, as if the feeling of his eyes alone was enough to undo her. When he couldn't stand it any longer, he kissed his way over her belly. She sighed and moved her thighs further apart, that sigh switching to a moan as he touched her, the feeling of her sliding beneath his skin and wrapping around his brain.

Slowly, he ran his tongue over her, wringing a gasp from her lips as she squirmed, her back arching off the mattress. He did it again, and again. He'd do it all night if she asked him to.

Her fingers threaded tight through his hair; she tugged.

'Be patient,' he murmured.

'Ordes, please.' Her voice was a strangled whisper. 'If you don't... I think I'll die.'

'That's dramatic,' he mumbled against her flesh.

She made a noise of protest.

He lifted his head to find her gazing down at him, her face flushed, lips parted, eyes shining in the moonlight. 'Say it,' he whispered. 'Tell me what you want.'

She bit her lip, then, so soft he had to strain to hear it, 'I want you inside me.'

With a groan that was almost a growl, he positioned himself over her, catching her mouth and kissing her deeply, letting her taste herself on his tongue, while his hand slid down her thigh, gripping her knee, lifting her leg and folding it around his hip. Slowly, gently, he eased himself inside her, watching her face shift – the quick flash of discomfort, where he stilled and gave her a moment, and, when he was buried completely, her lips parted and she sighed.

Soon, she was gulping and sobbing beneath him, her fingernails dug deep into his shoulders as she held as tight as she could, riding the wave of pleasure until she crashed over the edge, drawing him with her.

CHAPTER 55

Droplets of water billowed around her. They swirled through the air, insect-like, coming close but never touching her, a living storm pulled from the sea. Her hair hung like wet ink down her back and water pooled at her bare feet, sliding from her sodden shirt. *Ordes'* sodden shirt.

Two nights. She'd given them two, more than she was planning but, lying there, wrapped in his arms, their skin pressed together... it was hard, so much harder than she thought it would be. It was dark when she left, the dawn hours off, and the water was cool on her skin.

The Captain had been on watch, the deck silent. He'd not spoken to her as she'd climbed onto the railing and dove into the sea. And now, Jenyfer didn't know where she was, which town it was that lay before her. The landscape swept away from her in a gentle curve, the hills behind the buildings brushed blue and green and purple. A ship was anchored in the harbour and fishing boats were parked on the sand in an orderly row.

Jenyfer let her gaze slide over the buildings as dawn slowly crept over the village. Glancing down at her bare legs, she sucked in a breath.

Her skin shimmered silver in the sunlight, flecks of aquamarine and pearl flickering over her flesh in an oddly familiar pattern.

Scales. She had scales.

Jenyfer straightened, pushing back her dripping hair. She curled her toes into the cool sand. Beneath her feet, she could feel the heartbeat of the sea and, in her chest, alongside her heartbeat, another one, faint now, but still there.

A strangled sob rose in her throat, but she swallowed it down.

Movement in the corner of her eye made Jenyfer jump. A man was approaching. He was young, scruffily handsome, with wild, brown hair. Her blood was burning the closer he came – she wanted to run, she should run, but there was something in the way he was looking at her. The way his eyes moved over her.

Her song crept up her throat.

'Do you need help?' the man asked. His voice was soft, gentle, and some dark, cruel part of her wanted to crush him for his kindness. Instead, she smiled and held out her hand.

He hesitated.

She began to hum, her inner melody bursting forth into the air between them.

Glassy-eyed, mouth slightly open, the young man placed his hand in hers and, instantly, she could feel everything he felt, knew every thought that rushed through his head.

'I think I'm looking for someone,' Jenyfer heard herself ask, her voice low, melodious, a soothing purr. She wasn't sure what had led her here. Her thoughts, as she plunged into the sea from the deck of *The Excalibur*, were fixed on Lyonesse, but there had been a moment, a space in her thoughts, where things had shifted.

'I can be someone,' the young man breathed.

A slight tug on his hand was enough to draw him closer; his feet carried him forward, his eyes plastered to her face. He had nice eyes, she decided. They were green, with flecks of blue. Jenyfer placed her palm on his cheek. Those beautiful eyes closed, and she lifted herself onto her tiptoes and kissed him gently on the mouth.

'Yes,' she whispered. 'You could. But I don't think you're who I'm looking for.' She stroked the man's face, the brush of her fingers against his stubble echoing through the still of the morning. Soon, the village would wake. Jenyfer swallowed, not sure how much time she had. The young man's eyes remained closed and his body was slanted towards hers. 'Whose ship is that in the harbour?'

'Katarin Le Fey's,' he answered blissfully.

Jenyfer's heart sped up. 'Where is she?'

'The tavern.'

'Take me to her,' Jenyfer ordered softly. The young man nodded and, with his hand tightly in hers, Jenyfer let him lead her into the village. They passed guild houses and glided through a small market square. It was a pretty village, well-kept and neat. She wanted to ask him where exactly she was, but finding Katarin was more important.

Despite the early hour, the tavern door was unlocked. It was dark inside, no lanterns lit.

Her glassy-eyed guide stepped further into the room, Jenyfer behind him. He didn't take another step before a blonde woman with fierce eyes darted from the shadows and pressed a blade to the man's throat.

He acted like she wasn't there.

'Stop,' the woman demanded.

He ignored her, pressing forward. The blade bit into his skin; blood beaded like red jewels. The woman's eyes widened; her grip on the dagger tightened.

Jenyfer swallowed. 'Stop,' she commanded, and the man did.

The blonde woman looked at her suspiciously. 'Who are you?'

'I'm looking for Katarin Le Fey,' Jenyfer said, pitching her voice low, urging some of that music into her tone, but the woman simply narrowed her eyes.

'You're the girl from *The Excalibur*. The one Arthur spoke about.'

Jenyfer frowned. 'Arthur?'

'Arthur Tregarthen. He told us he knew you,' the woman answered.

Jenyfer's heart surged. 'Where is he?'

'The Captain can tell you that, if she decides it. What do you want Katarin for?'

'That's between the Captain and me.'

The woman threw back her head and laughed. 'Is it now?' She tucked her blade into her belt. 'Follow me. Not him,' she added, wrinkling her nose at the young man. 'What have you done to him?'

Jenyfer touched his cheek. He turned to her with vacant eyes and a blissful smile. 'Go home,' she told him. He nodded and left, not looking back at her, the tavern door easing shut behind him.

The blonde woman was watching Jenyfer, doing nothing to hide her interest. She opened her mouth to speak, then shook her head. 'I'll take you to the Captain – she can decide what to do with you.'

Jenyfer was led towards the rear of the tavern, where the woman pushed open a door to a large room – the Captain of *The Night Queen* sat at a long, wooden table, platters of food spread before her. Two other women were seated with her, one on either side, and there were others standing along the wall, their faces hidden by the shadows that lined the walls.

Katarin's beauty was well known, but Jenyfer hadn't been prepared for just how breathtaking she was up close. She tried not to stare, taking in the shining red hair, the colour of fresh cherries, and the creamy skin, plump red lips, and bright eyes. Katarin endured the scrutiny, running her eyes over Jenyfer's body, and she was painfully aware she was practically naked and still damp from the sea.

The blonde woman nudged her in the lower back, forcing her further into the room. The two women sitting with Katarin shifted slightly, their movements small, hands beneath the table-top. Jenyfer was more than certain they had drawn their weapons.

Katarin picked up her knife, spearing a piece of fruit and sliding it between her lips. She took her time chewing and swallowing, her eyes never leaving Jenyfer's face. 'If it isn't Ordes' little morsel,' she drawled eventually. Jenyfer started, and Katarin chuckled. 'Well, wasn't that a lucky guess?'

'She does look tasty.' The voice came from behind Jenyfer but she didn't turn to see who spoke. She kept her eyes on Katarin, who leant forward in her seat, her expression carefully composed as she stabbed another piece of fruit.

'What do you want, Little Morsel?'

'To join your crew,' Jenyfer said boldly.

'Ah,' the Captain said knowingly. She set the knife down, then picked up her mug, taking a long drink. 'Interesting.'

'I bet the faery got to taste her,' mumbled the same voice from before.

Katarin turned her mug around and around between long-fingered hands, her expression carefully composed. 'If I let you on my ship, what can you give me in return?'

Jenyfer took a deep breath, opened her mouth, and let it all go. She could see the music, see the notes suspended in the air before her, could watch as they danced around the small, dimly lit room and settled over faces and in ears.

Nothing happened. Jenyfer could feel her magic flowing through her, flowing into her voice as she sang, her inner song glorious and alive, but the women before her didn't move, didn't shift their expressions.

'I don't need a singer on my ship,' Katarin declared.

'Wait...' The blonde woman said. She moved to stand beside Jenyfer. 'What did you do to that man? The one who brought you here?'

'What man, Tahnet?' the Captain demanded.

Tahnet shook her head. 'Just one of the village lads, but this one'—she gestured at Jenyfer—'had him all doe-eyed and as obedient as a hound. He would have let me slit his throat if she didn't tell him to stop.'

Someone made a hissing sound.

A tall woman stepped into Jenyfer's line of sight. Her hair was bound in a loose knot, and her eyes were sharp, the shape of almonds. Jenyfer could feel her magic swirling around her, reaching out to stroke her skin.

The woman reached out and took hold of Jenyfer's chin, staring into her eyes. 'Arthur was right.'

'Get off me.' Jenyfer snapped, pushing the woman's hand away.

She hadn't wanted to believe it, not truly, not even after everything that had happened, but when she'd thrown herself into the sea... all was swirling water and waves of sand lifting from the sea bed as she sank to the floor of the ocean. There was a bright light behind her eyes, blue and silver combined in twirling, rippling hues, and as she opened her mouth and sucked the water into her lungs, Jenyfer could breathe.

She could breathe. Underwater. She flexed her fingers again; droplets of water appeared on her skin. She swallowed, forcing herself to look at Katarin.

The Captain of *The Night Queen* leant forward in her seat, studying Jenyfer with more interest than before. 'Why aren't you on *The Excalibur* anymore?'

'Tymis asked me to leave, so I did,' Jenyfer snapped, not bothering to hide her anger.

'Why?' Katarin asked, tracing the line of her jaw with the tip of a finger.

'Something to do with a prophecy, and how it wasn't the right time. He didn't make any sense, but he practically demanded I get off his ship,' Jenyfer replied.

Katarin and the tall woman with the almond eyes exchanged a meaningful look. 'You know what I do? Because if you're going to sail with me, you need to understand the risks,' she said. 'But, now, I'm looking for the Treasures of the Gods. Heard of them?'

'Yes,' Jenyfer answered swiftly. 'I've dreamt of the Grail as well. And I have this.' She pulled her sleeves up, revealing the lines of black ink flowing over her skin. 'A map. It's only half of it though...'

'Who has the other half?' Tahnet asked. A deep silence had seeped into the room. Outside the tavern, the sounds of a village coming to life floated through the air.

Jenyfer dropped her gaze. 'Ordes.'

Katarin sighed. 'Of course he bloody does. I'll add it to my list of things to ask him about when we speak next. Where does it lead?'

'No idea,' Jenyfer said simply. 'No one recognises anything.'

'Niniane would want to see it,' the almond-eyed woman said bluntly. Katarin shot her a look, and then nodded slowly.

'Where's Arthur?' Jenyfer asked, glancing quickly at the blonde woman who had brought her in. 'Is he here?'

Katarin stabbed another piece of fruit, raising it to her lips. 'He's busy.'

Jenyfer swallowed. 'With what?'

'That's not for you to know, not yet. I need to know if you can be trusted,' the Captain declared, running her eyes over Jenyfer's face. 'Can you be trusted, syhren? Know that if you lie to me, I'll slit your throat myself and dump you back into the sea.'

Jenyfer nodded, and Katarin's smile deepened.

'Well then. Welcome to *The Night Queen*, Little Morsel.'

CHAPTER 56

As the first rays of the sun kissed the beach, a woman washed ashore with the waves. Her long, blonde hair hung in streamers around her face and she dragged herself up the sand, coughing and vomiting saltwater, gagging and sobbing.

The fishermen on the beach gaped at her before one rushed forward, shedding his coat and draping it around her trembling shoulders. He helped her to stand on legs that had seemed to have forgotten how to stand. She was dressed in a ragged dress, her feet bare, her skin blue with cold.

With a shaking hand, she pushed her hair from her face, and he fell back in shock.

'Lamorna?'

She looked at him, frowning. 'Bryn?'

'Where...'

She sobbed, wrapping her arms around herself, her body shuddering with cold. Without another word, Bryn scooped her into his arms and carried her up the beach. She wanted to go to her aunt and her sister, but he took her to the Chif, and she didn't dare complain, didn't have the voice for it anyway. Her throat was burning.

Kernou was silent around them, the townspeople still sleeping, but soon, they would stir and the day would begin.

What would they think when they learned she'd returned?

With Lamorna in his arms, Bryn knocked on Ulrian Tregarthen's door. Lamorna trembled as footsteps approached – the door was flung open, and the Chif's eyes widened when he saw the prize Bryn Hawkens carried.

'Bring her in – to the fire,' the Chif ordered softly; Lamorna was ferried inside, still dripping. Bryn set her down gently on the lush carpet by the roaring fire in what she assumed was the Chif's living room. Towels appeared from nowhere, and the Chif himself draped them around her. She was vaguely aware of Bryn leaving.

There was no sound other than the crackling fire and Lamorna held her hands out to it. She couldn't remember what it was like to be warm.

Ulrian dropped to one knee, so he could stare into her face. She stared back, too cold and stunned to worry that she was not behaving appropriately. One side of the Chif's face was horribly scarred, the skin red and puckered. She wondered if it hurt, but she didn't ask, like she didn't ask what had happened to him.

'You've been gone a long time, Lamorna,' the Chif said softly. He tucked a chunk of her damp hair behind her ear. 'Where were you?'

'I don't know, exactly,' she whispered, wrapping the towels and Bryn's coat closer. 'I was in the Otherworld. I think.' She frowned. There was nothing but water and darkness and music in her head.

Ulrian stood and began to pace the room. Lamorna watched him warily. Something had happened, something that tugged at her mind, but she couldn't remember what.

'Your return presents me with a unique opportunity,' Ulrian said eventually. Lamorna waited, remembering that she was not to speak unless invited to do so. The Chif paused in his pacing, coming to kneel by her again. 'I have something to ask of you, Lamorna Astolat. Something great, something that might just change everything.'

'But... I'm a woman,' she protested softly. 'What can I possibly offer?'

The Chif touched her cheek gently. 'You're as perfect as the One God made you.' He stroked her skin, his fingers sliding around to grip her chin. She remained still. She did not try to pull away. 'I need someone with courage, with strength.'

'You tried to kill me,' she whispered, the words escaping without her consent. Memories of that night came flooding back at his touch. She could still feel the rope cutting into the tender skin of her wrists. She could still hear her sister screaming.

'The One God tests us in many ways,' Ulrian murmured. 'And you passed, Lamorna. You've been in the belly of the enemy. You've seen true evil. You faced it and you are stronger for it. The One God is very pleased with you, as am I.'

'I don't remember much about where I was,' she said softly.

Irritation flashed across his face momentarily, but the Chif smiled. 'It does not matter. You will remember in time. The Konsel and I will help you, if you help us.'

'I need to see my sister.'

'Your sister is no longer here,' Ulrian declared, still in that soft voice.

'Then where is she?'

'I do not know,' the Chif replied. 'But it does not matter. We shall prevail.'

Slowly, Lamorna nodded. She was tired and hungry, but such wants were not to be voiced. If this was what the One God willed, if she had indeed been tested and now chosen for some task He had set for her, who was she to question it?

Chapter 57

Jenyfer was gone.

Ordes sat up and threw back the bedclothes, searching for his pants and shirt. Half of her clothes were still on the floor, only a shirt gone – his shirt – which meant, wherever she was, she was practically naked. He froze, a dream, or maybe a memory, slicing through him. Her voice, soft and low, in the darkness. Two words, two tiny words that he grasped hold of.

I'm sorry.

He dressed quickly, then rushed out of his cabin and up the ladder, crashing head-first into the dawn.

There was no land on the horizon; the rising sun blazed golden fire across the face of the water. The deck was empty. Ordes rubbed at his face, frowning. He turned as footsteps echoed behind him. Kayrus yawned and stretched.

'There's no one on watch,' Ordes commented. His stomach was squirming.

'The Captain stood watch last night,' Kayrus replied, then headed to the helm. Ordes turned for the Captain's cabin, a horrible sinking feeling in his blood. Pounding on the door, he tucked his shirt in and ran his hand through his hair while waiting for his father to answer.

Ordes could hear the faint strains of music. He shook his head, pushing the sound away as, beneath the ship, something moved; a shifting of the ocean floor, a change in the currents. *The Excalibur* came to a halt. Ordes glanced up – the sails were still catching the wind, so what...

He didn't wait for Tymis – he flung open the door and stepped inside.

His father was sitting behind his desk, his brow furrowed. He didn't look up as Ordes entered.

'I can't find Jenyfer.'

'I know.'

'What do you mean you know?'

'I mean she's gone.'

'We're in the middle of the fucking ocean. How is she gone?'

'It wasn't time,' Tymis muttered. 'Everything happened too fast.'

Ordes approached the desk, fingers trembling. 'What happened?'

'She's part of the prophecy, of that I'm certain, but the Green Knight had it wrong. She wasn't supposed to be here yet.'

Ordes slammed his hand on the desk. His father didn't flinch, didn't look up. Music barrelled through Ordes' brain and following it, riding in on a wave of glorious sound, was blinding anger. He reached across the desk and grabbed Tymis by the shirt front, hauling him to his feet. 'What are you talking about? Where is Jenyfer?'

Tymis' hand shot out; his fist connected with Ordes' jaw. The pain of it, the shock of it, made him gasp and release the hold he had on his father. He stumbled back, falling into the seat.

'You hit me!'

'I'll do it again if you don't start thinking,' Tymis said. 'Everything I've ever told you, Ordes, was the truth. There are things happening beneath the surface of this world that are too difficult to explain right now – your mother would do this better than me,' he added.

Ordes rubbed at his jaw. 'My mother?'

Tymis sighed, resuming his seat. 'Your mother is not just a fey woman from the Isle. I've kept this truth from you since you were old enough to ask. Partly for my own, selfish reasons, because I didn't want you to leave, but I should have let you go,' he mumbled. 'All the times you asked me… but I couldn't, not when I knew what is yet to come.'

Ordes' insides, his muscles, everything he was, was so tight it was painful. 'Who is she?'

Tymis lifted his eyes. 'Your mother is the Queen of the Isle, the Witch of the Mists. The Goddess of Magic herself.'

Something washed over Ordes, a wave of something powerful and strong threatened to sweep him away. He swallowed. 'Niniane… is my *mother?*'

'Yes. I took you from her when I left the Isle, because I wanted to protect you,' Tymis said softly. 'Three sets of hands…' he muttered. 'Yours, hers, and…'

Niniane was his mother? What did that make him? Ordes flexed his fingers, feeling his magic – the magic he now understood belonged to an Old One – breathing beneath his skin. He could taste apples and smell fresh water and flowers, and could feel warm sunshine on his face. That deep space within him beckoned and, for a moment, all he wanted was to sink down into it, to see what lay at the bottom, but he shook his head and made himself focus on his father.

'Where is Jenyfer?'

'I've known who and what she is since the Green Knight threw a spanner in my works, only he got it wrong,' Tymis said, sighing. 'How? He's a god. But I guess if you didn't save her she'd be dead and the prophecy dead with her.'

Ordes grit his teeth so hard his jaw twinged. 'If you don't start explaining what the fuck you're talking about, I'll—'

497

'You'll what?'

'I'm going to find her,' Ordes declared.

'She'll come back – for you.'

'How do you know that?'

'Will you stop worrying about her and listen to me? The stories I told you, about the prophecies, and the one who made them,' Tymis paused, took a deep breath. 'It was me, Ordes. I was talking about myself. It was my story you were hearing.'

'As everything that comes out of your mouth is a gods-damned lie, you'll forgive me if I'm a bit sceptical,' Ordes shouted, startling himself, his voice rebounding from the walls of the cabin. His father didn't flinch and Ordes wanted to punch him, shatter that smooth calm right off Tymis' face.

'Long ago, a man dreamt of the Isle of Mists. He'd spent years wandering the forests of the world—'

Ordes shook his head. 'Stop.'

'—only to end up floating in the sea, where he hoped he'd die. Death had never been granted to him, you see, no matter how hard he'd sought it. But he washed onto a shore that sparkled like crystal and breathed air that tasted of apples.'

'Tymis—'

'This man had magic, but it was magic beyond that which the mortal world possessed. It was the magic of the Gods, but the man was not an Old One, nor was he a man at all, but something else.'

Ordes let his head fall into his hands and he was six again, a child enraptured with the way his father's voice rose and fell when he told his stories. He was six again, wishing with a child's imagination that everything his father said was true.

'The Witch of the Mists healed him, and she loved him. In his madness, his delirium, the man who was not a man at all told the Witch he could see what had not yet happened, and he spoke to her four prophecies.' Tymis stopped, then, softly, 'You know what they are, son.'

Ordes swallowed; his knees trembled, heart raced. His father's words, spoken almost every night for years – until Ordes decided he was too old for bedtime stories – echoed through his ears and when he spoke, it was a whisper. 'For the serpent to become the dragon, it must consume itself and be reborn.'

'Three sets of hands upon the stone, one set of hands to pass alone,' Tymis murmured. *The Excalibur* groaned, timbers shifting. Water lapped rhythmically at the sides of the ship.

'A song shall sing the Red Ones home, forever entombed in the House of Bone,' Ordes continued.

'Only on Camlann Field, will the red dragon yield, and the Once and Future King shall see the land healed.' Tymis held Ordes' gaze. His voice softened, until it sounded almost like regret. 'And the one who stands between the worlds shall bear the weight of them both.'

'Who are you?' Ordes whispered as the ship suddenly began to move. Behind his father, the window rattled violently, before it was flung open and the wind rushed inside, grabbing the papers and maps from the desk and tossing them about the cabin. Neither Ordes nor Tymis moved. The wind lifted Tymis' hair from his shoulders, setting it dancing around his face.

His eyes, so like the ones Ordes saw in the mirror, glowed with silver fire.

'I am the Myrddin – the son of a mortal woman and a being not of this earth anymore. I am as old as the forests of this world. I have seen through time and I know what is written, for all of us.'

Ordes could hardly breathe.

'My name is Merlin.'

ACKNOWLEDGMENTS

I would like to acknowledge that *The Call of the Sea* was conceptualised and written on the lands of the Widjabul people. I acknowledge and pay my respect to the traditional custodians, past, present and emerging, of the Bundjalung nation, and their continuous connection to the landscape and the rivers of this ancient place.

I have to thank my family first. We have been through a lot of upheaval over the last twelve months, and you still found a way to give me the time and space I needed to write. I don't have enough words to truly thank you for this – I love you guys.

My editor, cover designer, cartographer and blurb writer. Danikka, you are the best editor I could ever hope for – you seem to share my brain and know exactly what I want to say when I can't seem to find the words. Thank you for all your work and for your support. I am grateful to be able to call you a friend. Fran, my wonderful cover designer – once again you have come up with the most glorious cover for my book! Thank you for this work of art. Rachael, my cartographer – your art and your skill brought my world to life. My map is beyond amazing – it is perfect! Thank you so much! And to Jessie at Book Blurb Magic – thank you, once again, for untangling my tangly plot and making my blurb the best it can be!

My online friends and the writing community – I could not do this without you all. Your support and encouragement never ceases to amaze me. I am so thankful for all the time and effort members of the online writing community put into supporting each other, whether it be sharing tips or tricks or just simply offering feedback. You guys are amazing.

My beta and ARC teams – there are way too many of you to mention by name, but please know how grateful I am that you gave up your time to read for me, and for your support of me and my story. Thank you!

And lastly, to you, the reader, for choosing to dive into this world with me. I hope you enjoy your journey.

ABOUT THE AUTHOR

KATE SCHUMACHER is the author of *Shadow of Fire* and *Heart of Flame* (The Fires of Aileryan series).

When she isn't writing, Kate is reading her way through an ever-growing TBR pile. She has wanted to be an author since she was a child, and finds time to write in the in-between moments of life.

Kate completed a Bachelor of Arts in Creative Writing and Journalism, and an Honours degree in Screenwriting, followed by a Graduate Diploma in Education.

She lives in Northern NSW, Australia, with her partner, two children and three very spoiled cats.

Follow her on instagram @kate.schumacher.writer
or visit her website kateschumacherauthor.com